S
Card

Card, Orson Scott.

Earth afire.

| DATE | | | |
|---|---|---|---|
| | | | |
| | | | |
| | | | |
| | | | |
| | | | |
| | | | |
| | | | |
| | | | |
| | | | |
| | | | |
| | | | |
| | | | |

# EARTH AFIRE

## By Orson Scott Card from Tom Doherty Associates

*Empire*
*The Folk of the Fringe*
*Future on Fire* (editor)
*Future on Ice* (editor)
*Hidden Empire*
*Invasive Procedures* (with
    Aaron Johnston)
*Keeper of Dreams*
*The Lost Gate*
*Lovelock* (with Kathryn Kidd)
*Maps in a Mirror: The Short
    Fiction of Orson Scott Card*
*Orson Scott Card's InterGalactic
    Medicine Show*
*Pastwatch: The Redemption of
    Christopher Columbus*
*Saints*
*Songmaster*
*Treason*
*A War of Gifts*
*The Worthing Saga*
*Wyrms*

### THE TALES OF ALVIN MAKER
*Seventh Son*
*Red Prophet*
*Prentice Alvin*
*Alvin Journeyman*
*Heartfire*
*The Crystal City*

### ENDER
*Ender's Game*
*Ender's Shadow*
*Shadows in Flight*
*Shadow of the Hegemon*
*Shadow Puppets*
*Shadow of the Giant*
*Speaker for the Dead*
*Xenocide*
*Children of the Mind*
*First Meetings*
*Ender in Exile*

### HOMECOMING
*The Memory of Earth*
*The Call of Earth*
*The Ships of Earth*
*Earthfall*
*Earthborn*

### WOMEN OF GENESIS
*Sarah*
*Rebekah*
*Rachel & Leah*

### THE FORMIC WARS
*Earth Unaware* (with Aaron
    Johnston)

### From Other Publishers

*Enchantment*
*Homebody*
*Lost Boys*
*Magic Street*
*Stone Father*
*Stone Tables*

*Treasure Box*
*How to Write Science Fiction and
    Fantasy*
*Characters and Viewpoint*
*Pathfinder*
*Ruins*

# EARTH AFIRE

## THE FIRST FORMIC WAR

### Volume Two of the Formic Wars

# Orson Scott Card

## and Aaron Johnston

**TOR®**

A TOM DOHERTY ASSOCIATES BOOK
NEW YORK

EARTH AFIRE

Copyright © 2013 by Orson Scott Card and Aaron Johnston

A Tor Book
Published by Tom Doherty Associates, LLC
175 Fifth Avenue
New York, NY 10010

www.tor-forge.com

Tor® is a registered trademark of Tom Doherty Associates, LLC.

Library of Congress Cataloging-in-Publication Data

Card, Orson Scott.
    Earth Afire / Orson Scott Card and Aaron Johnston.—First edition.
        p. cm.
    "A Tom Doherty Associates book."
    ISBN 978-0-7653-2905-9 (hardcover)
    ISBN 978-1-4299-4384-0 (e-book)
    1. Space warfare—Fiction.  2. Science fiction.  I. Johnston, Aaron.  II. Title.
    PS3553.A655E35 2013
    813'.54—dc23

                                                                2012043815

Tor books may be purchased for educational, business, or promotional use. For information on bulk purchases, please contact Macmillan Corporate and Premium Sales Department at 1-800-221-7945, extension 5442, or write specialmarkets@macmillan.com.

First Edition: June 2013

Printed in the United States of America

0  9  8  7  6  5  4  3  2  1

To Stefan Rudnicki, for giving life to words on paper
and to those who call you friend

# ACKNOWLEDGMENTS

Many people helped make this novel happen, and they must be thanked.

Brett Rustand, a former Blackhawk helicopter pilot for the U.S. Army, helped us understand why rotor blades are more of a curse than a blessing and why combat birds in the future would be much better off without them. And his insight regarding sling-loading and tactical maneuvering helped shape our thinking as we developed the military hardware in these pages.

Special thanks also goes to artists Nick Greenwood and Giancarlo Caracuzzo, whose art gave life, color, and an eerie strangeness to the Formics, long before a page of this book was written.

Jordan D. White gave great counsel and encouragement when this story was still in its infancy. Thanks to Beth Meacham, our tireless editor at Tor, for her insight and wisdom. Kathleen Bellamy caught errors that you thankfully will never see.

Additional thanks goes to Melissa Frain, Aisha Cloud, Andy Mendelsohn, Rene Roberson, Karl Dunn, Rick Bryson, and everyone else at Tor and Erwin Penland who contributed in some way, large or small, to allow us to focus on writing.

Above all, thanks to our wives, Lauren and Kristine, and to our faithful children, for their endless patience, calm reassurance, and unflinching support. This is and always has been a story about family, the ones we're born into, the ones circumstance throws upon us, and the ones formed in battle and blood. That is what the Formics do not understand, the micro community, the strength of the few, the deep-rooted attachment we feel to those we love. *Somos familia. Somos uno.* We are family. We are one.

And that is why we win.

# CONTENTS

# EARTH AFIRE

# CHAPTER 1

# Bingwen

The librarian watched the vid on Bingwen's monitor and frowned and said, "This is your emergency, Bingwen? You pulled me away from my work to show me a spook vid about aliens? You should be studying for the exams. I have people waiting to use this computer." She pointed to the line of children by the door, all of them eager to get on a machine. "You're wasting my time and theirs."

"It's not a spook vid," said Bingwen. "It's real."

The librarian scoffed. "There are dozens of stories about aliens on the nets, Bingwen. When it isn't sex, it's aliens."

Bingwen nodded. He should have expected this. Of course the librarian wouldn't believe him. Something as serious as an alien threat would need to come from a credible source: the news or the government or other adults, not from an eight-year-old son of a rice farmer.

"Now you have three seconds to get back to your studies, or I'm giving your time to someone else."

Bingwen didn't argue. What good would it do? When adults became defiant in public, no amount of evidence, however irrefutable, would make them change their minds. He climbed back up into his chair and made two clicks on the keyboard. The vid of the alien disappeared, and a complex geometry proof appeared in its place. The librarian nodded, gave him one final disparaging look, then crossed the room back to her desk.

Bingwen pretended to busy himself with the proof until the librarian was occupied and her mind was elsewhere. Then he tapped the keypad and reopened the vid. The face of the alien stared back at him, frozen in place from when Bingwen had paused the vid. Had the librarian seen something he hadn't? Some glitch or inconsistency that flagged the vid as a fake? It was true that there were hundreds of such vids on the nets. Space duels, alien encounters, magical quests. Yet the mistakes and fakery of those were glaringly obvious. Comparing them to this one was like comparing a pencil sketch of fruit to the real thing.

No, this was real. No digital artist could create something this vivid and fluid and alive. The insectlike face had hair and musculature and blood vessels and eyes with depth. Eyes that seemed to bore right into Bingwen's and signal the end to everything. Bingwen felt himself getting sick to his stomach, not from the grotesque, unnatural look of the thing, but from the realness of it. The clarity of it. The undeniable truth of it.

"What is that?"

Bingwen turned around in his seat and saw Hopper standing behind him in that awkward way that Hopper had, leaning to one side because of his twisted foot. Bingwen smiled. A friend. And not just any friend, but Hopper. Someone who would talk to Bingwen straight and tell him that of course it's a fake, look, see right there, there's a glitch you missed, silly, there's proof that you're working yourself into a frenzy for no reason.

"Come look at this," said Bingwen.

Hopper limped forward. "Is that a spook vid?"

"What do *you* think?"

"Looks real. Where'd you get it?"

"Yanyu sent it to me. I just checked my mail."

Yanyu was one secret that he and Hopper shared. She was a research assistant to an astrophysicist on Luna. Bingwen had met her on the nets a few months ago in a forum for Chinese grad students looking to improve their English. Bingwen had tried other forums in the past, logging in as himself and showing no pretense. But as soon as he divulged his age, forum administrators always kicked him out and blocked his access.

Then he had found the forum for grad students. And rather than be himself, Bingwen had pretended to be a second-year grad student in Guangzhou studying agriculture, the only subject Bingwen thought he could speak to with any believable degree of competency. He and Yanyu had become friends almost immediately, e-mailing and instant messaging each other in English several times a week. Bingwen always felt a pang of guilt whenever they communicated; he was, after all, maintaining a lie. What's worse, now that he knew Yanyu well, he was fairly certain she was the type of person who would have befriended him anyway, whether he was eight years old or not.

But what could he say now? Hey, Yanyu. Guess what? I'm really a kid. Isn't that hilarious? What shall we talk about today?

No. That would be like admitting he was one of those pervs who pretended to be young boys so they could chat with teenage girls.

"What did she say in her message?" asked Hopper.

"Only that she had found this vid and that she had to talk to me about it."

"Did you message her?"

"She didn't respond. It's sleep time on Luna. Our schedules only cross in the morning."

Hopper nodded at the screen. "Play it."

Bingwen tapped the keyboard, and the vid began from the beginning.

On screen a figure emerged from a hatch on the side of a ship. Its pressure suit had an extra set of arms. A tube with plenty of slack extended from the figure's spacesuit and snaked its way down into the hatch, presumably carrying oxygen and heat and whatever else the creature needed to sustain itself in the cold vacuum of space.

For a moment the creature didn't move. It stayed there, sprawled on the side of the ship, stomach down, arms and legs out like an insect clinging to a wall. Then, slowly, it lifted its head and took in its surroundings. Whoever was filming was about twenty meters away, and the front of the creature's helmet was still in shadow, concealing its face.

In an instant the calm of the moment broke as the creature rushed toward the camera with a sudden urgency. Hopper jumped just as Bingwen had the first time he saw it. There was a burst of a foreign language on the vid—Spanish perhaps, or maybe Portuguese—and the man with the camera retreated a step. The creature drew closer, its head bobbing from side to side as it shuffle-crawled forward on its arms and legs. Then, when it was a few meters shy of the camera, it stopped and raised its head again. Lights from the camera operator's helmet fell across the creature's face, and Bingwen freeze-framed the image.

"Did you see how the hair and muscles of its face moved?" said Bingwen. "How fluid they were? Hair only moves that way in zero gravity. This had to have been filmed in space."

Hopper stared at the screen, saying nothing, mouth slightly agape.

"You two are asking for trouble," another voice said.

Bingwen turned around again. This time Meilin, his cousin, was behind him, arms folded across her chest, her expression one of disapproval. At seven years old, she was a year younger than Bingwen, but since she was so much taller than both him and Hopper, she acted as if she were older and thus in charge.

"Exams are in two weeks," she said, "and you two are goofing off."

Provincial exams were the only chance the children from rice villages had at getting a formal education. Schools were scarce along the river valley, the closest being north in Dawanzhen or south in Hanguangzhen. Space was limited, but every six months the district admitted a few students from the villages. To be eligible, you had to be at least eight years old and score at least in the ninety-fifth percentile on the exams. Those names were then thrown into a lottery, and the number of names chosen was based on the number of seats available, which was rarely more than three. Chances of getting in were slim, but school was a ticket out of the fields, and every child in the nearby villages, from the moment they turned four years old, spent all their spare time studying here at the library.

"This is your first chance to take the exam," said Meilin, "and you're going to blow it."

"Bingwen won't," said Hopper. "He aces every practice test. They won't even put his name in the lottery. They'll take him immediately."

"To ace a test means you get every answer right, mud brain," said Meilin. "That's impossible. The test self-adjusts. The more answers you get right, the more difficult the questions become. If you got every answer right, the questions by the end would be so complex nobody could answer them."

"Bingwen does."

Meilin smirked. "Sure he does."

"No, really," said Hopper. "Tell her, Bingwen."

Meilin turned to Bingwen, expecting the joke to end there, but Bingwen shrugged. "I get lucky, I guess."

Meilin's expression changed to one of disbelief. "Every answer? No wonder Mr. Nong gives you extra computer time and treats you like his little pet."

Mr. Nong was the head librarian, a kindly man in his seventies whose health was poor and who only came to the library two days of the week now as a result. His assistant, Ms. Yí, who despised children and Bingwen most of all, covered for Mr. Nong on days like today when he was out. "She hates you because she knows you're smarter than her," Hopper had once said. "She can't stand that."

Meilin suddenly looked on the verge of tears. "But you can't ace the test, Bingwen. You just can't. If you do, you'll raise the bar. They'll only consider children next year who ace the test. And that's when *I* take it. They won't even consider me." And then she *was* crying, burying her face in her hands. Several children nearby shushed her, and Hopper rolled his eyes. "Here we go," he said.

Bingwen hopped down from his seat and went to her, putting an arm around her and guiding her into his cubicle with Hopper. "Meilin, you're going to be fine. They won't change the requirements."

"How do you know?" she said through tears.

"Because Mr. Nong told me so. They've always done it this way."

"Hey, at least you have a fighting chance," Hopper told her. "They'd never take me. Even if I did ace the test."

"Why not?" said Bingwen.

"Because of my bad leg, mud brain. They're not going to waste government funds on a cripple."

"Sure they will," said Bingwen. "And you're not a cripple."

"No? Then what would you call me?"

"How do you know your legs aren't perfect and the rest of us have bad legs?" said Bingwen. "Maybe you're the only perfect human on Earth."

Hopper smiled at that.

"But seriously," said Bingwen. "They want minds, Hopper, not Olympic athletes. Look at Yanyu. She has a gimp arm, and she's working on Luna doing important research."

"She has a gimp arm?" Hopper asked, suddenly hopeful. "I didn't know that."

"And she types faster than I do," said Bingwen. "So don't say you don't have a chance, because you do."

"Who's Yanyu?" asked Meilin, wiping away the last of her tears.

"Bingwen's girlfriend," said Hopper. "But I didn't tell you that. It's a secret."

Bingwen slapped him lightly on the arm. "She's not my girlfriend. She's a friend."

"And she works on Luna?" said Meilin. "That doesn't make any sense. Why would anyone on Luna want to be *your* friend?"

"I'll try not to take offense at that," said Bingwen.

"She sent Bingwen something," said Hopper. "Tell us what you think. Show her, Bingwen."

Bingwen glanced at Ms. Yí, the librarian, saw that she was still busy, and hit play. As Meilin watched, more children gathered. When it finished, there were no less than twelve children around the monitor.

"It looks real," said Meilin.

"Told you," said Hopper.

"What do you know?" said Zihao, a twelve-year-old boy. "You wouldn't know an alien if it bit you on the butt."

"Yes, he would," said Meilin. "If something bites you on the butt, you're going to notice. There are nerve endings just below the surface."

"It's an American expression," said Bingwen.

"Which is why English is stupid," said Meilin, who always hated it when someone knew something she didn't.

"When was this vid made?" said Zihao. He climbed up into the chair, clicked back on the site, and checked the date. "See?" he said, turning back to them, smiling triumphantly. "This proves it's phony. It was uploaded a week ago."

"That doesn't prove anything," said Hopper.

"Yes, it does, mud brain," said Zihao. "You're forgetting about the interference in space. No communication is getting through. Radiation is crippling the satellites. If this was filmed in space a week ago, then how did it get to Earth with all the satellites down? Huh? Tell me that."

"It was *uploaded* a week ago," said Bingwen. "That doesn't mean it was *filmed* a week ago." He clicked through a series of screens and started scanning through pages of code.

"Now what are you doing?" asked Meilin.

"Every vid file has mountains of data embedded into it," said Bingwen. "You just have to know where to look." He found the numbers he was looking for and cursed himself for not checking this sooner. "Says here the vid was filmed over eight months ago."

"Eight months?" said Hopper.

"Let me see," said Zihao.

Bingwen pointed out the dates.

Zihao shrugged. "That's just further evidence that it's bogus. Why would someone record this and sit on it for eight months? That doesn't make sense. If this were real they'd want everyone to know about it immediately."

"Maybe they *couldn't* tell people immediately," said Bingwen. "Think about it. The interference has been going on for months now, right? Maybe these aliens are the ones causing it. Maybe their ship is what's emitting all that radiation. So the people who recorded this vid couldn't send it to Earth over laserline. Their communications lines were down."

"Then how did it get here?" said Meilin.

"Someone must have hand carried it," said Bingwen. "They got on a ship and they flew to Earth—or, more likely, they flew it to Luna. There's no atmosphere there, and gravity is less. So it would be much easier to land there. And since the Moon's close enough to us that communication between us and Luna is still getting through, we would hear about it here on Earth."

"Someone flew eight months to deliver a vid?" said Zihao.

"The discovery of alien life," said Bingwen. "What could be more important than that?" He tapped his monitor. "Think about the time line. It makes complete sense. Eight months on the fastest ship could take you pretty far out, maybe even to the Kuiper Belt. Precisely to the people who would first encounter something like this."

"Asteroid miners," said Hopper.

"Has to be," said Bingwen. "They've got the best view of deep space. They'd see something like this long before anyone else did."

Zihao laughed. "You pig faces think with your knees. You're all jabbering about stuff you don't know anything about. The vid is a fake. If it were real, it would be all over the news. The world would be in a panic." He put a cupped hand to his ear, as if listening. "So where are the sirens? Where are the government warnings?" He folded his arms and smirked. "You weed heads are idiots. Haven't you ever seen a spook vid before?"

"It's not a spooker," said Hopper. "That's a real alien."

"Oh?" said Zihao. "How do you know what a real alien looks like? Have you seen one before? Do you have a pen pal alien friend you've been swapping photos with?" A few of the boys laughed. "Who's to say aliens don't look exactly like paddy frogs or water buffalo or your armpit? If you guys believe this is real, you're a bunch of *bendans*." Dumb eggs.

Several of the children laughed, though Bingwen could tell that most of them weren't laughing with any confidence. They *wanted* Zihao to be right. They *wanted* to believe that the vid was a spooker. It had frightened them as much as it had frightened Bingwen, but it was easier to dismiss it than to accept it as real.

Meilin narrowed her eyes. "It is real. Bingwen wouldn't lie to us."

Zihao laughed and turned to Bingwen. "Cute. Your little girlfriend is sticking up for you." He looked at Meilin. "You know what aliens like to eat, Meilin? Little girl brains. They stick a straw in your ear and suck your head empty."

Meilin's eyes moistened with tears. "That's not true."

"Leave her alone," said Bingwen.

Zihao smirked. "See what you've done, Bingwen? You've scared all the kiddies." He bent down from the chair, got close to Meilin's face, and spoke in a singsongy voice, as if addressing an infant. "Aw, did Bingwen scare the little girl with his alien vid?"

"I said leave her alone." Bingwen stepped between them and extended a hand, nudging Zihao back. It wasn't a hard shove, but since Zihao was leaning forward in the chair and his center of gravity was off, the push was just enough to twist him off-balance. He stumbled, reached for the counter, missed, and fell to the floor, the chair scooting out and away from him. A few of the children laughed, but they instantly fell silent as Zihao jumped to his feet and seized Bingwen by the throat.

"You little mud sucker," said Zihao. "I'll cut out your tongue for that."

Bingwen felt his windpipe constrict and pulled hard at Zihao's wrists.

"Let him go," said Meilin.

"Girlfriend to the rescue again," said Zihao. He squeezed harder.

The other children did nothing. A few boys from Zihao's village were chuckling, but they didn't seem amused, more like relieved that it was Bingwen who was taking the abuse and not them.

Hopper grabbed Zihao from behind, but Zihao only scoffed. "Back off, cripple. Or we'll see how you do with two twisted feet."

More laughter from the other boys.

Bingwen's lungs were screaming for air. He kicked and pounded his fists on Zihao's shoulders, but the bigger boy seemed not to notice.

"What is going on over here?" Ms. Yí said.

Zihao released Bingwen, who fell to the floor, coughing and gasping and inhaling deeply.

Ms. Yí stood over them, holding her bamboo discipline stick. "Out!" she said, waving the stick. "All of you! Out!"

The children protested. It was Bingwen. He started it. He called us over here. He attacked Zihao.

Bingwen grabbed Meilin's hand, turned to Hopper, and said, "Meet us in the fields." Then he pushed through the crowd toward the exit, pulling Meilin along behind him.

"He was showing a spook vid," said one of the children.

"He was trying to scare us," said another.

"He pushed Zihao out of his chair."

"He started a fight."

Bingwen was through the front door, Meilin right at his heels. It was late in the afternoon, and the air outside was cool and damp, a light wind blowing up from the valley.

"Where are we going?" asked Meilin.

"Home," said Bingwen. He led her to the village staircase built into the side of the hill, and they began descending toward the rice fields below. Every village in the valley was built onto a hillside, the valley floor being too fertile and valuable to be used for anything other than rice. Meilin's village was three kilometers to the west. If Bingwen hurried, he might be able to escort her home and then cut south to his own village before it got too dark.

"Why are we running?" said Meilin.

"Because once Zihao gets outside," said Bingwen, "he'll come finish what he started."

"So I'm to be your human shield?"

Bingwen laughed, despite himself. "You're quite the little strategist."

"I'm not little. I'm taller than you."

"We're both little," said Bingwen. "I'm just littler. And I dragged you along because you're my cousin and I'd rather not see you get your head pounded in. You stood up to Zihao. He'll come for you, too."

"I can take care of myself, thank you."

He stopped and let go of her hand. "You want to go home alone?"

Meilin seemed ready to argue, but then her expression softened and she looked at the ground. "No."

Bingwen took her hand again, and they continued down the stairs.

Meilin was quiet a moment. "I shouldn't have cried back there. That was childish."

"It wasn't childish. Adults cry all the time. They just hide it better."

"I'm scared, Bingwen."

Her words surprised him. Meilin never admitted to weakness. If anything she went out of her way to prove how smart and strong and unafraid she was, always pointing out to Bingwen and Hopper and others how they were doing a math problem wrong or solving a thought puzzle incorrectly. And yet here she was, on the verge of tears, showing a fragility that Bingwen had never seen before.

For a moment he considered lying to her, telling her the whole vid had been a prank. That's what an adult would do, after all: laugh and shrug and dismiss the whole thing as fantasy. Children couldn't stomach the truth, adults believed. Children had to be protected from the harsh realities of the world.

But what good would that do Meilin? This wasn't a prank. It wasn't a game. That thing on screen was real and alive and dangerous.

"I'm scared too," said Bingwen.

She nodded, hurrying to keep pace beside him. "Do you think it's coming to Earth?"

"We shouldn't think of it as an 'it,'" said Bingwen. "There's probably more than one. And yes, it's coming to Earth. The interference is only getting worse, which suggests their ship is headed this way. Plus it looked intelligent. It *must* be intelligent. It built an interstellar spacecraft. Humans haven't done that."

They took the last turn in the staircase and reached the valley floor. Hopper was waiting for them, clothes soaked and covered in mud.

"Took you long enough," said Hopper.

"How did you get down before us?" asked Meilin. "And why are you so filthy?"

"Irrigation tube," said Hopper. He patted the side of his bad leg. "Steps take too long."

Meilin made a face. "People throw their dishwater in the tubes."

Hopper shrugged. "It was that or get beat to a pulp. And it rained yesterday, so the tubes aren't dirty. Much."

"That's disgusting," said Meilin.

"Agreed," said Hopper. "But it's easier to clean clothes than to clean wounds." He ran and jumped into the nearest rice paddy, which was filled waist-deep with water. He submerged himself, thrashed around a moment, getting most of the mud off, then shook his upper body and crawled back out of the paddy, dripping wet. "See? Fresh as a flower."

"I'm going to throw up," said Meilin.

"Not on me," said Hopper. "I just bathed."

They took off at a jog along the narrow bridge of earth that separated two of the paddies, heading out into the vast fields of rice. They ran slower so that Hopper could keep up, but it was a good steady pace for distance running.

After a few hundred yards Bingwen glanced back at the staircase to see if Zihao was following. There were a few children coming down, but Zihao wasn't among them. They didn't slow their pace.

"What's the plan?" said Hopper.

"For what?" asked Bingwen.

"Warning everyone," said Hopper.

Bingwen smiled. He could always count on Hopper. "I don't know that anyone's going to believe us. I showed Ms. Yí, and she shrugged it off."

"Ms. Yí's an old water buffalo," said Hopper.

They ran for half an hour, cutting across the fields that followed the bends and turns of the valley. When they reached Meilin's village, she stopped and faced them at the bottom of the stairs. "I can make it from here," she said, gesturing up to her house near the bottom of the hill. "What do I tell my parents?"

"The truth," said Bingwen. "Tell them what you saw. Tell them you believe it. Tell them to go to the library and see it for themselves."

Meilin looked up into the sky where the first few dozen stars had already appeared. "Maybe they don't mean us any harm. Maybe they're peaceful."

"Maybe," said Bingwen. "But you didn't see all of the vid. The alien attacked one of the humans."

Even in the low light Bingwen could see Meilin grow pale.

"Oh," she said.

"But maybe they won't come here to China," said Bingwen. "The world is a big place. We're only a tiny, microscopic dot on it."

"You're only telling me what I want to hear," said Meilin.

"I'm telling you the truth. There are a lot of unknowns at the moment."

"Even so," said Meilin, "we'd be stupid not to prepare for the worst."

"You're right," said Bingwen.

She nodded and looked more insecure than before. "Good luck. Stay safe."

They watched her ascend the stairs and waited until she was inside her home before they started running again. They stayed in the fields, jogging along the narrow earth bridges that crisscrossed the fields horizontally and vertically, creating a huge patchwork quilt of irrigated paddies. When they were almost to their own village, the first boy appeared behind them, several paddies back. Then a boy to their right appeared a few paddies over, matching their speed in a run. A third boy on their left appeared next, watching them as he kept pace with them.

"We're being corralled," said Hopper.

"Boxed in," said Bingwen.

Sure enough, the boys around them began closing in.

"Ideas?" said Hopper.

"They're taller than us," said Bingwen. "And faster. We can't outrun them."

"You mean *I* can't outrun them," said Hopper.

"No, I mean both of us. You actually have greater stamina than me. You have a better chance of getting through than I do."

"Plan," said Hopper.

"You run ahead and get my father. I hang back and keep them busy."

"Self-sacrifice. How noble. Forget it. I'm not leaving you."

"Think, Hopper. Stay and we both get pummeled. Run ahead, and we might not. I'm saving my skin as much as yours. Now go."

Hopper picked up his speed, and Bingwen stopped where he was. As expected, the other boys closed in, ignoring Hopper. Bingwen turned to his left and stepped down the embankment into the nearest paddy. The water was cold and reached his waist. The mud was thick and squishy beneath his feet. The rice shoots were packed tightly together and tall as his shoulders. Bingwen scanned the edge of the paddy until he found one of the paddy frogs half submerged near the embankment. He scooped it up, stuffed the frog into his pocket, and made his way to the center of the paddy. By the time he reached it, the boys had arrived. Each of them took up a position on one of the paddy's sides, leaving the northernmost side, the side toward Bingwen's village, unguarded. Less than a minute later Zihao arrived at that end of the paddy, breathing heavily from the run. It was almost full dark now.

"Out of the water," said Zihao.

Bingwen didn't move.

"You ruined our time at the library, mud brain," said Zihao. "How are we supposed to leave this hole if mud brains like you keep ruining our computer time?"

Bingwen kept his eyes toward the village, looking for an approaching lantern light to appear.

"I said out of the water," said Zihao.

Bingwen said nothing.

"Get out now or I'm coming in after you."

Bingwen stood still and silent.

"I swear to you I will break your fingers one by one if you don't get up here now."

Bingwen didn't move. He wasn't about to leave a defensive position. The water wasn't much, but it was all he had.

The boys around him shifted uncomfortably.

"You think you're so much smarter than everyone, don't you, Bingwen? I've heard you speaking English into your computer. I've seen what you study. You're a traitor." He spat into the water.

Bingwen didn't move.

Zihao was shouting now. "Get up here and face me, coward boy!"

Bingwen looked toward the village. No lantern light approached.

"I warned you," said Zihao. He charged into the paddy, splashing water and not caring what shoots he pushed aside and damaged.

Bingwen didn't flinch. He stood waiting, hands in his pockets.

Just before Zihao was within arm's reach—and therefore hitting range—Bingwen turned on the tears. "Please don't choke me. Please. Hit me if you want. Just don't choke me again."

Zihao smiled.

Poor Zihao, thought Bingwen. So loud and strong and yet so predictable.

Zihao's hands seized Bingwen by the throat, which Bingwen had extended and turned at a slight angle so that this time Zihao's thumbs would press against the side and muscle of Bingwen's throat instead of directly into his windpipe. Not that Bingwen expected to be choked for very long.

Bingwen allowed himself to look panicked and then muffled his words, as if begging for mercy. "Pleaskk akk."

Zihao's smile widened. "What's that, Bingwen. I can't hear—"

Bingwen shoved the paddy frog, face-first, directly into Zihao's mouth. He had needed Zihao to speak, and Zihao had walked right into it.

Zihao released Bingwen and recoiled, splashing backward and gagging, clawing at his face to get the frog free. But Bingwen was faster. Now he had his left hand behind Zihao's head to steady him while his right palm pressed the frog deeper into Zihao's mouth. The frog was too wide to fit completely, but that was ideal; Bingwen wasn't trying to choke Zihao; he only wanted to distract him. Zihao gave a muffled scream, and Bingwen released the frog, grabbed Zihao by the waist, and brought up his knee fast and hard into Zihao's crotch.

Zihao buckled and fell forward with a splash, his body limp, the frog slipping from his mouth and plopping into the water. Bingwen didn't wait to see how the others would respond. He had to act oblivious to them, as if so filled with rage, they weren't even a consideration. He screamed and raised a fist as if to bring it down hard on Zihao, who was now half submerged in the water and moaning. As intended, Bingwen's fist hit the water just to the left of Zihao's face and plunged downward, the momentum of the punch carrying his whole body straight down to the paddy floor, completely out of sight.

Before the water could settle, Bingwen turned his body and moved underwater in the direction Zihao had come. The shoots were parted and broken, giving Bingwen a wide enough path to move through without rustling many shoots and revealing his position. He didn't swim or kick or do anything to disturb the water, but rather crawled along the bottom with his fingers and toes, pushing himself forward, digging at the mud. Twice he paused and turned his head to get a silent gulp of air, but even then he kept moving forward.

He didn't know if they were coming for him, but he didn't rise out of the water to see. The darkness and shoots would conceal him or they wouldn't.

He reached the earth wall of the paddy, lifted his head, and allowed himself a look back. The boys were in the water around Zihao, helping him to his feet. Even if they ran for Bingwen now, they wouldn't catch him. They'd be too hampered by the water; he'd have too much of a lead.

He crawled out of the water and ran, his clothes heavy and wet.

There was shouting behind him but no pursuit.

He reached the stairs of the village just as Hopper and Father were coming down, a lantern in Father's hand.

"You're wet," said Father.

"But not bleeding," said Hopper. "That's a good sign."

Bingwen bent over, catching his breath, fighting back the urge to vomit. "Did you tell him about the vid?" he asked Hopper.

"There was no time," said Hopper.

"Tell me about it inside, where it's warm," said Father. He turned to Hopper. "My son is safe. Thank you. Your parents will want you home."

Hopper looked as if he wanted to object and tag along, but he knew Father well enough not to argue. They parted ways, and Father led Bingwen home, where Mother and Grandfather were waiting inside. Mother took Bingwen into her arms, and Grandfather went to fetch a towel.

"Are you hurt?" said Mother.

"No," said Bingwen.

"Here, by the fire," said Grandfather, wrapping him in the towel.

Bingwen took off his shirt and dried himself by the hearth. Mother, Father, and Grandfather watched him, their faces lines of worry. He told them about the vid then, letting it all pour out of him. The alien. The extra pair of arms. How the creature's hair and muscles moved in zero gravity. All the reasons why he believed it.

When he finished, Father was angry.

"I taught you better, Bingwen. I taught you to respect your elders."

"Respect?" said Bingwen. Why was Father angry? He hadn't even told them about Ms. Yí.

"Are you smarter than the government now?" Father said, his voice rising. "Smarter than the military?"

"Of course not, Father."

"Then why do you profess to be? Don't you realize that by reaching this conclusion on your own you are calling everyone who has seen the vid and *not* believed it a fool?"

"I call no man a fool, Father."

"There are experts for this, Bingwen. Educated men. If they thought it was real, they would have taken action. There is no action, therefore it is not real. Know your place."

Mother said nothing, but Bingwen could see that she took Father's side. There was only disappointment and shame for him in her expression.

Bingwen bent low, putting his face to the floor.

"Do not mock me," said Father.

"No mockery, Father. Only respect for those whose name I carry and whose approval I seek. Forgive me if I have brought offense."

He wanted to argue, he *had* to argue. Aliens were coming, whether Father believed it or not. Bingwen knew it sounded ridiculous, but facts were facts. They had to prepare.

But what could he say that wouldn't make Father angrier? The discussion was closed. Father would never watch the vid now, even if Bingwen brought it to him on a platter.

Bingwen remained prostrate for several minutes, saying nothing more. When he finally sat up, only Grandfather remained.

"Don't anger your father," said Grandfather. "It spoils the evening."

Bingwen bent low again, but Grandfather got a hand under his shoulder and sat him back up. "Enough of the bowing. I'm not going to talk to the back of your head."

Grandfather reached out to the table and took his cup of tea. They were silent a moment as Grandfather drank it.

"You believe me," said Bingwen. "Don't you?"

"I believe that *you* believe," said Grandfather.

"That's not a complete answer."

Grandfather sighed. "Let us assume for a moment that something like this *might* be possible."

Bingwen smiled.

"Might," repeated Grandfather, raising a finger for emphasis. "Extremely unlikely, but possible."

"You must go to the library, Grandfather, and see this vid for yourself."

"And anger your father? No, no, no. I would rather enjoy my tea and sit by the fire in peace."

Bingwen was crestfallen.

"What good would it do anyway?" said Grandfather. "Even if it were true, what could we do about it? Can we fight with sticks? Fly into space? Or should we pray?"

"Prepare to run away," said Bingwen. "Pack what we need, and then bury it where we can get it quickly."

Grandfather laughed. "Bury our belongings? Why? The aliens won't care about our traveling food and clothing and tools."

"We're hiding it from Father," said Bingwen. "Since he told me not to do this, I'm being very disrespectful, trying to save our family's lives by making it possible for us to run away at a moment's notice."

"Your father will be furious when he finds out," said Grandfather.

"He will only find out if and when we need the buried items," said Bingwen. "By then, he will be grateful for them."

They spoke quietly after that, making an inventory of the items they would need. It wasn't until much later, as Bingwen was climbing into bed, his pants long since dried, that he realized that no one had even asked him why he had been wet.

# CHAPTER 2

# Victor

"Look at them, Imala," said Victor. "They're all going about their business as if nothing is wrong, as if this were another day in paradise."

He was gazing out the window of the track car as it zipped by the buildings and pedestrians of Luna, Imala sitting opposite him, holding her holopad. "The whole world could be headed to ashes," said Victor, "and nobody cares."

Outside, the walkways were crowded with people: men and women in suits, maintenance crews, merchants at kiosks selling hot pastries and coffee. Nearly everyone wore magnetic greaves on their shins, which pulled their feet down to the metal walkway and forced them to move with a steady stop-and-go, robotlike gait. Only a few people were bounce-walking, relying solely on the Moon's low gravity to hop about, and these were getting plenty of annoyed looks from those in greaves, as if to move about in such fashion were indecorous.

"They don't know that anything is wrong, Victor," said Imala. "The vid still only has around two million hits. I checked the numbers before we left."

Victor closed his eyes and let himself gradually sink back into his chair. Two million hits. So few.

"It's been ten days, Imala. Ten. The whole world should know by now. You said it would go viral." He knew he was being unfair; Imala wasn't to blame. But it was maddening to think that billions of people were completely oblivious. It was like being in a burning ship and he was the only person acknowledging the flames.

No. He wasn't the only one. Imala believed him. Everyone in the recovery hospital thought he was certifiably loco, but not Imala. She had accepted the evidence the instant he had shown it to her. And here he was throwing her efforts back in her face.

"I'm sorry," he said. "I'm not blaming you. I'm grateful to you. Honest. I just thought more people would know by now."

"I thought everyone would see what I saw," said Imala. "I thought this thing would explode on the nets. I never imagined people would be this skeptical."

"Skeptical is putting it lightly, Imala." He gestured for the holopad.

"Don't read the comments, Victor. They'll only annoy you."

He gently took the pad from her, pulled up the posts under the vid, and started reading. " 'What a joke. This is the worst makeup and costuming I've ever seen. Who put this expletive expletive together? What a load of expletive.' "

"Thanks for the tasteful editing."

"They don't believe us, Imala. They're either dismissive, critical, or downright malicious. They think we made it up."

"There are people who do this kind of thing as a hobby, Victor. They dress up and make fan videos. Aliens, lost underwater cities, magical realms. They invent whole universes. I've followed a few of the links. Some of their vids look nearly as real as ours."

"Yes, but ours *is* real, Imala. The hormigas are living breathing things. The destruction they cause? Real. The weapons they have? Real. Their ship? Real. This isn't fantasy time."

"Not everyone dismisses the vid. Some people believe us."

"Some, yes. But have you gone to their sites? A lot of them are conspiracy theorists and *loquitos*. Crazies. They'd believe a cup of sour cream was an alien if someone told them so. They aren't earning us any credibility."

"They're not all conspiracy theorists, Victor. We have over twenty thousand followers now. The vast majority are intelligent, respectable people. They're stockpiling supplies, sharing ideas, alerting local governments, pushing the scientific community to get involved. We're not alone on this."

"We might as well be," said Victor. "Twenty thousand followers, Imala. From two million people that have seen the vid. That's a one percent success rate. And not one percent of the global population, mind you. On global terms, twenty thousand people is . . ." He paused to do the math in his head. "Point zero zero zero zero zero one six. That's not even a drop in the bucket, Imala. That's a water molecule clinging to the drop in the bucket.

No, that's the electron circling the hydrogen atom on the water molecule on the drop in the bucket."

"You've made your point."

"It's why I can't stand to look outside," said Victor. "I see all these people doing nothing, fearing nothing, preparing for nothing, and I think I've failed them. Their lives are in my hands, Imala, and I'm failing. I'm letting them die."

"You're doing everything you can, Victor."

"No I'm not. I'm not doing anything. I'm a prisoner in a recovery hospital. You're the one doing all the work. You're the one going to the press."

"And mostly getting ignored."

"Yes, but at least you're engaged. At least you're doing something. I've done nada."

"You've done plenty. You crossed the solar system in a tiny cargo rocket and nearly killed yourself in the process. You let yourself waste away to nothing to get here. You left your family and loved ones. You brought us critical evidence. I say that counts for something."

"I mean I'm not doing anything *now*. If no one pays attention, if no one takes us seriously, what I've done doesn't matter."

"Which is why we're going to the Lunar Trade Department and getting you released. You're healthy enough to walk now. Your strength is back. The adjudicator for your case has agreed to see you early. If we play this right, she'll throw out the charges against you, and you'll be a free man. Then you can help me. We have a few good leads, and if you're with me, if we can get you in front of the right audience, maybe we can get to someone with real authority."

"Who's the person we're seeing? What are our chances?" asked Victor.

"Her name's Mungwai. She's the department's chief adjudicator. I tried to get someone else, but she reviewed your file and insisted on seeing us both."

"Why did you want someone else?"

"Mungwai is a hard-liner. She's from West Africa. Don't speak unless she asks you a direct question, and keep your answers brief and factual. She's not a prosecutor, but she ought to be. She despises rule breakers."

"Wonderful," said Victor.

Three minutes later they reached the LTD, and Imala quickly led Victor through security and up a floor to Customs. They waited another ten minutes in the lobby before a young receptionist called them back and ushered them into Mungwai's office.

Mungwai was tall and slender with her hair braided tightly to her head in narrow rows. She stood at her desk, feet anchored to the floor, tapping her way through a series of holoscreens hovering at eye level. She didn't look up.

"Mr. Victor Delgado," she said. "You sure know how to make an entrance. In your first five minutes on Luna, you managed to commit one count of entering Luna airspace without a license, one count of improper flight entry, one count of failing to provide entry authorizations, one count of interrupting a government-restricted radio frequency, and one count of trespassing." She made a hand movement above the holofield, and all the windows of data vanished. Victor was still wearing the cotton scrubs the recovery hospital had supplied him, and when Mungwai looked him up and down disapprovingly, Victor felt self-conscious.

"The 'improper flight entry' is the most serious charge," Mungwai continued, "since failure to comply with Luna traffic controllers poses a safety risk to other vessels on approach and the fine upstanding citizens of Luna. People around here get quite upset when you drop ships on their heads."

"It wasn't a ship," said Victor. "At least not a passenger ship. It was a quickship, a cargo rocket, a lugger. As soon as I approached Luna, your lunar guidance system took over. It was on autopilot when it entered the warehouse. That's why the trespassing charge strikes me as unjust. I couldn't have stopped the ship if I had wanted to."

"Yes, but you piloted the quickship *to* Luna," said Mungwai. "You brought it here. That makes you responsible."

"It would have come here anyway," said Victor. "That's what luggers are programmed to do. They carry cylinders of mined minerals from the Kuiper Belt and Asteroid Belt on preprogrammed flight paths." Victor had actually changed the flight parameters by hacking the ship's system, but he wasn't about to point out that fact now. "The quickship would have acted exactly the same once it reached Luna airspace with or without me on board. The only difference is that I was the cargo instead of cylinders. Surely you wouldn't have arrested cylinders for trespassing."

Mungwai raised an eyebrow, and Victor sensed he had gone too far.

"What I mean," he said, keeping his voice calm, "is that I could make a very good case that I was not the pilot of the quickship. Which, it stands to reason, would render the charges dismissible."

"I'll determine the validity of the charges, Mr. Delgado. That's what the taxpaying citizens of Luna pay me for." She waved her hand through the holospace again, and windows of data appeared in front of her. "You disrupted a restricted radio frequency. Are you going to argue that the quickship made you do that as well?"

"That was clearly my own doing," said Victor, "but I had no idea the frequency was restricted. I was being buried in a warehouse by damaged quickships. I was desperate for help. Every frequency I had tried before was silent."

"Ignorance of the law is no excuse for breaking it, Mr. Delgado. This isn't the Kuiper Belt, where it's every man for himself and laws be damned. This is Luna. We maintain order. We're civilized."

Victor felt his face getting hot. "With all due respect, ma'am, free miners are not lawless barbarians. I'd argue that our society is far more civilized than Luna."

Imala cleared her throat, but Victor pretended not to have heard.

Mungwai looked amused. "Is that so?"

"In the Kuiper Belt if someone needs help, you help them," said Victor. "If their ship needs repairs, if they're low on supplies, if their lives are threatened, you rush to their aid and do whatever you can to keep them alive. And once you've helped them, they don't humiliate you or arrest you or threaten you with lengthy prison terms. They thank you. I find that more civilized than what I've experienced here."

"You have been given the finest medical attention at no cost to you, Mr. Delgado," said Mungwai. "Muscle- and bone-building medications. Rigorous physical therapy. Room and board. Your criticism of that treatment strikes me as incredibly ungrateful."

Victor exhaled. This wasn't going well. "I am grateful for the care I have received. But I would rather have a listening ear than a pill. I know what has crippled space communications. I know what's causing the interference. A near-lightspeed alien ship is heading to Earth. It's in our solar system already. It has weapons capabilities far beyond anything we've seen. It destroyed four ships of free miners and killed hundreds of people, including a member of my own family." He was trembling now but keeping his voice calm. "I saw the bodies. Women, children, all of them dead."

Mungwai raised a hand to silence him. "I've read your file, Mr. Delgado. I know what you claim to have seen."

"I don't *claim* anything. I don't have to. The vids and evidence speak for themselves."

"I've seen your vid," said Mungwai. "I also saw four other vids from the scientific community refuting yours as a likely hoax."

Victor opened his mouth to speak but Mungwai cut him off.

"However, rather than pass judgment, I forwarded your evidence to a friend at STASA."

Victor nearly leapt at the words. STASA, the Space Trade and Security Authority. Imala had been trying to get their attention for days. STASA monitored all space traffic and commerce and had deep ties with every government on Earth. If anyone could add credibility to Victor's evidence, it was STASA. Earth would instantly respond.

"What did they say?" asked Imala.

"My friend said he would pass the information on to the proper department. STASA apparently has a whole division dedicated to addressing these kinds of anomalies."

"Anomalies?" said Victor.

"Tricks of the light," said Mungwai. "Hallucinations. It happens all the time. A miner doesn't regulate his oxygen levels correctly or is suffering from fatigue, and he sees all sorts of things."

"These aren't hallucinations," said Victor. "This isn't based on testimony—"

Imala cut him off. "When will you hear back from your contact at STASA? Can we contact him directly?"

"You won't be contacting anyone, Imala," said Mungwai. "You are on administrative leave effective immediately. I'm removing you from this case. And don't look so surprised. You've been neglecting your other duties, and what's worse, you aided a criminal and uploaded his vids onto the nets."

"To warn Earth!" said Imala.

"That is not your job," said Mungwai. "Your job is to inform illegal entrants of their rights and to prepare the necessary documentation for their deportation."

"You're deporting me?" said Victor.

"You're an illegal entrant, Mr. Delgado. And a lawbreaker. I have decided not to give your case to the prosecutor, but I cannot allow you to remain on Luna. You will stay in the recovery hospital until the next ship

leaves for the Asteroid Belt in four days. If STASA wants to contact you or
request a stay before then, they may do so. Otherwise, you're on that ship.
Once you reach the Asteroid Belt you'll have to find your own passage back
to your family. I don't have a vessel going that far. As for the vids you uploaded onto the nets, I'm having them removed immediately."

"What!" said Victor.

"You can't," said Imala.

"I can and will," said Mungwai. "This department will not be held responsible for inducing a worldwide panic. You helped upload those vids,
Imala, which makes us partly responsible for any adverse effect they may
have on the citizenry. That showed extremely poor judgment on your part."

"People need to know," said Imala.

"There are protocols for this, Imala."

"Are you sure?" said Imala. "Because I don't recall reading 'How to
Warn Earth of an Alien Invasion' in the employee handbook."

Mungwai stiffened. "You are dismissed, Imala. And you're lucky I don't
have you fired outright. That is still a possibility. In which case, you would
be on the first ship back to Earth. I suggest you don't push the matter."

Imala said nothing, jaw clenched tight.

"You saw the vids," Victor said to Mungwai. "How can you do this?"

"What I am doing, Mr. Delgado, is keeping the peace and maintaining
order, what should have been done in the first place. Screaming 'fire' in a
crowded theater will only get people killed, even if there *is* a fire. Inform-
ing STASA is the best course of action. Isn't that what you wanted? They're
the best people to handle this."

"Unless they dismiss it," said Victor. "Unless they blow it off like everyone else."

"You are excused, Imala," said Mungwai. "I will see to it that Mr. Delgado is escorted back to the hospital."

She was dismissing them. The conversation was over.

Imala stood still a moment, then nodded, coming to a decision. "See
you around, Victor."

Victor watched her walk out and close the door behind her. Was she really abandoning him like this? Didn't she realize what was at stake here?
What if STASA didn't take it seriously? They needed to fight this. They
needed to see it through.

Mungwai spoke a command into her holofield, but Victor barely noticed. He was staring at the door, willing it to open. Without Imala he had nothing.

The door opened.

It wasn't Imala. It was two men in security uniforms. They took Victor outside to a car and put him in the back. One of the men climbed in after him, and the two of them rode in silence back to the hospital. The man then led Victor back to his room and made sure the door was locked before leaving Victor alone.

Victor sat on the side of his bed. They were sending him back. He had come all this way, risked everything, and they were tossing him out like space junk.

He thought of Janda, his cousin. If she were here, she would know what to do—or at least she would have Victor laughing and feeling confident again. He thought of Mother and Father and of Concepción and of the money they had left him to start his education on Earth. Now even school was impossible.

Later that evening an orderly brought dinner. As the man locked the tray down onto Victor's bedside table, Victor considered trying to subdue him and taking his key cards. It would be a pointless attempt, though, he knew. Victor was still getting his strength back, and the orderly looked strong enough to restrain four people at once. Besides, where would Victor go? His data cube held all the evidence and vids, and that was locked up at the nurses' station. He was useless without it.

When the door opened a half hour later, Victor was lying on his bed with his eyes closed. It would be the orderly, come to recover the untouched food.

"So you're giving up?" said Imala.

Victor opened his eyes. Imala stood before him, holding a small duffel bag. She tossed it onto the bed beside him. "I wasn't sure about your size. The clothes you came in didn't have tags on them."

Victor opened the bag. Pants, a shirt, undergarments, shoes, a heavy jacket, a pair of greaves.

"What, you've never seen new clothes before?" said Imala. "Don't just stand there. Get dressed."

She stepped away from the bed and turned around, putting her back to him.

"You're breaking me out?" he said.

"LTD records will show that you were moved to a holding facility for healthy illegals awaiting deportation. The holding facility will have no record of this, so unless Mungwai checks or the two offices compare records, we'll probably go unnoticed for a while."

"How long is a while?"

"A few days. Maybe less."

Victor began to change. "What about the cameras? There are three in this room and more throughout the building."

"I've taken care of the ones in here and those out in the hall. Once we're outside, it's a different story. Wear the hood."

There was a hood on the jacket. Victor slid it on over the shirt and hurried into the pants. She had taken care of the cameras. She had thought of everything, handled everything. And in only a few hours, no less. He suddenly felt a sense of awe toward Imala. She was more like a free miner than he had given her credit for.

"Is this smart?" he asked. "What if STASA comes looking for me for more intel?"

"I doubt they will," said Imala. "Not before your ship leaves anyway. I checked Mungwai's messages. Her contact at STASA is a low-level associate. No clout. His response to her didn't sound too promising."

"You hacked her messages?"

"It's not difficult. Point is, this guy didn't seem like a strong lead. If he passes the evidence along, it'll take time to move up the chain and be verified. But don't sweat it; I've built an alert into our system. If STASA tries to contact you, they'll do it through the LTD, and if that happens, my holopad will let me know. We'll go directly to STASA then."

"You really *have* thought of everything," he said, fastening the straps on his shoes. "But why don't we go to STASA now? We've got an in."

"We don't have an in. We have a halfhearted nobody with job preservation on the brain. I'm not putting the fate of the world in that guy's hands, and I'm not sitting around and waiting for STASA to get their act together. We're following another lead. Maybe a better one."

"Who?"

"She's waiting outside."

"What about Mungwai? If you do this your career is over."

"The fate of the world trumps any concerns about my career, Victor, though I appreciate the sentiment. Don't worry about Mungwai. She can't pull our vids down, not all of them anyway. They've been copied and re-posted far too many times. Two million hits may not seem like a lot on a global scale, but it means the train has left the station. You dressed yet?"

He snapped the greaves onto his shins. "How do I look?"

She turned and faced him. "Like a punk teenager. Put your hands behind you."

She pulled wrist restraints from her pocket and snapped them onto his wrists.

"I'm assuming this is part of the ruse," he said.

She took him by the arm and escorted him out into the hall. They moved straight for the exit, not rushing, but not poking along either. No one paid them any attention.

Victor stopped. "My data cube."

Imala pulled at his arm and got him moving again, keeping her voice low. "Already got it. Keep moving."

They were through the doors and outside. The domed canopy high above them was bright and blue like the skies of Earth, or at least like the skies of Earth Victor had seen in films. A car was at the curb. Imala opened the door and helped Victor inside. An Asian woman in her early twenties was waiting for them, sitting opposite, her right arm much smaller than her left. Imala crawled in next to Victor and closed the door. The car slipped onto the track and accelerated. Imala turned Victor's shoulder, reached behind him, and unfastened the restraints. "Victor, this is Yanyu. She contacted me after I left Mungwai's office. She's a grad assistant for an astrophysicist doing research for Juke Limited. She's here to help."

Yanyu leaned forward, smiling, and offered Victor her left hand, which he shook. "Nice to meet you, Victor. I recognize you from the vids."

Her English was good, but her accent was thick. "You've seen the vids?"

Yanyu smiled and nodded. "Many times. And I believe you."

Victor blinked. Another believer, and a seemingly intelligent, noncrazy one to boot. He felt like leaping across the seat and embracing her.

"I'm not the only one either," said Yanyu. "In the forums, a lot of researchers are talking about it, though most of them post anonymously so as not to damage their reputation in case the whole thing proves false."

"It's not false," said Victor.

"You don't have to convince me," said Yanyu, smiling.

"Yanyu has been studying the interference," said Imala.

"The media keeps broadcasting all kinds of theories," said Yanyu. "The prevailing one at the moment is that the interference is caused by CMEs."

Victor nodded, unsurprised. If he had to invent a theory, he'd probably go there as well. Coronal mass ejections, or CMEs, were huge magnetized clouds of electrified gas, or plasma, that burst out of the sun's atmosphere and shot across the solar system at millions of miles per hour, oftentimes expanding to ten millions times their original size. They had been known to disrupt power and communication in space before, though never on this scale.

"It's not CMEs," said Victor.

"No," said Yanyu. "But the idea is right. The gamma radiation this alien ship is emitting moves much like a CME, constantly expanding as it spreads across the solar system. If I had to guess, I'd say the ship has a ramscoop drive, sucking up hydrogen atoms at near-lightspeed and using the subsequent gamma radiation as a propellant, shooting it out the back to rocket the ship forward. It's brilliant engineering since the ship would have an infinite supply of fuel."

"If that's true," said Imala, "then why is the radiation coming in our direction, toward Earth? If it's propulsion, shouldn't it be emitting away from us, toward deep space?"

Yanyu smiled again. "That's just it. It's not accelerating. It's decelerating. It's desperately trying to slow down."

"It wouldn't emit the radiation from the front," said Victor. "Even to slow down. That would be suicide. It would fly right into its own destructive cloud of plasma."

"True," said Yanyu. "But the ship might emit the radiation from the *sides*. It would do so in equal bursts so as not to deviate it from its course, and that would explain why the interference happened so fast and spread so quickly in all directions before anyone knew what was happening."

Victor considered this. It made sense. He had known superficially that the hormiga ship was causing the radiation, yet until now he hadn't known how.

"So this ship," said Imala, "is acting like a volatile minisun rocketing toward us."

"Basically," said Yanyu.

"That's comforting," said Imala.

"How did you figure this out?" asked Victor.

Yanyu pulled a holopad from her bag. "It's the only explanation I could think of for this." She tapped a command and extended two thin poles from opposite corners on the holopad's surface. A moment later, a holo consisting of hundreds of tiny, random dots of light flickered to life above the pad. At first Victor thought he was looking at a star cluster, but as he leaned forward and got a closer look, a sickening feeling tugged at the pit of his stomach. He had seen such a cluster before. Deep in the Kuiper Belt.

"What is it?" asked Imala.

"Wreckage," said Victor.

Yanyu nodded, grave. "I'm still running scans because the readings from the scopes aren't particularly clear, but I think Victor's right. These objects appear to be moving away from each other at a constant speed from a center point. Like ship debris from an explosion."

"How many ships?" said Victor.

Yanyu shrugged. "No way to be certain, but probably dozens. If you trace the movement of all of the debris, the point of origin is here in the Asteroid Belt, near an asteroid named Kleopatra. Juke has facilities on the asteroid's surface, so there's always a lot of traffic there. If a burst of radiation from the alien ship took out the mining ships in that vicinity, then we have to assume that it took out all the facilities on Kleopatra as well."

"How many people are stationed there?" asked Imala.

"Between seven and eight hundred," said Yanyu.

Imala swore under her breath.

"And who knows how many people were on those ships," said Yanyu. "Maybe double that. We have no way of knowing."

"How old is this data?" said Victor.

"I got the first scans back this morning," said Yanyu.

"Who else knows about this?" said Victor.

"I shared it with my supervisor. He's reviewing the data now. He made me come find you and bring you back to the lab."

"We need to contact the media," said Imala. "Your supervisor needs to hold a press conference."

Yanyu frowned and shook her head. "No. I am sorry. That will not happen. We are not independent researchers. We work for Juke Limited. If anyone holds a press conference it has to be corporate."

"Corporates?" said Victor. "You want to bring in a lying snake like Ukko Jukes? He'll twist this somehow, he'll use it for his own gain. That's the last thing we need."

"I can't stand the man either, Victor," said Imala. "But these are his employees. He's responsible for these people. Their families on Luna or Earth deserve to know what has happened to them."

"We don't know what's happened to them, Imala," said Victor. "We're speculating."

"Ukko can help us, Victor. He has connections throughout the world. He's the most powerful man alive. If he knows the truth, the whole world will know."

Victor sat back. Ukko Jukes, father of Lem Jukes, the man who had crippled Victor's family's ship and killed his uncle. What had Father said at the time? The apple doesn't fall far from the tree? If Victor couldn't work with Lem, how could he possibly work with the father?

Yet what choice did Victor have? He was a fugitive, with nowhere to run and no other leads. It was only a matter of time before the LTD found him and Imala and sent them both packing.

"If we do this, I want to talk to Ukko Jukes myself," said Victor. "I want to tell him to his face that his son is a murdering bastard."

"Don't bother," said Imala. "Knowing Ukko, he might take that as a compliment."

# CHAPTER 3

# Lem

Lem Jukes stood before the crew of his asteroid-mining ship with his hands clasped reverently in front of him. He watched as the last people to arrive floated through the entrance and made their way to the back of the room where the rest of the crew was gathered. Each of them wore a blue jumpsuit with the Juke Limited corporate logo embroidered over the left breast. The magnetic greaves on their shins and vambraces on their forearms anchored them to the floor once they were in position. Other than the quiet rustle of fabric as everyone took their places, the helm was completely silent.

Lem hadn't made the memorial service mandatory, but he knew everyone on board would come, including those who didn't normally work in the helm: the cooks and miners and launderers and engineers. When you lived for nearly two years with people in a cramped environment, you got to know each of them rather well, even if your individual assignments didn't have you working alongside each other. Sooner or later, your paths would cross, and as a result, any loss of life on board was a loss felt by everyone. No one would miss the chance to pay their respects.

"I called this memorial service to honor those we have lost," said Lem. His voice was loud enough to reach the back of the room, yet calm and solemn enough for the occasion. "I speak not only of the members of our own crew who are gone, but also of the many others in space who have so selflessly fought and died trying to stop the Formics from reaching Earth."

Formics. The word still felt bitter and foreign in his mouth, like a large chalky tablet that he couldn't force himself to swallow. Dr. Benyawe, the leader of the science team, had suggested the name because of the creatures' antlike appearance, and as far as Lem was concerned it was as good a name as any. But he still hated it. The word gave the creatures legitimacy, an identity. It was a reminder that they were real, that this whole thing was not merely a dream.

"Nearly two years ago," Lem continued, "we left loved ones on Luna and set out for the Kuiper Belt. Our mission was simple: test the gravity laser. Point it at a few rocks and blow them to dust, prove to headquarters that the glaser can and will revolutionize the mineral-extraction process. Thanks to your diligence and unwavering commitment, we completed that task. It wasn't easy. It wasn't without mistakes and setbacks. But each of you persisted and did your duty. Each of you proved yourself. It has been my highest honor as your captain to serve beside you and watch you perform your tasks with such persistent exactness."

Lem knew he was laying it on thick, but he also knew that no one would doubt his sincerity. Mother had always said that were he not the heir to the largest asteroid-mining fortune in the solar system, he could have had a career on the stage. Lem had found that amusing; Mother was always thinking so small. The stage was for the pretentious and unattractive, all those who didn't have a face for the vids.

"But eight months ago our mission changed." Lem tapped his wrist pad, and the system chart behind him winked to life. A holo of the Formic ship appeared large and imposing. "*This* became our mission. This abomination. No one gave us the order to stop it. We gave that order to ourselves."

Technically, that was a half truth since it was the captain of the free-miner ship El Cavador who had asked Lem to help them stop the Formics. But what did that matter? Lem had accepted the invitation. No one had forced his hand.

He tapped his wrist pad again. The Formic ship vanished, and the faces of twenty-five men appeared. "Some of you may think that attacking the Formics was a mistake. We lost twenty-five of our crew, after all. Twenty-five good men. Twenty-five future husbands and fathers."

A woman near the front wiped at her eyes. A good sign, Lem thought. His real purpose here was not the memorial service, after all. It was to re-take command of the ship, *true* command, not to serve as captain in name only, but to have his orders followed, to hold absolute authority. To achieve that, he needed to stir up their emotions a bit.

"But I say attacking the Formics was not a mistake," Lem continued. "Sending a message to them that we would rather die than see our world taken from us was not a mistake. Proving to Earth that we would do anything to protect her was not a mistake. Taking steps to save our families back on Luna and Earth was not a mistake."

He could see he had them now. A few of them were nodding along.

"But then something changed," said Lem. "We stopped focusing on Earth. After following the Formic ship closely, we pulled back. We retreated way out here to the ecliptic, a great distance from the Formics and thus a great distance from those we could have warned and saved." He paused a moment and lowered his voice, as if it pained him to say the words.

"We knew more about the Formic ship than anyone. Its weapons capabilities, its speed, its likely destination. We had even calculated when and where it might emit its next burst of radiation. If we had stayed close to it, maybe we could've warned all those ships in its path."

He tapped his wrist pad. The faces in the holo vanished, and a cloud of debris appeared in the holofield.

"Like these ships. The ships at Kleopatra, home to a Juke outpost and processing facility. Nearly eight hundred of our own people lived on that rock, plus however many people were in the ships around it. Most of them free-miner families. Women, children, infants, the elderly. We could have warned them. But we didn't."

More taps. More holos. More wreckage. One by one, Lem displayed scenes of destruction. One by one he recounted the lives lost. Most of the crew had already seen these images; the ship had collected them over the past few months as they tracked the Formic ship by following its path of destruction toward Earth.

Lem described what it must have been like to be on those ships, explaining how a blast of gamma plasma at close range would vaporize blood and bone. And how, at longer ranges, flesh burned and cells broke down as a result of radiation poisoning.

"And while *we* were hiding in the shadows," he continued, "these people were fighting for Earth. While we retreated and protected *ourselves,* they faced the enemy, fighting for us, dying for us."

A few of the crew shifted uncomfortably. He was hitting a nerve.

A part of Lem felt a touch guilty for manipulating them this way. It was tacky and opportunistic to use a memorial service for personal gain, but then again this was war, not only between humans and Formics but also between Lem and Father, the great and glorious Ukko Jukes.

It had been Father who had given Chubs the secret orders to monitor everything Lem did as captain and to override Lem's orders should Lem do anything to put himself in danger, which made Chubs, in essence, a secret glorified babysitter.

Father would no doubt call this good parenting, looking out for his son, protecting him from the dangers of the Kuiper Belt. But Lem knew what was really at play here. Father was doing what he always did: asserting his control, pulling the strings, playing his little game of power, and making Lem look like the fool.

The whole thing had been especially humiliating since it was a year into the mission before Lem had realized that he wasn't exactly in charge. Chubs had been a stand-up guy about the whole situation. He had meant no hard feelings. He had even gone out of his way to keep Lem from losing face with the crew by keeping the whole thing a secret. But that hadn't taken the sting out of being made to look the fool. For a whole year, Lem had been convinced that Chubs was his most trusted adviser. And then surprise! I'm really working for your father, Lem, and no I won't relay your order to the crew because I can't allow you to make it. Sorry, your dear daddy said so.

Oh Father, you can't help yourself, can you? You can't stand the idea that I might actually accomplish something on my own without your involvement. You have to secretly insert yourself into my affairs. Sly, Father. Whatever the outcome, you win. If the mission fails, it's all my fault, if it succeeds, it only succeeded because you were there helping me along.

The thought was like a rod of steel added to Lem's spine. He was all the more convinced that he could never trust anyone on board and that the only way he would be free of Father was to beat Father at his own game, to take the company, to remove Father from his vaulted throne and politely show him the door.

That war began now, here on board Makarhu, weeks and months from Earth.

"Why did these people charge headlong into danger?" Lem continued, gesturing back at the debris cloud in the holofield. "Why did they risk their families? Because they felt a duty to protect the human race. A duty greater than themselves. I know many of you feel that same duty. I feel it too. I feel it so strongly that for the past several months I have lain in my hammock at night, overcome with shame."

Their faces showed their surprise.

"Yes, shame. I am ashamed that we sit here and do nothing except follow at a safe distance, while others fight to protect Earth. I wanted to warn Kleopatra. I wanted to rush in and tell them exactly what they were up against. But Chubs could not allow it." At the mention of his name, everyone turned to Chubs, who stood off to the side near the front, face forward, revealing nothing. "Yes," Lem continued, "that is a secret I recently learned that none of you know. Chubs was told by my father to keep me out of harm's way at all cost."

The crew exchanged glances.

"That's why we've been following the Formics at a safe distance," Lem continued. "That's why people have died. Because my father values me more than them, and thus prevents Chubs from helping them. That is why I am ashamed."

Here was the critical moment, he knew, the moment where he could let his own emotion show. Not as tears, of course—he couldn't look weak here. It would be much more powerful to give the appearance of *approaching* tears and then be strong and stoic enough to push them back. It wasn't easy. A lot of actors thought you had to go big, weeping and wailing and breaking a plate or two, but Lem knew better. It was the *contained* emotion that moved people. The grief and sadness that was threatening to rise up out of you, but dammit you weren't going to let it; you were going to be strong.

He pulled it off flawlessly, staying silent for slightly longer than normal so that they knew he was struggling to keep his emotions at bay. Then he cleared his throat, composed himself, and moved on. A few more near the front were crying.

"Were it up to me, we would be doing our duty to Earth," he said. "We would be doing more. We would be saving lives other than our own. But I am powerless. I see that now. With Chubs following his order from my father, I'm unable to do what I know is right. That is why, effective immediately, I am resigning my post as your captain."

Their faces said it all. Shock. Disbelief.

Lem couldn't have asked for a better reaction.

"You'll forgive me," he said, "but I can't continue to be the reason why we turn our backs on people. Should he accept the assignment, Chubs will serve as your captain. If he must adhere to my father's order, if he must put obedience to that rule above all concerns, then he must bear the shame of it. I hope he forgives me for giving him that burden, but I can't live with myself knowing that people are dying because he is protecting me."

Lem kicked off from the platform, floated over to Chubs, and offered his hand. Chubs saw that everyone was watching, some resentfully.

Chubs wisely took the offered hand and shook it, uneasy.

"You may not have allowed us to prevent those deaths," said Lem, "but you were doing what you thought was right. I commend you for that. I only pray God forgives us all."

Chubs didn't say a word. What could he say?

Lem launched across the room, climbed into the push tube, adjusted the polarity of his vambraces and shins, and said, "Fourteen."

The tube whooshed him away. When he reached his quarters, he moved straight to his holodesk. "Show me the helm."

Six video feeds appeared in the air above his desk, all taken from tiny cameras Lem had placed throughout the helm. He didn't have audio, but he didn't need it. He saw how some of the crew looked askance at Chubs with pure contempt.

Lem relaxed. All he had to do now was wait.

He didn't have to wait too long. Benyawe came to his quarters a few hours later. "That was quite a performance," she said. Lem was in his hammock, zipped to his waist, a box of chocolates floating in front of him. "Is that your reward to yourself?" she asked, gesturing to the chocolates.

"Nina. One of the cooks makes them for me. She brought me a box a little while ago."

"No doubt to comfort you as you deal with your *shame*." She forced a smile.

"They're quite good," said Lem, ignoring the jibe. "You should try one." Without waiting for her to answer he removed one from the box and pushed it through the air to her. It floated into her outstretched hand, and she popped it into her mouth and chewed.

"Little heavy for my taste," said Benyawe.

"The chocolate or my performance?"

"Both. When you almost cried, I thought that a bit much. Very convincing, mind you. But a bit much."

"Everything I said was true."

"Nearly everything," said Benyawe. "You said those people died because of us, that we would have warned them if not for Chubs. That's not
true. Most of them we wouldn't have reached before the Formics did. In
fact, in nearly every case, there's nothing we could have done. Had we not
fled the Formic ship and come out this far, we likely would have died from
the Formics venting their gamma plasma. Chubs was keeping us alive. And
yet you practically tied him to the stake and set the thing aflame. That wasn't
very sporting. He has been nothing but dutiful to you."

"Dutiful to my father, you mean."

"He saved your life, Lem," said Benyawe.

That was true enough, thought Lem. During the attack on the Formic
ship, Chubs had acted swiftly and saved Lem from a charging Formic who
seemed bent on ripping him limb from limb.

"When this is all over," said Lem, "I will see to it that my father rewards
Chubs for his service."

"If he gives you the captainship, that is," said Benyawe. "If he plays his
part in this little theatrical production of yours."

"Maybe you weren't paying attention at the memorial service, Benyawe.
I resigned the captainship."

She looked annoyed. "Please, Lem. What choice does Chubs have now
but to give it back to you and commit to the crew that he will never interfere with your orders again? If he doesn't do it, there's already talk of it
being taken from him."

Lem feigned shock. "Mutiny?"

"Don't pretend to be appalled, Lem. That's what you want, isn't it?"

Now he sincerely looked surprised. "You don't honestly think I want
mutiny, do you?"

She frowned and folded her arms. "Probably not. But you might not be
too quick to squelch it."

He smiled. "That is the captain's duty. Not mine."

She laughed. "You know, sometimes I look at you and see a younger version of your father, and sometimes I see a *better* version of your father."

"Yet you always see my father. I'm not sure how to take that."

"You are your father's son . . . whether you want to be or not."

He was surprised by that statement. Was it that evident that he hoped to
distance himself from Father? He had been careful never to disparage

Father in front of anyone, especially the crew. If anything, he had always spoken of his love for Father, which was not easily expressed but which was true nonetheless. He did love Father. Not in a traditional sense, perhaps, but the respect he held for Father was, he had to admit, a love of sorts.

There was a chime, and the female voice of the computer announced, "Chief Officer Patrick Chubs."

Benyawe smirked. "Shouldn't that be *Captain* Chubs?"

Lem ignored her. "Enter," he said.

The door slid open, and Chubs floated into the room. He looked tired and not at all surprised to see Benyawe. "So how do you want to do this exactly?" he asked Lem.

"Do what?" Lem asked.

"Finish this fiasco. We've got to see it through. I'll refuse the captainship and promise never to interfere with your orders again. How do you want to do it? You want me to make an announcement, write a mail message, or do we need to have another scene in front of the crew? Frankly whatever the plan is, I'd like to get it over with."

Lem felt a pang of guilt then. Benyawe was right. Chubs *had* been dutiful. He didn't deserve to be vilified. The man was only doing the job Father had hired him to do. Lem unzipped himself from the hammock and floated over to him. "You will always have a place in this company, Chubs. A good place. Your pick of it. I'll see to that. And should you refuse the captainship and insist that I take it, I would keep you as my chief officer. I'd be foolish not to. You're the most loyal and capable man on this ship."

"Is that safe?" asked Benyawe. "A few hours ago, you had the crew ready to string him up."

"He'd be working with the officers," said Lem. "They're completely loyal to Chubs."

"I wouldn't say completely," said Chubs. "Not anymore."

Again, a twinge of guilt pecked at Lem's conscience. He hadn't ruined Chubs per se, but he had severely damaged him, no question. Whatever friendship might have once existed between them was gone now. Lem could see that. There would forever be an awkward formality between them now.

"I'm sorry you felt the memorial service was a scene," said Lem. "And if you're choosing to refuse the captainship, you must understand that I cannot interfere with that decision in any way. I can't tell you how to proceed. That would imply I orchestrated all this, which of course is not true.

This must be your own decision. How and when you do it is entirely up to you."

It was unlikely that Chubs was recording their conversation in an effort to catch Lem in some confession, but it was better to be safe than sorry. They could never have any words between them that implied Lem had forced Chubs's hand.

Chubs nodded. He understood. Then he excused himself.

When he was gone Benyawe said, "When we return to Luna, I hope we hold another memorial service. One with a little more heart. The dead deserve that."

She launched off the floor and left without another word.

The holo from Chubs came a half hour later, sent out to all members of the crew. In it, he thanked Lem for thinking him worthy of so great an office, but he couldn't possibly accept. Nor would he interfere with Lem's commands. He agreed completely with Lem. Earth came first. If Ukko Jukes fired him for his insubordination, so be it. It was a small price to pay.

It was expertly done. Professional, sincere, and quite touching. Lem even found his eyes misting over, though his relief might have added to the emotion.

He waited an hour before recording his own holo. He humbly thanked Chubs for his selflessness and insisted that Chubs continue as his chief officer. It was a decent take, but he knew he could do better. Might as well get it right before sending it out. On the seventh take he had it. Every pause and breath and word was exactly as it needed to be. He sent it, waited another hour, then returned to the helm.

Chubs was waiting for him at the system chart. "What's your first unhindered command as captain?"

"Take us closer to the Formics' trajectory," said Lem. "Our scanners can't read much out here. Let's learn what we can and get back to Luna as soon as possible."

"You're the boss," said Chubs.

Yes, thought Lem. For the first time in two years, I am.

# CHAPTER 4

# Ukko

The track car sped east through the city of Imbrium, passing dormitories and government buildings and small industrial complexes. Victor sat by the window watching everything zip by, still amazed at the size and immensity of the city. "How do you fill all these domes and connector tunnels with oxygen?" he asked. "Where do you find that much air?"

Yanyu was still sitting opposite him, escorting Victor and Imala to the Juke observatory. "Lunar oxygen mostly comes from excavation," she said. "Everything you see is what we call the Old City. When people first came to Luna, they built the settlement on the surface. That required them to first build all these airtight domes to contain the oxygen and to protect the settlers from a constant bombardment of space particles. It was very expensive. These days all new construction takes place underground. That's where most people live now, as a matter of fact."

"*You* live aboveground," said Victor.

"Only because I'm on a budget and can't afford to live in the tunnels," said Yanyu. "But if I had the money I would. It's safer. You don't have to worry about bombardments or collision threats. And since there's no tectonic activity on the Moon, you don't have to worry about earthquakes either. Plus it's much quieter. The real benefit, though, is all the raw materials we extract from the excavated rock. Metals for construction of course, but also oxygen."

Victor looked surprised. "Oxygen from rocks? Is that possible?"

"You're breathing it," said Imala.

Victor sat back and shook his head. "Do you have any idea how useful that tech would be out in the Kuiper Belt? All of our $O_2$ came from mining ice. If we didn't find ice, we were *muerto*. Dead. A lot of families were lost that way."

"It's much easier to extract oxygen from ice," said Imala. "That doesn't take a lot of equipment. Pulling oxygen and nitrogen from rock, on the other hand, takes massive processing facilities. We don't build ships big enough to carry that tech out to the Deep. Someday perhaps, but not in our lifetime."

"What about fuel and energy for the tunnels?" asked Victor. "If the heat of the sun doesn't reach them, they must be freezing."

"All power on the moon is electric," said Imala. "It all comes from high-efficiency batteries powered by solar energy. There are solar arrays all over the surface, with the biggest ones in the equatorial area where the collectors lie flat on the ground. There are big ones at the poles, too, where rotating collectors on towers face the sun twenty-four/seven. Believe me, as long as the sun shines, power and heat aren't an issue."

Victor nodded, though he didn't share Imala's confidence. Batteries were unreliable. They failed all the time on El Cavador. "So this observatory we're going to, since it has telescopes, I'm assuming it's aboveground?"

"Oh no," said Yanyu. "It's below the surface. Almost all of the Juke facilities are. In fact, most of the tunnels outside the city belong to Juke Limited, although few people know how vast the company's tunnels really are. Mr. Jukes has secret R&D efforts in almost every industry, and yet few of those operations or departments appear on any tunnel maps. If I had to guess, I'd say the company's tunnel system is much bigger than the city itself."

"But if the observatory is underground, where are the scopes?" asked Victor.

"Far from here," said Yanyu, "positioned at various points around Luna, away from any light pollution. We tell them where to look, then we process all the images and data in our observation room. Traditional observatories like those on Earth don't exist on Luna. Up here they're all cubicles and office space. Not very interesting, I'm afraid."

The track car dipped suddenly into a tunnel entrance, and for a moment they found themselves in total darkness until the vehicle's interior lights turned on.

They maintained their speed for several minutes until the car took a fork in the track and began to decelerate. It took a series of turns and then pulled into a docking slot and stopped. Air tubes extended from the wall and encircled the vehicle. Then a chime sounded the all-clear, and the doors slid open. Victor, Imala, and Yanyu stepped out onto the docking platform. Yanyu then led them through a labyrinth of corridors and a series of locked doors. Victor was lost almost immediately.

At each door, a cubical holofield hovered by the doorjamb. Yanyu extended her hand into the holofield and did a series of wrist twists and finger movements that unlocked the door. At first Victor thought the movements were random, but then one of the doors buzzed in the negative and Yanyu had to retract her hand, reinsert it into the field, and begin the dance again. Finally they reached a simple, metal door adorned with the Juke Limited logo and the words:

ASTRONOMICAL OBSERVATORY

Yanyu led them into a low-lit observation room with a domed ceiling. Images of star clusters and nebulae and astronomical data were projected onto the ceiling, dissolving in and out like a screensaver. A dozen desks were scattered around the room with lamps and computer terminals and personal items. In the center of the room was a conference table, where a small crowd of researchers stood waiting. Yanyu stopped and gestured to the bearded man near the front. "Victor, Imala, I'd like you to meet Dr. Richard Prescott, the director of the observatory and our lead astrophysicist."

Prescott stepped forward and shook Imala's hand. He was younger than Victor had expected, midthirties maybe, with a mop of brown hair and casual street clothes. "Ms. Bootstamp. A privilege. Welcome. And Mr. Delgado, good to have you, as well. I hope you had no problems getting here."

"I had to sneak Victor out of the recovery hospital where he was being held," said Imala. "Which broke a few laws and makes both of us fugitives. Other than that, no problems."

Prescott seem unfazed by this. He put his hands in his pockets and smiled warmly. "Well, you're safe here."

Imala cut to the chase. "We need to get an audience with Ukko Jukes. With his backing, we can make a legitimate warning to Earth. Can you make that happen?"

"Probably," said Prescott. "But first things first." He gestured to the conference table. "Won't you sit down?"

"You don't believe us, do you?" said Victor.

Prescott smiled. "We wouldn't have brought you here if we didn't think you might be telling the truth, Victor. We all believe you to some extent. But before any of us act, we want to be absolutely certain. There are people outside this room who will need a lot more convincing than us. If we work together, we might be able to win them over." He gestured again to the table, and this time Victor and Imala each took a seat.

Prescott sat at the head of the table. "You have to realize, people in our field are even more skeptical of claims of extraterrestrial life than normal people. We have to be. Scientists are bred to doubt and question everything. Plus the prevailing belief has always been that we would *hear* extraterrestrial life before we saw it. We'd pick up their transmissions long before they showed up on our scopes. But so far no one in the science community has heard anything."

"You *can't* hear anything," said Imala. "The interference is crippling communications."

"True," said Prescott. "But that makes the whole claim of extraterrestrial life all the more difficult to believe. Impaired communications strike a lot of people as enormously convenient to a charlatan trying to justify the sky's silence."

"I'm not a charlatan," said Victor.

"I'm not saying you are," said Prescott. "I'm telling you what the chatter is out there. Nobody wants to back you because it's a claim they can't independently validate. So they keep quiet and hope someone else will take the risk. No one wants to look like a fool supporting what might be the biggest hoax of the century."

"The biggest *discovery* of the century," Victor corrected. "Not to mention the biggest threat to our species."

Prescott settled back in his chair. "That's the question, isn't it? Yanyu has shown us a few observations she's made. We've all seen the vids you and Imala uploaded. We've combed through the evidence. We've argued about it for hours. Now we want to hear it straight from you. If we believe you, we'll make things happen. The floor is yours, Victor. Convince us."

Victor glanced at Imala, who gave him an encouraging nod. Then he looked at the faces of the people gathered around the table, all of them older than him and well educated and experts in their field. Most of their expressions were unreadable, but a few had a hard time hiding their skepticism.

He cleared his throat and began to speak.

For the first hour no one said a word. Then Yanyu would occasionally speak up, throwing in astronomical data that seemed to validate Victor's story.

When he finished, the questions came fast. How is this ship causing the interference? Where is the ship now? Has anyone attempted to communicate with it, not with radio but by other means? Infrared light perhaps? What are the ship's intentions?

"I don't know," Victor said for the tenth time. "I don't know where the ship is or what damage it's caused or what lives it's taken. I wish I did know. I wish I had answers. I wish I knew my family was safe."

The mention of his family pricked some well of emotion inside him, and for a moment, he thought he might lose his composure. He swallowed, took a breath, and buried the emotion. "I don't have the answers. I'm not a navigator. I know basic fight mechanics and trajectory mapping, but that wasn't my job on my ship. I'm a mechanic. I build things, fix things. My family sent me because I was young and healthy. I had the best chance of withstanding the physical beating the trip would inflict on my body.

"Plus I could repair the quickship if anything went wrong. No one on board had that level of mechanical expertise. It had to be me. I know you'd rather have someone who understands science as much as you do, but I'm not that person. I'm the messenger." He paused and looked at each of the researchers in turn. "The ship is real and it's coming. A few days, a few months, I don't know. But it's coming. If we could talk to the ships in the Belt, we'd have thousands of people validating my claim. But since we don't, I recognize that it makes my story all the less believable. But ask yourself, do I look like I could orchestrate all this evidence? Do I seem like the kind of person who would invent all this for laughs? Do I seem like someone who could create vids and mountains of evidence that could withstand this level of scrutiny? I'm a free miner. We're scraping by out there, flying by the seat of our pants, and sometimes barely putting food in front of us. I'm not looking for money. I have nothing to gain here but saving lives. If you think you can shoot holes in my story, give it your best shot. But I promise you you'll fail. Every word I've said is true."

The room was silent. Everyone watched him. Imala found Victor's hand under the table and gave it a squeeze of encouragement. Finally Prescott leaned forward and put a hand on Victor's shoulder. "We believe you, Victor.

Some needed a little extra convincing, yes, but I think I speak for everyone when I say we're behind you. We'll help you as much as we can."

Victor felt such a rush of relief that he almost broke down again. It was going to work. The word would get out. He exhaled and grinned at Prescott. "Thank you."

"No, thank *you,* Victor. All of Earth owes you a debt of gratitude."

"This isn't going to be easy," said Imala. "I don't mean to dampen the mood here, but let's not forget that the media has already dismissed this idea. We've already been labeled phonies in some circles. I've been fighting this battle for a while now and losing. If you're with us, you need to be with us not only now, in the safety of this room, but also outside as well, where the rest of the world stands ready to mock and scorn. My career is likely over. Yours may be as well if you do this. I'm not trying to convince you to abandon us, I'm simply making sure you understand what we're up against."

"Your point's well made," said Prescott. "I can only safely speak for myself, Imala, but I assure you I'm with you."

"Me too," said Yanyu.

The others in the room nodded.

"Then what do we do?" asked Imala.

"Two things," said Prescott. "We continue validating Victor's story by searching the sky and getting all of our friends in the field doing the same. We do a full-court press on that. Secondly, and more immediately, I'll make some calls. Getting an audience with Mr. Jukes isn't easy. He has an army of people who resolve issues for him and deflect people like us. But considering the circumstances, I think we can break through."

They didn't break through. Not immediately anyway. They were told that Ukko Jukes was otherwise occupied and inaccessible.

"Can't *we* just go to the press?" Victor asked Prescott. "With your added credibility, someone would listen."

"While I appreciate you putting so much weight in my endorsement, the fact is, it's not enough. There are ten people out there with the same degree of notoriety and credentials that I have who would counter me and discredit the idea. Sad but true. Some of these people are wolves. I've disproved a lot of their theories, and that hasn't exactly endeared me to them. They'd all be quite happy to put a shot across my bow. If we go without

Ukko, we have to be ironclad. We have to be so convincing, that the doubters are the ones who look like irrational crazies and not us. That may take time. The team is working on it, and we're getting there, but I think Yanyu and Imala are right. Ukko is our fastest recourse. If we can get him, we're golden."

Hours later, long into the evening, Prescott pulled Victor and Imala aside. "The staff is staying here tonight. It doesn't look like we'll get word on Ukko until tomorrow. I can have someone take you to your apartment, Imala, but that might not be a good idea. I'd rather keep Victor here, and frankly it's probably better if you stay as well. We have extra cots. They're not terribly comfortable, but they're yours if you want them."

Yanyu showed Victor and Imala where two adjacent offices were being used for storage. Two cots had been set up, one in each office. Yanyu brought Imala and Victor each a pillow, blanket, emergency pack of toiletries, and a clean Juke jumpsuit. Victor found the men's restroom down the hall, showered, then dressed in the jumpsuit. He felt like a traitor wearing it, like he was disavowing his family somehow. But the suit fit well, and it felt good to get into clean clothes.

He returned to his room and lay down on the cot. He tried to get comfortable but sleep wouldn't come. Rehashing his experience to the observatory staff had turned his mind to home.

Nine months. Had it really been that long since he had last seen Mother and Father?

The images from Yanyu's holopad of the destruction in the Belt weighed on him. He knew that none of the destroyed ships at Kleopatra could possibly be El Cavador—there was no way his family could have beaten the alien ship to the inner Belt. Yet the mere existence of the debris had unleashed a flood of dark possibilities in his mind. What if the alien ship had caused the same level of destruction in the Kuiper Belt? Victor's family had been rushing to a depot to warn the people there that the hormiga ship was coming. What if the hormigas had attacked the depot just as El Cavador arrived?

It wasn't the first time Victor had imagined worst-case scenarios. A day hadn't gone by since leaving El Cavador that he hadn't pictured some horrendous accident befalling the ship.

Yet in every instance, whenever such thoughts surfaced, Victor's confidence in his family had always allowed him to push the fears aside. Father would keep them safe, he told himself. Everyone would work together. They would be fine. That's what the family did. They survived. They always had. When critical systems failed and the worst outcome seemed imminent, the family always found a way to overcome it. Father had never failed in that regard.

I shouldn't worry, he had always told himself. Not yet. Not until I have cause.

Well, now he had cause. The images of the destroyed ships in the inner Belt gave new life to every horrendous outcome he had imagined.

Victor pressed the palms of his hands into his closed eye sockets. Please God, let them be alive. Let Mother and Father and Mono and Edimar and all of them be alive.

He pulled the blanket up and tried to shake the thoughts away. Father would keep them safe. Father had never failed them.

When sleep took him, he saw hundreds of hormigas crawling over the surface of El Cavador, twisting open the hatches and peeling back the armor. They scurried into the holes they created, pouring in, climbing and clawing over each other, rushing through the cargo bay, flying down the corridors, hungry, determined, maws open, arms outstretched, wriggling in a massive wave of scurrying bodies and pattering bug feet. They burst through the door of the helm and rushed inside, where Mother and Father and the whole family were crowded in a corner, cowering, screaming, desperate, arms raised up to protect their faces.


Word came back from Ukko's office the following morning as Victor was having breakfast with Imala in the observation room. "He's agreed to see us," said Prescott. "He's giving a presentation to the press this afternoon, and his assistant said he'd grant us five minutes afterwards."

"Five whole minutes?" said Imala. "Well, I'm glad to hear the fate of the world should warrant so much of Ukko Jukes's precious time."

"We're lucky to get this much," said Prescott. "I had to argue with his assistant to even get on his calendar. She wanted to schedule us two weeks from now."

"Luna may not exist two weeks from now," said Imala.

"That's what I told her. It got her attention."

"Did you tell her it was an alien invasion?" asked Victor.

"If I had she would have laughed me to scorn and terminated the holo. The words 'alien invasion' sound ridiculous."

"Yet true nonetheless," said Imala.

"I could only bait the hook," said Prescott. "I told her we had made the greatest scientific discovery in centuries and that if Mr. Jukes made the announcement to the world, he'd be considered an international hero. That piqued her interest."

"If he already has an appointment with the press," said Victor, "we should see him before he meets with them. That way he can pass on the warning immediately."

"No chance of that," said Prescott. "For starters, this isn't the right type of press. They're all tech journalists and industry bloggers. Ukko's unveiling something the company's been developing. When we go to the world with *our* story it needs to be with all the big news feeds and networks. Ukko will want to make a show of it. Besides, he won't want to go to the press today, even if he believes us. He'll want further evidence first."

"More evidence?" said Victor. "How much evidence do people need?"

"Ukko's cautious," said Prescott. "He'll want incontrovertible evidence from his own people. Evidence from a free miner will hold little weight. He'll regard it warily. I mean no offence. That's just how it is."

"But you *have* gathered evidence," said Imala.

"Evidence of destroyed ships," said Prescott. "That proves there's been an incident. It doesn't prove who's responsible."

"Five minutes isn't a lot of time to convince him," said Victor.

"You only have to hook him. Once he believes this is possible, he'll wipe the rest of his schedule clean and give you all the time in the world."

Prescott called for a skimmer, and he, Yanyu, Victor, and Imala boarded it and returned to the surface. Ukko's office was underground within the Juke tunnel system, but it was located at such a distance away that Prescott thought it faster to fly to the docking station nearest the office than to weave their way through the tunnels.

After the short flight, they descended underground again and entered a wing of the tunnels that was far more elegant and brightly lit. Here the floors were hardwood with strong magnets underneath that pulled on everyone's greaves and allowed them to walk normally despite Luna's low gravity. There were leather sofas and chairs, potted plants and abstract art, tapestries and vaulted ceilings, massive sculptures made of iron ore mined from asteroids deep in the Belt, all lit by soft recessed lights that gave the whole wing a prestigious air.

Prescott led them into the waiting room to Ukko's office, where a tank of tropical fish consumed an entire wall. Inside it, the tunneled rock of Luna had been carved out to resemble a coral reef, and eels and other vibrantly colored water creatures swam in and out of crevices and holes barely bigger than Victor's fist.

The site of it all made Victor sick. All this money, all this extravagance. Out in the Belt free-miner families slaved over asteroids to pull out enough lumps to feed their children, only to have corporates like Juke Limited sweep in, jump their claim, and toss the family aside. And what did the Juke bastards do with that money? They bought fish tanks and sculptures and hardwood floors and pranced around in their palaces while honest people went hungry.

"They're beautiful, aren't they?"

Victor turned away from the glass and came face to face with a woman in her midthirties. She wore a long, modest business skirt and loose-fitting blouse and clutched a holopad tight to her chest. "That one's a leopard moray eel," she said, pointing to one with vivid red stripes and black and white splotches. "They look vicious with that snout and sharp teeth of theirs, but they're really quite harmless. They never bother humans, preferring instead really tiny fish."

"The big preying on the weak," said Victor. "He must feel right at home."

She regarded him curiously, then extended her hand. "I'm Simona, Mr. Jukes's personal assistant. I'm assuming you're with Dr. Prescott?" She gestured to the desk across the room where Imala, Yanyu, and Prescott had gone to speak to the receptionist.

"We're to meet with Mr. Jukes," said Victor.

Simona appraised the Juke jumpsuit he was wearing. "Do you work in the observatory? I don't recall seeing your photo on file."

"I'm not with the observatory," he said simply. He didn't like her questioning him. She appeared friendly enough, but she was fishing for information.

"Dr. Prescott says this news of his is the biggest discovery in centuries," said Simona.

"He's not exaggerating."

A dot of red light on the back of her holopad flashed for an instant, and then Simona looked down at her holopad. She tapped through it for a moment then looked back up at him. "Victor Delgado. That's your name, isn't it?" She turned her screen around and showed him his mug shot, which the LTD had taken upon arresting him. Beside it was the photo she had just snapped of him. Facial-recognition software had put the two together. "It says here that you're in a holding facility with the LTD awaiting deportation back to the Belt. But seeing as how you're standing in front of me, I'm going to assume you granted yourself an early dismissal." She glanced back at the desk. The receptionist was pointing Prescott and the others toward Simona. "Dr. Prescott and Yanyu I know," said Simona. "But the other one is a mystery." She pointed her holopad, snapped another photo, and read the results. "Imala Bootstamp. Currently on probation from the LTD. This grows more curious by the moment."

Prescott and the others approached.

Simona greeted them warmly, though her smile struck Victor as insincere. "You made it," she said. "Good. Here's how this will work. Mr. Jukes's schedule is very tight. You will sit in the back of the studio and make nary a sound during the presentation. Once the holo transmission is done, Mr. Jukes will approach you. You'll have five minutes. But before we go a step further, I need to know how these two are involved." She gestured to Victor and Imala.

"They brought the subject to our attention," Prescott said.

"And what subject is that?" asked Simona.

"We went over this on the holo, Simona. Our message is for Mr. Jukes."

She pointed to Victor. "This young man has a rather extensive criminal record and might be a fugitive. I'm not bringing him into Mr. Jukes's presence until I get some answers." She crossed her arms across her chest and raised her eyebrows, waiting for someone to speak.

"I saw something in the Deep," Victor said. "Out in the Kuiper Belt. I took a quickship to Luna to warn everyone, and I was arrested on ludicrous charges. You have them there in front of you. You can read them yourself. They don't make my story untrue."

"What did you see?"

Victor looked at the others. He didn't know how far to take this. Imala saved him the trouble. "I know you think you're only doing your job here, Simona," she said, "but we don't have time for it. Thousands of people in the Belt are dead. We have proof and we know why. If you don't take us to

Ukko Jukes and he doesn't do something to help us warn the world, thousands and millions and maybe even billions of people on Earth could be next. If that happens, then people are going to look up from the corpses of their dead wives and children and ask why didn't Ukko Jukes do something when he had the chance. And do you know what we'll tell them? We'll tell them the truth. We'll tell them Simona played gatekeeper and shooed us away because busy-as-a-bee Ukko Jukes didn't have five minutes to save the world."

Simona stared at Imala, lips pursed, considering. Finally she said, "Very well. Follow me." She snapped her fingers, turned on her heels, and led them down a corridor behind the receptionist desk and into a vast, mostly empty room. The lights were off in the room save for a series of spotlights that hung from a rig at the far end of the room. Beneath the spotlights was a large spherical holofield three meters in diameter. Ukko Jukes was standing motionless in the center of it while a makeup artist dabbed at his forehead with a small white pad. Floating words scrolled upward in the air in front of Ukko, and he seemed to be mouthing the text to himself, rehearsing.

As a child on board El Cavador, Victor had feared the name Ukko Jukes. Whenever spotters spied a Juke ship in the vicinity, Victor knew it meant trouble and sometimes even violence. As a boy of four or five, Victor had assumed that Ukko captained all those ships himself, shouting orders from the helm like a giant menacing warrior. And even later, when Victor had learned the truth of who Ukko Jukes was, the name still carried an air of dread and danger.

Yet here was the man now, shorter than Victor had expected, with thinning white hair and a trim white beard and a woman at his side dabbing his cheeks with makeup. It made Victor almost laugh to think that he had ever feared such a man.

Simona put a finger to her lips and led Victor and the others to the back of the room where a few dozen chairs had been set up in the darkness. Most of the chairs were empty, but a handful were occupied by people who appeared to be helping with the production. Victor took a chair beside Imala and waited. It galled him to sit here and watch these people fret over something so insignificant. Whatever this production was, it was completely meaningless compared to what was coming.

A woman with a headset and a holopad called for quiet, and Ukko dismissed the makeup lady with a brusque wave of his hand. The lady scurried off as someone in the shadows counted down from ten. At zero, a dozen heads appeared in the holofield in front of Ukko, all of them smiling and courteous. Ukko greeted them warmly, thanked them for their time, then the text of Ukko's presentation appeared in front of him.

"Today is a special day in the history of our organization. For the past twenty-five years, Juke Limited has been the leader in space mining, extracting hundreds of millions of tons of minerals a year and growing every economy in the world. Some might say, if it ain't broke don't fix it. But Juke Limited will never stop innovating. We continuously look for ways to make our industry more efficient and more productive. Today I give you proof of that. Today the space-mining industry takes a revolutionary leap forward."

A family portrait appeared in the air beside him: a father, mother, and three young children, all sitting under a tree and smiling for the camera. "Ask yourself, what is the one resource we waste the most in space? Is it oxygen? Fuel? . . . No. It's time. We waste millions of man-hours prospecting for viable asteroids. Each of our prospecting ships has a crew of ten to twenty men and women, who spend months in space, oftentimes with little or nothing to show for it. That translates into lost time with spouses and little ones. What we need is a smarter, faster, less expensive way to determine an asteroid's mineral content. Is it full of rich ferromagnetic metals? Or is it a worthless rock? Today, ladies and gentlemen, I give you the solution. The answer to all that wasted time."

The family portrait disappeared. Ukko walked to his left, and the holofield and light rig moved with him. He stopped at a large object no bigger than a skimmer covered with a black sheet. Victor hadn't noticed it before in the darkness. The light rig shot up into the air, and the holofield expanded to five times its original size so that it now included the draped object.

"Ladies and gentlemen, I give you the world's first space-mining drone . . . the Vanguard!"

Ukko made a sweeping gesture with his arm, and the black sheet flew backward out of the holofield, unveiling a small, white, seamless vessel that sparkled in the rotating spotlights. "Working as a scout, the Vanguard will seek out mineral-rich asteroids via remote control and preprogrammed flight paths. By firing digger bots no larger than an apple down into the surface of the asteroid from space, the Vanguard can determine the asteroid's approximate mineral content. That information is then relayed back to Juke. If the mineral content is high enough and the asteroid large enough, a mining crew is dispatched for immediate mineral extraction."

The floating heads in the holofield began asking questions. As each one did, Ukko brought the head forward and made it larger than the others. What is its fuel source? How soon will these be operational? How do you safely fly it via remote control if there's a time lag between it and headquarters? What will happen to all the prospecting crews? Are these people out of a job?

Ukko answered them all deftly, as if he expected each one. No, the crews would not lose their jobs. Drones would increase the discovery of minerals and thus increase the need for mining crews. All those employees would be transitioned to mining vessels.

Well, doesn't that debunk the whole "saving time" argument? Victor wanted to ask. How are you giving people more time with Daddy dearest if you're moving him from one ship to another and keeping him in space just as long?

But none of the journalists seemed concerned with that detail. The technical specs and increased efficiency potential had them practically salivating. By the time the questions ended, the journalists were all applauding enthusiastically. Ukko thanked them for their time, promised them each packets with further specs and photos for their stories, and bid them all good-bye.

When the last journalist winked out, the holofield disappeared, the lights in the room came on, and the small production crew rushed forward to congratulate Ukko on a job well done. He took an offered water bottle and downed a long drink, mostly ignoring the praise around him. When Simona approached and whispered in his ear, Ukko stopped, listened, and looked in Victor's direction. A moment later Simona was ushering the production crew out of the room.

When they were alone, Ukko smiled, approached Prescott, and put a hand on the man's shoulder. "Richard, this is a wonderful surprise. I haven't seen you since the Deep Space Expo. Linda is well, I hope."

"Yes, sir. Thank you for asking."

Ukko continued down the receiving line. Without looking at Yanyu's gimpy right arm or giving any sign that he noticed it, Ukko deftly offered her his left hand instead, which was the hand she preferred to greet people with. "And Yanyu," he said, smiling affectionately, "one of our prized grad assistants. I hear only good things about the research you're doing for us at the observatory. Keep it up. There will always be a place at Juke for the best and the brightest. Or as my finance team likes to call them, *profit pro-ducers*." He winked and moved on.

Ukko turned to Imala and didn't appear at all surprised to see her. He took her hand gently in both of his. "Imala Bootstamp. When last we spoke I believe you were turning down my generous job offer."

At the LTD, Imala had learned that auditors were being paid under the table by Juke Limited to ignore the company's tax and tariff evasions. Ukko had offered Imala a job within the company to silence the scandal, but Imala had refused and left Ukko with a few colorful remarks instead.

"You're wearing a Juke jumpsuit, Imala. And running with my scientists now. I'm confused. What could pique the interest of the Customs Department and two of my finest astrophysicists?"

"A matter of mutual interest."

"Clearly. And tell me, Imala, how are things at Customs? Are you regretting turning down my offer?"

"I'm no longer with Customs, Mr. Jukes. At least that's my suspicion. I was on administrative leave, but after yesterday's events, I suspect they've since given me the ax."

"I'm sorry to hear that. You must stop this habit of getting fired, Imala. Your résumé is turning into a list of terminations. It will make recruiters nervous."

Victor could tell Ukko was enjoying this.

"If I can do anything to help," said Ukko, "be a reference perhaps, just let Simona know. I'd like to think my opinion still holds a little weight in the world."

"How generous of you to offer," said Imala. "I'm sure you'd be all too eager to give others your opinion of me."

"I would indeed."

They stood there facing each other a moment longer, hand in hand, each of them maintaining a mask of politeness. Ukko finally broke his gaze and turned to Victor, offering his hand. "And who is this fine-looking young man?"

"Victor Delgado."

"A pleasure to meet you, Victor. And are you on my payroll, or is this a loaner as well?" He gestured at the jumpsuit.

"A loaner. I'm a free miner actually."

Ukko raised an eyebrow. "Free miner? Interesting. The surprises never cease. Tell me, are you with a clan I may have heard of?"

"We only have one ship. My family's not big enough to be considered a clan."

"I see."

"We work the Kuiper Belt. Our ship is called El Cavador."

"A Spanish name."

"We're Venezuelan. It means 'The Digger.' "

"An appropriate name for a mining vessel. Kuiper Belt, you say. You're a long toss from home, aren't you?"

"You could say that."

"I've never been out that deep myself. I never saw the appeal, quite frankly."

"There are fewer corporates," said Victor. "That's what makes it so attractive. My family used to work the Asteroid Belt, but we were bumped by Juke ships so often, we could no longer survive there. It's hard to make a living, Mr. Jukes, when someone is always stealing your mine shafts."

Simona stiffened slightly. Ukko's expression remained pleasant. "Yes, well I'm sorry to hear your family had a hard time. I'm glad to hear they're doing better deeper out."

"I didn't say we were doing better, Mr. Jukes. We're not. We *were* doing better, but then your son Lem bumped us off an asteroid, crippled our ship, and killed a member of our crew."

"Victor," Imala protested. "This isn't why we came here."

The smile on Ukko's face had vanished. He shot a look to Simona, who was now wide-eyed with shock. "I assure you, Mr. Jukes, I don't know what this man is talking about!"

"What the hell is this?" said Ukko, rounding on Prescott.

Prescott opened his mouth to speak, but Ukko was already back at Victor. "What do you know of my son? Is this some kind of extortion attempt?"

"Marcus!" said Simona.

A bodyguard lumbered into the room. Ukko held up a hand, stopping him, his eyes now boring into Victor. "You have three seconds to explain yourself, boy, or you will not like where this conversation goes."

"Like father like son," said Victor. The words came out of him before he had even considered what he was saying.

Ukko's cheeks flushed, and his expression hardened. "You rock suckers are all the same. Ignorant, pompous heathens."

"This isn't helping, Victor," said Prescott. "We need him."

Victor looked at Prescott, considered his words, exhaled, then turned back to Ukko. "We didn't come hear to talk about your son. We came here to discuss—"

"To hell with whatever you came here to discuss," said Ukko. "If you mention my son, you explain yourself."

"Fine. About ten months ago, your son's ship jumped ours during our sleep-shift, cut our anchor lines, and bumped us off a rock. One of his lasers sliced off an external sensor, which then struck and killed my uncle."

"That's a lie."

"It's not a lie. It happened right in front of me."

Ukko shook his head. "My son wouldn't bump you. He had no reason to. He isn't on a mining mission. If you think for an instant you can muscle money out of me with some made-up story—"

"I can describe the ship," said Victor. "I was out on spacewalk when it struck us. It hit me as well. I got a very good look at it."

"Anyone with access to flight records here on Luna could find out what type of ship my son is on. That doesn't prove anything." He stepped closer to Victor, his smile acid. "You think you're the first pebble pusher to try to blackmail me?"

Victor didn't flinch, though he realized now how foolish he was being. If they lost Ukko as an ally, or worse, if they made him an enemy, they would never get a warning out in time. "If you don't believe me," said Victor, "you can ask him when he returns to Luna. Assuming he isn't dead already."

The color drained from Ukko's face. "What are you saying? Are you threatening my son?"

"I'm not threatening anyone, Mr. Jukes. But something out there is. The same thing that has threatened every ship in the Belt and destroyed a good number of them. That's why we're here. I know what's causing the interference. And if you don't help us do something about it soon, we're all in a world of hurt."

# CHAPTER 5

# Mazer

Lieutenant Mazer Rackham jogged across the tarmac to where the HERC sat on the landing pad and climbed up into the copilot's seat. It was three o'clock in the morning, and cloud cover from the west off the Tasman Sea had blotted out the Moon and left all of Papakura Military Camp in near total darkness. Mazer put on his helmet and switched on his HUD while the other three members of his unit climbed into the HERC and did the same. A holo of the HERC appeared in the air in front of Mazer, covered with blinking dots. Six months ago it had taken the team ten minutes to run through the preflight sequence. Now they could do it in twenty-seven seconds flat.

Mazer blinked the appropriate commands to begin the sequence and saw that Reinhardt, the pilot, was doing the same. Avionics? Check. Load talons? Check. Gravity lens? Check.

The HERC—or heavy equipment recovery copter—was a scooper, a low-flying aircraft designed to rush into hostile territory; scoop up troops, vehicles, or supplies; and get out as quickly as possible. Since it was primarily used for extraction and not direct combat, it didn't pack a lot of heavy air support. Yet what it lacked in big guns, it made up for in armor. The standing joke on base was that a tank and a helicopter had done the funky watusi in the bushes, and the HERC had popped out nine months later.

Yet to call the HERC a mere flying tank was an insult to its design. Engineered by Juke Limited, the HERC was the world's first gravity-lensing aircraft, which used lenses to deflect gravity waves from Earth and send them around the aircraft. The lenses were not mechanical lenses like glass lenses that refracted light, but rather fields created by a center point. By adjusting the shape of the field, it adjusted the direction that gravity waves were focused or deflected. The result was the aircraft felt less gravity. It hovered. It flew without rotor blades. And because gravity lensing adjusted continuously to provide vertical placement above the Earth's surface, all that was needed to make the HERC fly forward was a means of propulsion, which the rear jet engine provided.

It took very powerful computers to constantly adjust the direction, focus, and strength of the gravlens, however. And computers, when rattled in combat, tended to fail. As a backup, in case the gravlens gave out and the aircraft dropped like a stone, Juke Limited had installed rotor blades as well. When not in use the blades folded into a single blade that tied back parallel to the main line of the aircraft like a cockroach's wings. These could deploy in 0.3 seconds, which, in high altitude, was more than enough time to keep the HERC airborne. But since the HERC was almost exclusively a low-flying aircraft, normally going no higher than twenty meters above the trees to avoid detection and enemy fire, the backup rotor blades wouldn't deploy fast enough to save the crew. If anything, they would merely lessen the impact. And even then the rotors would do as much harm as good. Once you hit the ground the torque effects from the blades would take over and flop the bird around or try to drill it into the ground. You were almost better off deploying the huge emergency chutes, keeping the rotor blades off, and praying the airbags kept you alive.

Mazer tried not to think about crashing, focusing instead on the assignment at hand. The order had come directly from the Ministry of Defence six months ago. The NZSAS—or New Zealand Special Air Services, the special forces branch of the kiwi military based out of South Auckland—was to put the HERC through rigorous field tests to determine the aircraft's combat readiness.

Mazer had been tasked as flight-team leader, and the commission had come as a surprise. He had no training as a test pilot, and he had been in the NZSAS for less than two years. As far as he could tell, there was a line of men a kilometer long who were far more qualified.

"Don't let it go to your head," Reinhardt had told him. "When the colonel gives assignments like this, it doesn't mean he likes you. It means you're expendable. You think they want their best guys dying in field tests? Hell no. They want us getting the bugs out. We're guinea pigs, Rackham. Crash-test dummies. Bottom of the totem pole."

It was a joke of course. In the NZSAS, there *were* no totem poles. Every man was equal. There were chains of command, yes, but no one pulled rank or dumped unfavorable assignments on greenies. In the unit, no job was beneath any soldier. If a ditch needed digging, Colonel Napatu was as likely to grab a shovel as anyone else.

"Check and clear," said Reinhardt, finishing up the preflight sequence.

"Check and clear," Mazer repeated.

Behind the cockpit, Patu banged the butt of her rifle twice on the floor. "Let's get a move on and get this over with. I haven't slept in thirty-six hours."

Beside her, Fatani closed his eyes and laid his head against the headrest. "None of us have slept in that long, Patu. We all need our beauty sleep." Fatani was a hundred and twenty kilos of Polynesian muscle, well over two meters tall. The safety restraints around his chest were extended to maximum length, but even so the fit was tight.

"You try to get *beauty* sleep, Fatani?" Reinhardt asked with mock surprise. "You must suffer from some serious insomnia."

"Keep it up, Reinhardt," said Fatani. "We'll see how long you laugh when I drop your skinny butt from this bucket at three hundred and twenty kilometers per hour."

"You'd only kill yourself," said Reinhardt. "Birds tend to crash without a pilot."

"I can pilot as well as you can."

"Yeah, and by the time you crawled up here into the seat, you'd be crashing into the ground."

"Then I'd die with a smile on my face, knowing I had just dropped you."

"Enough with the testosterone," Patu said. "Can we go now, please?"

"Blue River, Blue River," Mazer said into his helmet. "This is Jackrabbit. We are clear and flight-ready, over."

"Roger that, Jackrabbit," came the voice over the radio. "You are clear to go. Mission sequence code: lima tango four zero seven foxtrot, over."

Mazer entered the code into his HUD and repeated the sequence back to the controller. Windows of data popped up as the computer accepted the code and opened the mission file. Mazer blinked the command to forward the files to everyone else. A timer in the upper right corner of his HUD began ticking up the seconds from zero. It was a timed mission, apparently.

Reinhardt initiated the gravlens, and the HERC lifted a few meters into the air. Even after all these months, the silence of the whole operation un-nerved Mazer. He had done hundreds of hours in traditional helicopters, and his mind had become accustomed to the roar of the engines and the *thump thump thump* of rotor blades. To hear nothing but the almost imper-ceptible purr of the computers felt completely unnatural.

Then Reinhardt initiated the rear engine, and Mazer got that all-too-familiar sick feeling in his stomach as the HERC shot forward over the tarmac and headed north. Mazer pushed the sensation aside and focused on the intel. "Target is latitude negative thirty-seven degrees, zero minutes, twenty-one point seven seven two two seconds. Longitude one hundred seventy-five degrees, ten minutes, thirty-seven point five one six two sec-onds."

"Coordinates confirmed," said Patu.

"Identify target," said Fatani.

The HERC shot up another fifteen meters as they approached the tree line, heading up into the hills of the Hunua Ranges and leaving the airfield behind them. Mazer instinctively put a hand on the instrument panel to steady himself. "Target is an AT-90 Copperhead. Crew of two. Both seri-ously wounded."

Copperheads were squat assault tanks loaded with enough firepower to level a small city. They were also ridiculously heavy and hard to carry be-cause of their wide, shallow design.

"Whose turn is it to play medic?" asked Fatani.

"Yours," said Patu. "And don't ask me to cover for you. I bandaged up the last two rounds of guys."

"They better not be bleeders," said Fatani. "I hate the bleeders."

For field tests and war exercises like this one, the NZSAS used rubber-ized dummies for their casualties. Mazer and his unit were to treat the dummies like real soldiers and administer lifesaving first aid as part of the exercise. The bleeders were the worst. Loaded with red syrupy paint, they added a good two to three hours to cleanup time and put everyone in a bad mood.

The Copperhead tank would be a dummy as well. Probably a burned-out bus or ATV pulled from the scrap heap and loaded with enough weight to resemble a Copperhead. The Colonel wouldn't use a real one and risk damaging it.

"So what's the deal, Lieutenant?" asked Reinhardt. "Is this operation a final exam or something? Why all the secrecy?"

"No idea," said Mazer. "Colonel said to be ready to fly at 0300, and we'd get our orders then."

"Seems strange to me," said Fatani. "Normally we're the ones designing the field tests. Now all of a sudden the colonel's doing it for us. No briefing. No prep. Just strap in and wait for orders."

"Combat's no different," said Patu. "Makes perfect sense to me. Brass wants to see how the HERC manages when we're not controlling all the variables. Think about it. Before we run a test, we determine everything. Where it flies, what the weather's like, where the enemy is located, what their capabilities are. But what team in real combat is going to have all that intel?"

"Pilots would at least know what the weather was like," said Reinhardt. "It's the first thing they teach you in pilot school. When the windshield wipers are on, it's raining outside."

"You're hilarious," said Patu.

"All I'm saying," said Fatani, "is that if this is some kind of exam, it would've been nice to have known that ahead of time."

"Has to be," said Patu. "That's why they didn't let us sleep. They want to know if exhausted pilots flying with limited intel can pull off a HERC mission."

"If that's the case, they're testing *us* as much as the HERC," said Fatani.

"It doesn't matter," said Mazer. "We do what we always do. We scoop up the target and we bring it home."

The secretive nature of the operation didn't bother Mazer. He was used to sporadic psychological tests like this; it went with the territory in special forces. Someone was always running you to the point of exhaustion and then denying you water and keeping you up for another twenty-four hours. Or they were messing with your head in some other way: isolating you, or dropping you in the middle of nowhere with a blindfold over your eyes and telling you to return to base using only your other senses. Compared to those tests, this surprise mission with the HERC was a cakewalk.

A message appeared on Mazer's HUD.

"Hostile territory in three point four kilometers," said Mazer.

A second later there was a flash and a boom to their right as a flare exploded not ten meters from the cockpit. Flares were used as surface-to-air missiles—or STAs—in war games. It was all show and no shrapnel, but it still startled everyone on board.

"Whoa!" said Reinhardt, pushing the stick forward and dipping the HERC into a stomach-churning descent.

"Hey!" said Patu, slamming back into her seat. "Easy on the dips."

Mazer grabbed the window bar to his right and tried to keep his focus on the data on his HUD.

"I'd say we got bad intel," said Reinhardt. "We're in hostile territory already." Two more explosions lit up the night sky, one on each side of the aircraft.

"Fatani!" shouted Mazer.

"I'm going, I'm going," said Fatani.

A section of the floor beneath Fatani slid away, exposing the gunnery dome on the underside of the HERC. Fatani worked the joystick on his seat and lowered himself into the dome, seat and all. The thickly forested hills of the Hunua Ranges rushed beneath him, the treetops just visible in the darkness. Fatani made a final adjustment, and the top hook of his seat latched into the swivel mount, suspending him in place and giving him the ability to spin and maneuver in any direction. A small window on Mazer's HUD showed him Fatani's POV, and Mazer watched as the butt of the laser cannon slid into position and locked on to Fatani's chest harness.

"Locked!" shouted Fatani.

"Acquiring targets," said Mazer.

More of the dummy STAs were shooting off around them, and Fatani picked them out of the sky before the flares could explode.

"Brass is dropping some serious cash on this op," said Reinhardt.

Mazer was thinking the same thing. These hills had long been the playground for SAS exercises, but Mazer had never heard of a team getting this much heat in a single war game.

Tracer fire arced into the sky from the northeast. The glowing paint pellets whizzed by the windshield, narrowly missing the HERC. Fatani was on the source a half second later, hitting the tracer gun with the cannon's laser, rendering the ground gun inoperable. Mazer saw the other three tracer guns on his HUD just before their arcing fire erupted upward. He blinked them as targets for Fatani, and the chair in the gunnery box spun and swiveled at a sickening pace as Fatani clicked off several more shots.

Reinhardt dipped lower, weaving right and left to avoid the tracers—flying only a few meters above the tree line.

"Let's not forget I'm down here," said Fatani. "These pines will take my boots off if you go any lower."

"Relax," said Reinhardt. "If we hit a tree, you'd be a human bag of jelly so fast, you wouldn't feel a thing."

For three more kilometers they dipped and maneuvered and took out tracers and STAs. Patu kept swearing at Reinhardt for bobbing them around so violently and nearly getting them all killed. Mazer was beginning to agree; the motion-sickness pills could only do so much.

Then the HERC crested a hill and they saw it—there in a treeless valley—not a scrapyard vehicle pretending to be a Copperhead tank, but an actual Copperhead. Stranger still, it was taking heavy fire from the tree line to the north.

Patu and Fatani responded without hesitation, laying down cover fire into the trees. The lasers were harmless, nothing more than a game of tag, but everyone took the exercise as seriously as real combat.

"Put us over the tank," said Mazer.

A barrage of pellets smacked into and ricocheted off the HERC's armor as Reinhardt got them into position over the tank. Since the gravlens had no effect on anything below the HERC but only on things above it, the tank didn't so much as twitch. Thick bumper bars lowered from the underbelly of the HERC on either side of the gunnery bubble to keep it from being crushed by the payload.

"Bars are down," said Fatani.

"Initiating load talons," said Mazer. He blinked the command, and the massive talons on either side of the HERC extended outward and unfolded themselves. There were three talons on either side, each a hooked blade with heavy rubber padding along its edges. Mazer extended his hands into the holofield in front of him on the dash. The talons responded to his hand gestures, diving downward and acting as a claw, wrapping around the tank and scooping it off the ground. Reinhardt compensated with the gravlens and suddenly the tank was airborne.

"Locking payload," said Mazer, blinking out the command. Beneath the tank, opposing talons extended farther until they reached one another and locked in to place.

The enemy fire from the trees had stopped by now, but Patu continued to lay down cover fire as the HERC banked hard to the south and headed home.

Fatani and his seat rose up from the floor and returned to their original position. He then snapped the safety harness and cable winch to his vest and unbuckled himself from the seat. Steadying himself against the wall, he punched in the command to retract the bubble. The bubble's sections of glass separated and folded away, leaving a gaping hole in the middle of the HERC's floor. The ceiling hatch to the Copperhead was two meters below it. Fatani turned to Patu and yelled over the roar of the wind. "You sure you don't want to take care of the wounded?"

"Positive. I wouldn't want to deprive you of the opportunity to show off your keen medical skills."

Fatani sighed. "They better not be bleeders." He positioned himself over the hole and used the winch to lower himself down the hatch.

Mazer watched the feed from Fatani's helmetcam as Fatani opened the hatch and lowered himself into the tank. There were no bleeders inside. There weren't even dummies. There were two live men, both in safety helmets and heavy padding. Mazer didn't recognize either of them. One was in a business suit, and the other was in a tan uniform Mazer didn't recognize.

"Sergeant Fatani," said the one in the suit. "So good to see you. I was just telling Captain Shenzu here that you're the finest gunner in the NZSAS."

To Fatani's credit, he didn't respond with a stunned silence. Rigorous training and a cool head will do that for you. "Are either of you wounded?" he asked.

The man in the suit laughed and waved a hand. "No, no. We're fine. We had Colonel Napatu put in that bit of intel to get you to come down here and pull us out. Shall we go up? Captain Shenzu would very much like to see the cockpit."

"Of course," said Fatani, as if this were the most natural of requests in the world.

In under a minute, Fatani had the recovery straps around each of the men's chests. He then carefully powered up the winch and raised them into the HERC. By then, Mazer was out of the copilot's seat and giving the men a hand, helping them into the cabin.

"Lieutenant Mazer Rackham," said the man in the suit. "An honor to meet you. I hope our little Hercules has met your expectations."

His accent was European, but Mazer couldn't place it. "You seem to know all of us, sir. Yet we don't have the honor of knowing you."

"Where are my manners?" He extended a hand. "Heinrich Burnzel. Global sales. Juke Limited."

A salesman. This was getting stranger by the moment.

"And this is Captain Shenzu of the People's Liberation Army," said Burnzel. "A most respected officer of the Chinese military."

Shenzu bowed slightly and shook Mazer's hand. "Very impressive flying, Lieutenant. We watched the whole approach on Mr. Burnzel's holopad." His English was flawless and completely without an accent.

Burnzel was all smiles as he held up his holopad as if proof of the claim.

"Lieutenant Reinhardt is our pilot," said Mazer, "but I'll be sure to pass on your praise. Please, won't you be seated? The safety harnesses are there in the jump seats. We should have a smooth ride in, but we'd appreciate you buckling up as a precaution."

"Of course," said Burnzel, the smile still plastered across his face. He sat in the jump seat and began buckling the straps. "We were also hoping you could demonstrate to Captain Shenzu how fast the HERC could go with a heavy payload."

"I beg your pardon?"

"Oh you know. Give us a little show, Lieutenant. Zip around the valley for a minute. Impress us. No loop-the-loops, though," he said with a laugh. "Go upside down and we lose antigrav." Then he laughed as if that were the funniest joke in the world.

Fatani was back inside by now. He and Mazer exchanged glances, and Fatani shrugged. Mazer hit the command to seal the hole in the floor and made his way back to the copilot's seat.

"You want to tell me what's going on?" Reinhardt said under his breath.

"I'm finding out," said Mazer. He slid his helmet visor back down into place. "Blue River, Blue River. This is Jackrabbit. Target is secure and airborne, over."

This time the voice on the radio was Colonel Napatu's. "Jackrabbit this is Blue River. Have you secured the passengers?"

"Affirmative. They're retrieved and buckled in the cabin, sir."

"Good. Don't jostle them. Bring her in nice and easy."

"They're asking that I come in hot, sir. Give them a show."

"Negative. You bring her in slow. We're not bowing to some corporate jackass any more than we have to."

"A sales demonstration?" said Reinhardt. He, Patu, Fatani, and Mazer were all standing in Napatu's office, still wearing their flight suits. "The mission was a sales demonstration?"

"The Chinese are interested in the HERC," said Colonel Napatu. "They wanted to see it in action before they cut any deal with Juke Limited."

"Since when does the SAS give test-drives to the Chinese?" said Reinhardt. "Look, no offense, sir, but we were taking some heat out there. Nothing but flares, yes, but we all took this op rather seriously. I was flying like a bumblebee to avoid that flack. We could have buried that bird in a hillside. And for what? To show off to a Chinese captain and some suit from sales trying to meet his monthly quota? Pardon me for saying so, sir, but this whole thing strikes me as incredibly negligent."

Napatu leaned back in his chair, folded his hands across his stomach, and cocked his head to the side. "Are you finished, Lieutenant?"

Reinhardt straightened and retreated a step, his cheeks flushed. He put his hands behind his back in parade-rest position. "Yes, sir. Pardon me for speaking candidly, sir."

"Since I happen to believe you're justified in being annoyed, I'll forgive that candor, Lieutenant. But I'll kindly remind you that an SAS officer holds his tongue as well as he holds a rifle, especially when addressing a senior officer."

"Yes, sir. Begging your pardon, sir."

Colonel Napatu sighed and swiveled in his chair for a moment. "All of you sit down. I don't like you hovering over my desk like that."

Mazer and the others took a seat in the armchairs and sofa opposite Napatu's desk.

Napatu put his elbows on his desk and rubbed his eyes, suggesting he was as sleep deprived as the others. "I would love for you all to believe that the SAS is immune to the bureaucratic crap that so plagues the rest of the military," he said. "And I would love for you to believe that I as the CO of this unit have the authority to tell the defense department where they can stick the asinine orders they so often toss in our laps. But since you all tested so highly for intelligence, you know both statements are false."

He leaned back in his chair. "Fact is, we are a branch of the NZ military, and when we receive orders we follow them. That is our duty. We do not question them. We do not voice our disapproval. We obey. This business with the HERC came straight from General Gresham. He called me himself two days ago. His orders were clear. Give this Chinese captain and his Juke sales rep a real show. The natural assumption was that I would have you fly the HERC around the tarmac a lap or two. Not so, said the general. I was to coordinate a full heavy-vehicle extraction. Lots of noise, lots of daring piloting, and the two guests of honor were to be waiting inside the Copperhead. That was their explicit request. They didn't want to observe. They wanted to experience."

He sighed and rubbed at his eyes again. "As you might expect, I expressed my concerns regarding safety and liability. The last thing this country needs is for a Chinese officer to die under our care. That would read just dandily on the news nets. But my objections were ignored. I was to follow orders to the letter. Nor was I to inform the extraction team of the uniqueness of their mission. While I agree that you all took a lot of heat, I was not for a moment concerned. Reinhardt can dance circles around any other pilot in this unit."

"Thank you, sir."

"He's buttering you up so you won't be mad at him," said Patu.

"I'm ashamed to admit it's working," said Reinhardt.

"What was this about, sir?" asked Mazer. "Why should the SAS be involved in a sale to the Chinese? If Juke wanted to show off the HERC why not do it at their own facilities? Our HERC isn't the only one in existence. Why bring the Chinese here?"

"Several reasons. One, Juke pilots aren't nearly as good as you. I'm not buttering you up, that's simply a fact. Juke knew they'd get a much more dramatic presentation here. Second, the Chinese wanted to see soldiers in action. That's who will be flying theirs, and they happen to have a lot of respect for the SAS. That is why, in fact, they wanted all of you sleep deprived. They figure a sleep-deprived SAS officer is equal to a well-rested Chinese one."

Fatani grunted. "Hardly."

"You're an exception to any such comparison, Fatani," said Colonel Napatu. "You're equal to four Chinese officers. And I don't mean simply in terms of mass."

"I can see why the Chinese might like this arrangement," said Mazer, "but why would the defense department agree to it? Why do a favor for the Chinese? I thought we were hoping to keep this tech proprietary."

"I asked those same questions. First off, we couldn't keep the HERC for ourselves even if we wanted to. Juke will sell the tech to whoever will pay for it. The U.S. military is big enough to make stipulations like that to their contractors, but not us. We're small potatoes. We'll buy a few dozen HERCs at the most, which is barely enough to break a sweat on the Juke assembly line. China is a big buyer. Juke would hang us out to dry and leave us with nothing if it meant snagging a deal with the Chinese. My point? We never had a chance of keeping this proprietary. As to why we agreed to do the show, it turns out the SAS is getting a few HERCs for free for our troubles."

Fatani whistled. "For free? Considering the price tag of a HERC is more than the GDP of most third-world countries, I'd say we got a good deal. Not bad for an hour's worth of work."

Napatu leaned forward and frowned. "Well, that's the sour part of this conversation. The Chinese didn't ask for just a single hour of work."

"That look on your face makes me think I'm not going to like the next thing out of your mouth," said Reinhardt.

Mazer thought the same, but he kept quiet.

"The primary reason why we gave a show to the Chinese," said Napatu, "was because they were testing *you* as much as the HERC."

"Told you," said Fatani.

"Testing us for what?" said Patu.

Mazer answered. "The Chinese not only want to purchase a fleet of HERCs, they also want an experienced HERC team to train their pilots how to fly it."

"Say it ain't so," said Reinhardt. "We have to babysit a bunch of Chinese pilots?"

"How many pilots are they sending us?" asked Fatani.

"None," said Colonel Napatu. "The Chinese aren't coming here. You're going to them. Guangdong province. Southeast China. It'll be a six-month op."

Nobody spoke. It wasn't uncommon for an SAS team to be given orders to conduct a joint cooperative engagement training—or JCET—but that didn't mean everyone was thrilled by the idea.

Sensing disappointment in the others, Mazer said, "It's China, Reinhardt. They have hair dryers and silk sheets. I think you'll survive."

Napatu took a data cube from his desk and offered it to Mazer. "Captain Rackham, you'll continue as team leader. Your mission objectives are there on the cube. You'll brief the others on the plane. You fly out at 0900."

Mazer took the cube, surprised. *"Captain,* sir?"

"You've just been promoted. I'm not having some Chinese officer thinking he outranks everyone on your team."

It was six o'clock in the morning when Mazer left Colonel Napatu's office and made his way across base toward the motor pool. Three hours. Napatu had given them three hours to arrange their affairs before getting on a plane for an overseas six-month assignment.

This is why it would never work with Kim, he told himself. This is why it was ridiculous to even consider marriage. No relationship can operate this way.

They had never discussed marriage, but Mazer knew Kim was thinking about it as much as he was. It was evident in the little things she did: the way she smiled at any baby they passed in the market, or how she casually mentioned her goals for the future, like how she wanted a bay window in her home when she settled down, or how she would grow her own vegetables when she settled down. That was her phrase: "When I settle down." It was never "When *we* settle down," but the subtext was there nonetheless. The implication was obvious. She was putting her toe in the marriage waters and seeing what ripples it produced.

Mazer always responded as if he sensed no subtext at all. They were making conversation, nothing more. Why yes, a bay window would be lovely. But no, gardens were a pain; there were weeds to be pulled and bugs to be sprayed and dirt to be tilled. That was time, and time was money. I'll *buy* my vegetables, thank you very much.

It was a game they played, a game of compatibility. And the more they played it, the more convinced Mazer became that he would never find a better match.

He woke the officer on duty at the motor pool and checked out a vehicle. The drive from Papakura to East Tamaki was quick, and he parked across the street of Medicus Industries at ten minutes to seven. She would already be up in her office, he knew; she always came in early to get a jump on the day.

He didn't call her. Instead, he tapped his wrist pad three times to ping her, then he watched her office window on the fifth floor. She appeared a moment later, smiled, and waved him to come up. He walked to the front door, waited for the holo to appear in the box, and typed in the sequence she had taught him. The door opened, and he crossed through the empty lobby to the lifts.

She met him on the fifth floor and gave him a light kiss on the cheek. She looked as beautiful as ever, her hair pulled back in a ponytail to keep it out of her face while she worked over her holos all day. "This is a pleasant surprise, Lieutenant," she said. Her American accent always made him smile.

"I'm a captain now actually," he said.

"As of when?"

"This morning."

She raised an eyebrow. "Really? With a captain's pay?"

"I assume so. There wasn't much time to discuss it. Why, you need a loan?"

She smiled, though he could see that the promotion made her uneasy. An unexpected early-morning promotion was a bad sign. It might mean they were shipping him out.

He waited for her to ask, but instead she cocked her head to the side and said, "You look tired."

"I haven't slept in thirty-something hours," he said.

"And yet you came to tell me about your promotion before getting some sleep. I feel special."

"I didn't come to tell you about my promotion," he said.

She sensed bad news coming and held up a hand. "Before I get the whole story, let's eat first. There are pastries in the conference room."

She hooked her arm in his and led him down a corridor. All the offices they passed were dark and empty of people. They reached a glass-paneled room with a long table and a wide marble counter at the far end loaded with fresh fruit, pastries, and self-cooling containers of juice and milk. Kim handed him a plate, grabbed one for herself, and started loading up.

"Are these yesterday's pastries?" Mazer asked, picking up an apple turnover and giving it a sniff.

"A caterer brings them in early. They're fresh. And why should you care? You're supposed to be able to survive off the land, eating worms and roasted field mice. Day-old pastries are luxury food."

He didn't feel like eating, but he put the turnover on his plate anyway and followed her back to her office.

A holo of an adult-sized human skeleton was floating on its back in the air above Kim's holodesk. Windows of data surrounded it, along with handwritten notes in Kim's squiggly shorthand.

"Looks like we're a party of three for breakfast," said Mazer.

Kim waved her hand through the holofield, and the skeleton disappeared. "Sorry. Not exactly what you want to see before eating."

There was always something floating above Kim's desk. If not bones, then muscles or the circulatory system or some cross section of damaged tissue. She had studied medicine at Johns Hopkins in the U.S. and done her residency at one of the most notoriously brutal trauma centers in Baltimore. Despite being one of the youngest doctors on staff, she quickly built a reputation for being coolheaded and smart in the most gruesome situations. Several medical associations honored her, and it was those citations that had brought her to the attention of Medicus, which had offered her a position at their corporate offices in New Zealand with the promise that she would be helping far more people by working as a medical consultant.

The company made the Med-Assist device, a holopad designed to help soldiers treat battle wounds. It could do anything: bone scans, blood work, give surgery tutorials, even administer drugs. It was like having a medic in your pocket, only you had to do all the work. The U.S. military had funded the initial development and now used the device extensively throughout all branches of their service. Other countries had since jumped on board. A device for the New Zealand Army was near completion.

"Is that the new Kiwi version you've been working on?" Mazer asked, gesturing to a Med-Assist on the corner of her desk.

"Latest prototype," she said, handing it to him. "Tell me what do you think of the voice."

He turned on the device, clicked through the first few layers of commands, and placed it over his leg. A scan of his femur appeared on screen, the image tinged in green. A woman's voice with a New Zealand accent said, "Femur. No trauma detected."

"Why isn't it *your* voice?" he asked.

Kim's voice had been used in the American version. The U.S. Defense Department had asked that the voice be that of a real doctor, and Medicus thought Kim the perfect fit. She was already on staff, she was American, she had great bedside manner, and she was brilliant. Kim had agreed to do it only on the condition that Medicus test several voices along with hers before making the final decision. Medicus complied, recording samples from Kim and other doctors and then bringing in several soldiers from the NZSAS for a focus group. Mazer had been among them, and he was the most outspoken in the group for why the voice should be Kim's: She sounds like a doctor; she sounds like she knows what she's talking about; soldiers will be anxious and afraid and at the height of emotional distress; a voice like hers will calm them; I believe every word she says.

The executives had been delighted, and afterward they had made a point of introducing Mazer to Kim, citing him as proof that she had a lot of recording to do. She had scowled at Mazer playfully and blamed him for giving her more work than she had time for. He had apologized, and in a moment of uncharacteristic spontaneity that surprised himself more than anyone, he asked her to dinner to make it up to her.

It seemed like such a long time ago now.

Mazer sat on the sofa opposite her desk. Kim removed her shoes, sat beside him, and draped her legs across his lap.

"The Kiwi version can't be my voice," she said. "New Zealand soldiers want to hear a New Zealander."

"I don't," said Mazer. "I'd much rather hear yours."

She smiled. "It's a matter of clarity. Americans pronounce words differently. You don't want a soldier administering the wrong drug or performing an incorrect action because he or she misunderstood the directions."

"True," said Mazer. "But the real reason why it can't be you is because your voice is so intoxicating. You're like the sea sirens in *The Odyssey*. Soldiers become so enchanted by the music of your voice that they get all dreamy and starry-eyed and completely forget about their fellow soldier bleeding out in front of them."

She smiled again. "Yes. Tragic when that happens."

Why was he being playful? It would only make this more difficult.

"I'm leaving for China," he said. "For six months."

It was like a slap. She stared at him. "Why so long?"

"Exercises with the Chinese. We're training them on some new equipment." He couldn't speak of the HERC. It was still classified.

"Not a hostile op?"

"No," he said, reassuring her. "Purely training."

"Those can be dangerous too."

"This one won't be. It will be boring."

"How often will you get to come back?"

"I won't. Six months solid. No leave time."

She stared at him then looked down at her half-eaten pastry and pushed it around her plate. "I see. When do you leave?"

He checked the time on his wrist pad. "Less than two hours. I only found out an hour ago."

She put the plate aside, angry. "That's how much time they gave you? That's ridiculous. Not to mention insensitive. It shows a complete disregard for people. Doesn't it make you angry?"

"I'm a soldier, Kim. This is what I do. I go places."

"Why does it have to be you? I thought you were in the middle of some important training here."

"I am. It's the training here that's now taking me there."

She pulled her legs off his lap. "Can you request that someone else go in your place? I know that's unorthodox, but surely they make exceptions."

"I don't have extenuating circumstances."

"Tell them I need you here to help with the development of the Med-Assist."

"You've never needed my help before, and the military doesn't make exceptions, especially with private contractors. If you needed a soldier, they would argue that it doesn't have to be me."

She got up, crossed to the window, and looked out over the city. "Don't you *want* to fight this?"

"You know I can't, Kim."

"That's not what I asked."

"Do I want to go to China? Of course not. But I don't get a say in these matters. That's the problem. It's always going to be like this. They're always going to send me away."

She turned and faced him. "What are you saying?"

"I'm saying this is a moment of decision. I know we've never discussed marriage, but you and I both know that's where this relationship is headed. We dance around the word, but we're both thinking about it."

"Of course I think about it," she said. "That's what people our age do, Mazer. They look for someone with whom to spend the rest of their life."

"And is this the kind of marriage you want?" Mazer asked. "Do you want a husband who goes off for six months or years at a time? Is that the kind of father you want for your children? One who's absent most of the time? People don't get married to live apart, Kim."

"No, people get married because they love each other and want to make babies together, Mazer. People get married because they see happiness ahead of them with someone."

"Yes, but you don't see that with me," said Mazer. "You see a world of lonely, sleepless nights, worrying about whether or not I'm bleeding to death in a ditch somewhere."

"Don't say that."

"You're proving my point, Kim. Whenever I leave on assignment, you're near crazy with worry. At first I thought it was endearing because it meant you deeply cared for me. Now it makes me sick to think about it. I can't stand that I make you feel that way."

She turned away, back to the window.

"I've always been afraid to start a family for this reason, Kim. When I joined up I resigned myself to being single. I wasn't going to be an absent father and husband. Then I met you, and I convinced myself that I could make it work. I told myself that our commitment to each other and to our children would be strong enough to endure any separation. But now I see that I was only being selfish. I was thinking about my happiness, not yours. You deserve someone who can be with you and share the load every day of your life."

She didn't turn around.

"I can't leave the military," he said. "I'm in for at least five more years. I don't have a choice on that. Asking you to wait until I get back from China is the same as asking you to wait five years, which I won't do. That's not fair to you."

He waited for her to move, to look at him, to say something. She didn't.

"Marriage to me wouldn't be marriage, Kim. You'd be committed to someone who wasn't there. You'd be raising children by yourself. I saw my father do that when my mother died and he moved us to London. He was not a happy man, Kim. Without my mother, he was a shell of who he was. He tried to stamp out all the Maori culture my mother had ingrained into me as a kid because it reminded him of her and it pained him too much to see it. The songs, the stories, the dances, he outlawed them all. I was to be a proper Englishman like him. An Anglo. As if Mother had never existed. Only, he couldn't change the color of my skin. That stayed dark no matter how many boarding schools he put me in."

He crossed the room and stood behind her.

"You don't want your children to have only one parent, Kim. I know that life. I don't want it for my kids, either."

She turned to him. She was crying but her voice was steady. "I'd like to believe that you're being noble and self-sacrificing, Mazer, but all I'm hearing is that you don't want a life with me."

He didn't know how to respond. Of course he wanted a life with her. Didn't she see that? The issue was it wasn't a life they could have. It would be a life *without* each other.

But before he could form a response, she went to her shelf, pulled down a Med-Assist device, and handed it to him. "One of the American versions," she said. "With my voice. You said you wanted one, so there you are. Something to remember me by."

It was a dismissal. Everything they had built between them was brushed aside in that one gesture.

It was what he had come to do, what he knew he *needed* to do for her sake, but now that it was done, now that the business was over, a sick empty feeling sank in his gut like a dead weight. He had to explain himself better.

He didn't get a chance.

She walked out and left him there. He waited twenty minutes but she never returned. When employees started showing up and turning on the lights to the offices all around him, he tucked the Med-Assist under his arm and made his way to the lifts.

It was the right thing to do, he kept telling himself. For her happiness, long-term, it was the right thing to do.

# CHAPTER 6

# China

Mazer boarded the C-200 moments before takeoff and found five new HERCs strapped down in the cargo bay, each of them adorned with Chinese characters and the red-and-gold starred emblem of the People's Liberation Army. Apparently he and his team were not only tasked with training the Chinese, but they were also to hand deliver the HERCs as well. It annoyed Mazer. It meant the deal with Juke and the Chinese had been in the works for some time and that the SAS could have told him sooner that he was likely shipping out.

Not that it would have made much difference, he admitted. He still would have felt the need to cut ties with Kim, and having more time to do so would have only prolonged the inevitable. Either that or his courage would have failed him, and he would have convinced himself yet again that they could make it work. This way was best for her. Harsh and fast and then he was gone and she could get on with her life.

He moved through the cargo bay and saw that the rest of his team was already aboard, each of them asleep in one of the bunks recessed into the walls. Mazer stowed his bags in one of the lockers and climbed into an empty bunk. His whole body felt heavy and fatigued and ready for sleep, but thoughts of Kim kept him awake long after takeoff. He kept replaying the scene with her in his mind, thinking of all the things he should have said differently. He took out the Med-Assist she had given him and clicked through it randomly until he came upon a tutorial on how to give rescue breaths. He hit play, laid the Med-Assist on his chest, and listened to the sound of her voice.

He woke six hours later. His team was still asleep. He took the data cube Colonel Napatu had given him and attached it to his wrist pad. The computer read him the entire mission file as he prepared a large pot of chicken pasta in the aircraft's kitchen area, using ingredients he found in the supply closet.

When he was done, he woke the others, and they gathered around a table in a small room near the cockpit where the engine noise was less.

"The mission's a true JCET," said Mazer. "Usually it's just us training the host nation. This time, the Chinese will be training us, as well."

"On what?" asked Fatani. "How to use chopsticks?"

"Oh, you're real classy," said Patu.

"We'll be trained on a digging vehicle they've developed," said Mazer.

Reinhardt made a face. "Digging vehicle? We're giving them the world's first antigrav bird, an aircraft that will revolutionize flight, and they're giving us a bulldozer? Lame."

"Double lame," Patu agreed.

"We don't know it's a dozer," said Mazer. "We don't know anything about it, in fact. There was next to nothing on it in the cube."

"A digging machine," Reinhardt repeated. "Six months away from home to learn how to dig with a fancy Chinese shovel. I hate this mission already."

They landed a little over an hour later at a military airfield northeast of Qingyuan. Two lines of Chinese soldiers in full-parade dress faced each other at attention at the end of the plane's cargo ramp. Captain Shenzu, the Chinese officer from the HERC mission, stood at the bottom of the ramp and saluted. "Welcome to China, Captain Rackham."

"You beat us here," said Mazer.

"You'll forgive me for taking more comfortable accommodations. The Chinese government would have granted you the same convenience, but we would much rather have you guarding our precious cargo."

Mazer gestured back to the HERCs. "There they are. All dolled up and ready for action. When it's convenient for you and your commanding officer, I'd like to discuss our training regimen."

Captain Shenzu smiled and waved the suggestion aside. "All in good time, Captain. Come." He motioned to a skimmer parked to their right. "The drill sledges are about to surface. Your timing could not have been better."

They flew northeast out of the airfield, cut across open country, and pulled up to an aboveground concrete bunker on the crest of a shallow, barren valley. The valley floor was riddled with deep gaping holes, each big enough to fly the skimmer into. Shenzu parked, hopped out, and escorted them around the bunker to the opposite side overlooking the valley floor.

"You said 'drill sledges,'" Mazer said in Chinese. "Are these the drilling machines you'll train us to operate?"

"Your pronunciation is quite good," said Shenzu.

"We all speak Chinese," said Mazer. "Part of our training."

Shenzu seemed pleased. "China is flattered that you would think our language important enough to learn, Captain."

"You are the largest country in the world," said Reinhardt.

"The largest, yes," said Shenzu, "but sadly not the most technologically advanced. The U.S. and a few countries in Europe have us beat on that front. As well as the Russians, though they don't have the economic stability that we do. It's only a matter of time before we leave them all behind."

"You sound rather confident," said Mazer.

Shenzu was looking at something on his holopad. "In three seconds, Captain, I think you'll see why."

Mazer felt slight tremors in the earth beneath him and heard a muffled rumbling noise. He turned and scanned the valley but saw nothing. Then a massive spinning drill bit burst through the surface, slinging dirt and detritus in every direction in a violent shower of debris. The drill shot upward in a blur of motion, and Mazer saw that it was the front half of a massive tunneling vehicle, rocketing upward from the ground. The engines screamed, and red hot ejecta erupted from the rear of the vehicle as it soared three meters in the air and then slammed back down to the surface. The lavalike spew from the rear continued to bubble out and drip to the ground as the engines whined down and the drill began to slow. Smoke rose from the spew, and Mazer heard the sizzling heat of it even from this distance. A felled tree that had caught a shot of the spew crackled and began to burn.

Mazer opened his mouth to speak just as two more of the tunneling vehicles burst from the ground elsewhere in the valley, one of them getting a little more elevation on its exit than the first one had.

After the sledges landed and began to quiet, Shenzu smiled and said, "You'll have to excuse them. They're showing off. They know they have an audience."

"What are they?" asked Patu.

"We call them self-propelled drill sledges, but they're tactical earth bur-rowers. Quite extraordinary, aren't they?"

That was putting it lightly, thought Mazer. The HERC might revolution-ize flight, but the drill sledge revolutionized warfare, introducing an entirely new landscape to the battlefield. He immediately understood why the Chi-nese wanted the HERCs. The HERC could carry the sledges behind enemy lines, drop them off, and leave them to their digging. The two vehicles made the perfect assault team.

"What's their range?" asked Mazer.

"Only ten kilometers," said Shenzu. "But we're hoping to improve that."

Ten kilometers. That was more than Mazer would have suspected. "Are they weaponized?"

Shenzu laughed. "We'll have plenty of time for questions later. Come. I'd like you to see them up close."

They descended the valley and approached the nearest drill sledge. The entire cockpit was now encased in a thin layer of frost.

"It's cold," said Reinhardt, touching the surface.

"We keep the cockpit as cold as possible," said Shenzu. "We have to. Otherwise the pilot would be cremated, as in burned to ashes, bones and all."

There was a cracking sound as ice broke away from where the cockpit hatch sealed against the sledge's roof. The hatch opened, and a pilot climbed out and waved. He wore a helmet with a wide visor and lights on the top and sides. Mazer could see a hint of frost around the visor's edges as the pilot nimbly climbed down from the sledge. His thin body suit was lined with small coils that ran up and down his body and around his ap-pendages like a continuous nest of very thin snakes. Every part of him, head to toe, wafted cool mist like a hunk of meat pulled straight from the freezer.

"It's called a 'cool-suit,'" said Shenzu. "The drill sledges work like an earthworm. Whatever it digs through in the front, be it clay or rock or what-ever, is ejected out the back. The propulsion doesn't come from the biting action at the front. It actually comes from the backward ejection of the su-perheated debris."

Off to the side, a team of Chinese soldiers was putting out the fire on the felled tree and spraying the other mounds of spew with canisters of com-pressed chemicals, sending hissing clouds of steam into the air.

"When the sledge is moving fast through solid stone, it spews back lava," said Shenzu. "You don't want to follow one when that happens."

"How does it handle such lava-hot ejecta?" asked Mazer. "Seems like the spew would burn through any piping system."

"Very observant," said Shenzu. "That was one of the most difficult challenges. It's like the problem of the universal solvent: What do you store it in?" He pointed to the rear of the drill bit. "A series of internal tubes begins here at the nose and extends back to the spew end. The tubes are continuously water cooled. Each is wrapped in a network of thin water pipes that are pumped from a refrigeration unit at the rear of the sledge.

"But even with the cooling system, the entire cockpit is superheated when the sledge is chewing rock. That's why we have the cool-suits. We keep the cockpit as cold as possible because when you hit rock and go into hyperfast mode, the heat produced is incredible, well above boiling temperature. The suits kick in to cool the body and counter the heat. Then, when the sledge slows down, and the heat descends, the cockpit has excess cooling and the temperature drops to freezing. At that point the cool-suit reverses its process and channels warmth to the body."

"Sounds like a temperature roller coaster for the pilot," said Fatani.

"It takes some getting used to," admitted Shenzu. "Sweltering heat one moment, teeth-chattering cold the next."

"I've been doing this for months," said the pilot, "and I'm still not used to it. But it's a such a ride, I'd dig all day if they'd let me."

"You said it had *hyperfast* mode?" asked Mazer.

"Speed is relative," said Shenzu. "We consider it fast for a drill sledge."

"How fast?" asked Mazer.

"We've topped them out at twenty-four kilometers per hour."

"Through rock?" Mazer was stunned.

"Oh yes. When it's gophering along, going normal speed, it runs about half that. But if you hit rock and punch it, if you go hot, she burns a hole through the ground."

"So rock is faster?" asked Patu.

"More propulsion," said Shenzu.

"What about communication?" asked Fatani. "Radio doesn't go through dirt."

"Infrasound," said the pilot. "Elephant speech. It's slower than regular speech, so the receiver speeds it up so you can hear it. There's a time lag, though, as if you were talking to someone on the moon. Rocks carry the infrasound digitally, but you can't receive anything when you're going hot. Gophering you can hear. But when you punch it, you're on your own."

Shenzu waved over a Chinese soldier. The man approached carrying a helmet atop a neatly folded cool-suit. Shenzu took them both and handed them to Mazer. "We took the liberty of pulling your sizes from your files and making you each a suit. As the commanding officer of your team, Captain Rackham, we thought you'd like the honor of going first."

"Now?" said Mazer. "I have no idea how to drive it yet."

"This drill sledge fits two," said Shenzu. "Not comfortably, I'm afraid, but it's how we train our pilots. Lieutenant Wong here will take you for your first dig."

"Relieve your bladder first," said Wong. "Once we start digging we can't pull over, and you do not want to go in your suit. Nothing's worse than ice crotch."

Mazer changed in the bunker and returned a few minutes later. The suit was tight, and the coils felt awkward. The ones on his inner thighs kept rubbing against each other, so he waddled and stepped bowleggedly.

"How does the suit feel?" asked Shenzu.

"It's not freezing yet," said Mazer, "so I can't complain."

The drill sledge was now held up in the air at a fifty-degree angle by long spindly legs that extended from the sides of it like legs on a grand-daddy long-leg spider. The drill bit was pointed down toward the earth, less than a meter off the ground.

"The legs get it into a diving position," said Shenzu. "It can't dig down when it's horizontal on the surface unless it's entering into the side of a mountain."

A collapsible ladder extended down from the cockpit. Lieutenant Wong was already up in the forward seat waiting. Mazer ascended the ladder and awkwardly climbed into the narrow seat behind him, nearly kicking Wong in the head as he brought his foot around. It was extremely close quarters, with only Wong's seatback between them. Mazer found the chest harness and buckled in as Wong retracted the ladder and closed the cockpit, cutting out all exterior light. The glow from the cockpit instrumentation bathed them both in red and green, and Mazer leaned as far as he could to the side to see the front. A small holo of the drill sledge appeared in the air above the console.

"How do you know what's ahead of you?" asked Mazer.

"Depth gauges," said Wong. "They measure the density of mass ahead." He made an adjustment to the holofield, and a colorful cross section of the earth appeared. "The darker areas are thickest," he said, gesturing at the holo. "Probably granite. Hit those and you go hot, really cruising. The brighter spots like these here and here are soft earth, such as clay."

"What about those white lines that crisscross through the image?"

"Those are tunnels we've dug with the drill sledges in the past. They're all over this valley. It's like a man-sized anthill beneath us."

"What happens if you hit water? Like an underground lake or spring?"

"Better to avoid those. We try not to screw up the water table, but sometimes it's unavoidable. Hit a water source on a dive, and the water chases you down the hole, like pulling the plug in the bathtub. Water isn't much of a propulsion, either. It all goes to steam. So hitting water is like hitting the brakes. That's why you always want to aim for rock. You ready?"

"Go easy on me."

"There's nothing easy about these babies."

He made a few hand gestures in the holofield, and the drill bit roared to life, spinning quickly almost immediately and getting up to a screaming whine in less than ten seconds. The cockpit vibrated. Mazer felt as if his bones were rattling.

"What about the legs outside?" Mazer said into his radio.

"They'll fold in automatically once we start down," said Wong. "Get ready for a burst of cold. The suit cools instantly the moment we start digging. It's kind of a shock."

"Roger that," said Mazer, though in fact he wasn't the least bit ready. Diving underground felt unnatural. This is what we do with our dead, he told himself. Suddenly a dozen questions sprang to his mind. What happens if there's a malfunction and the drilling stops? How do you repair that? How could anyone rescue you? Had that happened before? Was there a Chinese pilot somewhere deep underground, buried with his stalled drill sledge, dead of asphyxiation?

And then there was a brief drop and a momentary jolt forward as the drill bit hit the earth and tore into the surface.

Then spew shot out the back, and they were surging downward.

An instant later a blast of cold hit Mazer so quickly that he felt as if he had fallen into icy water. His muscles constricted; his teeth clenched; his hands clung to the armrests. He wasn't going to die, he knew, and yet the fear of it wrapped its tendrils around his heart and squeezed.

Kim would love this, he told himself. She was like a kid when it came to amusement park rides. The scarier the better.

The drill sledge dropped a few meters as it hit a tunnel, and Mazer felt momentarily weightless. Then the drill sledge hit earth again, and Mazer strained against his chest harness.

"Granite ahead," said Wong. "Prepare to go hot."

A second later another burst of cold hit Mazer's suit as the drill picked up speed and surged forward through rock.

The engine roared, and the drill bit screamed, and Mazer realized he was laughing, laughing with tears in his eyes, just like Kim would do.

# CHAPTER 7

# Rena

The helm of the space station looked nothing like the helm of El Cavador, but it reminded Rena of what she had lost nonetheless. It was the energy of the room that felt familiar—the hustle and chatter from the crew as they flew from one console to another, sharing intel or relaying orders or checking the various holocharts. It was the same energy Rena had felt every day of her life on board El Cavador. Except, in that life she had been surrounded by family, people who valued her and loved her and called her La Gallina, or Mother Hen, because she was a listening ear and a comforting friend to everyone on board. Here, aboard a depot owned and operated by WU-HU, the largest of the Chinese space-mining corporations, somewhere in the outer rim of the Asteroid Belt, Rena was no one. An outsider. A stranger.

She floated through the hatch and waited for someone to notice her, not daring to interrupt a member of the crew. After a moment, a young Chinese officer spotted her and came over, catching a handhold near her.

"You here about the nav sensor?" the man asked. His English was good, but his Chinese accent was thicker than most.

Rena nodded.

The man pointed. "Over there. Fourth workstation on the right."

Rena thanked him and moved in that direction. Ever since she and the other survivors of El Cavador had arrived, carried here by Captain Doashang and his WU-HU vessel, they had earned their room and board by making repairs throughout the station and on whatever WU-HU ships docked here. Captain Doashang had vouched for them to the station chief, a kindly woman named Magashi, who had given them one of the storage rooms to sleep in. It was a zoo every night, all of them cramped in that tiny space, with little ones and infants waking up at all hours, crying to be held or breast-fed or reassured that their nightmares were nothing more than dreams.

Rena had dreams as well, though she never spoke of them to anyone. In them, Segundo, her husband, was always alive, stretched out beside her in her hammock, his arms wrapped around her, holding her close, telling her about a repair he had made or something he had overheard on the ship that day. Sometimes they laughed. Other times they marveled at how blessed they were to have Victor as a son. Other times he threatened to tickle her, and she threatened him serious bodily harm if he tried. Other times they said nothing at all; it was enough to simply be together, floating there side by side.

In every instance she could feel the thickness of his arms around her and the warmth of his breath on the nape of her neck. It was real, as real as it had ever been.

And then she would wake, and it was as if he had died all over again.

She kept her tears silent and unseen. Even in the cramped quarters of the storage room no one saw her as anything but calm, confident, and optimistic. She couldn't allow herself to seem otherwise. There were too many younger mothers who looked to her for reassurance and comfort and strength.

Of course there were those who despised her as well, regardless of what she did. Julexi whispered discontent whenever she had the chance. Her husband, Pitoso, had been the first to die in the attack on the alien ship. His explosive had detonated prematurely, killing him instantly and alerting the hormigas of the attack. The battle had been a disaster after that. The hormigas had poured out of the hole the explosion had created, literally throwing themselves at the men of El Cavador.

And since it had been Segundo who had modified the explosives and prepared them for the attack, Julexi was convinced that it was Segundo who had, in essence, killed her husband and set them all on the path to ruin. Segundo was the reason why El Cavador was destroyed. Segundo was the reason why they were cramped in this hellhole of a room one step above a closet. It was Segundo Segundo Segundo.

Abbi felt no different. Her son Mono had secretly stayed on El Cavador instead of coming with her onto the WU-HU ship. Had Segundo and Victor not filled her son's head with foolish ideas and convinced him that he was a mechanic, Mono wouldn't have died on El Cavador with the others. He would've stayed with his mother where he belonged. He'd be here, alive, helping her, holding her, speaking softly to her. He was only a boy, after all. He had no business as Victor's apprentice. He was too young. Shame on Victor. Shame on Segundo.

A few others despised Rena as well, though why exactly Rena could only guess. Perhaps they felt the need to blame someone. Or perhaps they thought *they* should be making decisions for the group. Or perhaps they resented how some mothers came to Rena for comfort and not to them.

Whatever the reason, it didn't matter. Rena ignored them all. The women never confronted her directly with their grievances, so Rena let it go. Bringing it up would only escalate their complaints and divide them further. And division wouldn't help them. Divided they might not survive.

She found the broken nav sensor at the helm and immediately got to work. It was an easy fix if you knew what you were doing. Corporate ships and stations like WU-HU or Juke had crewmen who knew next to nothing about how the ship functioned; they each had a single task, and that's all they did. But on a free-miner ship, families couldn't afford that luxury. Everyone had to know everything.

And so on El Cavador they constantly taught each other, shadowing each other for a day or a week, or putting together trainings and seminars. Rena knew navigation of course, but she learned all other duties as well, mining and maintenance and cooking and piloting, every chore that kept the family functioning and alive. No one stops learning, Concepción used to say. Our strength is one when our mind is one.

Captain Doashang had learned this principle quickly. Every task he had given to Rena and the other women had been completed with exactness. There was no learning curve, no trial and error; the women of El Cavador simply did precisely what was needed as soon as it was asked. Sometimes before it was asked. Wait until something's broken, and you've waited too long, Segundo had said.

Rena disassembled the nav sensor and swapped out the burned component. As she worked she noticed three crewmen nearby glancing in her direction and talking quietly. They spoke in Chinese, thinking she didn't understand them, but El Cavador had snogged Shoshan, a Chinese bride, years ago, and she and Rena had become dear friends. Shoshan didn't speak Spanish, and the two of them had set about teaching each other their native languages. Rena still couldn't speak Chinese to save her life, but she could pick up words and phrases here and there if she listened close enough.

". . . babies screaming at all hours of the night . . ."

". . . we can't keep feeding them . . ."

". . . you should talk to Magashi . . . problems if they stay here much longer . . ."

". . . supplies won't last forever . . ."

". . . feed one clan and then everyone wants a handout . . ."

Rena gave no sign that she understood and kept her eyes on her work. It wasn't the first time she had heard such things. Many of the crew resented the fact that Magashi had let the women and children of El Cavador stay. Most of the station crew was kind and generous and eager to share the food they had in storage if the women of El Cavador worked for their share. But a few of the crew spread resentment like wildfire.

We can't stay here, Rena told herself for the hundredth time.

Rena and the other women were already doing double the workload of the typical crewmember in some instances, but Rena knew that would never be enough. Those who spoke against them would always speak ill, no matter how much Rena and the others helped.

In fact, it would only get worse, she knew. As supplies continued to diminish, and as fewer supply ships from Luna arrived, the complaints would get louder and more frequent and sooner or later someone would take action. Rena didn't think the crew would turn violent, but she didn't rule out that possibility. People became desperate when they were hungry.

Yet where could they go? All the WU-HU ships that came in were ordered to stay docked. Everyone was on inactive status.

And whenever a free-miner ship approached the station, it was always to beg for food. The supply depots were hoarding their storage, the free miners said. "We have money. We'll pay for food. Please. We have nowhere else to go."

Initially Magashi had sold what little food she could. But she had faced such a fierce backlash by some of the crew, that she now turned every approaching ship away.

Rena couldn't ask passage on a starving ship anyway. She had nineteen women and several dozen children. If the ship didn't have the food to feed them, going with them would be suicide.

It was a problem without a solution, and the clock was ticking.

"Incoming vessel," said the spotter.

"Can you identify it?" asked one of the officers.

"Looks like a vulture, sir."

Rena felt the hairs on the back of her neck stand on end. Several of the helmsmen looked uneasy as well, and for good reason. Vultures were recovery crews who salvaged dead ships for profit. Most of them were mining crews who had given up on rocks and found easier money stripping ships to the bone.

The rule was, if you found an abandoned or crippled ship unoccupied by living persons, then the laws of salvage applied: Whoever takes it, owns it.

The problem was, the rule invited fierce competition among vulture crews. Once a crew found a ship, they had to strip it of its most valuable parts as quickly as possible before another crew swooped in and tried stripping it as well. It was a feeding frenzy that always turned violent if the stories were true, and Rena had every reason to believe them. On more than one occasion El Cavador had found a salvaged ship that included dead vultures among the ship's dead crew, suggesting that a competing crew of vultures had come in during the salvage and taken everything for themselves, killing everyone who stood in their way.

*Piratas* was the word Segundo had for them. Pirates.

"They're pinging us," said the spotter.

"Open a frequency," said the officer. He moved to the holodesk and put his head into the field.

A head appeared in the air in front of the officer. It was the blackest man Rena had ever seen, skin so dark that the whites of his eyes were as bright as moons by comparison. His expression was fierce and unfriendly. "I am Arjuna," he said. "I seek audience with the station chief."

"For what purpose?" the officer asked.

"Are you the station chief?"

"No. I'm one of her officers."

"Her? Your chief is a woman?"

"A very capable one. What's your business?"

"That is for me to discuss with the station chief."

"We're not giving out food if that's your request."

"We do not seek food. I come with grievous news. And an offer. One that will help you extend the life of your supplies."

"What news?" asked the officer.

"The destruction of more than fifty mining ships. All of them killed by the Pembunuh, as we call them. I can give you the coordinates. You can turn your eye there and see that I speak the truth."

Pembunuh. Rena hadn't heard the word before, but she knew what it meant. Every ship and crew seemed to have their own name for the aliens. Hormigas, Wageni, Bugs.

But fifty ships? The thought of it left Rena cold. So many people. So many families. Fifty versions of El Cavador. It was unthinkable.

"Give us the coordinates," said the officer.

Arjuna complied, rattling off a string of numbers. The spotter put them in his computer, and everyone in the helm gathered around his screen. Rena hung back, craning her neck to catch a glimpse, but everyone was clumped together so closely she couldn't see. It took several minutes to move the eye and zoom in on the coordinates, but eventually the images came through.

The crew fell silent. Hands covered mouths. Eyes widened. Rena pushed her way through the crowd to see. No one stopped her or seemed to even notice.

It was more wreckage than Rena had ever seen, most of it mere dots on the readout, stretched out across tens of thousands of kilometers of space and still moving.

"I do not lie," said Arjuna.

The wreckage was between them and Earth, and the first of it was surprisingly close to their position. Only two to three weeks away perhaps.

"I will connect you to the station chief," said the officer.

"I do not wish to speak to her via holo," said Arjuna. "I want to speak to her in person."

"You can't dock your ship here. This is a private station."

"My ship will not approach. I will come in a shuttle. Alone. You are free to search me when I arrive. Anyone who wants to return with me is welcome."

Return with him? Why would anyone want to return with him?

The officer put Arjuna on hold, conferred with Magashi, and made the necessary arrangements. Four hours later, the shuttle docked in the cargo bay, and Arjuna floated from the airlock and turned on his greaves. The magnets pulled his feet to the deck plates, and he stood facing Magashi who had come with four of her armed guards. Rena stood off to the side, out of sight but within earshot.

Arjuna was a big man, well over two meters tall and wide in the shoulders. He wore a heavy coat cinched tight at the waist, thick boots, and padded pants. "Put your guns away, friends," he said. "I come with money, not violence." He reached into his pocket, and the guards flinched, their hands on their weapons. Arjuna slowed and delicately pulled out a money stick. "Relax. Five thousand credits can hardly harm you." He pushed the stick through the air to Magashi, who caught it and examined it.

"We're not selling any food," said Magashi.

"I'm not here for food," said Arjuna. "I've come for men. Twenty if you can spare them. These ships the Pembunuh have destroyed are there for the taking. I mean to salvage them for what parts we can find. I will give five thousand credits to every man who joins us."

"My crew are employees of WU-HU," said Magashi. "They have jobs."

"Yes, jobs at a station that does nothing at present but burn up supplies. I can take them off your hands for a few months. They can earn a great deal, and you can save on supplies. How long do you think your food will last if you continue as you are? The interference has driven most supply ships back to Luna. The Pembunuh have destroyed others. Ask other travelers if what I say is not true. It will be months, maybe even a year before more supplies come. If the Pembunuh wage war on Earth, supplies may never come again. Your station is overpopulated. I can help alleviate that issue."

"By taking my crew?"

"Borrowing them," said Arjuna. "I doubt any of them wants to starve to death."

"You've made your offer," said Magashi. "We're not interested."

"The wreckage is a gold mine. You have a problem. I have a solution."

"The wreckage is a battlefield. Will you pilfer from the dead?"

"The dead have no use for their ships. I do."

"Why not use your own crew?" asked Magashi.

"I will use my crew. But with more men I can double our efforts and salvage more before others arrive."

"Other vultures, you mean?"

A flash of anger came to Arjuna's eyes. "We are not vultures, madam. We are crows. Ours is an honest trade. There are buzzards and vultures in the Black, but my crew and I follow none of their ways. We harm no one and we abhor those who poison our industry. Ask any tradesman or salvage dealer. Arjuna is a man of his word. His methods are as gentle as a lamb."

"Even lambs bite," said Magashi.

"Yes, but we bite only to chew the food we have earned by the sweat of our labors."

"We're not interested," Magashi repeated.

"And what of the men who hold those weapons?" asked Arjuna. "Does the woman speak for them? Would they like not five thousand credits and a job that pays better than the ones they have?"

The men glanced at each other, curious how the others would respond. After a moment, when no one responded, Arjuna said, "Very well. Then I will ask you to return my money stick."

Magashi pushed it back to him. He caught it, slid it in his pocket, and bowed. "May your shelves never empty and your bellies never hunger." He pushed off the floor and launched back toward the airlock.

"Wait!" The word was out of Rena's mouth before she could stop herself.

Arjuna caught a handhold at the airlock and turned back. Rena flew to him and landed beside him. "You say men, but will you take women? Free-miner women?"

"I would take one free-miner woman over four corporate men. Free-miners are skilled and hard laborers. Are you from a clan?"

"Not a clan. A single ship. El Cavador. Or rather, that *was* our ship. It was destroyed in the Kuiper Belt by those you call the Pembunuh."

"Then you have my condolences. But if your ship was destroyed, how is it that you are alive?"

"It's a long story. But there are many of us here, and we are wearing out our welcome. If you can promise us protection from your crew and trans-portation to a depot, I can give you skilled laborers." She had no idea why she trusted this man, but she did.

Arjuna smiled. "You need not worry about my crew, Lady of El Cava-dor. What I have spoken is true. We are a family of crows, not vultures."

Family. The word reassured her. But only for a moment. Who was this man? Was she ready to put the women and children in his hands? He could be a murderer, for all she knew.

No, there was kindness in those moon eyes.

"As for taking you to a depot," he said, "I give you my word on that as well. Once we salvage, we will make for a depot to trade. Should we part ways there, you are doing me a favor as well. I wouldn't have to fly you all the way back here. Where are you headed?"

"I don't know," she said. "But wherever home is, it's not here."

"What is your name, Lady of El Cavador?"

"Rena Delgado."

"And do you speak for your crew?"

"I speak for no one but myself, but I believe my crew will come if I ask them to."

"Then you are not a woman to be trifled with if you have such sway and influence." He gave her a measuring look. "Tell me how to safely remove an oxygen processor."

He was testing her. But the question was simple enough. There were four steps and three precautions to be mindful of. She recited them all, throwing in a few secrets that Segundo had taught that she doubted Arjuna knew about.

The crow tried to hide that he was impressed. After a moment, as if considering her further, he said, "If you have twenty men and women as sharp as you, I will take them."

"We have more than twenty people," said Rena. "And you will not get a single one of us unless you agree to take us all."

"How many?"

"There are fifty-six of us."

Arjuna scoffed. "My shuttle isn't that big, Rena of El Cavador."

"Then you can make two shuttle trips."

"And are all these people skilled laborers, or can I expect children and invalids among them?"

"No invalids. But thirty-seven of them are children, yes. Some of them infants."

He scoffed again. "And what am I to do with thirty-seven more children on my ship? I have enough little mouths to feed already."

She was glad to hear that he had children on board. That was further evidence of family. Pirates didn't carry children.

"Our children work, sir. Not outside the ship, but many of them clean and wash and cook as well as any man or woman in your crew. They'll earn their food."

"I need salvagers, not dishwashers."

"And you'll get salvagers. Nineteen of them."

"How many of them are men?"

"None," said Rena. "We lost all our men."

She saw a hint of pity in his eyes. "Yours is a tale of sorrow, I see," he said. He folded his arms and considered a moment. "Nineteen women and thirty-seven children. Most captains would laugh at such an offer."

"Most might. But you know better. By your own math, nineteen free-miner women are equal to seventy-six corporate men."

He threw back his head and laughed at that. A big booming laugh that surprised her. She didn't think he had any humor in him, but there it was. "You use my own words against me, Rena of El Cavador. Very well. Come. Bring your nineteen women and thirty-seven children. If you salvage as quickly as you do calculations, I have need of you among my crew."


"Are you out of your mind?" said Julexi.

Rena was floating outside the storage room in the corridor with most of the women. A few others were inside the room, feeding and tending the children. "Keep your voice down," said Rena. "You'll frighten the children."

"*I'll* frighten the children? *I'll* frighten them? A ship of murdering vultures is what will frighten them, Rena."

"They're not vultures," said Rena. "They're crows."

Julexi threw her hands up. "Vultures, crows, seagulls. What's the difference? They're all the same. They're parasites. They feed off the dead and they kill whoever they fancy. We used to run from these ships in the K Belt, Rena. And now you want to *join* one of them? Have you lost your senses? We know nothing about this man. He could take us back to his ship and have his way with us."

"He has a family. They're a lot like us."

"How would you know?" asked Abbi. "He'll tell you anything to get us on his ship."

"I know because I met his family," said Rena.

The women stared at her. "What do you mean you met them?"

"I made him take me back to his ship on his shuttle. I insisted on inspecting the vessel and meeting his family."

"You went on his ship?" said Julexi. "Alone?"

"I wasn't going to rush us all over there without knowing what we'd be getting ourselves into. They'll put us in the cargo bay. It's slightly bigger than the storage room here. I saw it. It's clean. There are hammocks in there. And there's food as well. I saw their supplies. There's enough for all of us. If we work hard, we'll be fine."

"There's food here," said Abbi. "We're safer here."

"I don't think we are," said Rena. "Sooner or later we will make all the needed repairs. It's only a matter of time before they ask us to leave. I've heard things."

"Gossip and the whisperings of a handful of people," said Julexi. "Magashi likes us. We do more work than most of her crew."

"Magashi may not have the say for much longer," said Rena. "This is more than idle chatter I'm hearing. It's not safe. I worry for the children."

"And throwing them to a flock of vultures *doesn't* worry you?" said Abbi.

"They're not *your* children anyway," said Julexi. "They're *ours*."

Yes, thought Rena. They're not mine. I gave up my only child. I sent Victor to Luna to warn the world. I have lost him just as I have lost Segundo.

Aloud she said, "*Somos familia*. We are family. These children may not have come from my womb, but I love them like my own. Arjuna's family is like that as well. I could sense it. They're *familia*."

"You expect us to trust these people with our lives after one visit?" said Abbi.

"We've been putting our lives in other people's hands from the moment we left El Cavador," said Rena.

"That's different," said Julexi. "That was WU-HU. These are scavengers."

"He has offered to give any one of you a tour of his ship to meet his family. But we need to move quickly if we're going to do that. He grows impatient."

"Impatient?" said Julexi. "And what other emotions of his should we fear? His rage? His lust?"

"Will you shut up?" said Edimar. The fifteen-year-old popped out of the shadows. Rena hadn't even noticed that Edimar had been listening. "I am so sick of you cutting everyone down. Everyone's wrong but you. Everyone's to blame. Well you know what? If you actually said something positive every once in a while, you might not be so miserable and people might actually find you tolerable."

Lola, Edimar's mother, looked aghast. "Edimar! You will apologize to Julexi this instant!"

"No," said Edimar. "I won't. Because every one of you knows it's true, and you're all too polite to say so. Well I'm not. If you want to stay here and wait for the Chinese to kick us out, Julexi, fine, but I'm going with Rena."

Julexi narrowed her eyes. "You spoiled little child. You're worse than your dogging sister."

Lola slapped Julexi so fast and so hard, that it spun Julexi into the wall. Several women gasped. Julexi steadied herself, a hand to her cheek, shocked.

Edimar's sister had been Alejandra, whom the family had sent away when they feared that Alejandra and Victor might fall in love. Dogging, or marrying within the clan, was taboo, and even though Alejandra and Victor had done nothing wrong, the family had taken precautions. To accuse Alejandra of any impropriety was cruel and heartless. Rena was tempted to slap Julexi too.

Lola's voice was like ice. "You will never speak of my daughter again. Do you understand me? If you had a drop of Alejandra's goodness and decency, it would be double what you have now."

Edimar stared, mouth agape. Rena was no less shocked. Lola was always so mild-mannered. She had never lashed out at anyone.

Lola turned to Rena. "Edimar and I will do whatever the council decides. I trust your judgment. If you think it's best to leave with this crow, if this is how we can get back on our feet, then I will salvage a hundred ships at your side." She pushed off the wall toward the storage room door. "Come, Edimar. We've said our peace. Let the other women say theirs."

Edimar was still too stunned to move, staring at her mother as if seeing her for the first time. Then after a moment she came to herself and followed Lola inside.

When they were gone Julexi said, "Did you see that? Did you see her slap me? She's trying to divide us."

The hypocrisy of that statement almost made Rena laugh. But it would have been a sad and tired laugh had she done so. The sense of family was fading, she realized; the thread that stitched them together was unraveling and fraying at the edges. She couldn't allow that. Segundo had asked her to keep them together, to keep everyone alive.

"I'll tell you what I want," Rena said, realizing it was true as the words came to her. "I want us on a ship again. Not a crow's ship or a corporate ship, but *our* ship. Just as El Cavador was and always will be. That is where we belong. We're not going to get there by staying here. Here we have no future. Our work and welcome are drying up. Arjuna can help us move in the right direction. If you disagree speak up now."

They discussed it and then voted. A handful dug in their heels, but the majority—though nervous of the idea—was for going. Anything to get them closer to their own ship, they said. And in the end, even those who were against leaving came along. Staying with the group seemed safer than staying alone with WU-HU.

Later, as the second group boarded the shuttle for Arjuna's ship, Julexi stepped to the airlock with her bag and faced Rena. "If they rape us and kill our children, I hope God has mercy on you."

"I hope God has mercy on us anyway," said Rena. "We need all the help we can get."

# CHAPTER 8

# Beacon

The blueprints on the wall in the engineering room looked nothing like what Lem had imagined in his head.

"It's still your idea, Lem," said Benyawe. "Trust me. The design may look different from what you initially envisioned, but the principle is the same." She was floating in front of him at the wall, stylus in hand.

"I don't care if it's *my* idea," said Lem. "Throw out my idea if it's rubbish. Don't feel handcuffed to anything I suggested. I only care that it works. I'm not conceited enough to think I have a better grasp of this than you do, Benyawe. Do whatever you think is best."

In truth it stung him slightly that she had changed the design a bit, even though he had fully expected her to do so. He wasn't an engineer after all, and he only understood the science on the most fundamental level. Of course she was going to change it.

He had commissioned her months ago to develop a replacement for the glaser, and at the time he had given her a suggestion for its design, fully expecting her to dismiss his idea outright, pat him on his little head, and tell him to stop playing in her sandbox. Instead, she had thought the idea worth pursuing and assembled a team of engineers to make it work. Now that nugget of an idea had grown into schematics and actual plans.

"We call them 'shatter boxes,'" said Benyawe. "As you know, the problem with the current glaser is that the gravity field spreads outward too quickly and too wide."

Lem hardly needed reminding of that. It had almost meant his life. Back in the Kuiper Belt, when they had fired the glaser at a large asteroid, the gravity field had grown so quickly and stretched outward so far that it had nearly consumed the ship and turned them all to space dust. Lem's quick thinking was all that had saved them.

Benyawe pointed to some crude drawings on the wall that looked like two cubes connected to each other by a long, coiling string. "Your initial idea was a device like a bola, with two small glasers on both ends that attach themselves to opposite poles of an asteroid." She wiped the crude drawing away with a flick of her stylus, and floated over to the detailed schematics. "The shatter boxes operate the same way."

The cubes were now thick discs, and one of them was disassembled in the air, as if the whole thing had been photographed a microsecond after it exploded apart, revealing each of the individual pieces inside. "When they're fired from the mining ship, they spin through space like a bola, which as it turns out, is a brilliant mechanism if we detach the cable from each glaser at just the right instant. The spinning motion and additional guidance from us will sling them to opposite sides of the asteroid, where these anchor braces will dig into the rock." She indicated the teethlike claws on the sides of the shatter boxes. "All that's left is pushing the button and letting the glasers rip the rock to shreds. The two gravity fields will interact, counter each other, and keep the destructive reach of the fields to a minimum."

"So it works," said Lem.

"In the computer models, yes. It's much safer than the current design."

"Then why aren't you clicking your heels in glee?" said Lem. "Or am I missing something?"

"There is a problem, yes," said Benyawe.

"Which is?"

"Money. The original glaser isn't destroyed every time we use it. The shatter boxes are. They're consumed in the gravity field along with everything else. That's enormously expensive and would offset most of the profit we'd reap from mining the asteroid. It's not cost effective."

"Then make it cost effective," said Lem. "Use cheaper components and materials, shrink the size of the shatter boxes, remove anything that's not absolutely essential. Do whatever it takes."

She was quiet a moment then asked, "Are you sure this is how we should be spending our time, Lem?"

"How else would you be spending it?"

"Finding a way to fight the Formics."

"My dear sweet Dr. Benyawe, what do you think you've been doing?"

She seemed confused. "You want to fire these at the Formic ship?"

"I want to use them however we can. If they can safely destroy asteroids, maybe they can safely destroy the ship or whatever happens to be inside it."

"We'll never catch it before it reaches Earth. And if it enters Earth's atmosphere, it's beyond our reach. Plus it will take months to build these once we arrive at Luna."

"We'll need to move this through production much faster than that," said Lem. "We may not have months."

Lem's wrist pad vibrated, signaling a message from the helm. He tapped it. "Go ahead."

Chubs's voice said, "Long-range sensors have detected an emergency beacon."

"From where?"

"We can't determine its point of origin. Considering its trajectory however, it appears to have come from the Battle of the Belt."

Lem glanced at Benyawe and saw that her interest was piqued as well. The Battle of the Belt was the name the crew had given to the massive line of wreckage the sensors had found since flying closer to the Formics' trajectory. The *Massacre* of the Belt would have been a more fitting name in Lem's opinion, considering how one-sided the outcome had been. It was impossible to say what had happened exactly, but the amount of wreckage suggested that anywhere between fifty to one hundred mining ships had attacked the Formics in a coordinated assault. Sensors couldn't identify the ships at this distance, but they were likely free miners and corporates alike, allied for once against a common enemy.

A beacon sent from one of the ships in the battle might hold critical, useful intel. Maybe they had discovered a weakness in the Formics' defenses. Or perhaps they had more information about the Formics' weapons capabilities. Any nugget of information could be helpful.

"Is the beacon broadcasting a message?" asked Lem.

"Affirmative," said Chubs. "But sensors are only getting a billionth of it through the interference. We can't make it out. The light sequence suggests it's a STASA beacon, though."

Every satellite used blinking lights to identify itself from a distance in case radio had failed. No sequence was more familiar to anyone than that of the Space Trade and Security Authority.

"I'm on my way," said Lem. He clicked off and launched toward the push tube. Benyawe, as he expected, followed close behind. When they reached the helm, a rendering of the beacon spun in the system chart in front of them, its lights dancing across its surface.

"Can you determine *when* it was sent?" asked Lem. "Was it before or after the battle?"

"Impossible to say," said Chubs. "It may have nothing to do with the battle. We don't know."

"Where is it now? Could we intercept it?"

"It's not along our current trajectory. If we alter our course, we could snag it in about eighteen hours."

"Would that delay our arrival to Luna?" asked Benyawe.

"By twelve days at least," said Chubs.

"Twelve days?" asked Lem.

Chubs shrugged. "That's the math. We'd have to decelerate to intercept the beacon and then accelerate back up to our current speed. Twelve days minimum."

Lem considered a moment. "You think we should go for it?"

"In all honesty, it's probably not worth pursuing," said Chubs. "If it were a free-miner or corporate ship, I might expect intel on Formic defenses or weapons, something useful. But this is a STASA beacon. It's probably a worthless emergency announcement."

"Maybe it's a distress signal," said Benyawe.

"If it is, it was sent from the ship before the ship was destroyed," said Chubs. "There's nothing left from the battle but debris. And even if by some miracle a few people survived in a scrap of wreckage and fired off a beacon, they couldn't have held out this long. Too much time has passed. There's no one out there we can save."

"Maybe it has information about the battle," said Benyawe. "Which ships were engaged, crew manifests. That would allow us to at least document the battle for historical purposes."

"We're not historians," said Chubs. "That's not our mission."

"Even so," said Benyawe, "thousands of people lost their lives. Their families on Earth have a right to know what happened to them. That battle is a testament to human courage."

"And a testament to human inadequacy," said Chubs. "You're not going to boost morale on Earth by pointing out how our new alien friends wiped out dozens of heavily armed ships."

"We're not going to keep it a secret either," said Benyawe. "Earth needs to know what it's up against."

"The Formics will reach Earth long before we do," said Chubs. "By then Earth will know exactly what it's up against."

"I say we go for it," said Lem. "Right now we don't have any critical intel that's going to make any difference in the coming conflict. With that beacon we might. If we show up twelve days late, so be it. It's not like they're expecting us."

Eighteen hours later a crewman extended one of the ship's claws normally used for mineral extraction and snagged the beacon from space. Lem watched from the helm as the claw brought the beacon into a holding bay. There crewmen attached cables to the beacon's data ports. Three seconds later the download was complete.

Lem went to the conference room beside the helm with Benyawe and Chubs and pulled up the beacon's files and projected them in the holofield above the table. There were images of the Formic ship; 3-D models; information about the ship's trajectory, speed, and estimated date of arrival at Earth, but nothing new, nothing Lem didn't know already. No weapons analysis. No identified weakness. Lem waved his hand through the field, pushing files aside and bringing others to the forefront to take a closer look. Worthless, worthless, worthless. It was all old news. His hand moved faster. He was getting impatient.

A man's head appeared. It was a vid. Lem stopped.

The man looked to be in his fifties—old for a space commission, but not that abnormal for high-ranking officers. Lem made the appropriate hand gesture, and the vid began to play.

"I am Captain Dionetti of the Space Trade and Security Authority, commanding officer of The Star Seer. As the evidence in these files shows, an alien vessel is approaching Earth at incredible speed. We have been tracking alongside it for the past three days, and we will continue to match its speed and monitor it until it reaches Earth."

"Don't monitor it, you idiot," said Lem. "Destroy it."

The captain continued uninterrupted. "Two weeks ago, reports circulated among the ships here in the inner Belt that an alien vessel had attacked an unspecified number of ships near Kleopatra. News of this engagement spread quickly among the ships in the area. Several clans and corporate vessels decided to stage an offensive against the alien vessel once it reached our position. I and other STASA officers made repeated attempts to quell such an illegal and unprovoked attack—"

"Unprovoked?" said Lem.

"We reminded miners that attacking any ship is against space trade law established by STASA and ratified by the U.N. Security Council. We do not know this alien ship's intentions, and such aggression might justifiably provoke it to defend itself or retaliate, thus putting all of Earth in jeopardy.

"Sadly, the mining ships ignored our counsel, and a total of sixty-two ships joined in the assault. Our vessel recorded the events from a distance, and the vids of that battle are included amongst these files. I am saddened to report that all sixty-two ships appear to have been destroyed. As you will see from the vids, the alien vessel is fully capable of defending itself if provoked. Therefore, by the authority invested in me by the Space Peace Act and the Space Emergency Response Act, STASA is issuing a cease-fire against the alien vessel. Any mining ship which fires upon or attempts to obstruct the alien vessel will be subject to arrest."

"Cease-fire?" said Lem. "Tell me this is a joke."

"Typical STASA," said Chubs.

"The human race is a peaceful species," continued the captain, "and STASA will do everything in its power to maintain that peace. Rather than provoke our alien visitors and assume malicious intent, we will extend to them the hand of welcome and begin diplomatic efforts to establish a lasting, peaceful relationship between our two species. If the intel in this beacon reaches Earth before we do, we implore you to notify STASA of our escort and to make preparations to greet the alien ship with the proper delegates and peace offering. God protect us. End of transmission."

The man's head winked out.

"Are they insane?" Lem said. "A peace offering? He watched the Formics wipe out sixty-two ships, and he wants to shower them with gifts? Unbelievable."

"He saw the Formics' firepower," said Benyawe. "He's trying to prevent another massacre and maintain calm. Firing on the Formics is only going to lead to more deaths. You can't argue with that. He's doing what he thinks is best for Earth."

"He's wrong," said Lem. "We saw their firepower too. We saw what they did to El Cavador. That doesn't mean we're suddenly going to crawl into bed with them."

"I'm not saying I agree with him," said Benyawe. "I'm saying he's asking for diplomacy over rash action. I see his point of view."

"His point of view is boneheaded arrogance. You didn't see these creatures up close, Benyawe. I did. And believe me, a nice present in a pretty pink bow isn't going to make them our best friends."

"What do we do now?" said Chubs.

"We get to Luna as fast as we can and pray the political idiots don't roll out the red carpet."

"Faster than our previous speed?" asked Chubs.

"We can bump it up a notch," said Lem. "We're trying to avoid collision threats, I know, but our previous speed was still a little cautious. Let's push the safety parameters."

Chubs nodded. "I'll give the order immediately." He hurried back to the helm.

Lem returned his attention to the holofield where the captain's head had been. "How could someone be so asinine? An escort? The man watched all those people die and he has the audacity to give the Formics an escort?"

Benyawe shook her head, her voice barely above a whisper. "Sixty-two ships."

"We thought it might be more than that," said Lem.

"So many people."

Lem wiped his hand through the holofield, searching through the files for the vid of the battle. He found it and played it.

A massive cluster of ships appeared in the holofield. In the center was the Formic ship, huge and imposing, like a giant red moon hurtling through space. Dozens of mining ships were matching its speed, buzzing around it like bees at a hive, firing at the Formics with everything they had, which despite their numbers, seemed woefully inadequate.

Even at a distance Lem recognized several ships from his father's fleet, all of them armored with additional plates crudely welded to their hulls. They had apparently hastily readied themselves for war, but the added armor did nothing for them. One by one, the Formic guns picked off the ships, slinging hundreds of globules of laserized gamma plasma with perfect accuracy, vaporizing whole clusters of ships in flashes that sent debris hurtling in every direction.

Those ships are nothing to them, Lem realized. We're gnats. Mild annoyances. Easily pushed away, barely worth the effort.

As Lem and Benyawe watched, ship after ship broke apart into nothing, spilling their innards and crew into space. Most of the debris vanished as it moved out in every direction, but some of it continued forward in the direction the ship had been moving, carried by inertia as if it refused to accept it was dead and leave the fight.

Other pieces of debris were caught in an invisible field behind the Formic ship and pulled along, as if a giant magnet at the rear of the Formic ship caused the debris to change course and follow the ship.

The surviving ships pressed on, undeterred, firing relentlessly, pounding away at the Formics with everything in their arsenal. The outcome was always the same. Death, death, death. In moments, the hive of bees was diminishing, thinning out, leaving only a few persistent ships. Don't you see it's useless? Lem wanted to scream at them. Don't you see you're going to die? You're not even damaging them. Pull away. Dying accomplishes nothing.

But the ships in the holofield ignored him, firing and hammering away. It was pathetic now. A mere handful of ships remained. And then in a flurry of Formic fire, they were gone, leaving nothing but the Formic ship itself, unscathed and unflinching, silent once again as it bored through space like a bullet toward Earth, dragging a line of wreckage behind it.

The vid stopped.

Benyawe wiped at her eyes.

And to Lem's surprise, he realized that his own eyes were wet as well. He wiped at them quickly, furious with himself.

Fools, he thought. They had all been fools. Why had they persisted? Why had they wasted it all? Didn't they see they weren't making a dent? Didn't they know their loved ones on Earth would be devastated?

Of course they knew, he realized. It was their loved ones on Earth that had driven them. That's what had kept them in the fight, a desperation to save those back home.

I could have done the same, he thought. I could've stayed in the fight as well when we confronted them. But I didn't. I ran. I scurried away like a frightened mouse. Does that make me the wise man or the greater fool?

"I need to get word to my father," he said. "Laserlines aren't getting through, but we need to send something, anything. And we need to send it repeatedly, nonstop, a continuous broadcast. Maybe we'll hit a pocket where the interference is thin. Maybe someone will hear us and relay it through. Maybe it won't work, but we have to try."

He waited for her to respond, to say something, anything.

Finally when she spoke, her voice was trembling. "What will they do when they reach Earth, Lem?"

He shook his head. "I don't know. But they won't do it for long. I'm going to destroy it. With or without my father's help, I am going to destroy it."

# CHAPTER 9

# Announcement

Victor stepped through the doorway and into the small furnished apartment. It was a company suite, located underground in Juke's tunnel system and normally reserved for employees from Earth when they visited corporate headquarters. The lights came on, and an image of the Imbrium skyline at night appeared on the wall where a window should be.

"Someone will bring you your meals," said Simona. "If you get hungry before then, there's a kitchenette and a fully stocked pantry. Help yourself."

"What about Imala? Are you putting her up somewhere as well? She can't go back to her apartment. She helped me escape. The authorities might be looking for her."

"You needn't worry about Ms. Bootstamp. Mr. Jukes will provide for her. The police won't be a problem."

"Meaning what? Ukko controls the police?"

Simona ignored the question. "I'll bring you some fresh clothes. Stay presentable and keep the room neat. You'll probably have visitors."

"Who?"

"Specialists. Scientists. People with questions."

"I told you everything I know."

"Mr. Jukes will want to verify your claims with his own people."

"Prescott and Yanyu are already working on that."

"Mr. Jukes has specialists in all fields. He'll want many of them to talk to you."

"Every moment counts," said Victor. "Why is everyone dragging their feet on this? Did I not make it clear what's at stake here? Militaries need time to prepare."

"Mr. Jukes is an intelligent man, Victor. I assure you he knows what he's doing."

Victor shook his head. More delays. More inaction.

Simona stepped back out into the hallway. "This door will remain locked at all times. If you need anything, use the holopad there on the nightstand. Someone will assist you."

"So I'm a prisoner here?"

"We're keeping you here for your own safety. The LTD doesn't know you're here, and we want to keep it that way." She punched the code into the wall and sealed the door without another word.

That evening a group of technicians came and administered a lie detector test. Victor didn't object; he had nothing to hide. Once they had all the patches and sensors on him, however, he began to worry that the machine would misinterpret his brain activity somehow and conclude he was deceiving them. Then he feared that all the anxiety he felt over this possibility would skew the results even further. When the machine finished, the technicians said nothing and packed up the equipment.

"What were the results?" he asked.

"Don't know," said the tech. "We administer the test. Someone else reads it."

The test must have strengthened his case because the next morning small groups of people began visiting him every hour. Engineers. Psychologists. Biologists. Victor answered their questions as best as he could, though more often than not he had no answer to give. No, he hadn't seen the ship up close. No, he didn't know how many hormigas were inside.

He could tell many of them were skeptical. They listened intently and took studious notes, but some had a hard time hiding their disbelief and disdain. A few of them returned for a second, third, and fourth time, repeating the same questions over and over again.

By the fourth day Victor was losing his patience. "I've already answered these questions multiple times," he told them. "I know what you're doing. You're trying to catch me in a lie. You're throwing in details I didn't give you to see if I'll notice or change my story. You're desperately looking for signs of deception because some of you are so pompous and wrapped up in your own self-importance that you can't accept the fact that a man without all your college degrees could possibly know something you don't."

Some of the scientists laughed. Others scoffed and stormed out. Victor didn't care. He preferred to be alone anyway.

On the fifth day it happened. Simona came to the apartment with Imala, who was so relieved to see Victor that she embraced him. "They've been drilling me for days," she said. "I can only assume you were getting the same." She smiled at him. "They found it, Victor. Prescott and Yanyu found it."

Simona set her holopad on the table and extended the bars in the corners. A live news broadcast projected in the field. Ukko stood at a lectern crested with the Juke corporate logo. Behind him, clustered together, was a crowd of people, most of whom had come to Victor's apartment in the past few days. Prescott was among them, as was Yanyu.

"Ladies and gentlemen of the press," said Ukko. "Citizens of Earth and Luna. We are not alone in the universe."

Victor felt a weight lift. In that one sentence, his task was complete. The burden was someone else's now. He was free.

Cameras flashed as Ukko continued. "An intelligent and hostile alien species is at this moment approaching Earth in a ship unlike anything we've ever seen." He gestured to his left, where a holofield resided above a platform. The alien ship appeared, suspended in space. "This holo and others I supplied to STASA this morning leave no doubt in my mind that our planet is in grave danger." The alien ship minimized, and Yanyu's wreckage from the Belt appeared. "Dedicated members of my staff have discovered evidence that this alien vessel is responsible for the destruction of an unknown number of mining vessels in the Asteroid Belt and beyond. We fear the loss of human life may already be in the thousands. We can also prove definitively that this alien ship is the cause of the communications interference that has crippled space commerce for months. My team is tracking the ship as we speak, and if its current rate of deceleration continues, it will reach Earth in approximately eleven days."

There were murmurs from the media.

Ukko signaled them to quiet. "We must do all in our power to remain calm and prevent a worldwide panic. I call upon all governments of Earth to convene an emergency summit at the United Nations so that immediate precautionary measures can be taken. And I vow that Juke Limited will continue to do everything in its power to keep the world informed and to assist in whatever preparations will be made. I'll now turn the microphone over to members of my team who will take you through the evidence and answer all of your questions." He stepped away from the lectern, and ges-tured to Prescott, who came forward and introduced himself.

"It's running on every feed," said Simona, who was tapping at her wrist pad.

"Our investigation began," said Prescott, "when we initiated an analysis of purported evidence uploaded onto the nets concerning an alleged alien vessel. Much of this evidence was dismissed by members of the press, but our team of researchers continued to analyze it nonetheless."

It was a bold statement to make. Yet Victor saw the wisdom of it. The world would want to place blame; people would be angry. They'd demand to know why they hadn't been told sooner and why they had been given so little time to prepare. By subtly slapping the media on the wrist, Ukko was doing preemptive damage control and deflecting any blame from himself.

The press conference went on for an hour, with various members of Ukko's team taking the microphone to present evidence and answer ques-tions. Victor and Imala watched the subsequent news coverage as anchors regurgitated Ukko's announcement. There were rumors that the director of STASA was preparing a statement. The president of the U.S. had called a press conference. The Politburo in Beijing was deliberating. The secretary-general of the United Nations would be making a statement shortly. Even-tually Victor turned off the broadcast, and the room went silent.

"What's going to happen now?" he asked Simona.

"The U.N. will hold its summit. STASA will spring into action. Nations of the world will pledge their support, and every politician with a spark of intelligence and an eye on the next election will scramble to praise Mr. Jukes and his team."

"What about the ship?" Victor asked. "Will they ready a fleet to de-stroy it?"

Simona shrugged. "Too early to say. What matters is that it's not your problem anymore. You two are free to go. As of right now, your services with Juke Limited are no longer required. Mr. Jukes wishes to express his deep gratitude for your tireless assistance, and as a token of his thanks he is giving you the use of a Juke shuttle to fly you to Midway station. You'll re-turn the shuttle there and secure your own passage out to the Kuiper Belt."

Victor couldn't believe what he was hearing. "You're giving me a shuttle?"

"On loan. To get you to Midway. You said yourself you wanted to find your family."

"Yes but . . . what's the catch?"

"No catch. Mr. Jukes recognizes the sacrifices you've made, and he is all too eager to return the favor and reunite you with your family. I'm to take you both to the dock immediately."

"Both of us?" said Victor.

"Imala will be accompanying you. She'll pilot the shuttle. It's not a ship you're familiar with."

Victor looked at Imala and saw at once from her expression that she had already agreed to this. "How can you possibly consider this?" he asked. "Your career. Your family. You don't want to come with me. It's a six-, seven-month trip to Midway."

"They asked me," said Imala. "It's the least I could do after everything you've done for us. You shouldn't be traveling alone."

"But I don't have to travel alone," said Victor. "A ship to myself is generous, but it's unnecessary. Surely there are still transports leaving for the Belt. And if not, there will be now. A lot of people will want to get as far away from Earth and Luna as possible until this is over. Why not put me on one of those ships and be done with it? Why give me a whole shuttle?"

"Mr. Jukes wants you riding in comfort," said Simona. "Money is no object."

Victor didn't know what to say. A shuttle. All the way to Midway. For free. It was more than he could have asked for. It was too good to be true.

And then he realized it *was* too good to be true.

"Ukko isn't doing this out of generosity," he said. "He's doing it to get rid of me. That's what this is. He keeps me here under house arrest and then he ships me out as soon as the announcement is made? On a shuttle with just Imala? Away from anyone I might relay my story to? This isn't a gift. It's a muzzle. He doesn't want me talking to anyone, especially the press. He doesn't want me telling them that his son is a murderer. He's protecting Lem by making me disappear. Tell me if I'm getting warm here."

"Or perhaps Mr. Jukes is genuinely grateful and you've misjudged him," said Simona.

"Oh yes, I've misjudged the man who has been attacking families like mine for decades, the man who called me a heathen and threatened me and kept me as a prisoner—"

"Who protected you from the authorities," Simona corrected.

"For his own gain! Do you honestly think I'm stupid enough to believe that Ukko Jukes would do anything out of the goodness of his own heart?"

"Victor," said Imala. "Think for a moment. Does it really matter what Ukko's motivations are? You're getting a shuttle back to your family. You're getting out. That's what's important."

He rounded on her. "You're siding with them?"

"I'm not siding with anyone. I'm thinking of your interests. So what if Ukko wants to protect his son? Fine. Don't make it your concern."

"It *is* my concern. It most definitely is my concern. Lem killed my uncle."

"And what are you going to do about it?" asked Imala. "Go to the police? Press charges? There's a warrant out for your arrest. And even if the police listened to you, which they wouldn't, do you think you have a legal leg to stand on? You have no corpse. No proof. No other witnesses. Do you think Ukko doesn't employ the most powerful legal army in the world? Do you think he would stand by while you made these accusations? He owns this city, Victor. He owns all of Luna. Probably judges as well. I'm telling you now, as someone who knows, if you go to war on this, you will lose. It's that simple."

"What happened to you, Imala? What happened to the fire? Two weeks ago you were trying to take down the man all by yourself. Now you're tucking tail and running."

He could see the words were like a slap to her face, and he regretted them instantly.

Imala's eyes narrowed. "What happened? An alien ship coming to Earth, that's what happened. I don't like this any more than you do, Victor. Believe me, no one despises Ukko more than me, but this is not the way to hurt him. It will fail. The only person who would come out of this a loser would be you."

"She's talking sense, Victor," said Simona.

"Don't take my side," said Imala.

"So you knew they wanted to get rid of me?" Victor asked Imala. "You knew this was their motivation? And you agreed to it?"

"Of course I knew. It's obvious, isn't it? And I knew you'd figure it out as well. We get what we want, Ukko gets what he wants—"

"And Lem gets away with murder."

"You didn't come here seeking vengeance, Victor. You came here to do a job, and that job is done."

Victor turned to Simona. "If Ukko is doing this solely as a token of gratitude, then he would honor my request to go with a transport."

"That's not an option," said Simona.

Victor smiled sardonically. "Yeah. Didn't think so."

They took a skimmer to a small, private spaceport north of Imbrium, well beyond the watchful eye of the Lunar Trade Department. Imala pointed out that she had never heard of the place and didn't remember seeing it listed in any official registry at the Customs Department. Simona brushed the observation aside and assured them both the port was legal.

The skimmer slid into a slot near the terminal entrance, and Simona led them inside. It was a narrow terminal with a dozen gates, six to a side. Other than a few technicians moving about, preparing shuttles and loading supplies, the terminal was empty.

Simona guided them to their gate and wiped her hand in a holofield beside the gate exit. The door to the umbilical opened, and Simona led them inside.

The shuttle was small, with most of the space dedicated to the cargo bay, which measured ten by twenty meters. Several pallets of wrapped supplies had been tied down in the center.

"Supplies for Midway," said Simona. "Just leave them on the ship when you turn in the shuttle." She then showed them where their supplies and hammocks were located and asked Imala if she had any questions with the flight controls. Imala didn't.

Simona extended a hand. "Then good luck to you both. I hope you find your family, Victor."

Victor shook her hand. "Thanks. And I hope you wise up and get a new employer."

Simona winked. "Someday perhaps. The sun to your back, Imala."

"And to yours," said Imala.

Simona left them then and sealed the umbilical door behind her.

Imala buckled into the pilot's seat, entered a few commands into the console, and turned on the virtual windshield.

Victor climbed into the copilot's seat beside her. "You sure you know how to fly this thing? I thought you were an auditor."

She threw more switches and punched in more commands. "My father's a pilot back in Arizona. He did everything he could to convince me to follow in his footsteps. Flying lessons, low-grav flight training. He even took me on an orbiting shuttle cruise when I was a kid and talked the pilot into letting me take the helm for a few minutes. I think he thought I'd have some magical experience that would convince me to pursue piloting. I broke his heart when I told him I wanted to work in tax and tariffs."

"A far cry from flying."

"And not the most glamorous of careers either, in his opinion. What can I say? Macroeconomics and financial structures fascinate me. My father called it a 'cataclysmic mistake.'" She smiled. "You have to know my father. He's not the most open-minded of men. He even tried to marry me off to another Apache to keep me from coming to Luna. A real tribesman like my father. Pride of the people and all that. Preserving our heritage.

"Despite all that, though, I really liked the guy. If my father hadn't been the one to introduce us and if he hadn't been pushing the whole thing, I'm not sure what would have happened. My mother said I broke it off to spite my father, which is probably true. When I left home, it wasn't a fond farewell. My dad and I both said a few things we probably shouldn't have."

"Is that why you're not going back to Arizona? Is that why you're coming with me?"

"I'm coming with you, Victor, because you shouldn't do this alone and because I think the world owes it to you."

"It's not your debt to pay, Imala. I got here on my own, remember? I'm not helpless."

"Yes, but what you seem to forget is that you nearly wasted away to nothing and you've failed miserably on your own ever since you arrived. If I hadn't helped, you'd still be stuck in the recovery hospital awaiting trial, with the world none the wiser about what's coming."

Victor put his feet up on the dash and his hands behind his head. "My hero. Whatever would I do without you?"

"Not much," said Imala.

The anchors detached, and Imala pulled the shuttle up and away from the terminal.

Victor sat up, suddenly serious. "Are you sure about this, Imala? This is a year-long trip. Six months out, six months back."

"I can do the math, Victor."

"Yes, but you're being rushed into this. It's not too late to change your mind."

"You're saying you don't want the company?"

"No, I'm saying this is a sacrifice you don't have to make."

"I can't stay on Luna, Victor. And I'm not going home. If I go home, I'm useless. Here, I can do something. I may not be able to stop the hormiga ship, but I can contribute in some small way. Will you let me do that please? Will you at least give me that courtesy?"

He smiled and pushed off the seat, weightless now. "On one condition: My family calls me Vico for short. If we're going to be in this can for six months, we should at least treat each other like family."

She grinned, testing the sound of the word. "Vico. I'll see if I can remember that."

They flew for seven days toward Last Chance, a small supply depot that was the last stop in this quadrant for those traveling to the Belt. From here, crews could anticipate several months and two hundred million kilometers of nothing. Victor and Imala didn't need supplies, but they were desperate for news. Their shuttle had lost contact with Luna after the first day because of the interference, and they had no idea what preparations Earth and Luna had made since then.

As they approached the depot, still several hours away, Victor said, "You realize of course that in all likelihood the ships docked at this place are going to know less about what's going on than we do. They won't have had communication for the same reason we don't. They'll be pumping *us* for information, not the other way around."

"Probably," agreed Imala. "But our shuttle is hardly the fastest thing out here. Maybe there are ships at the depot that left Luna after us and arrived before us. In which case they might know something we don't."

The shuttle's flight data said that Last Chance had ten docking stations with umbilicals, but when the depot came into view, Victor saw that there were at least four times that many ships clustered around it.

"It's packed," said Victor. "No way we're getting on board."

"Maybe we don't have to," said Imala. "Laserlines work over short distances. If we get close enough, maybe they can feed us news directly to the ship."

When they were less than a hundred klicks away, Imala used the laser-line to hail the station.

The head of a portly woman appeared in the holofield.

"I'd ask for a docking tube," said Imala, "but it doesn't look like you have one available."

"We don't. You're welcome to patch in to our news feeds, though."

"You're getting broadcasts from Luna?"

"We're getting text only," said the woman. "The bandwidth doesn't handle voice or video."

"How are you getting even that?" said Imala. "We can't get anything."

"We've set up a string of ships between us and Luna," said the woman, "with a ship every million klicks or so. Like a bucket brigade. They're pass-ing up information via laserline as it becomes available. It's not a perfect system, mind you. The deterioration you usually get in ten million klicks happens in a hundred thousand now. So in a million klicks you can barely make out a very slow transmission. The ships have to repeat the message three times and make the best guess about some passages, but even so you're going to get some deterioration and holes in the text. Shall I send you the codes for the uplink?"

"Yes. Please," said Imala.

"There's a fee," said the woman.

"You're charging me for the news?"

"Keeping relay ships out there isn't cheap. News wouldn't get through otherwise."

"How much?" asked Imala.

The woman told them a ridiculous amount. Imala wanted to argue, but Victor said, "I'll pay it." His family had left him money for his education at a university. He could spare some of it here.

Five minutes later text from various news feeds appeared on their mon-itor. The reports were riddled with holes and sentence fragments, but Vic-tor and Imala got the gist of each report.

Victor had hoped that a fleet had been assembled, but it quickly became evident that such wasn't the case. STASA was calling for calm and pushing for diplomacy, seeking for ways to communicate with the hormigas when they arrived. The U.N. had conducted an emergency summit as Ukko Jukes had suggested, but all that political circus had accomplished was to appoint the Egyptian ambassador, Kenwe Zubeka, as the secretary of alien affairs, a new position with zero power or influence. Zubeka seemed not to notice how insignificant his position was and kept making asinine statements to the press.

When asked about the destroyed ships in the Belt, Zubeka had said, "We don't know what kind of misunderstanding or provocation our alien visitors were responding to. As soon as we can talk to them, I'm sure we can have a peaceful conversation that will benefit both our species."

"Are you kidding me?" said Victor. "A misunderstanding? He's calling the murder of thousands of people a misunderstanding? When they killed the Italians, it wasn't a misunderstanding. It was deliberate. They knew what they were doing."

"It's typical geopolitics, Vico. Few countries have any military presence in space. Most of the bigger powers have shuttles and cargo vessels that are space-ready and could be weaponized, but to form a fleet, to amass enough ships to stage an assault or form a blockade, we need a coalition. The U.S., Russia, China, India, France. These countries don't work well together. The Chinese don't trust the Russians, India doesn't trust the Chinese, and the U.S. doesn't trust anybody, except for maybe a few countries in Europe. And no country wants to act on their own. If they go alone they risk crippling their ships and weakening their arsenal. That would make them vulnerable to other powers."

"So they're going to do nothing? Why does everyone seem to believe that inaction is the best course of action?"

"Caution is their action, Vico. Or at least that's their justification. They're sitting tight to see what happens. Everyone is hoping this will resolve itself. They're acting like humans always act when war seems inevitable and most of the variables are still unknown. They're playing the good-guy card and waiting for the other guy to shoot first."

"The Formics don't shoot first, Imala. They rip apart. They find life and they destroy it. They're not interested in diplomacy or gathering around a table and making friends. They're interested in breaking us wide open and bleeding us dry."

They read on, but the situation only worsened. Riots were springing up all over the world—people taking to the streets to demand that governments take action. Deaths were reported. Governments continued to call for calm. The media discussed the vids Victor and Imala had uploaded as well. Experts scrutinized every detail, spending far too much time excusing the media for initially ignoring the vids. The vids did, after all, look like so many spookers out there.

When they finished reading, Victor said, "We can't move on, Imala. We're not leaving this depot. Not yet. Not until we see how this plays out."

None of the other ships at the depot moved on either. And over the next few days, the number of ships only grew. Victor and Imala programmed the monitor to alert them whenever a new message came through, regardless of whether they were sleeping or not.

They stayed for days, reading the reports aloud to each other the moment they came in. Sometimes Victor became so frustrated with the idiocy of governments or the press that he would tell Imala to stop reading. Then he would retreat to the back of the shuttle to cool off.

"All that effort," he told her, "all that time spent in the quickship so that Earth could prepare, so that countries could muster enough resources to take action, and nobody is doing anything." He wanted to cry. He wanted to reach down through space and shake someone. "How can they be so fundamentally wrong?"

"Because the world doesn't think like a free-miner family, Vico," Imala said. "We're not one people. We're splintered, too concerned about our own people and agendas and borders. We're one planet, but you wouldn't know it by looking at us."

Among all the idiocy, there were voices of reason as well. Several governments were as incensed and baffled by the inaction as Victor was. Germany, Australia, New Zealand, Argentina, South Africa. All were advocating forming a coalition to build an immediate defense. But Russia and China and the U.S. beat down the idea in the U.N. Security Council. Further provocation would only lead to further violence.

On the fourth day, with a small cadre of STASA ships acting as escorts, the hormiga ship reached Earth's geosynchronous orbit and came to a full stop.

# CHAPTER 10

# Mothership

"What do you see?" said Bingwen. "Are they letting people inside the library?"

Above him, Hopper clung to a drainpipe on the side of one of the village houses. Even with his gimp leg, Hopper had always been a better climber. It was the position of his bad foot that gave him the advantage. Since the foot was turned slightly inward, Hopper got more of the sole of his foot on the surface of things without having to bow his legs. It allowed him to scurry up rickety pipes like this one despite it being wet and narrow. "There's got to be at least four hundred people here," said Hopper.

It was dark, well into evening, and the crowd was dotted with lanterns. Nearly everyone from the nearby villages had come to the library to see what would happen when the alien ship arrived. Bingwen's parents were somewhere in the crowd, as was Grandfather. Bingwen had been standing with them, clinging to Mother's hand. But as the crowd grew and shuffled forward toward the library, bodies began to push against each other, and Bingwen felt as if he might be crushed. Before Mother could stop him, he had ducked down and crawled through people's legs behind him until he came out the back and found Hopper.

"Ms. Yí's got the door closed," said Hopper. "She's getting up on a chair."

Bingwen was desperate to see. He looked around him. There was a rain barrel to his right below a windowsill. He grabbed a fruit box from the trash pile and used it as a stepping stool to climb up onto the barrel. From there he pulled himself up into the windowsill. He didn't have nearly as good a view as Hopper, but he could see over the crowd well enough.

Ms. Yí, the librarian, was motioning for quiet. "Please. Everyone, please.

The library is closed. We will reopen tomorrow for the news feeds at normal business hours."

The uproar from the crowd was immediate. "Let us inside!" someone shouted.

"We want to see the feeds!"

Ms. Yí waved for quiet again. "Even if I could let you in, we don't have enough machines. You wouldn't fit. If we hear any news, I'll post it on the door."

"You'll *open* the door!" someone shouted.

"This is our library!"

"Push her out of the way."

"They're going to rip her arms off any second now," said Hopper.

It was true. It was about to get ugly. Bingwen had to do something fast. "Hop, we need to get on the roof of the library."

Hopper gave him a mischievous grin. "I don't know what you have in mind, but I like it already."

Bingwen lowered himself to the ground, and Hopper followed. They ran around the crowd to the back of the library. There were no doors or windows in the back, just a smooth stucco wall.

"No way to get to the roof," said Hopper. "Nothing to climb. I could give you a boost, but the roof is four meters up."

Bingwen was hardly paying attention. He had run past Hopper to a stretch of tall grass behind the building. The bamboo ladder was right where he had left it, anchored to the ground with two hooked stakes. Even if someone had stood right where Bingwen was standing, they likely wouldn't have seen the ladder; it was too well concealed beneath the thick net of grass and undergrowth. Bingwen lifted it free of the stakes and dragged it toward the back of the building.

Hopper blinked. "What is *that?*"

"A ladder."

"Obviously. Where did it come from?"

"I made it."

"When?"

"About a year ago."

"And when were you going to tell *me* about it?"

Bingwen gestured with his hand. "Hopper, I'd like you to meet my ladder. Ladder, Hopper."

"Very funny. You mean to tell me you've been sneaking into the library for a year now?"

"A few years actually," said Bingwen. "This is the third ladder I've made."

Bingwen leaned the ladder against the lip of the roof, placing the bamboo poles neatly into the two small grooves on the roof he had chiseled out for that purpose. He gave the ladder a tentative shake to determine it was steady, then gestured to the lowest rung. "After you."

Hopper shook his head. "A few years? Why am I not surprised?" He climbed the ladder, and Bingwen followed.

The top of the roof was flat. Bingwen pulled up the ladder and laid it to the side.

"This is why you ace all the practice tests," said Hopper. "You've been cheating for years."

"I don't cheat," said Bingwen. "I study more."

"When?"

"Three or four in the morning most days. You'd love it. It's very quiet."

"That explains how you learned English."

"What did you think, Hop, that I could pick up English during the paltry hours of study they give us? It's the most backwards language in the world."

"Stop using words like 'paltry.' You're only making me feel dumber."

Bingwen smiled and put a hand on Hopper's shoulder. "You're not dumb, Hop. You're smart. I study more because I have to. I don't grasp concepts as quickly as you do."

Hopper folded his arms and scowled. "You're only trying to make me feel better."

Bingwen made scissors with his fingers and snipped the air. "Let's cut this wonderful bonding moment short and get inside, shall we?"

Bingwen hurried to a spinning, bulbous air vent. He knelt beside it and peeled away the rubber skirt around the vent's base. Then he wrapped his arms around the base, twisted, and lifted. The vent came free easily, leaving a gaping hole in the roof.

"How did you lift that thing when you first started coming up here?" asked Hopper. "Your arms weren't long enough to wrap around the thing."

"Pulley system," said Bingwen. "Little rope, little bamboo, lot of work. Believe me, this is much easier."

Hopper shook his head again. "Unbelievable."

Bingwen set the vent aside.

Hopper leaned forward and peered into the hole. "It's a four-meter drop to the floor. How are we managing that? No, let me guess. Winches and scaffolding made from rice shoots and bubblegum?"

Bingwen grinned. "Hopper. We have a ladder."

Hopper flushed. "Right."

They retrieved the ladder, lowered it into the hole, and shimmied down. They were in the southwest corner of the building, obscured from the rest of the library by tall shelves of books.

Bingwen could hear voices.

"Now what?" whispered Hopper.

Bingwen crept forward to the end of the shelf and looked down the aisle. The front door was barred, and Ms. Yí was inside now, seated at a terminal, flanked by two of her assistants, watching the news feed.

"That mud sucker," said Hopper. "She gets to watch the feed and we don't?"

"Follow me," said Bingwen.

They crept along the back wall to the main office. Bingwen pulled back a corner of carpet and took out a concealed access card.

"I'm not even going to ask how you got that," said Hopper.

Bingwen opened the door, rehid the card, and they went inside. The projector and antenna box were in a cabinet. "Hold out your arms," said Bingwen. Hopper obeyed, and Bingwen loaded Hopper's arms with both devices. The amp and speaker were in a drawer in the back. Bingwen slid them into his pocket and motioned for Hopper to follow him out.

When they reached the ladder, Hopper said, "So you get the light stuff, and I get the heavy stuff?"

Bingwen put a finger to his lips, took the antenna box, and scaled the ladder. When they both reached the top, Bingwen pulled up the ladder and resealed the hole.

"If you had told me theft was your plan from the beginning," said Hopper, "I could have saved us both a little jail time by telling you what a yak's ass of an idea this is."

"Not stealing," said Bingwen. "This equipment will never leave the library." He carried everything over to the opposite side of the roof above the front door. Most of the crowd was still present, but they had calmed and were sitting in small groups along the village staircase or in the few patches of grass, conversing quietly and waiting for the librarian to bring them news. No one noticed Bingwen setting up the equipment.

It took him only a moment. When it was ready, he popped the lens cap, and the news feed projected onto the side of the house opposite the library. A reporter was standing in the streets of Beijing. Thousands of people were behind him, all of them watching the massive screens on the sides of buildings. The screens all showed live images of a red ship shaped like a giant teardrop.

Below Bingwen, someone shouted and pointed to the projection. "Look!"

The voice of the street reporter boomed from the speaker. Bingwen adjusted the volume, and the crowd of villagers quickly congregated in front of the house. Several of them applauded and whistled and briefly shined their lights up to the roof to see who had done them the favor. Hopper was standing at the roof's edge, chest out, waving to the crowd like a general returning from war.

Bingwen caught site of Grandfather, who gave him a wink.

". . . tens of thousands of people have taken to the streets," the reporter said. "All of them here to see and experience this historic event together. I've stopped several people, and their feelings span the emotional spectrum. Some told me they're afraid, that the destruction of mining ships in the Belt troubles them deeply . . ."

The reporter prattled on.

"Are you frightened, Bingwen?" Hopper asked.

They were sitting beside each other on the roof now, hugging their knees tight to their chests to stay warm in the chilled night air.

Bingwen made a slight adjustment on the speaker in front of him so that the sound in their direction lessened but that the audio for those below remained the same.

"Aren't you?" Bingwen asked.

"I'd never say so to my father or to Meilin . . . but I have dreams now. Nightmares. My mother says I scream at night. The dream is so real. It's right there in my room, standing over me."

"The creature?"

Hopper nodded. "Only it's not wearing a compression suit. It's not wearing anything. It just stands there, looking down at me." He looked skyward, as if he could see the ship beyond the blackness.

"It's a dream, Hop. I have them, too."

Hopper turned, surprised.

"A lot of people do," said Bingwen. "Even my father. He had to splash water in his face the other night and sit by the fire. Couldn't go back to sleep. I'd never seen him like that. But they're dreams, Hop. That's all they'll be. That ship looks big in the projection, but the world is much bigger. Twelve billion people strong. Whatever the creatures are, they won't touch us here."

"You don't believe that. You've been stockpiling supplies. You've been preparing for the worst. You told me to *expect* the worst."

It was true. Bingwen had been scrambling ever since Yanyu sent him the vid. And he'd been telling Hopper to do the same. But gloom and doom wasn't what Hopper needed to hear now. The time for prep was over. All they could do now was stay even keeled and alert.

"It's food storage," said Bingwen. "I'm playing it safe. I mostly do it in case supplies run short and the trucks don't come. Grandfather and I have a lot, we'll share."

"You're only trying to make me feel better again," said Hopper.

"You're right," said Bingwen. "I take back everything I've said today, especially the part about you being smart." Then he gave Hopper his toothiest grin.

Hopper rolled his eyes and shoved Bingwen lightly on the shoulder.

The shouting below startled them both.

"Stop!" Ms. Yí stormed out of the building, waving her arms. "Stop!" She ran in front of the projection and faced the crowd. "You can't do this. All of you, go home!" She pointed a finger up at Bingwen. "You little rat, you put everything back."

Someone threw a shoe. The light from the projection was in Ms. Yí's eyes, so she only recoiled at the last moment. The shoe lightly bounced off her chest, but Ms. Yí squealed as if it had taken off her arm. Several people laughed.

"Go back inside," someone yelled.

"Leave us alone."

"Get out of the light."

Ms. Yí looked defiant. "The regional director will hear about this!"

Another shoe flew, and Ms. Yí squealed again and retreated, covering her face with her arm. More laughter. Bingwen watched her go, feeling sorry for her.

Ms. Yí stopped at the library door and shined her light toward the roof. "You will never set foot in this building again, Bingwen. You understand? You either, cripple."

"Eat farts, pig face!" Hopper shouted.

More people laughed and Ms. Yí disappeared inside.

"Smart," said Bingwen. "Now you'll never get to take the test."

"She wasn't going to let us take it anyway. Besides, we don't need her. We'll come back at three in the morning and take the test then. Right, ladder boy?"

They went back to watching the broadcast. The street reporter was interviewing someone when the anchor interrupted him and the feed switched to live coverage of the alien ship in space. Several news shuttles had tentatively approached it, and these gave the alien ship a sense of scale. It was bigger than Bingwen expected. He had seen all the evidence Yanyu had forwarded him; he had examined all the data and holos the free miner had uploaded. Yet numbers were merely numbers. This was the real thing, larger than anything humans had ever dreamed of building.

The crowd of villagers was silent now. No one moved. Hopper was wide-eyed and rigid with fear.

The commentator's voice said, "An envoy from the United Nations is now approaching the alien ship, which for the past forty minutes has not changed its position or moved."

What is it doing? Bingwen wondered. Why is it just sitting there? Is it waiting for us? Attempting to communicate?

In space, a distance from the alien ship, a small ship approached, escorted by two news shuttles. The feed switched to cameras from the shuttle escorts, and Bingwen saw that the approaching ship was light blue and emblazoned with the mark of the United Nations. The feed switched again to cameras inside the ship, where a dark-skinned man stood anchored to the floor in formal attire, smiling like an idiot.

The commentator's voice was almost a whisper now. "We go now to U.N. Secretary of Alien Affairs Kenwe Zubeka, who carries with him gifts and tokens of peace from a hundred and eighty-seven countries."

The U.N. ship stopped within a few kilometers of the alien ship. A platform detached itself from the underside of the U.N. ship and floated forward. A massive disc-shaped holo flickered to life above the platform like a Frisbee.

The news broadcaster said, "U.N. delegates from twelve different nations insisted that Secretary Zubeka have a military escort, but Zubeka refused, saying quote, 'We will not aim a gun with one hand and offer a token of peace with the other.'"

Inside the ship, Zubeka spread his arms. "Welcome. On behalf of the people of Earth, I extend a hand of fellowship to you, our brethren of the universe."

A voice on the feed translated Zubeka's words into Mandarin.

"We present you with this hologram, a show of our hope for peace and mutual respect between our species."

Above the disc a giant holo of a dove with an olive branch in its beak flapped it wings, as if taking flight.

Bingwen sighed. A dove? That means nothing to this species. They've never seen one and have no idea what it represents.

"This creature is a dove," said Zubeka. "A symbol of our—"

Hundreds of globules of light exploded from a point on the alien ship and rained down on the dove, disintegrating the platform beneath it. The hologram winked out, and the villagers watching gasped and recoiled.

Zubeka's smile waned, but he strained to keep his composure. "They must be offended that I didn't come forward in person."

The cameras from the news shuttles swiveled and zoomed in on the alien ship, where a section of the hull had slid open and a strange, elongated device was protruding from inside. Clearly a weapon of sorts. Zubeka kept his eyes forward but gestured to the captain of the ship to his right. "Captain, perhaps we should give the ship some space."

The captain spun to one of the flight controllers. "Back us up! Get us out of—"

A second burst of light shot forth, engulfed the U.N. ship, and shattered it to bits.

The villagers screamed. Hopper scrabbled backward, screaming, frantic. The alien gun rotated, fired again. A news shuttle vaporized. Then another. A third one turned and tried to flee, but the aliens hit it from behind. Dust. The gun swiveled again. Screams from inside the last shuttle remaining, the one broadcasting. The camera shook. The image spun as the ship turned, unsteady, frantic, desperate. There were noises off screen, people screaming, scrambling, engines gaining power, preparing to run.

A searing burst of light punctuated the chaos, and the projected feed went to black.

For a brief moment the villagers were too shocked to speak. Then everyone began shouting out at once, getting to their feet, calling out names, searching for others in the crowd, picking up children, telling loved ones to hurry, rushing for the village stairs that led down to the fields. Several of the men were calling for calm, but no one seemed to be listening.

"Bingwen!"

Bingwen looked down. Mother was below, frantically waving for him to get off the roof.

"I'm coming!"

"What do we do?" said Hopper. Tears were running down his cheeks, but he seemed not to notice.

Bingwen grabbed him by the arms. "Hop! Look at me. Look at my face. That ship is in space and we are down here. You understand? It's far away. We're safe."

Hop blinked, nodded.

"We need to help everyone stay calm. All right? Someone's going to get hurt if we don't. I need you to have a clear head."

Hopper blinked again, nodding, coming to himself. He wiped at his eyes with his sleeve. "Right. Yes. Sorry. What do you want me to do?"

"Come with me."

They ran and retrieved the ladder, lowered it over the side, then slid to the ground. Bingwen hastily hid the ladder in the grass, then he and Hopper sprinted to the front of the building. Mother was there. She scooped Bingwen up into her arms. Father arrived a moment later, half carrying, half dragging Grandfather, who was holding his side and wincing.

"What happened?" said Mother.

"Crowd pushed him over on the stairs," said Father. "Nearly trampled him. It's madness. They would've killed him if I hadn't pulled him out."

He lowered Grandfather to the ground, who clutched at his chest, gritting his teeth.

"Your heart," said Mother. There was panic in her voice.

"I'm fine," said Grandfather, waving the concern away. "Bruises is all."

"Broken ribs is more like it," said Father. "Maybe more."

A toddler nearby, a young girl, stood alone, crying. People ran by her, oblivious, ignoring her. Bingwen nodded to Hopper, who understood at once and ran to the girl, kneeling beside her, putting an arm around her, comforting her, scanning the crowd for her mother. The child screamed on.

"Bastards," wheezed Grandfather. "No respect for their elders. Knocked me over like a herd of water buffalo. I should carry a cane. I could've beat a few of them." He turned his head to Bingwen. "That mud sucker who gives you problems. The one that's all bluster."

"Zihao," said Bingwen.

"That's the one. Stepped on my kidney. Looked me right in the eye, too. No honor. I'll cut his liver out if I ever see him again."

"Don't talk," said Mother.

"I'm fine," said Grandfather. "I can walk. Give me a minute." He tried to sit up, winced, and fell back.

"I'll stay with him," said Bingwen. "We'll catch up with you later."

Mother looked uncertain.

"Nobody's staying with me," said Grandfather. "I'm going at my own speed and pace. Don't know what all the rush is anyway. Alien ship blows up a few news shuttles, and everyone pisses their britches. Running around like fools won't accomplish anything."

"He's right," said Bingwen. "This panic is only making things worse."

"I'll stay with him," said Father. "Bingwen, get your mother home."

"We're staying together," said Mother.

"Only person who's staying is me," says Grandfather. "Am I not to be respected?"

"Not this time," said Father.

"Then leave me with Bingwen," said Grandfather. He pointed at Father. "If I go with you, I'll never hear the end of your complaints. All the way home, it'll be how I should be more careful, how it's my fault I fell, how I'm a burden."

"You *should* be more careful," said Father.

"You're no burden, Father," said Mother.

"Leave me with the boy," said Grandfather.

"You can't even walk," said Father. "Bingwen can't carry you."

Grandfather pushed himself up, wincing, but he got to his feet this time. "I don't need carrying. We'll be right behind you. Go. Before someone ransacks our home and takes what little food we have."

Mother and Father exchanged nervous glances.

"What," said Grandfather, "you think these people will suddenly be civilized when they go home? They're stirred up like hornets. If they fear there's a fight ahead, they'll think only of themselves and stockpile whatever they get their hands on."

Father looked back toward the retreating crowd. Mother covered her mouth with a hand, afraid. Bingwen almost told them then. Don't worry. I have supplies. I know you told me not to, Father, but I buried some tools and cans and rice sacks up at the top of the hill above the village. We'll be fine. For a little while at least.

But before Bingwen could muster the courage to admit that he had defied Father, the moment was past and Father was pulling Mother by the hand back toward the stairs.

"Get home as fast as you can, Bingwen," Father called back over his shoulder. Then he shouldered his way into the crowd, hurrying down the stairs, pulling Mother along. In seconds, Bingwen lost sight of them completely. He turned back to Grandfather, who had seated himself on the ground again, resting.

Hopper was still with the little girl. But now Meilin, Bingwen's cousin, was with him also. The little girl clung to Meilin's shirt, her eyes wet and wild with fear.

A young woman broke through the crowd, running back up the stairs. The little girl saw her, tore away from Meilin, and ran into the woman's arms. The woman embraced the child and lifted her up, crying, terrified, relieved.

"How could you run off without your own child?" Hopper scolded.

Meilin rounded on him, eyes wide with shock. Bingwen was surprised as well. It was unthinkable to address an adult like that.

The woman was shaking her head, ashamed, clinging to her daughter. She mumbled her thanks and ran back the way she had come, the girl in her arms.

"You see?" Grandfather said to Bingwen. "No respect for one's elders."

When the woman was gone, Meilin poked Hopper hard in the chest. "You had no right to say that to her."

"She had no right to abandon a two-year-old," said Hopper.

"She might not have abandoned her. Maybe she thought her husband had her. Maybe she was helping someone."

"She should have taken the child with her."

"Oh *you* know so much about parenting."

"Enough," said Grandfather. "Both of you. A sack of rice knows more about rearing children than either of you two. And where are *your* parents, hmm? Would you scorn your own mother so, boy?"

Hopper hung his head, ashamed. "No, Ye Ye Danwen," he said, addressing Grandfather with the proper respect.

"I should think not," said Grandfather. He motioned for Bingwen. "Help me up."

Bingwen offered a hand and pulled, but it was Grandfather who did most of the work, getting one foot under him and then another, slowly, painfully getting to his feet.

"Don't let me sit and rest again," he said. "Hurts too much to get back up." He inhaled deep and winced. "Hurts to breathe, too." He gingerly raised his arms above his head, stretching, testing the threshold of his pain. Then he lowered them, out of breath. "I need a length of fabric, Bingwen. To tie around my chest and keep my breaths shallow. And a staff."

Bingwen looked around him. The area outside the library was deserted now except for the four of them. Homes lined both sides of the staircase that twisted up the hillside, and the lights inside the homes were mostly on. Bingwen could hear people talking in hushed, hurried voices. Fear, their voices said. Fear and death.

Two houses up, a clothesline stretched between two homes. A sheet flapped on the line, lifting and falling with the updrafts from the valley below. Bingwen ran to the sheet, listened a moment, then yanked it down and threw it over his shoulder. At the same home, by the edge of the roof, a two-meter length of bamboo stretched from the corner of the roof to the rain barrel, directing the runoff. Bingwen turned the bamboo and pulled it free of its lashings, then carried both items to Grandfather.

"That's stealing," said Meilin.

"No," said Grandfather. "That's minding your elders. Rip the sheets into long strips, Bingwen."

Bingwen dug in the dirt for a stone, found one with an edge, then worked it in the sheet enough to tear it. Then he got his fingers in the hole and ripped the sheet easily.

They made long strips, wrapping them tight around Grandfather's chest and putting the knot far from the wound. "Tighter," Grandfather kept telling them, until it was so tight Bingwen was afraid Grandfather might not be able to breathe at all. But it was only then that Grandfather's face finally relaxed.

"Good. Yes, good," he said. He sounded old and tired and leaned on the bamboo. "Now down the stairs with us."

The four of them took to the stairs, moving at Grandfather's pace, taking each step slowly, one at a time. Grandfather's free hand rested on Bingwen's shoulder for support, clutching at the boy's shirt.

"You two run on home," said Grandfather, nodding to Hopper and Meilin. "I'll not keep you. Your families will fear for you."

"We're staying with you," said Meilin. "If you fall down the stairs, Bingwen will never get you home."

Grandfather leaned on his staff and laughed, which instantly brought on a new wave of pain that nearly buckled him. "Don't make me laugh, child. Or I *will* fall."

Bingwen grabbed Grandfather's belt to steady him more, and Grandfather nodded his thanks. Then Grandfather took a breath and, moving slower than before, continued down the staircase.

We won't get home before sunrise, Bingwen realized. Not at this pace. Not with three kilometers of rice fields to traverse. He watched Grandfather's feet, shuffling forward, carefully maneuvering each step.

Step. Shuffle. Step. Shuffle.

Bingwen looked up. It was a cloudless night. The Milky Way and millions of stars arced across the sky. One of the stars seemed particularly bright. At first Bingwen thought it might be a plane or a high-altitude skimmer. But the light didn't move. It didn't blink. It stayed there, staring down at him, unflinching. Bingwen kept his eyes on it, waiting for it to drop from the sky and spill fire.

# CHAPTER 11

# HERC

Mazer doubted he would get through to the NZSAS, but he went to his office to try contacting them anyway. It was the middle of the night, and the administration building was dark and deserted when he arrived. The holodesk was on and waiting for him, cycling through images of Chinese soldiers in combat gear. Mazer wiped his hand through the field, and the images disappeared, replaced with a menu of Chinese characters. The base didn't have an English model, but Mazer knew enough characters to operate the thing. He tapped out the appropriate commands and waited.

The star icon spun in the field, indicating the uplink was pinging Auckland. Mazer had tried this hours ago, but the grid had been too congested then. Trying now, moments after the alien ship had fired upon news shuttles and essentially declared war on the human race, would almost certainly prove a waste of time; every secure link in the New Zealand Army would be in use now.

To Mazer's surprise, there was a chime, and a New Zealand comms technician appeared in the holofield. The tech was young, barely eighteen, and looked frazzled.

"NZ comms," said the tech. "You are connected. Identify. Over."

"Captain Mazer Rackham requesting immediate contact with Colonel Napatu at Papakura. NZSAS."

"One moment, sir." The tech busied himself with offscreen controls.

Mazer watched him. He's not frazzled, Mazer realized. He's afraid. He's scared out of his buck-private mind because the world he thought he knew, a world in which nothing questioned our position at the top of the food chain, was just thrown out with the bathwater.

The tech finished whatever he was doing. "I'm sorry, Captain. Colonel Napatu is inaccessible. Shall I patch you through to the SAS switchboard?"

"Yes, please."

"One moment."

The kid disappeared. The star icon returned. Mazer waited for ten minutes. Finally Sergeant Major Manaware, Colonel Napatu's assistant, answered. Before Mazer could say a word, the sergeant major said, "Your orders are to maintain your position, Captain."

The holofield chimed, and a memo from Colonel Napatu appeared as an icon in the field. A form order, no doubt.

Mazer exhaled to keep his cool. "Sergeant Major, if the SAS deploys, my team needs to be on hand. No one knows the HERC like we do."

"Captain, I know you're frustrated, but the colonel's got seventeen strike teams on assignment all over the planet, and right now we don't have the means to bring you all home. And even if we did, the colonel is asking everyone to stay put. We don't know what we're up against, and we are not yet in a state of war. The alien ship remains in geosynchronous orbit. We're not circling the wagons just yet. Colonel Napatu is on conference with the admiral and other unit chiefs as we speak. In the meantime, watch the feeds and stay informed."

"That's just it," said Mazer. "We can't watch the feeds anymore. After the alien ship destroyed the news shuttles, the Chinese blocked all public access to the feeds. We're in the dark. We have no idea what's going on now. I think the Chinese are trying to prevent a panic, but they're liable to only make things worse."

"Then check in with us on the switchboard every few hours, we'll keep you informed."

"I usually can't get through," said Mazer. "It's a miracle I got through this time. Request permission to keep this line open."

"Negative. I need every available line. If you can't check in with us, then use your receivers to access one of our satellites."

"We can't do that either. The Chinese only allow access to their own satellites. They jam everything else. It's been that way ever since we got here."

Manaware was getting impatient. "Then talk to the Chinese. Even if they've blocked public access, the military will still have access to feeds. Ask them to keep you informed."

"Yes, but—"

"Captain, I've got twenty holos in my queue to answer. Excuse me."

He clicked off.

Mazer tried reconnecting with the switchboard, but he couldn't get through. He waited ten minutes, tried again, then slammed his fist on the desk when the transmission failed. He switched off the machine, closed his eyes, and exhaled. The SAS wasn't getting them out. And now Mazer and his team were cut off from the world, right when they needed minute-by-minute intel.

He tapped the memo Manaware had sent and opened it. He skimmed through it in five seconds and saw exactly what he had expected. Carry on. Continue in your duty. We'll keep you informed. Blah blah blah.

He couldn't take much more of this. The world had known for eleven days now that the ship was coming, and all anyone wanted to do was wait and see. Let's not *act,* everyone was saying. Let's wait and see. Let's *observe* this alien ship. Let's watch it and see what it does.

Well guess what, geniuses, "waiting and seeing" is the same as "waiting and *getting blown up.*" Did the U.N. actually think all that wreckage in the Belt was the *miners'* fault? And now the aliens had just disintegrated the secretary of alien affairs. A clown to be sure, but the man was an emissary of the human race. These creatures, whatever they are, just took our little flag of peace and pissed all over it.

And what does the SAS do? Do they bring Mazer and his team home at all speed and prepare for the worst? No. They park us in China and have us whistle our way through our training exercises.

Mazer got up. and headed back toward the barracks. He knew exactly how the world would respond. The Chinese would shy away from any coalition agreement and claim that the protection of their own people was their first priority. In other words, China would look out for China. The Russians would almost certainly bow out as well, though for different reasons. Why help the U.S. and other superpowers retain their strength? Why not let the aliens hammer the coalition? That would suit the Russians just fine. Their military is the weakest it's been in decades. They'd love to see everyone else brought down to their level.

Mazer entered the barracks and found his team waiting for him.

"Did you get through?" said Fatani.

"What did the colonel say?" said Reinhardt.

"Quiet," said Patu. "Let him talk."

"I spoke to Manaware," said Mazer. "Our orders are to stay put."

"Stay put?" said Reinhardt. "Are you kidding me? They just blew up the damn reception party."

"The colonel is in council," said Mazer. "If orders change, they'll ping us."

"Well that's fine and dandy," said Reinhardt. "That's just roses and pansies. And what are we supposed to do when this thing starts blowing up cities? Sit here and eat our rice and wave in the general direction of the destruction?"

"You watch too many movies," said Patu. "Nobody's blowing up cities."

"How do you know?" said Reinhardt. "It blew up those shuttles easily enough. And with a single gun no less. Who knows what it can do?"

"Why keep us here?" said Fatani. "We need to be back home, ready to deploy."

"Agreed," said Mazer. "But Manaware says there's no means to bring us home at the moment. There are too many strike teams on assignment. It would be a logistical nightmare."

"We're the army," said Patu. "We're experts on logistics."

"It's a matter of resources," said Mazer. "We're a handful of soldiers in a very big army. The military isn't going to use a good portion of the air force to gather up a hundred soldiers or less. We're a drop in the bucket. Those fighters are on high alert and could be needed at any moment."

"Then let us get home on our own," said Fatani. "Don't command us to stay here. They can't afford to send a plane? Fine. Let us get back our own way."

"Those aren't our orders," said Mazer.

"So what do we do?" said Patu.

"First," said Mazer, "we get intel. We need a visual on that ship."

Patu shook her head. "I've tried." She gestured to the holoscreen and the two satellite receivers she had set up on tripods. "I've got three discs on the roof right now, and they're not picking up a thing. The Chinese are still jamming other satellites and silencing the public feeds."

"What about shortwave radio?" said Fatani.

"I already tried," said Patu. "I can't pick up anything useful. The base is surrounded by rice farmland. Not exactly a hotspot for rogue radio operators."

"And you can't crack the jammers?" Mazer asked Patu.

"If I knew what devices they were using and where they were located, I could probably figure out how to disable them. As is, I got nothing."

"So we're in a bubble?" said Reinhardt.

"It's like we're in the eighteenth century," said Fatani.

"The jamming is probably localized," said Patu. "They can't cover all of China. It's probably only for military use. If I had to guess, I'd say it only covers the boundaries of the base and a few kilometers of spillover."

"So if we go outside the base," said Mazer, "and set up our dishes, we should get an uplink?"

Patu shrugged. "Maybe. No way to be sure until we try."

"The Chinese have us on lockdown," said Fatani. "We're not supposed to leave the base."

"Who cares about the rules?" said Reinhardt. "This is an international emergency. I say we load up a HERC and get airborne."

"If we take a HERC, they'll be all over us," said Mazer. "Let me talk to Captain Shenzu. Maybe they'll give us an uplink to their military feeds."

"And maybe a pig will jump out of my armpit and sing the national anthem," said Reinhardt. "They'll have all kinds of classified intel pumping through those feeds. They won't let us touch that with a ten-foot pole."

"Doesn't hurt to ask," said Mazer. "Where are all the brass now?"

"Holed up in the comms building," said Fatani. "We don't have access."

"Then I'll knock," said Mazer. He left them and crossed the courtyard to the comms building. The door was solid steel. Mazer found a rock among the bushes and pounded on the metal. It was loud. The banging echoed through the courtyard. He kept pounding for five minutes until a guard threw open the door and yelled at him to stop.

"Bring me Captain Shenzu, and I'll stop," Mazer said.

The guard objected. Mazer started pounding on the door again. The guard tried to rip the rock from Mazer's hand. Mazer swept the guard's legs out and dropped him on his ass. Then he started pounding on the door again.

"All right," said the guard, getting to his feet. "I'll get him. Just stop."

Mazer tossed the rock back into the bushes and gave the man a friendly smile.

Shenzu arrived two minutes later.

"We're in the dark," said Mazer. "We need updates. Either stop jamming and let us access our own satellites or give us access to your military's feeds. Please, as a courtesy from one soldier to another."

"I'm afraid I can't do that, Captain Rackham. The Politburo has given strict instructions on how information is disseminated. We're hoping they'll broadcast to the public again soon. In the meantime, we'll keep you informed."

"Not good enough," said Mazer. "We don't want filtered data given when it's convenient. We want uncensored intel immediately as it happens. My team and I deserve that. This ship is a threat to our people as much as it is to yours."

"Then use the uplink in your office."

"I can't get through anymore. There's too much traffic."

"That's an issue with your own military, Captain Rackham, not mine. I assure you, we will do our best to keep you informed."

Before Mazer could respond Shenzu turned and walked away, nodding at the two armed guards who had accompanied him. The guards stayed behind. They closed the metal door and stood outside facing Mazer, daring him to start knocking again. They were both bigger than the guard who had come the first time, but Mazer figured he could take them down easily enough. But what would that accomplish?

He returned to his office and tried his holodesk again. He didn't get through. He tried five more times, and every time the connection failed. The ship could be moving toward Earth right this very moment, he realized. It could be happening right now. It could be headed toward home, guns ready. He thought of Kim, sitting in her office, watching the news feeds, unprotected. He got to his feet and returned to the barracks, trying to appear calm. "Shenzu said he'd keep us informed."

"Not bloody likely," said Reinhardt.

"We'll give the man the benefit of the doubt."

They waited three hours, but no word from Shenzu came. Mazer replayed the scene over and over in his mind. The U.N. ship being vaporized. The news shuttles taking fire, shattering, ripping apart, the screams of the crew. He pictured Kim again. He saw the bright flashes of light ripping through her building, vaporizing her office. It was his imagination, he knew. Kim was safe. The world was a big place. If the alien ship attacked, it wouldn't go to New Zealand. The island was too small and insignificant a target. Kim was safe. Shenzu would come. Shenzu would bring them intel. He waited another hour, but that was all he could take. He couldn't just sit here and do nothing. He motioned his team to follow him. "Patu, bring the transmitter and satellite receiver. Everyone else, get your gear. We're taking a HERC."

Ten minutes later they were walking across the tarmac on the airfield to where all the HERCs were parked. They moved quickly and saw no one. They climbed aboard a HERC, stowed their gear, buckled in, and lifted off.

"Head east, low to the ground," said Mazer. "We'll only go a few kilometers outside the base. Hopefully we'll be beyond the jamming out there."

Reinhardt turned the HERC east and accelerated, flying only a few meters above the tarmac. "You think anyone will follow us?"

"They'll know we're airborne by now, but it will take a few minutes for them to scramble a crew. We'll be long gone by then. Patu, can you remove the tracker?"

She unbuckled her harness and came forward. "As long as Mr. Ace Pilot here can keep us steady." She slid on a headband light, grabbed a few tools, and lay down on her back under the dash. When they reached the end of the airfield, Reinhardt lifted the HERC a few meters into the air to clear the fence and then continued east across open country. Ten seconds later Patu came out from under the dash holding a small box. She handed it to Mazer and returned to her seat.

They cut north for another two kilometers before Mazer pointed to a field and said, "Park us over there, keep the gravlens running."

Reinhardt banked to the left, descended, and slowed the HERC to a stop, a meter above the ground. Mazer opened his door and dropped the tracker box onto a thick clump of grass, hoping not to damage it. He then closed his door, lowered his visor, and called up the map on his HUD. They were still on base, and none of the other HERCs were airborne yet. They still had a lead.

"Take us northeast to the river," Mazer said. "Fast. We need distance between us and the box."

The HERC lifted and shot forward in that direction. The base was roughly ten square kilometers, most of it grassy flatland, which wouldn't provide much cover. The river, however, with its canopy of trees and narrow valley walls would give them some decent concealment.

"Patu," said Mazer. "Have that sat receiver ready. I want us getting a feed as soon as we're clear of their jammers."

"Assuming we *can* get clear of the jammers," said Fatani. "We're only guessing at their range."

"The Chinese aren't going to invest money and equipment to jam feeds over farmland," said Mazer. "I think Patu's right. We go far enough off base, and we'll pick up something."

Reinhardt crested a hilltop and descended quickly down into the river valley. It was still full dark, but the night-vision feature inside their helmets gave them a clear view of everything. The HERC dipped down between the trees directly above the river. Using the water like a road, Reinhardt took them north, weaving them back and forth with the curvature of the water. Twice he had to quickly lift them over the trees where the canopy was too thick to squeeze through. Another time he hopped up to avoid a bridge.

"Hey," said Patu. "How about a little warning on the hops? I'm holding sensitive equipment here."

Reinhardt gave the stick a little wiggle, wobbling the HERC and jostling Patu in her seat.

"Funny," said Patu. "Real funny. How would you like my boot, Reinhardt? Up your ass or in your teeth?"

"On a bun with mustard please," said Reinhardt.

Patu only shook her head.

They moved north through the river valley for another five minutes and then suddenly they were over rice fields. No fence marked the end of the base's borders, but the difference in landscape couldn't have been more distinct.

"Anything, Patu?" asked Mazer.

"Not yet."

"Northeast," Mazer said to Reinhardt. "Keep your eyes open for a spot with decent elevation and a place to hide the HERC. As soon as Patu gets a clear signal we'll land."

Captain Shenzu's head appeared in the holofield above the dash. "Captain Rackham. You and your team will kindly return to the airfield immediately. You are not authorized to seize government property whenever you choose. Disengaging the tracker box is a serious offense. Please, for your own safety, return to the airfield. If you fail to comply, we will be forced to take action to recover our property. I repeat, we will be forced—"

Mazer shut off the holofield. "Patu?"

"Working on it. Still no signal. But the jamming is weakening the farther we go out. That's a good sign."

"Keep on it."

"So what are we going to do if we *do* get a signal and nothing is happening?" said Reinhardt. "What if that ship is just parked there in space doing nothing? We can't sit out here and watch it forever."

"Couple of options," said Mazer. "Once we run out of rations, we could fly the HERC back to base and face the fury of the Chinese, who, worst-case scenario, arrest us and imprison us for life, or best-case scenario, throw us out of the country."

"Getting tossed out of China is preferable," said Reinhardt, "since it gets us home. But, since we'll also likely be court-martialed, stripped of our rank, and humiliated upon arrival in Auckland, I'm not too keen on that either. Other options?"

"We fly the HERC south until we hit the South China Sea," said Mazer. "We dump the aircraft somewhere on the coastline where it can be recovered, then we find passage on a freighter back to New Zealand."

"Where we'll promptly be court-martialed, stripped of our rank, and humiliated," said Reinhardt. "Option C?"

"You take Patu as your bride," said Mazer. "We buy a few rice paddies and live among the peasants. I'll pass as your handsome, inexplicably old, inexplicably dark-skinned son of two white parents, and Fatani will be your water buffalo, plowing the fields with you in the blazing sun."

"Do I get to whip Fatani?" asked Reinhardt.

"Naturally," said Mazer. "But he also gets to bite you and poop wherever he pleases."

"Why don't *I* get to marry Patu?" said Fatani.

"Because you're the *size* of a water buffalo," said Reinhardt. "We all must play to our types."

"I'd rather marry a *real* water buffalo than any of you," said Patu.

Fatani laughed.

"Your words sting me, Patu, queen of the rice lands," said Reinhardt.

Patu rolled her eyes, and Reinhardt maneuvered them slightly to the east, heading toward a low range of mountains covered in lush tropical forests.

After a moment there was a beep from the backseat.

"I got something," said Patu. "A visual. Not the best image, but it's getting clearer by the moment. An American news satellite. There's no audio though."

"Patch it to our HUDs," said Mazer. "Reinhardt, take us a few more kilometers along this mountain, then find a high place to land."

"You got it," said Reinhardt.

A fuzzy video feed appeared in Mazer's HUD. The superimposed text on screen read LIVE.

The vid was of space. The alien ship was there in the center, small and distant and unmoving. The satellite wasn't directly between the ship and Earth, but rather off to the side, at an angle, giving Mazer a slight view of the ship's profile.

"I see a place to land," said Reinhardt. "I'm taking her down."

The HERC descended through a break in the tree canopy. Mazer allowed himself a glance outside. They were on the crest of a wide, lush mountain ridge, almost entirely consumed with dense jungle forest. The air was thick with the scent of flowers and composting vegetation.

The HERC set down gently, and Reinhardt killed the gravlens. There was a slight jolt as normal gravity took over, and the aircraft sunk a centimeter or two into the soft jungle topsoil. No one spoke or moved. They sat there, watching their HUDs.

They waited for half an hour. Nothing happened. They got out of the HERC and stretched. Mazer ordered them to take sleep-shifts. Two would stay awake and two would sleep in two-hour shifts.

A hand shook Mazer awake. It was dawn. Sunlight dappled the ground around them, shining through the tree canopy overhead. Fatani said, "Something's happening."

Mazer pulled on his helmet and switched on his HUD. There was the alien ship. Only now the stars around the ship were shimmering, like heat rising off a stretch of asphalt in the summer sun. At first it seemed like a glitch in the broadcast. Then the alien ship began to rotate, turning its nose away from Earth, and Mazer understood. The ship was emitting something, radiation perhaps, or heated particles, using the expulsion of the emissions to change its position.

It turned ninety degrees then stopped, with its profile now facing Earth.

"What's it doing?" said Fatani.

Slowly the ship began to spin on its axis. At first Mazer didn't notice; the surface was so smooth. Then a giant ring of light appeared on the side of the ship at the bulbous end, as if the surface of the ship had cracked and was emitting light from inside.

"What is that?" asked Fatani. "What's that circle?"

The ship continued to rotate. Once. Twice. Three times.

Another circle of light appeared on the bulbous end beside the first one. Then a third circle appeared. The alien ship continued to spin. Around. And around. And around. Then, moving in unison, the three giant circles began to rise upward like columns from the ship.

"I don't like this," Fatani said.

Then, in an instant, one of the columns broke free, slung down toward Earth by the spinning motion, leaving a massive recessed hole in the side of the ship.

It's not a column, Mazer realized. It's a wheel. Tall and metallic and enormously wide, with flat sides and a turtlelike top that had been part of the skin of the ship. It was shooting straight toward Earth.

"The hell it that?" said Fatani. "A weapon? A bomb?"

As Mazer watched, the second wheel broke away, slung to Earth, chasing the first. Then the third wheel followed, right behind the other two.

"What are they?" said Patu.

"Whatever they are, they'll burn up as soon as they hit the atmosphere," said Reinhardt. "They're huge."

"They won't burn," said Mazer. "They can generate fields. They'll deflect the heat." He spoke Chinese then. "Computer, digitize the sat feed into a holo that includes Earth and the three alien projectiles. And do it to scale."

A construct appeared in the holofield. Crudely made. A white sphere representing Earth and three small wheel-shaped projectiles quickly approaching it.

"Skin the Earth's surface to match current time zones and the Earth's rotation in relation to the position of the projectiles."

The surface of the Earth appeared on the sphere. Oceans, continents, atmosphere, all slowly spinning on an axis.

"Can you determine the speed of the three projectiles based on what we see from the sat feed, perhaps using the starfield as reference?"

"Affirmative."

"Are they decelerating?"

"Negative. Speed is constant."

"Vector their trajectory," said Mazer.

In the holofield, a dotted line extended from the wheels, hitting Earth at a sharp angle, as a reentry vector should.

"I don't think they're bombs," Mazer said in English. "Look at their approach. Coming in at that sharp of an angle. I think they're landers."

In Chinese Mazer said, "Computer, can you guess what their deceleration would be as they hit the atmosphere?"

"Insufficient data."

Mazer figured as much. Fine. He would make do with the information he had.

"All right," he said. "Let's assume they decelerate in the atmosphere at a constant rate that puts their speed at zero by the time they make landfall. Can you calculate that?"

"Affirmative."

"Okay. Then based on that tentative rate of deceleration and the current speed and position of the landers in relation to the speed, tilt, and orbital eccentricity of Earth, can you determine exactly where the first lander will touch down on the surface?"

"Negative. There are too many other variables."

"Can you approximate?" asked Mazer.

"Affirmative. The landers will likely touch down within this circle."

A large red transparent dot appeared on the surface of the Earth.

"Enlarge three hundred percent," said Mazer.

Earth zoomed toward them in the holofield and stopped. The dot was massive. Roughly two thousand kilometers wide. Its center was in the middle of the South China Sea. To the east it covered the northern half of the Philippines. To the west it engulfed most of Vietnam, nearly touching Ho Chi Minh City to the south and Hanoi to the north. Plus the northeastern tip of Cambodia and all of southern Laos. But the largest mass of land was in southern China, including all of Guangdong province.

"We're in that circle," said Patu.

"It's a big area," said Reinhardt. "They could be going anywhere."

"It's eighty percent water," said Mazer. "They're not headed for water. And you can probably cross off the Philippines, Vietnam, and Laos as well."

"Why?" said Fatani.

"Computer," said Mazer. "Show population density within this circle."

Hundreds of tiny blue dots appeared, the vast majority of which were in southern China, where the dots were so thick along the coast and a hundred kilometers inland that they had coalesced into a solid blob of blue.

"You think they're headed for populated areas?" asked Fatani.

"You saw what they did in the Belt," said Mazer. "Computer, how much time do we have before the projectiles reach Earth?"

"Approximately seventeen minutes."

Fatani swore.

"Patu, I need a sat uplink to NZSAS immediately," said Mazer.

"I'll try," she said.

"What do we do?" said Reinhardt.

"We warn as many people as we can," said Mazer. He waved his hand through the holofield, reconnecting with the Chinese base. "Red Dragon, Red Dragon. Acknowledge. This is Captain Mazer Rackham. Do you read? Over."

A Chinese soldier's head appeared. Mazer knew the face but not the name. One of the flight controllers.

"Red Dragon acknowledge," said the soldier. "We've been trying to hail you, Captain. You're in a bit of trouble with the base commander, I'm afraid."

"Patch me through to him."

The controller looked surprised. "To Colonel Tuan?"

"Yes, immediately. It's an emergency."

"Yes, Captain, but I doubt he'll answer." The soldier busied himself, then returned a few seconds later. "I'm sorry, Captain. Colonel Tuan is not available, but Captain Shenzu is here."

"Put him on."

Shenzu replaced the controller in the holofield. "We have a situation, Captain Rackham. Return to the base immediately."

"The landers are headed for us," said Mazer. "They'll make landfall in southeast China. I'm almost certain of it."

"Landers?"

"The giant discs in the sky. Descending to Earth. Are you watching the feeds?"

"We have a broadcast, yes."

"Vector them. Track them. They'll make landfall here."

"How can you know this?"

"We did the math with our AI. You've got less than seventeen minutes."

"Captain, bring the HERC back to base immediately."

"You're going to need us in this, Captain. We can help. Your HERC teams aren't ready. You know that as well as I do."

"You have violated our trust and stolen government property, Captain Rackham. Return to base."

From the backseat, Patu said, "I've got the NZSAS switchboard."

"I'll call you back," Mazer said to Shenzu, then he waved his hand through the holo to make Shenzu disappear. "Patch the switchboard to the holofield," he shouted back to Patu.

The same frazzled buck private from hours earlier appeared in the holo-field.

"Switchboard. It's Captain Mazer Rackham. Connect me with Colonel Napatu."

"He's inaccessible, sir."

"Then get me Sergeant Major Manaware. Anybody. Now!"

"One moment." The tech busied himself, then disappeared. Manaware appeared.

"Captain Rackham—"

Mazer cut him off. "Listen to me. The landers, the discs, they're headed to southeast China. I can't be certain, but I think they're coming to us."

"We've calculated a huge landfall radius," said Manaware. "They could be going to anywhere in Southeast Asia. Hell, they could stop in the middle of the sky and switch directions. There's no telling, Captain. We can't be sure where they're going."

Mazer didn't have time to argue. "Fine. Contact Colonel Napatu. I need permission to engage the landers if they do land here and prove hostile."

Manaware looked at someone off screen and said, "Colonel, he's asking permission to engage."

"Is Napatu there?" said Mazer, incredulous. "Then put him on the line!"

Manaware stepped away and Colonel Napatu appeared. "Captain Rackham, what the hell is going on? I got China on the other line saying you've run off with two billion credits worth of tech."

"Colonel, they cut off all the feeds. We were without any contact to—"

"You are on a diplomatic training mission, Captain Rackham. You are representing your country. And in case you didn't know, our government and most of the free world is trying desperately to convince China to trust us and join a coalition against this alien ship. We need the Chinese, Captain. We need their shuttles and we need their firepower. Stealing their property and angering Chinese brass is not helping our cause. We are in the middle of a global security crisis. This is bigger than you and your team. Now fly that HERC back to base and kiss the feet of their commander. That is an order."

Napatu winked out.

They were silent inside the HERC for a moment. Finally Reinhardt said, "So what do we do?"

"You heard the colonel," said Fatani. "We have our orders. We return to base."

"Yes," said Mazer. "But the colonel was a little unclear on *when* to return to base. Did anyone else catch that?"

Reinhardt smiled. "I don't recall a time. Surely an order like that can wait sixteen minutes, give or take."

Mazer looked at the others. They nodded.

"All right," said Mazer. "Buckle up. Patu get that news feed back on the sat uplink. Reinhardt, take us up. Way up. A few thousand feet. I want us in a position to see anything. Seal the windows. Pressurize us."

"Hold on to something," said Reinhardt. He engaged the gravlens, and the HERC shot straight up as if yanked upward on a string. It climbed higher and higher, the altimeter numbers clicking through fast. Two thousand meters. Three thousand. Six. Seven. In a minute they were higher than they had ever taken the aircraft. Mazer's stomach churned. His ears popped. His head swam. He blinked, kept himself focused, and ignored the queasy feeling.

Below them, the landscape was green and lush, filled with tiny, watery squares of rice paddies like a green tiled mosaic laid across the Earth.

"Computer," said Mazer. "Follow the projectiles. Monitor their speed. Then update the landfall radius in real time as they approach. Tighten that circle as much as you can."

"Understood," said the computer.

They hovered there, waiting, watching the landfall radius on the map, watching the sky.

The sat feed in Mazer's HUD showed the first projectile hit the atmosphere, a glow of orange heat encircling the front. The speed of the lander immediately slowed, and the computer instantly made modifications to the

map. The giant red circle that was the landfall radius suddenly jumped inward, becoming a smaller circle, a third of its original size. The circle no
longer included the Philippines or Vietnam or Cambodia or Laos. Only
southeast China remained.

"Mazer," said Reinhardt.

"I see it," said Mazer looking at the map.

"No, not there," said Reinhardt. "There." He pointed east out the windshield.

Mazer looked. A distance away, almost to the edge of the horizon, a
long white contrail stretched behind the alien lander, the front of it a bright
hot wall of heat.

# CHAPTER 12

# Mud

"We're nearly there, Grandfather. We shouldn't rest now. Look, you can see the village stairs from here. A kilometer at the most. Here, I'll help you." Bingwen extended his hand.

Grandfather swatted it away. "Did your parents teach you nothing, boy? Do your elders mean so little to you? If I say I need a rest, I will take one, and no *boy,* however closely related, will command me not to." He muttered something under his breath, a curse perhaps, then leaned heavily on his staff, groaning and wincing and scowling as he lowered himself toward the ground. His strength failed him just before he reached it, and he fell with a *thud* onto his backside. Another wince. Another curse. Then he exhaled deeply, as if the air he had been carrying in his lungs had only added to his burden and he was glad to be rid of it.

After the chaos of the night, the morning seemed strangely normal. The sun had been up for only half an hour at the most, but already there were small groups of people in the rice fields all along the valley, bent over the shoots, working, chatting, going about their labor as if the previous night had been a dream. There were fewer people than usual though, Bingwen noticed. And those who were close enough for him to see their faces were all elders, hunched and wrinkled like Grandfather with their coned straw hats and sun-faded garments.

"You told him not to let you rest, Ye Ye Danwen," said Hopper. "You've been saying it for hours. It's not fair of you to scold him for doing exactly what you commanded."

Grandfather swung his cane out, not hard, not intending to hit Hopper, but fast enough and with enough force behind it to scare Hopper and send him shuffling backward. Hopper's bad foot tripped him up, and he fell back onto the dirt, nearly tumbling into the nearest rice paddy.

"Enough from you," said Grandfather. "You've been chattering all night and I'm done with it. Home with you."

He waved his hand wide, as if sending Hopper away.

Hopper rolled his eyes when Grandfather wasn't looking, dusted himself off, and went back to sit by Meilin, who was squatting on an embankment nearby, poking at the nearest rice shoots with a stick.

Hopper was right of course. Grandfather *had* told Bingwen on multiple occasions throughout the night that he was not to let Grandfather sit down again. "Keep me moving, Bingwen," he had said. "It hurts too much to get back up again."

And so Bingwen had tried: rushing over whenever Grandfather made a move to sit down, urging Grandfather on, pleading, pulling, reminding Grandfather of the pain that awaited him when he got up again. But on every occasion Grandfather had only grunted and resisted and cursed and scolded and sat down anyway.

And an hour or so later—because Grandfather would always take that long, regardless of how many times Bingwen urged him up again— Grandfather would struggle upward, his bones creaking and paining him so deeply that he'd apologize to Bingwen for being old and foolish and "Please please please, don't let me sit down again."

It was maddening. Stop me, Bingwen. Don't stop me, Bingwen. Do as I say, Bingwen. Don't do as I say. Bingwen would give anything for a truck or a skimmer.

Grandfather began to lie down in the dirt, and Bingwen came over and helped him, getting his hands under Grandfather shoulders and lowering him gently down.

"There are people in the fields, Grandfather. Let me find some who can carry you the rest of the way."

"I have two feet, boy. Let me use them. I will not be the burden of any man."

Oh, you won't burden any man, thought Bingwen, but you will burden *me*.

Then he instantly felt ashamed for having thought such a wretched thing. It was Grandfather who had believed him about the aliens when no other adult had, Grandfather who had helped him pilfer cans of food and bags of rice and bury it all in the earth, Grandfather who had shown him how to build the ladder to get into the library many years ago. Always Grandfather.

For a moment Bingwen considered running ahead to the village and getting Father anyway. But then the thought of Father only angered him. He shouldn't have left us, thought Bingwen. He should have come back for us after getting Mother home.

No, if Father didn't come on his own accord, Bingwen wasn't going to get him.

Hopper and Meilin giggled, poking the stick at a paddy frog who hopped away from them and splashed in the water.

Bingwen got up and went to them. "He's asleep again. You should both go home. Your parents will be sick with worry. Grandfather and I don't need you now."

"And do what at home?" said Hopper. "Get a lashing for staying out? A fist to the ear. No thanks."

"I told you to go home hours ago. You should have listened."

Hopper shrugged. "This is fun."

"Fun?" Bingwen wanted to shake him. "Dragging Grandfather through the valley is fun? You're being stubborn and stupid, Hopper. Both of you. Wasting your time out here laughing and teasing each other. You should be home, helping."

Hopper was on his feet, angry. "Helping do what? You said we were fine, Bingwen. You said nothing was going to happen. You said it's a big world and we're a tiny part of it."

Bingwen could feel his face flushing with fury, tears welling up in his eyes. Everything was building up and crashing down inside him all at once. Grandfather's stupid old bones and the aliens and Father not coming and the cold of the night and Hopper giggling. "I said that on the roof to keep you from crying, Hopper. I said that to help. Which is more than you're doing for me. All night long you and Meilin have been yapping and telling stories and poking with sticks, like this is all a game. Don't you realize what's going on? Don't you see the danger we're in? There are creatures above us, monsters with maws and claws and muscles and strength, hanging over us like spiders, and you skip and giggle and chase frogs like we're having a birthday."

Hopper glared. "Oh some friend you are. I go with you into the library,

I *steal* for you, I freeze my butt off out here so you won't be alone, and this is the thanks I get." He poked Bingwen in the chest. "You're just mad because Meilin is having more fun with me than she ever had with you."

Bingwen blinked. What? Meilin? What did any of this have to do with Meilin? But then he saw Meilin's cheeks flush with embarrassment before she turned away and Bingwen understood at once. Why hadn't he seen it before? All through the night as Hopper and Meilin had lagged behind, the two had chased each other and needled each other and laughed and seemed oblivious to Bingwen and Grandfather. It had annoyed Bingwen, but for none of the reasons that Hopper thought. Did he honestly think Bingwen was . . . what? Jealous? How could Hopper imagine even for an instant that Bingwen and Meilin could ever be anything other than cousins?

"You know what?" said Hopper. "I *will* go home. Because I'd rather get boxed on the ear by my father than yelled at and insulted by someone I *thought* was my best friend."

He turned and began limping away.

Bingwen opened his mouth but no words came out. What would he say? That he was sorry? That he hadn't meant to lash out? That he was grateful that Hopper had come? That Hopper *was* his best friend and that it was he, Bingwen, who was acting like a fool? Yes, he would say all of that.

Someone was shouting in the valley, their voice frantic.

Bingwen turned. A distance away some workers were pointing in the sky, shouting. Bingwen's eyes followed their fingers and he saw it. A ball of fire in the sky. Burning through the atmosphere.

It was the ship, he told himself. The ship was coming down on them.

He ran to Grandfather, kneeling beside him, shaking him. "Wake up! Grandfather! Wake up!"

The old man roused, confused, disoriented.

Bingwen looked up again. The ship was still a distance away, bearing down on them, aiming for them. It seemed low to the ground, but Bingwen knew better. That was the curvature of the Earth playing tricks. The ship was still high in the air. They had a few seconds.

He shook Grandfather again. "Get up!"

"Wha . . . what is it?" Grandfather said, coming to himself.

"It's coming!"

Bingwen pointed. Grandfather looked, his eyes widening.

Bingwen wanted to scream to Hopper and Meilin to run, but where would they run to? If the ship hit the Earth like an asteroid with enough force, they were all dead. Everything would be decimated. The shockwave would kill them instantly.

Hopper had stopped cold, standing there stupidly, staring up into the sky. Meilin was beside him, too afraid to move.

Grandfather tried to get up, but cried out and fell back again.

Bingwen looked behind them. The embankment. They were lying on the top of the earthen bridge between two paddies. He had to get Grandfather to the far embankment, away from the ship. He hooked his fingers under Grandfather's armpits and pulled. Grandfather cried out, but Bingwen didn't care. He pulled, straining, gritting his teeth. Grandfather barely moved, edging inch by inch toward the embankment. They weren't moving fast enough, Bingwen realized. He needed help.

"Hopper!" Bingwen shouted.

Hopper didn't respond. Didn't move.

Bingwen strained, pulling, digging his feet in the ground for purchase. He wasn't going to make it. The ship was going to crush them.

He glanced up at it. The fire in the front had vanished; it was free of the outer atmosphere; it was right on top of them, bearing down, growing larger by the second, as big as a village, as ten villages, twenty.

Meilin was screaming.

Bingwen pulled. Grandfather howled at the pain. Hopper was a statue.

Then the sound of it reached them. A sound like nothing Bingwen had ever heard. Like the roar of an engine and the scream of a monkey and the cry of a thousand different things at once, deep and resonating that shook the earth.

Five seconds to impact.

Bingwen screamed, pulled at Grandfather, finding a strength he didn't have before, sliding him, yanking him back. Then they were both rolling down the embankment, tumbling, limbs flailing. They hit water, Bingwen went under, the deafening sound was muffled. Then Bingwen got his feet under him, pushed up, breaking through the water again. A hand grabbed him, slammed him against the embankment. Grandfather.

Bingwen looked above him. Hopper and Meilin hadn't moved. They were stones. Frozen with fear.

"Hopper! Meilin!"

But nothing could be heard over the sound.

And then the sound exploded into a noise a hundred times louder because the thing hit the earth somewhere close by, and the world shook so hard Bingwen thought it had split apart, and a wave of air and dirt and water exploded across the valley, and Hopper was gone, and Meilin was gone, and mud and blackness and debris rained down and buried Bingwen and Grandfather alive.

Pain.

It swam at the edges of Bingwen's awareness. Distant at first, blurred, unfocused. Then slowly the murkiness rippled away, clarified, and the pain became acute. Then suddenly it was piercing, searing.

Bingwen's eyes snapped open and he cried out, awake, aware. His arm. Something was crushing his arm. He couldn't see. There was darkness all around him. He was in a cave. No, not a cave, a pocket of air buried in the dirt and mud. Branches and trees were above him, blocking out much of the sun and shielding him from more dirt and debris. How was that possible? How was he under a tree? There were no trees in the fields.

Where was Grandfather? He turned his head. A tree branch was crushing his arm. He tried to pull the arm free, but pain stabbed through him like a bolt of electricity, taking his breath away. He took in air and cried out again. His left arm was broken. He had never broken a bone before, but he knew at once that's what it was. He twisted his upper body, trying to reach his right arm across his chest to dig the dirt away from under his penned arm and free it, but the movement caused another punch of pain that made him howl yet again.

He lay there on his back, breathing hard. "Grandfather?" His voice was only a whisper. Then louder, "Grandfather!"

"Here."

The voice was weak but nearby. Bingwen lifted his head and looked around. All around him were shadows and dirt and tree limbs.

A branch to his left moved. "Bingwen?" The voice was raspy and pained.

"Here," said Bingwen. "I'm here."

The branch moved again and this time a hand emerged, old and muddy, reaching out, searching. Bingwen extended his good arm and seized Grandfather's hand. Grandfather's grip tightened around his.

"I'm here, boy. I'm here."

Bingwen couldn't help it. Tears came then, busting out from deep inside him. He tried to push them back, biting his lower lip to suppress them, but they fought their way out, and in seconds he was sobbing and shaking and only making the pain in his arm worse.

"Are you hurt?" said Grandfather.

"Yes," Bingwen managed to say. "My arm. It's broken, I think."

"I'm going to get you out."

"How? You could barely move before."

"Your grandfather isn't as weak as he looks."

It was a lie, and Bingwen knew it.

"I'm going to get help," said Grandfather.

Grandfather's hand released his, pulled back.

Bingwen scrabbled for it with his good hand. "No! Don't leave me."

Grandfather's hand returned and grabbed Bingwen's again. "I'll be right back, Bingwen. On my father's name I swear it."

The hand tried to pull back again, but Bingwen clutched it tightly this time, not letting go. "Wait. Please. Don't go. I'm . . . afraid." He hated himself for saying it, felt the shame of it like a slap. But it was true. He could feel the darkness now, not just see it, like a stranger was just behind him, standing over, ready to strike. He was going to die here, he knew. If he released Grandfather's hand they were both going to die. He would be crushed by the tree and the mud and the darkness.

Grandfather gave Bingwen's hand a reassuring squeeze. "I can make it to the village, Bingwen. I'll come back with your father."

"No." Bingwen's voice was a panic. "You can't. You couldn't walk."

"Then I'll crawl. I won't leave you under this—"

But the rest was cut off because then the deafening roar of a machine tore through the world like a grinding thunderclap and the earth shook like a hundred earthquakes, and Bingwen clutched Grandfather's hand and screamed.

# CHAPTER 13

# Survivors

The HERC was moving fast, flying at an altitude of four thousand meters toward a billowing cloud of dust far ahead of it in the distance. Mazer zoomed in as far as his HUD would allow, but he still couldn't see the downed lander from here. It was hidden behind several crests of mountains. "Patu, talk to me. What's going on? I need a sat feed on that lander. I need video."

"I'm trying, I'm trying," said Patu. "The whole network is going berserk. Everyone in the world is piggybacking on all the satellites pointed at southern China. I'm only picking up bits of intel here and there. All three landers are down. I know that much. They're roughly three hundred klicks apart and form a line that starts in the southeast corner of Guangdong province and crosses up to the northeast corner of Guangxi province. We're heading toward the second lander. The first one set down east of the Nangao Reservoir in Luhe County, about sixty klicks north of the coast."

"Populated area?"

"Not at the point of impact, no. It's mostly forested mountains. There are several villages nearby. A few towns. But nothing densely populated. We lucked out on that one."

"What's the lander doing?"

"Right now, near as I can tell, it's not doing anything. It's just sitting there."

"What about the second lander?"

"Impact site is in a valley south of a town called Dawanzhen. Mostly rice lands. Several villages are clustered in that area. Again, not densely populated, but certainly more people than where the first lander put down. Casualties are likely."

Mazer turned to the pilot's seat. "Reinhardt, what's our ETA?"

"We'll be on top of that thing in under three minutes," said Reinhardt. "What I want to know is: What do we plan on doing once we get there? We're not packing a lot of heat, Mazer. This thing is a training aircraft, remember? We're not carrying any rockets. We got a few slicers and that's it, no heavy air support. If we get in a fight, we could be in trouble."

"We're not looking for a fight," said Mazer. "Our job is recon and rescue. We help people on the ground and learn as much as we can about the lander. We'll send live feeds back to Auckland and to the Chinese. The more they know, the better they can prepare. Patu, what about the third lander?"

"Not good. It set down right outside a city named Guilin on the west bank of the Li River. Population two-point-seven million."

Mazer winced. A dense population compounded their problems a hundredfold. It had landed outside the city, though; that was some comfort. At least the lander hadn't parked downtown. "Fatani, find every emergency and news feed you can coming out of that city and relay it to Auckland and to base command. Also see if you can patch in to any seismographic feeds. My guess is that thing felt like an earthquake when it hit. There may be buildings down, utilities disabled."

"I'll see what I can find," said Fatani. "But don't hold your breath. It won't be easy to breach their system in under three minutes. And don't forget it's all in Chinese."

"Do the best you can," said Mazer. He clicked over to the radio. "Red Dragon, Red Dragon, this is Captain Rackham, do you read, over?"

Shenzu's head appeared in the holofield. He looked furious. "Captain Rackham, turn your aircraft around immediately. Do not approach the alien landers. I repeat, change your course at once and return to base. The landers are on Chinese soil. That makes them our concern, not yours."

"They're on Earth," said Mazer. "That makes them everyone's concern."

Shenzu said, "Captain, you are flying in a stolen aircraft. You have zero authorization to be in Chinese airspace. You are violating international law. Your commanding officer in Auckland has conveyed to us that he has ordered you to return to base. We have given you the same order. Unless you comply immediately we will have no choice but to shoot you down. We will not allow you to provoke the landers and endanger our citizens."

"We're trying to *help* your citizens," said Mazer. "The second lander is right in front of us. There might be casualties. We can be there in under two minutes and provide immediate medical assistance. There are no airfields or bases remotely close to here. It will take medevacs a while to reach that position. We're the best you've got for emergency air support."

"That is not your concern."

"You want us to abandon these people?"

"You are thinking about a handful of individuals, Captain Rackham. I am thinking about all of China. Flying a military aircraft toward that lander could be perceived as an act of aggression and exacerbate the situation. We are trying to maintain peace, and your blatant insubordination is threatening our efforts. You have ten seconds to comply and change your course, or we will drop you from the sky."

Mazer waved his hand through the holofield to make Shenzu disappear. Then he blinked out a quick command to start a ten-second countdown on his HUD. "Reinhardt, get us close to the ground. Stay on course, but keep us low and use as much cover as you can find."

Reinhardt put the HERC into a manageable dive. "We won't be invisible, mate. It's broad daylight. If they're sat-tracking us, they can put a precision-guided missile on us and drop us like a rock."

"Then go faster," said Mazer.

Reinhardt scoffed. "Get lower and go faster? These are jungle mountains, Mazer. You want me flying us into a cliff face?"

"Then fly as fast as you can as safely as you can. The closer we get to the lander, the better our chances are with the Chinese."

"Isn't the opposite true?" said Patu.

"Technically, yes," said Mazer. "But the Chinese's biggest fear is that we'll provoke the aliens. If they fire on us when we're close to the lander, they risk it looking like a provocation to the aliens. So the closer we get, the safer we are. Hopefully. Punch it, Reinhardt."

"You sound unsure," said Fatani.

"I *am* unsure," said Mazer. "I could be completely wrong. But I think the Chinese are smarter than that."

"We'll know in three seconds," said Patu.

The second countdown reached zero just as the HERC leveled out from its dive above the trees at the crest of a low-level mountain. The aircraft flew straight for a moment, then the mountainside dropped away, descending toward the valley below. Reinhardt dropped the nose of the HERC as well, level with the terrain. They plummeted down the mountainside like the front car of a roller coaster on its first big drop. Mazer felt himself rise slightly in his seat and tighten against his restraining harness, the valley floor rushing up toward them at a sickening pace. Reinhardt pulled up at the last instant, and they all dropped back into their seats, Mazer exhaling and unclenching his fists.

"Easy," said Patu. "He said faster, not suicidal."

Reinhardt hit the throttle, taking advantage of the flat valley floor to pick up speed. "They're one and the same, Patu, my queen of the rice. One and the same."

The next mountain was coming up fast. Mazer scanned the radar and heat sensors displayed on his HUD. He didn't see any incomings.

"Sky looks clear," said Mazer.

"That doesn't mean we're home free," said Fatani. "They could have fired a missile from Beijing for all we know. Might take a minute to get here."

"Which is exactly why they won't fire at all," said Mazer.

The HERC rose sharply up the mountainside. They flew in silence, rising and falling with the landscape, shifting slightly off course here and there in the hope of evading detection, always scanning the sky around them, watching for incoming threats. None came. A minute passed. Then two.

"Looks like you called their bluff," said Fatani.

"Or they fired something our sensors can't detect," said Reinhardt, "and it'll blow us up any second now."

"Not funny," said Patu.

"Hey, if the Chinese can make a mole vehicle that drills through solid rock," said Reinhardt, "nothing would surprise me."

"What if Shenzu's right, Mazer?" said Fatani. "What if we're kicking the hornet's nest here? This species doesn't know what we are. They might think we're a missile fired on them. We could start a war."

"The war is already on," said Mazer, "despite what the Chinese would like to think. If any of you disagree speak up now. I can't force you to come along. You heard the colonel. He gave us direct orders. If you come, you will almost certainly be court-martialed when this is over. You need to know that. Your career will be over. If you want to back out now, say the word and I'll set you down here. You can tell them I forced you to come this far. That goes for you, too, Reinhardt. If you want to sit out, say so. I can fly this thing if I have to."

Reinhardt snorted. "You can't fly the HERC, Mazer. Keeping it in the air and landing it when you need to is not flying. That's driving. Flying is what *I* do. It's an art. And you, sir, are no artist."

"We're all in, Mazer," said Fatani. "Nobody's for turning back. But Shenzu has a point. We might incite a response."

"It can't be avoided," said Mazer. "We're not abandoning the people on the ground. Patu, any luck with that sat feed?"

"You don't need one," she said. "We're there."

Reinhardt crested the last mountain, and the lander came into view, a massive, metallic discoid, shrouded in a cloud of dust. Mazer stared. It was larger than anything he had imagined. An engineering impossibility. Perhaps sixty stories high and nearly a kilometer wide. The top of it was smooth, shiny, and slightly rotund. But the side was crude, made from thousands of metal plates of various sizes arranged in a seemingly random fashion, as if the builders had no regard for symmetry or aesthetics.

Beneath the lander was a ring of displaced earth several hundred meters wide, tallest near the lander and tapering off near the edges, as if the lander had stepped on a giant mud pie and spilled its contents in every direction. No, not a mud pie, Mazer realized. A mountain. The lander had crushed a small mountain or large hill, leveling it to the ground and displacing dirt and unearthed trees in a mudslide that had buried much of the valley floor.

"Patu," Mazer shouted, "turn on all external cameras and broadcast a live feed to every satellite you can access. Then get on the radio with Auckland and the Chinese and tell them the landers have shields."

"How can you be sure?" said Patu.

"That must be how it crushed the mountain," said Mazer. "It couldn't have been the force of the impact. The lander was moving too slow when it set down. And look at the landscape. No shockwave evidence, just the wall of displaced earth. That has to be from shields."

"What does that mean?" said Fatani.

"Means we may not be able to hurt it even if we try," said Mazer. "Reinhardt, circle this thing. Help Patu capture it from every angle. Fatani, you and I will scan for survivors. There's a rice field to the immediate north. There were probably workers down there when this thing hit. Look there first."

Mazer gave his shoulder harness a shake to make sure it was tight then blinked out the command to open his door. A gust of wind and dust blew into the cockpit as Mazer's door slid back. He leaned out as far as his straps would allow and looked down, zooming in with his HUD.

The mudslide was a blanket of brown, with broken trees and the shattered remains of houses jutting up here and there through the muck. It was total devastation. If there were survivors, there wouldn't be many. Mazer activated his thermal scanner, but the screen showed nothing promising. If there were people trapped under the muck, Mazer couldn't see them.

He lifted his head and looked farther west, to the edge of the mudslide. There he saw his first body. Someone lay facedown in the water of a rice paddy, arms extended, half submerged, not moving. Mazer couldn't tell if it was a child or an adult, but either way, the person was beyond help.

He looked farther west toward a village built into the side of a neighboring mountain, a kilometer away. A few people were running from their homes, heading down into the valley, presumably looking for loved ones who had been working in the fields. The rest of the villagers were scrambling up the mountain, fleeing in the opposite direction, away from the lander, their arms full of meager supplies.

Mazer's eyes returned to the rice fields, scanning right and left. He figured he was best off sticking to the edge of the mudslide. Or even just beyond it. That's where he had the greatest likelihood of finding someone alive.

Then he saw it.

A large tree near the edge, half buried, branches broken. From under it, right at the edge of the mudslide, a pair of legs emerged, skinny and barefoot. The head and upper torso appeared buried. For a moment Mazer was certain the person was dead, suffocated under the mountain of mud and debris. Then the legs kicked, moved.

"I got somebody," Mazer shouted. "Computer, lock on this position."

The HERC's AI tracked where Mazer's eyes were looking and put a targeting icon on the moving legs. The coordinates were immediately entered into the computer, and the image of the survivor was shared with the team.

"I see him," said Reinhardt. He banked the HERC to the right, moving in that direction. "How are we going to get him out?"

"Drop me at the site," said Mazer. "I'll get him an oxygen mask, then we'll use the talons to lift the tree away and pull him out. Patu, get the triage kit ready."

A deafening noise filled the air. Metal creaking, screeching, grinding. A machine as big as a city coming to life.

"What is that?" said Fatani

"Swing us back around," said Mazer.

Reinhardt rotated the HERC until they were facing the lander again. They hovered there, high in the air, a hundred meters away from it, with a clear view of its top, watching it.

The noise was unbearable. Piercing, painful stabs of volume. Mazer wanted to rip off his helmet and press his palms to his ears.

Then in an instant everything changed. The lander began to spin clockwise like a top. Fast, urgent, and easy, as if it lay atop water or air instead of earth and stone.

"What's it doing?" shouted Patu.

The lander picked up speed, spinning faster, screaming like a turbine, slinging up dirt and debris. Small clods of earth and crushed stone pinged against the windshield.

"Take us higher," shouted Mazer.

Reinhardt didn't need to be told twice. He yanked up on the stick, and they flew straight up, well beyond the reach of the slung dirt.

The lander was a blur of motion. The sound was worse than before, high and shrill. Mazer could feel it in his teeth. He looked west. The people running into the fields from the village were falling over, screaming, unable to stay on their feet, the earth shaking beneath them.

"It's digging into the ground," said Fatani.

It was true. The lander was burying itself into the surface, sinking deeper and deeper, spraying gravel and dirt across the valley like hail. Is this its weapon? Mazer wondered. To cause earthquakes? Or will it dig with its shields straight through us, putting a hole through the center of the Earth like a bullet through the brain?

Mazer looked back at the valley floor. The fallen villagers were curled up on the ground, their arms raised protectively over their faces as dirt and stone rained down on top of them. The villagers fleeing up the mountainside were doing no better, stumbling, falling, dumping their possessions from their arms, scrabbling to get purchase and keep from tumbling down the mountainside.

Mazer shouted over the roar of the noise and pointed to the villagers getting pounded in the valley. "Reinhardt! Get us down there to those people."

Reinhardt turned the HERC and dove straight into the maelstrom of flying dirt. Clods of it slammed into the sides and top of the aircraft. Fatani and Mazer closed their doors, cowering under the onslaught. A rock hit Reinhardt's window hard, spiderweb cracking an area of it a half-meter wide.

"There," Mazer shouted, pointing to a cluster of women huddled together.

Reinhardt flew in fast.

"Patu," Mazer shouted. "Help me get them inside."

The HERC leveled out and touched down beside the women, using the side of the aircraft as a shield against the dirt. Mazer and Patu were out in an instant, helping the women climb aboard. To Mazer's relief no one resisted. The women practically jumped inside. Fatani made room for them and told them where to hold on. In seconds, the doors were closed and the HERC was airborne again. They stayed low to the ground and picked up four more people on three more stops. One of the men had a bad head wound where a stone had hit him. He was dazed and in shock, and his face was covered in blood. Patu cradled his head, while Fatani dressed the wound.

"Take us up," said Mazer. "I don't see any more, and this is all we can carry."

"Where to?" said Reinhardt.

"Over this ridge to the north," said Mazer. "Not far. These people will need to hook up later with the others from the village. We'll set them down somewhere safe and then go back and search for others."

"We need a hospital," said Reinhardt.

"We need a lot more than that," said Mazer.

Reinhardt hopped the HERC over the ridge. Two women in the back clung to each other crying, their bodies bloody and filthy, their clothes bedraggled. They looked like the end of the world. Mazer didn't want to leave them anywhere; he wanted to rush them into a triage center where doctors would tend to their wounds and nurses would calm and reassure them. But what choice did he have?

Reinhardt found a clearing on the far side of the ridge and set down the aircraft. Patu slung open the door, and she and Fatani carried out the man with the dressed head wound and set him down gently in the grass. The others followed. The lander was over a klick away, but the screeching digging noise was still so loud that Mazer had to shout to be heard. He spoke in Mandarin, his voice clipped and authoritative, not to be questioned. "We're going back for more people. Stay here and stay together. Help each other. We'll be back."

One of the village women knelt beside the wounded man, taking over for Patu and Fatani. Patu pulled more sterile dressings and pain meds from the med kit, gave them to the women, then followed the rest of the team back into the HERC. Seconds later, they were airborne again, heading back over the mountain.

Once again, the lander came into view. Spinning, screaming, digging like a drill. Two-thirds of it was now submerged into the ground. Mazer turned his thermal scans back on and leaned out his window, combing the valley for more survivors. Then, as if a switch had been flipped, the deafening noise began to diminish, like giant turbines winding down.

"It's slowing," said Reinhardt.

Mazer turned back to the lander. It was true. The spinning was decelerating. The slung detritus wasn't getting as much altitude. It dropped even lower as the spinning continued to slow. Then, like a top in its final rotations, the lander went around once, twice, then stopped, settling firmly into the earth as the noise died away.

In an instant Mazer realized what the lander was doing. "It's a fortress," he said. "They were digging in. Literally. Anchoring their position. Getting ready."

"For what?" said Reinhardt.

"For whatever is inside that thing," said Mazer.

They hovered there a moment, waiting, watching.

Nothing happened.

A tree near the lander caught Mazer's attention, and the site of it sprung a memory in his mind. The legs. "Reinhardt," he said. "Swing us west again. Pull up those coordinates of the first survivor we saw."

The HERC turned to the west. Mazer leaned out, searching, suddenly afraid that he had been too late. Then he saw it. There, in the same place, was the tree. Only now the legs weren't sticking out. A man was standing beside the wall of mud, leaning on the exposed trunk of the tree, injured or exhausted or both.

"There!" Mazer said, pointing.

"I see him," said Reinhardt. He brought the HERC down quickly. There wasn't any level ground to land on among the paddies, so he stopped the HERC just above the paddy nearest the old man, hovering there, holding his position. Mazer took off his helmet and hopped out, sinking to his knees in the water and muck of the rice paddy.

The old man was short and bald and covered in mud, his eyes wide, his cheeks streaked with tears. He looked to be in his seventies or eighties. How he had survived, Mazer could only guess.

"My grandson," said the old man, gesturing at the tree. "He's stuck. I can reach his hand, but I can't pull him out. Please. Hurry."

"Where?" said Mazer.

The old man crouched down and pointed into a hollow impression in the mud beneath the felled tree. Mazer got down on all fours in the water to get a closer look. The hole was small, not even big enough for him to squeeze his shoulders in. He couldn't see anything in the darkness. He unclipped the small light from his hip and shined it inside. There was the boy, maybe two meters in, pinned down.

Mazer turned to the old man. "What's the boy's name?"

"Bingwen. But hurry. He's in pain. His arm is broken."

Mazer stuck his head in the hole and shined the light on his own face so the boy could see him. "Bingwen. My name is Mazer Rackham. We're going to get you out."

The boy turned his head to him. He looked weak.

Mazer turned back to the HERC. "Patu, throw me the shovel."

Patu unhooked a collapsible shovel from the back wall and brought it out, sinking in the muck of the paddy beside him. Mazer took it. "Bring me an oxygen mask and the winch cable, too." He clicked on the radio on his collar. "Reinhardt, get the talons ready. We're going to have to gently pull this tree away."

Mazer gripped the shovel and worked quickly, digging around the hole to make it wider without unsettling the mud above the tree. The boy inside was in a little bubble of protection thanks to the thick branches above him, and Mazer had to be careful not to cause an avalanche and bury him alive.

Patu returned with the winch cable and oxygen.

Mazer looped the cable around his waist. "If it caves in when I go in there, use the cable to pull me out."

"That might rip you in half," said Patu. "Let me go in. I'm thinner."

She was right. She was the more logical choice. But Mazer didn't want her taking the risk. "I've got it," he said. "Get the med kit ready."

He chiseled away at the mud with the shovel. The earth fell away easily. When it was big enough, he crawled in up to his waist, one hand carrying the oxygen mask. "Bingwen. Can you hear me?"

The boy looked at him, blinked as if waking, and—to Mazer's surprise—spoke in English. "My grandfather. Is he all right?"

"He's right outside. We're getting you both out of here. But first I need to put this mask over your mouth. I want you to take some deep breaths for me when it's on, okay?"

Mazer placed the adult-sized mask over the boy's face and turned on the oxygen. Bingwen took a shallow breath. Then another, stronger this time. Then a deep one, filling his lungs. The color slowly returned to his face. He blinked again, getting his bearings, waking up.

Mazer pulled his stylus from his pocket, turned on the light beam, and passed it over Bingwen and then himself. "Reinhardt, I'm sending you our position. When you bring in the talons, be sure to avoid us."

"I see you. Stay put and you'll be fine. Talons are ready."

"Go," said Mazer. "Straight up if you can."

There was movement to Mazer's left and right as the tips of the talons dipped into the earth, grabbing at the tree. The boy seized Mazer's hand and shut his eyes tight. The talons shifted, clawing, tightening their grip. Mud rained down. Bingwen turned his head away. Mazer leaned forward, shielding the boy's face.

Then the whole tree lifted up and away, branches swaying, cracking, dumping dirt. Sunlight poured into the hole. Bingwen blinked at the light.

Patu was beside them with the med kit in an instant. Mazer took out the Med-Assist Kim had given him and examined Bingwen's arm. There was a hairline fracture on the boy's lower radius. Mazer scanned again to be certain and smiled. "Your arm's going to be fine, Bingwen. Lieutenant Patu here is going to give you something for the pain, then we'll slip a cast on you. Have you ever had a cast before?"

"No."

"You'll love it. It's like having a giant muscle on your arm."

Patu readied a syringe, wiped at a spot on the boy's arm, and administered the shot. Bingwen flinched. The drug worked quickly. Mazer could see the boy relax, as if a knot inside him was unraveling. The old man hovered over them, watching their every move.

"Let's get him in the HERC," said Mazer. He got his arms under Bingwen's back and legs and lifted, holding the boy's frail body close to his chest. He weighed next to nothing.

Bingwen winced, cradling his arm.

Reinhardt flew the HERC in close. The talons were tucked away and secure, the tree tossed off to the side in the mud.

Patu helped the old man aboard, and Mazer and Bingwen followed. Fatani slammed the door shut behind them, and they were soaring upward again, leaving the valley far below.

Mazer lay Bingwen gingerly on the floor and secured him with a strap. Patu knelt beside him, carefully taking the boy's arm in her hand and wiping it clean with gauze.

"What's the status on the lander?" said Mazer.

"No movement," said Fatani. "All's quiet. But if it so much as flinches, the whole world will know. Every major network is running our feed live."

"Good," said Mazer. "Keep the cameras rolling."

Patu took the sleeve cast out of its bag. It was long and loose and fibrous and made for an adult. She dug a pair of scissors out of the med kit, eyed the length of Bingwen's arm, and cut the cast down to his size. Then, moving slowly so as not to jostle his arm, she slid Bingwen's hand into the sleeve cast. "Now hold your arm up a bit so I can slide this on. That's it, nice and straight."

She slipped the sleeve cast up his arm, stopping just below the shoulder. Then she pulled the pin. The cast inflated, molding to Bingwen's arm. Then the fibrous exterior tightened and went rigid. A single beep issued, signaling the cast had set.

"How does that feel?" asked Patu.

Bingwen gave it a tentative wiggle. "Heavy."

Then his eyes widened, and he tried to sit up. "Stop! We have to go back. My friends. Hopper and Meilin. They're still down there. Turn around. Please. We have to go back."

Mazer exchanged a glance with Patu.

The old man came over and put an arm around Bingwen. "Lay down, boy."

"No, Grandfather. We have to dig them out. We have to." The boy looked desperate, his eyes welling with tears, his good hand clutching the old man's filthy shirt. "Hopper and Meilin, Grandfather. Hopper and Meilin."

The old man shook his head sadly, wrapped his arms around the boy, and pulled him close. Bingwen buried his face in his grandfather's chest and began to sob.

Mazer watched, feeling helpless. There had been two other people down there. Children, probably. But where? Mazer hadn't seen anyone near the tree. And his scanners hadn't picked up anyone either. He wanted to reach out to the boy, calm him, reassure him, tell him that his friends had gotten out in time, that they had escaped the mudslide. But he knew it wasn't true. The old man's face said as much.

"I got aircraft coming in from the northwest," said Reinhardt. "Helicopters and VTOLs. Twelve of them. All medevacs from the military."

"About time," said Fatani.

They were coming because of the camera feeds, Mazer knew. They're coming because of us, because of what we were showing the world. The video the HERC was taking of the lander and villagers in distress had forced the Chinese to act. The whole world was watching. In homes all over the planet, families stared in horror as Chinese rice farmers screamed and cowered under the onslaught of the lander. But where was the Chinese military? the viewers at home would ask. Where were the emergency crews? Where was the help? Why wasn't China doing more?

Mazer had given them no other option. They either had to act and help or face a public-relations nightmare.

As if on cue, Shenzu appeared in the holofield. His composure completely different than it had been before. "Captain Rackham. You are to be commended for following our orders so thoroughly and assisting the wounded as we requested you to do. China praises your rescue efforts. We, of course, have been doing the same at the other landers."

He's performing for the recording equipment, Mazer realized. He's covering China's butt in case we're also broadcasting radio chatter. Mazer played along, eager to do whatever was necessary to keep the Chinese help coming.

"Thank you for getting here as soon as you could. We have wounded. Where should we take them?"

"There's a ridge to the northeast. An old farming barn at its peak. We'll use that as a temporary hospital. I'm sending you the coordinates now."

There was a chime, and the data appeared in the holofield.

Reinhardt gave a thumbs-up, signaling that he had the coordinates. Then he turned the HERC northeast.

"Good luck," said Shenzu. Then he clicked off the holo.

"Maybe they won't shoot us down after all," said Reinhardt.

"Fingers crossed," said Mazer.

They flew for three klicks until they reached the coordinates. The barn proved to be two buildings, one an actual barn and the other a wide hut that was likely the farmhouse. Both were made of bamboo and thatch and local timber, weathered and worn and faded in the sun. A strong gust of wind seemed capable of blowing them both over, but they were apparently stronger than they looked. They stood atop a wide ridge of terraced rice fields filled with water. In the morning sun, the water glistened, making the terraces look like giant staircases of glass. The wind in Mazer's face was light and cool and free of dust, carrying with it the sweet, green smells of the jungle to the west. To his right a flock of sparrows swooped down into the valley. It was quiet and peaceful and felt like a world away from the lander.

Reinhardt set the HERC down between the two buildings on an access road. An old pickup truck, with its hood up, was parked nearby, rusted and dented and tilting to one side, a few leafy vines twisting up the side of it. A dead relic.

The barn was to the right. It was three-sided, open in the front, with two water buffalo tied up inside beside a few bales of hay. Crude hand tools and farming implements hung on nails along the interior wall.

Mazer got out and took Bingwen into his arms. Patu ran ahead to the farmhouse and banged on the door. No one answered. The door was unlocked. Mazer carried Bingwen inside. The house was empty. A single room, twenty meters squared, void of any furniture. It smelled of smoke and age and dust. Holes like windows in the far wall offered a sweeping view of the valley.

Mazer lay Bingwen down on the concrete floor and told him to lie still.

The grandfather thanked Mazer profusely. Mazer noted how the old man struggled to walk and the bandages wrapped around the man's chest.

"You're hurt."

The old man shrugged. "I'm old. The two go together."

Mazer went back to the HERC for the Med-Assist. He returned, cut the man's bandages away, and scanned his chest. "Two cracked ribs."

"I could have told you that without the fancy equipment," said the old man.

Mazer pulled a handful of pill packets from the kit and offered them to the old man. "Take these for the pain."

The old man waved them away. "I'll be fine."

Mazer took the man's hand and closed the old, weathered fingers around the pill packets. "Your hands are withered with arthritis. Your chest probably burns with every breath. These pills speed the healing and help you rest. Your body needs both. Save your strength to care for Bingwen. Don't argue. And here, take these."

Mazer emptied his pockets of his rations and pulled two emergency water bags from the kit. "This should hold you until the doctors arrive."

The old man accepted the items, his eyes wet, and nodded his thanks.

"Mazer!"

It was Patu, shouting from the HERC. "We've got to move."

Mazer hurried outside and climbed aboard. Reinhardt had them up before Mazer was buckled.

"The lander," said Patu. "It's opening."

# CHAPTER 14

# India

Captain Wit O'Toole stepped out of the command tent and into the frigid morning air of the Kashmir Valley roughly 350 kilometers west of the Chinese border. To the east the sun was just beginning to rise over the outer Himalayas, casting long shadows across the valley floor and bathing Wit in a golden glow. Soon this would all be snow, a thick blanket of white that would cover the landscape until next summer. But for now it was steep green meadows and thick pine forests and vibrant wildflowers living out their brief existence before the snows came. It was a sight Wit would never tire of seeing. Earth in its purest form. No industry, no buildings, no people. Just mountains and green and a river at the bottom. It was breathtaking and beautiful and worth fighting for.

Wit looked down again at the images on his wrist pad. Three alien landers in China. He flipped the images away and called up a button, one that when pressed would alert everyone in his unit and call them to assembly. Wit pressed it.

Around him were twenty two-man tents, clustered together on the hillside. Almost immediately there was movement inside the tents. Seconds later men began to emerge, their hair unkempt, their clothes disheveled. Many of them were barefoot. But they were all alert and eager for news.

Six hours ago Wit had ordered his men to get some sleep. They would have preferred to stay up and watch the live coverage of the alien ship in space, but they had already been awake for thirty-six hours at that point, and they needed their rest. They were MOPs—or Mobile Operations Police—the most elite special forces unit in the world. Yet even soldiers as skilled and lethal as they were needed sleep.

The men gathered around Wit, some of them wearing only their long underwear, hugging themselves in the morning chill. They were a diverse group. Forty men from thirty different countries. Europeans, Asians, North and South Americans, Africans, Middle Easterners—all of them hand-picked from special forces units in their respective countries. They had all discarded their old ranks and uniforms and agreed to represent their country in an international force in which they were all equal and all devoted to a single cause: stop human suffering, anywhere in the world.

Wit thought it unfortunate that there were no Chinese soldiers among them. He could use one right about now. He had tried over the years to recruit from China, but the military there had always patently refused his offer. They would stand independent and not insert themselves into international matters. Or so said the official memo Wit had received from China. He would not have access to their soldiers under any circumstances. Period.

"The aliens have sent three large landing crafts down into China," said Wit. He removed his holopad from the pouch at his hip and held it in the palm of his hand. He then extended the projection antennas at each of the four corners and turned on the holo. An image of one of the landers appeared in the air. Some of the soldiers in the back strained to look over the heads of those in front of them.

A supply truck was to Wit's left. He climbed up onto the back bumper to give everyone a better look.

"You can't tell from the holo," Wit said, "but these landers are massive, many times larger than the world's biggest sports arena. Each of them could easily hold tens of thousands of troops or hundreds of aircraft or land vehicles. We don't yet know what's inside them. At the moment, they're just sitting there. They landed only a moment ago."

"Where in China?" said Calinga. "We're close to the border."

"Nowhere near us," said Wit. "Southeast China, north of Guangzhou."

"When do we deploy?" asked Calinga.

"I haven't asked Strategos for orders," said Wit. "And I won't be asking them either. In fact, I cut off all communications with Strategos three minutes ago."

The men exchanged looks.

Strategos was the high commander of the Mobile Operations Police. The general, so to speak. Except, instead of being a single person, Strategos was actually thirty people. Twenty-two men and eight women, each from a different nation, and each with a wealth of experience in black ops and peacekeeping operations. Some had been leaders of intelligence agencies. Others were military leaders still in active duty. Together they identified and planned MOPs missions and gave Wit his orders. Sanctioned by the U.N. Security Council, Strategos was a model of international military cooperation, a fraction of the size of NATO and far more effective on small-scale ops. Where NATO was a show of force, MOPs was a lightning strike, hard and fast and out before the enemy knew what hit him.

"You cut off lines with Strategos?" said Calinga. "Far be it from me to tell you how to do your job, Captain, but won't that make it difficult for us to get our deployment orders?"

"You won't get deployment orders," said Wit. "Even if the lines were open. Strategos won't send us to China. If orders come through it will be for us to stay put and maintain our position."

"Why?" said Deen. "The war's in China."

"China is the reason why," said Wit. "They're a stable state. Strategos won't send us in without a referendum from the U.N. Security Council and the blessing of the Chinese government, neither of which will likely happen any time soon, if at all. China won't ask for help."

"Why not?" asked Deen.

"Because they're China," said Wit. "If the landers had set down in Europe or Australia, we'd already be on a plane. China will be less cooperative. They'll want to handle this alone. Accepting help would be a show of weakness. Their military would take it as an insult. They won't abide that."

"This isn't solely their problem," said Calinga. "It's everybody's."

"China won't see it that way. If anything, they'll see this as an opportunity to assert their strength. If they rid the world of invading aliens, suddenly they're the strongest nation on Earth. Everyone would think twice before crossing them."

"Who's stupid enough to mess with China anyway?" said Calinga.

"The U.S. would have done the same thing," said Wit. "They don't want foreign troops on U.S. soil. It feels like a loss of sovereignty. It spooks the civilians and it implies that the nation helping you is stronger than you are. It's selfish and asinine, but that's national pride for you. A month from now, after a few million Chinese civilians have died, China may reconsider."

"You think it will get that bad?" asked Lobo.

"Probably worse," said Wit. "Think about our approach to alien combat."

Calinga said, "Analyze before we act and presume hostile intent."

"Right," said Wit. "And hostile intent is now a foregone conclusion. They wiped out a few thousand space miners and they turned a U.N. secretary and a few shuttles of reporters into space dust. We can safely assume they're not carrying gift baskets in those landers."

"So why did you cut communications with Strategos?" asked Calinga.

"Because I don't want to disobey a direct order," said Wit. "I'm going into China. If I never get the order to stay put, then I'm not disobeying it."

"You're obviously not going alone," said Deen. "We're coming with you."

"I can't order any of you to do that," said Wit. "I can only ask for volunteers. Getting across the border will be difficult. Relations between India and China aren't rosy. The borders are tight. We won't be able to take weapons. The Chinese would never let us in. We have to cross as civilians. We can acquire new weapons and gear once we're in the country."

"And do what exactly?" asked Deen.

"What we've trained to do," said Wit. "We'll be fighting an asymmetrical war. Instead of us being the high-tech masters of the battlefield, we will be the low-tech guerrillas trying to sabotage, interfere, strike at key points. We'll demoralize the enemy so badly, they'll want to quit. Like the Viet Cong against the U.S., or Castro against Batista, or the Fedayeen against the Soviet Union in Afghanistan. It will require a much different approach to combat than what we're used to waging. And we'll have to make it up and improvise as we go along. We still have no idea what the aliens' capabilities are."

"So forty guys against an alien army?" said Deen. "Don't get me wrong, I like a good fight, but those aren't promising odds."

"We won't be alone," said Wit. "Everything we learn about the enemy, every effective combat tactic we develop, we'll share with the Chinese military. If they're smart, they'll implement them. And we'll be watching the Chinese as well. If they do something that works, we'll implement it. The more we help each other, the more effective we both can be."

"I thought they didn't want help," said Lobo.

"They can't *ask* for help," said Wit. "They don't *officially* want help. But the individual squadrons in the thick of things will be grateful to have us. I hope."

"Where will we get supplies?" asked Calinga.

"Does this mean you're volunteering?" asked Wit.

"Hell yes," said Calinga. He turned to the others, "Anyone here *not* volunteering?"

No one raised their hand.

Calinga turned back and smiled. "Seems unanimous to me. I say we get moving."

"Not yet," said Wit. "I need to be clear about what the consequences of this will be. If we trudge off into China, we'll likely be labeled deserters and court-martialed."

"The consequences of us *not* going might be the end of the world," said Lobo.

"He's right, Captain," said Mabuzza. "We go where you go."

"So what if they court-martial us," said Deen. "Beats turning our backs on the people in China. I'd rather have a clear conscience as a deserter than a lifelong guilt trip as a soldier in good standing."

The men murmured their consent.

"All right," said Wit. "I see you're all as bullheaded as I am. You've got ten minutes to strike camp. Move!"

They moved.

Nine minutes later, the vehicles were pulling out, heading down the mountain pass toward Srinagar. Wit and Calinga sat in the cab of the lead truck, with Calinga at the wheel and Wit watching the sat feeds from China on the dashboard monitor. On screen the landers had spun into the ground, digging in. An aircraft was on site, recording it from every angle. Wit opened his holopad. A map of northern India appeared in the air in front of him, a small pin marking their current location.

"I think our chances are better if we cross into China from Pakistan in the Karakoram Mountains," said Wit. "Here at Khunjerab Pass."

"Pakistan?" said Calinga. "Now we have to cross two borders?"

"Getting into Pakistan won't be a problem. It's still the Kashmir region. And the borders between Pakistan and China are far more lax than those between India and China. Plus Khunjerab Pass is a cargo hub. Lots of commercial traffic. Big trucks. Freight loads. There will be cargo planes on the China side carrying freight east. Short runways. Dangerous flights. We'll hitch a ride."

"What about the vehicles?" asked Calinga.

"We'll ditch them in Srinagar," said Wit. "Roads are bad and fuel is scarce in that part of western China. We'd be abandoning them anyway. Plus it's hard to pass as civilians when you're driving military trucks."

"What's the elevation there?"

"Close to five thousand meters."

"You've got to be an insane pilot to take a job like that," said Calinga. "Winds in the mountains. The constant threat of storms. Big cargo planes. That's asking for a nosedive into a mountainside."

"That will work to our advantage," said Wit.

Calinga made a face. "How you figure?"

"A pilot who takes a job like that is interested in one thing only. Money. And money we have."

They drove into Srinagar and found a warehouse where they could store their trucks and supplies. Wit had the men lock up everything tight, though he doubted he would ever see any of the equipment again. His men were all in fatigues, which pegged them as soldiers. The trucks were clearly military as well. Which meant they were probably filled with valuable tech. Guns almost certainly. And military weapons on the black market would catch a very good price in Srinagar. Pakistan was only a hop, skip, and a jump away. Afghanistan wasn't much farther. Ten to one, thought Wit, the owner of this warehouse will have a burglary in the next few days, a burglary he secretly arranges himself for a decent cut of the profits.

But what could Wit do? If they approached the border as soldiers, they had zero chance of getting through.

They left the warehouse carrying only personal items in their pockets: holopads, passports, radio communicators, sat receivers. Small items. Inconspicuous.

They walked to a street market nearby and looked for clothes. Merchants shouted to them, offering their wares and promising incredible prices. Fruit, fish, jewelry, pirated music. Wit walked on, ignoring them.

They found a merchant selling men's clothing, but the designs were all wrong. Too small and too festive. The merchant held up a bright, shimmering pair of pants and a multicolored kurta. Wit forced a smile. If he and his men showed up at a Chinese border wearing that, they'd be mistaken for a troupe of acrobats.

"We need plain clothes," said Wit.

The merchant smiled and held up a finger. "Ah. Plain. These are too flashy for you, yes? Perhaps this is more to your liking." He pulled down a bright yellow kurta that hung down to Wit's knees and hurt his eyes.

"Not my style," said Wit. "Is there a dry cleaners near here?"

The merchant's smile vanished—Wit was no longer a potential sale. The merchant cocked a thumb down the street then turned his attention to someone else. Wit and his men pushed on. As they left the market, people began to stare. Mothers grabbed their children and pulled them out of the street. Pedestrians stopped and watched them with narrow eyes. Old men scowled.

"Not the friendliest of neighborhoods," said Calinga.

"We look like soldiers," said Wit. "Merchants love us because soldiers have money. Civilians like soldiers as much as they like a hole in the head, which is what soldiers in this region of the world sometimes give."

"Why a dry cleaners?" asked Calinga.

"Clothes obviously," said Wit. "And more importantly used clothes."

"We can't buy other people's clothes," said Calinga.

"You can buy anything if you've got the money for it," said Wit. "But we might not have to buy other people's clothes. Cleaners have unclaimed stuff, too. Shirts and pants people forgot they sent there or didn't pick up. And we're close to the university. So we've got a better chance of finding something functional."

They found the dry cleaners two blocks later. The owner was a small man sitting behind the counter, watching a sat feed of the landers in China. He heard the door ring as Wit and the men entered, but he didn't look up from the monitor. He was riveted.

Wit waited a moment, then cleared his throat. The man looked up at them, took in their number and size, and his eyes widened in surprise.

"We need clothes," said Wit. "For forty men. Mostly big sizes. Warm and comfortable. With lots of pockets, preferably. We'll pay well and we'll throw in the uniforms we're wearing. A nice trade. Probably the best sale you'll make this year. You could probably shut the place down for a week after we leave and still come out ahead. That is, assuming you have what we need."

The man had plenty. A whole storage room full. There were unclaimed items, yes, but new items as well. Smuggled stuff. A lot of Chinese knock-offs. Thick cargo pants with plenty of pockets, cotton undershirts, socks, heavy wool shirts, knit caps. Wit even found a baseball cap for a Major League team back in the States. Wit hated baseball—one guy throws a ball, one guy swings, and twenty other guys stand around watching and spitting— but the cap was precisely the type of thing a civilian would wear.

They were careful to mix up the wardrobe. Matching civilian clothes could look like uniforms too. So not everyone wore cargo pants, and those who did wore different colors, black or khaki or navy. Their shirts were different too. Similar, but not identical.

Wit paid the man in full and threw in a healthy tip. He and the men then changed and left their uniforms in a pile back in the storage room. Wit then split the men into ten groups of four and had them take different routes to the rail station. He had no worries about being seen in India—he had every authorization to be here. But now everyone around them was a potential fellow traveler to Pakistan, and suspicious passengers were likely to alert authorities, which Wit wanted to avoid at all costs.

They set out. Wit left with Calinga, Deen, and Lobo, and they got no suspicious looks whatsoever on the way.

They bought their tickets in their small groups and took the first train heading west into Pakistan, all ten of the four-men groups taking separate cars on the train. No one paid them any attention. Everyone on the train was watching news feeds from China on their holopads.

Wit pulled out his own holopad and dug around on the net until he found recent footage from China. It was more video from the first aircraft on the scene.

Wit watched. The constantly moving camera from the underside of the aircraft was a little nauseating, however, and Wit was about to abandon it and look for other footage from another source, when something on screen caught his eye. He tapped the screen and rewound the video. The aircraft was setting down and attempting a rescue. A soldier was out, pulling some- one from the mudslide. A small child, a boy perhaps. The soldier had him in his arms and was moving back toward the aircraft. For only a few seconds, the soldier's face came into view. Wit froze the video and showed the image to Calinga, seated beside him. "Look familiar?"

"That's the Maori," said Calinga. "The one we tested."

"Mazer Rackham," said Wit.

"How did he get into China that fast?"

"He must have been there already."

"He's working with the Chinese?"

"Not when this was recorded," said Wit. "He can't be. The Chinese would never allow a New Zealander to make a rescue like that. Not with the whole world watching. Saving a child from disaster? That's the holy grail of PR. If Mazer were flying with the Chinese, it would be a Chinese soldier saving that kid. Mazer is spoiling their moment in the sun."

"So who's in the aircraft with him?"

"No idea," said Wit. "But it's not the Chinese."

# CHAPTER 15

# Formics

Mazer leaned out of the HERC and looked back one last time at the farmhouse, getting smaller behind them in the distance. The boy, Bingwen, had been lucky. Another meter or two to the right or left underneath that tree, and the dirt would have buried him alive. How many like him were stuck in those fields, Mazer wondered, trapped in some pocket of air, waiting for rescue that probably wasn't coming?

Mazer leaned back inside and flipped on his HUD. Patu was sending him several feeds, each positioned at one of the corners of his field of vision. They were all satellite feeds, taken from above, giving him a clear view of the top of the lander, which had opened. A large dark circle was now in the center, like the hole of a doughnut, exposing a vast space inside mostly hidden in shadow.

"What are we looking at?" said Mazer. "Can we see what's inside?"

"Negative," said Patu. "I've tried various spectrums. The sun's too low. Not enough light is getting in."

They crested the final hill and the lander came into view. There was a cluster of aircraft gathered around it now, the medevacs as well as a few other military birds. All with Chinese markings. A few of them hovered over the hole.

"Patu," said Mazer. "Are there any feeds coming from the aircraft over the lander?"

"Negative. If they're filming anything, they're not broadcasting it."

Shenzu, the Chinese liaison, appeared in the holofield. "We'll take it from here, Captain Rackham. China appreciates your assistance. Please keep your distance."

"There may be other survivors," said Mazer.

"We will see to them," said Shenzu. His voice was firm, unquestioning. He winked out.

"What do we do now?" said Reinhardt.

"We obey," said Mazer. "We hang back. We let them do their job. Fatani, patch us in to their radio chatter. I want to know what they're saying to each other. Reinhardt, take us back to where we dropped off the first of the wounded. We can carry them up to where the hospital will be set up."

A beam of light shot out of the center of the lander from deep inside the hole and hit one of the helicopters above it. The laser punched through as if the helicopter weren't even there, slicing off the spinning rotor blades in an instant. The helicopter dropped like a stone, smoking and burning, twisting, careening. It bounced off the side of the lander and spiraled to the ground where it crashed in a heap and burst into flames.

The other helicopters near the hole began to retreat. They didn't move fast enough. Three more lasers shot up, slicing the aircraft in half. They each fell from the sky, burning. One of them was a medevac, a big bird. A crew of ten at least. Doctors and nurses. The aircraft exploded before it hit the ground.

Fatani found the radio frequency. Frantic shouts and screams assaulted Mazer's ears. The Chinese were in a panic.

The last of the helicopters above the lander fell away. It crashed on the top of the lander near the open hole on a flat surface and stayed there, churning out so much black smoke that the helicopter was no longer visible.

Then they came.

At first there were so many of them that Mazer didn't realize what he was looking at. They were like a colony of bats shooting up out of a cave. Or a swarm of insects erupting upward from their hive in a single column of twisting movement, packed close together and yet not touching one another. They were aircraft, Mazer realized, shooting up from the hole in the lander. A column of fast-moving metal, sharp and dark and frightening, rising quickly, moving as one.

There were two kinds, Mazer realized. One small, the other large, maybe three times the size of the HERC. There were hundreds of them, rising up like water in a straw. Then at an altitude high above the lander they split up, like the roots of an upside-down tree, shooting off in every direction, creating a canopy across the entire landscape that covered the valley with shadows.

One flew directly above the HERC. Mazer craned his neck to watch it pass. It was silent, he realized. They all were silent. No engine noise. No rotors. No sound whatsoever. Like ghosts.

Gunfire erupted from one of the Chinese aircraft to Mazer's right—an arc of tracer fire that twisted, readjusted, then found its mark. One of the larger retreating alien aircraft took the fire. Bullets pinged off the hull in a shower of sparks, knocking the aircraft out of its flight path and sending it spinning toward the ground. It hit the surface then bounced up momentarily, spinning end over end, reeling, completely out of control. Then it landed again and slid to a stop, leaving a trench behind it where it had dug into the earth.

At once, as if moving as one, seven alien aircraft changed course and descended on the Chinese helicopter that had fired. The Chinese gunner rotated and spewed his tracer fire upward at his attackers, but the aliens maneuvered swiftly to avoid it, juking right and left. Then they opened their own guns: brief bursts of laserized material hit the Chinese aircraft from all sides at once. The helicopter twisted and ripped apart like a crushed can, sending debris and shrapnel and fire in every direction. The burning heap plunged to the ground and slammed onto a hillside, where gravity continued to pull it downward. It rolled end over end and crashed into a tree, scattering ashes and more debris.

"Get us to the ground!" Mazer shouted. "Now!"

Reinhardt slammed the stick to the side, turning them away, dropping them fast.

Ahead of them, the downed alien aircraft smoldered in the grass.

Mazer pointed. "There! Put us down by their wrecked aircraft!"

Reinhardt shot Mazer a look. "You want me to land near that thing?"

"Do it!" shouted Mazer.

Reinhardt obeyed, cutting right and setting them down close to the wreckage. Mazer hopped out, and looked up, unholstering his sidearm and aiming above him. A weapon that small would do nothing against a big aircraft, but it felt better in his hand. The alien crafts that were behind them pushed on, ignoring them, soaring overhead, heading north.

Mazer watched them go and exhaled, his shoulders relaxing. There was a brief explosion of gunfire to the south, and he spun around in that direction. He saw nothing; the mountain south of his position blocked his view of the lander and other aircraft. He listened. After a brief silence, more gunfire, followed by a deep explosion—a ripping, booming sound that seemed to echo off the sky. Metal twisting, engines dying, the brief clatter of loosed parts colliding in the air and tinkling downward like a burning wind chime.

Mazer looked east and west. There were alien crafts heading in both directions, some moving fast, others proceeding slowly as if patrolling or scanning the ground below them. None of them was dangerously close or seemed to be paying him any attention. The frantic chatter on the radio continued, although now there was clearly less of it. Mazer strained to make it out, but the shouting was fast and frantic and all in Chinese, with only bits and pieces coming through, all jumbled on top of each other.

Another explosion boomed from the south.

The radio chatter went silent. A dull static took its place.

Mazer stood there a moment, listening, willing more voices to return to the frequency and check in. None did. He slowly did a 360, taking in the landscape, searching the sky for Chinese aircraft, seeing none.

He spoke into his comlink. "Red Dragon, this is Captain Mazer Rackham, do you read, over?"

No response.

"Red Dragon, do you copy?"

Nothing.

Mazer turned to his left. The downed alien aircraft lay on its side twenty meters away. Mazer had expected it to be a bent and twisted wreck bearing little resemblance to its original shape. But the aircraft appeared intact and undamaged, as if constructed by some impenetrable material. The only sign of duress was a thin line of smoke slowly seeping from a vent in the back.

He turned to Reinhardt. "Keep the HERC running. Be ready to take off in an instant. Fatani, Patu, helmetcams on, weapons up. Record everything. Reinhardt, watch the skies. Warn us if anything comes our direction."

Mazer cautiously moved toward the downed aircraft, his weapon up, safety off, finger by the trigger, ready.

"You sure about this, Mazer?" said Reinhardt. "We don't know what that thing is or what it's capable of."

"Nor does anyone else," said Mazer, "which is exactly why we have to find out."

Cautiously he stepped forward. Patu appeared at his side, her assault rifle up to one shoulder, ready to fire. Fatani came around the HERC and joined then, his sidearm in hand, aiming forward.

All of them wore their helmets, recording the scene.

"Spread out," said Mazer.

They parted, Mazer going to the left, Fatani going wide to the right, Patu continuing forward.

"Are we broadcasting, Patu?" asked Mazer.

"All three feeds are live."

"Good."

They drew closer to the aircraft. It was clear that the same engineers who had built the lander had built this. The metal hull was dark maroon, almost a rusty color, unpolished and spotted with patches of corrosion. The lines and corners were rough as well, as if no consideration had been given to aerodynamics or style. It was like a boxcar, ugly and bulky and strictly utilitarian.

The aircraft lay on its side so that the top of it faced Mazer. It was taller than he was. He approached it and kicked the metal with his boot. It gave a light, hollow *clang*. He moved around it to the opposite side. Fatani was there, standing on a slight rise in the earth, affording him a better view of the aircraft's side, now its top. Mazer climbed up beside him and saw where the bullets from the Chinese helicopter had hit it. Nothing had penetrated the hull, but the bullets had left small, near-imperceptible depressions in the metal. It struck Mazer as strange.

Fatani must have been thinking the same. "This doesn't make sense," he said. "The bullets didn't break through. There's no leaking fluid. No visible damage at all from the gunfire. Why did it go down?"

"Maybe the sheer force of the impact knocked it out of whack. Like a punch to the side of the head. The pilot wasn't expecting it. Or maybe the aircraft is difficult to realign once shaken. Any number of reasons."

The craft moved: A large piece of metal on the top, like a bay door, rose up twenty centimeters.

Mazer stumbled backward, startled, nearly tripping over himself. Patu and Fatani stumbled back as well, guns up and tight in their hands.

"What's it doing?" said Fatani.

The door was a wide, flat section of hull nearly as tall as the aircraft. Another grinding noise sounded, and the door—now the roof—slid backward, revealing a deep empty space inside.

"I don't like this," said Patu.

The door slid all the way to the back and stopped. The interior was wide like a cargo bay. Mazer couldn't see far enough inside to see the bottom. He stepped toward it.

"Easy," said Fatani. "That door's not opening on its own."

Mazer drew closer. One meter, then two. His gun up and aimed. He was right at the side of the thing. He stood on his tiptoes, trying to see inside.

A red hand to his right reached up out of the space and grabbed the edge.

Fatani swore. Mazer stumbled back again. Patu stepped forward, ready to fire.

Mazer threw up a hand. "Wait! Don't shoot." He backed up, getting his feet back under him, his heart racing.

The red hand was muscled and hard, with fine wisps of short hair. It was maybe two-thirds the size of Mazer's hand and was a claw as much as anything. Mazer watched it and heard a sound inside. A hiss. Not a mechanical sound, but a biological one. Breaths. Shallow and raspy. The sound an animal makes when it's in pain.

"Back up," said Mazer.

They retreated a few steps.

The red hand clinging to the edge strained again, tightening, clutching, pulling. The breathing was heavier, more labored. The animal was trying to lift itself.

A second, smaller hand appeared near the first.

Then the creature's leg came over the edge, and the body quickly followed. Now Mazer could see that the smaller arm and hand wasn't an opposing limb, but a second, smaller arm on the same side beneath the first. Or perhaps the middle appendages were an extra set of legs. It was difficult to say; there didn't appear to be much anatomical difference between the two.

The creature lay there on the narrow edge, catching its breath, rasping, like a tightrope walker taking a break mid performance. It wore no clothing. Strapped to its back was a large semitransparent canister filled with fluid that sloshed around inside. Its head was turned away from them. It looked to be about four feet tall. It's skin was covered in a short, fuzzy fur, yet the hair was thin, like the hair on a man's arm, affording Mazer a clear view of the creature's skin, which was earth tones, mostly deep reds with splotches of orange and yellow and green. Like an insect.

"Let me shoot it," said Patu.

"Wait," said Mazer. "Let's see what it does."

After a moment the creature seemed to compose itself and gather strength. It tried to maneuver its hands in such a way to lower itself to the ground, but when it shifted its weight, it tumbled over the side and fell hard to the ground. The creature inhaled sharply as if stabbed with pain but made no other sound. It lay still for a moment, breathing. Then slowly, with great effort, it tried to get to its feet. At first it failed. The arms on its left side were limp and apparently broken. The left leg was twisted slightly, bent at an angle that didn't match the right leg it was using. It must have been thrown around violently during the wreck.

Mazer could now see that a tube extended from the bottom of the canister on the creature's back. At the end of the tube was a short wand, not unlike the pack a pest-control worker might wear.

The creature got its good leg under it. Then, pushing upward with that leg, putting its back against the aircraft as support, it slowly got to its feet. Mazer almost pitied it then. It was such a short, broken thing. But the feeling lasted only an instant. He tightened his grip on his gun, aiming at the creature's head.

The creature hobbled forward, still oblivious to their presence. One painful step after another it put weight on its bad leg as it shuffled along. It reached the end of the lander and continued moving forward in the grass.

"Where's it going?" said Fatani.

"Don't know," said Mazer. "Keep on eye on the aircraft in case another one comes out."

He stepped toward the alien walking away from them, his gun still up, following it. The creature was moving slow. It couldn't go far. Mazer knew he needed to kill it. But what then? Should they try to recover the body? Surely China would want to study it. And if not the alien then at least whatever the alien was carrying in its container.

The creature reached behind it with its good, smaller hand and found the tube from the canister. It passed the tube up to its larger hand. The two hands worked in tandem, sliding down the tube until they found the wand, which the creature grabbed and pointed at the grass in front of it. A yellow mist emanated. The grass immediately wilted and turned black, dying.

Alarms started going off in Mazer's helmet. A biohazard alert.

"Masks!" shouted Mazer, retreating a few steps. He blinked the command, and the oxygen mask inside his helmet pressed against his face, covering his mouth and nose. He felt the suction of it and knew the seal was tight. Fresh oxygen poured in.

"Back off," he said. "It's spraying some kind of defoliant."

"It's in the air," said Fatani. "My helmet's going berserk."

The creature continued spraying. Wide swaths of grass around it died. The mist swirled and grew, carried away from them by the wind.

"We've got to do something," said Patu.

Mazer hesitated a moment longer then pulled the trigger. His gun discharged. The creature took the round to the head and dropped. The wand stopped spraying.

"It's the defoliant," said Mazer. "There are traces of it in the air. Get back to the HERC. Reinhardt, move the HERC upwind."

The HERC lifted slightly into the air and moved thirty meters north before it set down again.

"What if that thing isn't dead?" said Fatani.

"I got it," said Mazer. "Get back inside. Touch nothing. Don't sit down. Whatever it was spraying may be on your clothes."

They moved. Mazer blinked a command and turned on the thermal imaging. The creature on the ground showed a slight heat signature. Faint but it was clearly warm-blooded. Mazer squeezed off four more rounds, just to be sure. The creature took each in the back, jerking slightly as if kicked. Otherwise it didn't move. The head wound was bleeding out in the grass.

Mazer turned to the alien aircraft and climbed up on top of it. He stood at the edge of the door and looked down inside. At the bottom, clumped together in a heap was a mass of alien bodies, all of them armed with the same defoliant canisters on their backs. "It's a troop carrier. It's hard to get an exact count of how many creatures are in here. The bodies are all clumped together. I'm going to guess nine."

Mazer did the math in his head. He wasn't sure how many troop carriers had come out of the lander, but it had to have been at least a hundred and maybe double that. If each of them were filled with ten troops armed with defoliants, the casualty count to the Chinese could be enormous, to say nothing of the ecological implications.

One of the aliens moved, still alive. Mazer emptied his gun into it.

The pile went still.

He knelt down, took out his laser cutter, and began slicing away at a corner of the troop carrier, trying to cut a piece of the metal off for analysis. The laser, which normally sliced through steel with ease, cut slowly, having a hard time with the metal. Mazer had hoped for a larger piece, but the pace of the cut prompted him to settle for a tiny piece no bigger than a coin. He blew on it, letting the metal cool, then dropped it into a small container at his hip. Then he stepped off the door and tried to push it forward back into place, hoping to seal the aircraft closed and thus lock the chemical inside. The door didn't move. He briefly looked inside for a lever or switch or button but saw none.

He lowered himself from the troop carrier and ran for the HERC.

He stepped up onto the landing skid and grabbed a handhold. "Take us up," he told Reinhardt. "Directly over the dead grass."

The HERC rose.

With his free hand, Mazer dug under the dash until he found the flare gun. There were several signal flares attached to its base. He would have preferred another method, a more reliable incendiary that was easier to control—flares were so unpredictable—but it was all he had and he didn't want to get any closer to the dead grass. He loaded a flare and fired it straight down into the black patch of grass. The flare bounced once and ricocheted off to the side, landing a distance away, spinning like a firework in a patch of perfectly healthy grass, spewing sparks and flame.

Mazer loaded another flare and tried again. This time the flare hit the ground and spun wildly in place, spewing sparks in every direction before it shot off elsewhere. It wasn't as accurate as Mazer had hoped, but it was enough; the dead grass caught the flames and began to burn.

Mazer turned to Reinhardt. "Find us a flat surface nearby, preferably away from vegetation. A road maybe. Fast."

The HERC banked east. Mazer scanned the skies. The troop carriers and smaller aircraft were elsewhere, moving away from them.

Reinhardt brought the HERC down onto a dirt road, the first one Mazer had seen in a while.

Mazer hopped out, removed his helmet, and set it on the ground. "Patu and Fatani, we need to strip down. Whatever was exposed to the air, whatever may have come in contact with the defoliant, starting with your fatigues. Dump them here in a pile. Don't let your clothes touch another part of your skin or anything inside the HERC, if it can be avoided. Keep your boots."

Mazer undressed quickly, keeping on his undershirt, shorts, and socks. He left his fatigues in the dirt. Fatani and Patu stripped down as well. Mazer then removed a first-aid kit from under his seat and took out a bottle of surgical antiseptic. He poured it into Patu and Fatani's cupped hands and told them to wash their hands and neck thoroughly. Mazer then did the same. The liquid was cold and brown and smelled like a hospital. When they finished they used gauze loaded with the antiseptic to wipe down their helmets, boots, and weapons.

Mazer then grabbed another of the flares and pulled the igniter pin. The end of the flare spewed hot sparks. Mazer bent down and set the sparks to the clothes. They caught fire and burned. He tossed the flare into a nearby rice paddy, where it sizzled and extinguished.

"Now what?" said Reinhardt. "We've got no one on the radio. No extra clothes. Barely any weapons."

"We need extra clothing," said Mazer. "More of our skin is exposed now. And there could be hundreds of troops out there putting that mist in the air. We need to cover up."

"We need to reassess what the hell we're doing out here," said Reinhardt. "We're not equipped for aerial combat, Mazer. This is out of our league now. Rescue effort is one thing. Aerial assaults is another. We are officially over our heads here."

"Everyone's over their head," said Mazer. "Nobody's prepared for this."

"If we go back to base, they'll confiscate the HERC," said Fatani. "We'll be out of the fight."

"We're not *armed* for a fight," said Reinhardt. "That's my point. Load this baby with missiles and bigger guns, and it can do some good. As a rescue aircraft, we're target practice. We need to give this back to the Chinese and let them use it for what it was made for. This is their resource, not ours."

"We can still do some good out here," said Patu. "There were a lot of people on the ground back there. Still on foot. We need to get them centrally located, away from the chaos. Up to the makeshift hospital maybe. At least until they can be extracted properly."

"There isn't going to be a hospital," said Reinhardt. "Did you miss the events of the last twenty minutes? Those medevacs are down, Patu. Toast. No one's building a hospital. Right now we're it. If we take those people up to the hospital, they're no better off up there than where they are."

A beeping noise sounded in Mazer's helmet.

Reinhardt turned to the dash, suddenly alert. "I got two incomings. Moving fast. Chinese fighters."

Mazer could hear their jet engines now. He looked up and saw them coming from the south, flying low, screaming across the sky. They flew almost directly overhead a moment later. One of them opened fire at a cluster of alien troop carriers in the distance. The other fighter launched a missile, which hit its target. A troop carrier exploded, its wreckage twisting, falling, burning. Mazer and the others couldn't help but cheer.

Then the tables turned. All of the alien aircraft in the vicinity suddenly changed course, as if moving as one organism, and converged on the Chinese fighters. Mazer quickly put on his helmet and zoomed in, following the dogfight. The Chinese fighters saw the danger and climbed, trying to shake their pursuers, banking left and right. The smaller alien skimmers, which likely only held a single pilot, were much faster and more maneuverable than the troop carriers. A cluster of the skimmers soon caught up with one of the fighters and fired in unison. The Chinese fighter exploded, sending a spray of shrapnel and fire in every direction.

Mazer and the others went quiet, watching the burning wreckage cascade down from the sky.

"We're over our heads here, Mazer," Reinhardt repeated. "We should talk with the Chinese. They'll be desperate for help now. They'll put us back out here."

Patu, Fatani, and Reinhardt watched him, waiting for him to make a decision. Good sense said to go. The sooner they armed the HERC, the sooner someone could be in the air with it, putting it to good use. He looked south. He could still see people coming down from the hills, fleeing the lander on foot, scattering across the landscape in groups of four or less, completely disorganized. Mazer couldn't see their faces from this distance, but he knew what he would see if he could. Fear, grief, confusion, helplessness.

"We need to move as many people up to that farmhouse as we can," said Mazer. "We can't leave them out here unorganized. It doesn't matter if the medevacs are down. We can make it a hospital."

"We don't have supplies," said Reinhardt.

"We have a few," said Mazer. "And we have more medical training than any of them likely do. We can help. And we can organize the ones who are unhurt to help as well. These people are fragmented and terrified. They need to gather, get their bearings, and get out of the open. Who knows how much of that defoliant has been sprayed. They could run right into a cloud of it. The best place for them is up high, out of the valleys, where there's more wind. That farmhouse is as good a place as any."

"We're not a transporter," said Reinhardt. "This thing can only take a few people at once."

"Then we'll take a few people at once," said Mazer. He climbed up into the cockpit. "Take us up. Fatani, watch the skies for incomings. Patu, you and I will help the survivors into the HERC and get them fastened in."

They all acknowledged, and Reinhardt took them up again.

They flew south but didn't have to go far. They landed near a family running across a field. The woman had an infant in her arms. Both she and the baby were crying. The father carried two toddlers, both of them clinging desperately to his neck. The children were maybe two and three years old. The family was poor and barefoot and dirty and terrified. They came to the HERC without hesitating. Mazer and Patu were out and helping them inside. The children were frightened and screaming. The mother huddled with her infant inside, knees up, trembling.

When everyone was secure, Reinhardt took them up again. They didn't go far before he was setting the HERC down once more, this time for an older couple. Each of them was carrying a bag. Their clothes were muddy and ripped. They looked as if they were still in a state of shock. Mazer and Patu helped them inside.

"We've only got room for one or two more," said Reinhardt.

Mazer saw a group of five people running toward them, waving their arms.

"Wait!" they were shouting. "Wait for us." They were crying and desperate.

"We can't fit all those people," Reinhardt said to Mazer.

"We'll squeeze them in," said Mazer.

The last group was a mix of people, likely unrelated. A teenage girl. An old woman. A child, maybe ten years old. A middle-aged man. A woman in her twenties. Some of them looked injured, limping or favoring an arm, but nothing looked serious. They had likely fallen during the earthquake or in the mad rush of it all.

Mazer squeezed them all in tight, putting the child and teenage girl up front in his seat, while he stood in the back. Reinhardt took them up and headed toward the farmhouse. Mazer addressed the people inside. He and his team were taking them to a farmhouse. They would make it a hospital. They would bring more people. Real doctors would likely come later. In the meantime, he needed everyone's help. Those who were uninjured would assist those who were. He asked about the ten-year-old boy: Was anyone related to him? No one was. He told the boy to stick with one of the women. She would tend to him. The woman agreed. Mazer told them to cover their skin once they reached the farmhouse, explaining as best he could about the defoliants. They needed to stay indoors. Supplies would come later. Water and food. There was already some of that at the farmhouse. He distributed what little other supplies he had in the HERC.

By then they had reached the farmhouse. Mazer slid back the door and began helping everyone inside. The middle-aged man assisted as much as he and Patu did, carrying in children and lifting the bags for the elderly. The old man and Bingwen were inside. They seemed grateful that Mazer had returned. They were happy to see the others. The old man recognized several of the people. They embraced.

Mazer turned to the middle-aged man. "What's your name?"

"Ping," the man said.

Mazer put a hand on his shoulder and addressed the crowd. "Everyone, Ping here is in charge until we get back with the others. Remember, stay indoors."

"We're not safe here," said the father of the young family. "Those planes. They could come back."

"You're safer here than where you were," said Mazer. "The military will come."

"Why aren't they already here?" said the man. "Why do foreigners save us?"

"Your military is desperately fighting to protect you," said Mazer. "It was their idea to make this location a hospital. They'll send someone. Supplies will come."

"You can't be sure of that," said the man. "You don't know. You can't be sure of anything. I saw the helicopters, the ones with the doctors, the ones the military had sent. They blew up. They went down. No doctors are coming. I saw it happen. I saw it with my own eyes."

He was getting upset, his voice rising.

Mazer made a calming gesture with his hands, patting the air in front of him. "Right now we need to stay calm, friend. We will tell the military you are here. They will send assistance as soon as they can. You're stronger together here than you were out there alone. We'll bring more people."

"More people means more mouths to feed, more water to share," said the man. "There isn't enough of that to go around already. If you bring more people, you will kill us all."

The man was terrified, in shock, irrational. And thinking only of his family.

The boy Bingwen surprised Mazer by speaking up. "This man pulled me from the mud," he said, gesturing to Mazer. "I was trapped under the dirt, and he pulled me out. He risked his life for me and my grandfather. He told us he would come back, and he did. He keeps his word, a man of honor. He and his team are trained. We should listen to them and trust them."

The young father turned on Bingwen, furious. "What do you know of anything? You, a boy. Do you have little mouths to feed? A wife to tend to? No. You speak of honor, and yet you show none to your elders, speaking out of turn, giving me orders as if I were a child. Were I your father I would lash you for your loose tongue."

"You are not his father," said Bingwen's grandfather, rising to his feet and putting a protective hand around the boy. "And you speak out of turn, sir. Be grateful your wife is alive. Be grateful you have three of your children. The rest of us don't know what has become of our loved ones. These men are willing to help us, to reunite us all. We will listen to them."

The father's face was twisted with anger. He regarded the grandfather and Bingwen with contempt. Then he turned to the others, gesturing to Mazer. "These men are foreigners. We know nothing about them. They are not like us. We do not have to take orders from them."

"We're not giving you orders," said Mazer.

"You are making promises you can't keep. Just like all foreigners do. Talk and more talk. Can you command our military? Can you make them come? No. Can you make food and water appear? No." He turned back to the others. "I am not staying here. How are we better off here in this dump of a farmhouse than we were back in our village?"

"We're farther from the invaders," said Ping.

The young father scoffed. "Farther? Are you such a fool that you think this is far enough? We are a few kilometers away at most. That is nothing to a skimmer. They can reach us in a second. The big disc is right over those mountains. Is that far enough for you?"

No one answered.

"We need to keep moving," said the man, "get as far away from here as possible. On foot if we have to. We need to find military of our kind. My family and I are pushing on. Any of you are welcome to join us, but don't expect us to slow down for you."

He waited. No one moved.

The man's mouth tightened in a hard line. "Fine. If you want to stay here and die, that is your choice." He moved to the container of water bottles. "But we are taking our fair share of supplies with us." He grabbed several bottles of water—far more than was their share—and put them in his sack, which he looped over his shoulder. Then he picked up one of the toddlers and took the hand of the other. He moved toward the door without looking back at his wife. "Come, Daiyu."

The wife was still holding the infant in her arms, rocking it gently. It had stopped crying. The woman looked torn, afraid. She clearly didn't want to go.

Her husband's voice was like a whip. "Come, Daiyu!"

The woman hesitated. She looked into the faces of the people in the room as if they might have an answer for her, a way out, a way to stay and go at the same time.

"You dishonor me, wife. Come! For the sake of our children."

She looked at her husband. His stare was like a knife. She cowed, pulled the baby tight to her chest, bowed her head, and shuffled toward the door. As she passed Mazer she lifted her eyes and met his. She stopped. Mazer could see she was on the verge of tears. She looked down at her infant, then back up at Mazer, as if considering leaving the child with him, as if she knew she would not live out in the open and wanted at least one member of their family to survive.

Mazer couldn't bear it. It was a breach of a protocol, perhaps even a cultural offense, but he said it anyway. "You don't have to go. You can stay here with your children."

The young father exploded with fury. "How dare you! How dare you speak to my wife, to separate us." He spat at Mazer, grabbed his wife's wrist, and pulled her toward the door. "You see?" he said to the others.

"You see what foreigners will get us? They cannot be trusted." He spat again at Mazer.

The two toddlers stood framed in the doorway, confused and frightened. They had started to cry.

"Quiet!" said the father. He grabbed one by the hand, a boy, and pulled him out into the sunlight. The wife followed reluctantly, pulling the second toddler behind her. The father led them toward a trail that curved down the terraced fields. He moved quickly, not looking back, dragging the toddler along, who stumbled and hurried to keep up. Just before they were out of sight, the wife looked back. Mazer thought she would cry out then, ask to be rescued. If she did, he would go to her. He would scoop up her children and bring them inside. All she had to do was say the word.

Then the trail descended, and the woman and her children disappeared from view and were gone.

The villagers in the house all looked at Mazer, waiting for him to respond.

"You don't have to stay," said Mazer. "Any of you. You're free to go at any moment. But staying together and helping each other will improve all of our chances. My team and I will keep our word. We'll be back with others as soon as we can."

"Wait."

Mazer turned. It was the old woman with the bag. She had it open and was digging through it. She pulled out a shirt. "Here. You are not covered as well as you should be. An undershirt and shorts will not protect you from the mist." She gave the shirt to Mazer then turned to Patu. "And for you, too. A woman needs better covering." She snapped at her husband. "Huang Fu. Help me find clothes for these half-naked soldiers."

The old man, who had been sitting on his bag, catching his breath, slowly got to his feet and opened the bag, searching.

"Here you are," said the old woman, giving Patu a simple cotton shirt with a floral print. It was worn and heavily faded from the sun, all of its brilliance and color nothing but a memory. "I have picked more seasons of rice in that shirt than there are years in your life," said the old woman.

Patu nodded, accepting it. "Thank you."

"And here," said the old woman. "Pants. As much as my husband would like to see those legs of yours, you had better cover up before his heart fails him."

Patu took them. They were loose and wide with a drawstring at the waist. "Again I thank you."

The old woman stepped to Fatani, took one look at his broad shoulders and thick neck, and shook her head. "How can I dress a water buffalo? What do you eat for breakfast? Your wife and children? Huang Fu, how do we dress this man?"

"I have nothing that will fit him," said the old man.

She turned on him, annoyed. "Of course you don't, mud brain. None of us do. Give me your blanket." She snapped her fingers, impatient.

The man hurried over, carrying a thin blanket.

"You need not give me that," said Fatani. "You'll need it to—"

"Shut up, water buffalo," the old woman said. She opened the blanket onto the floor then produced a knife from her pocket. She snapped open the blade. It had been sharpened so many times over the years that the blade looked half the size it had probably originally been. Her cuts were swift and sure. She ripped off long strips. She cut a hole in the middle for his head. She then gave him the poncho and tied one of the straps around his waist. Then she tore strips of fabric from a sheet and tied them around his arms. The old man gave her another two pair of loose pants for Mazer and Fatani, and the old woman nodded her approval. "There. Now you don't look like foreigners at all."

Mazer and the others nodded their thanks and rushed to the HERC, eager to get airborne again. As Mazer climbed up into the cockpit and took his helmet from the seat, he saw that the boy Bingwen had followed him out.

"What should we do if you don't come back?" Bingwen said in English. "If something happens to you, I mean?"

"We'll be back," said Mazer.

"You'll *try* to come back. I don't doubt that. But that's not the same thing. These people need direction. They need a leader."

"Ping will know what to do," said Mazer.

"No, he won't," said Bingwen. "I know him. He's from my village. He's strong and willing, but he's not very smart."

"And you are?"

"I'm not asking to be the leader," said Bingwen. "I'm asking for a contingency plan. I'm asking for your expertise in dealing with frightened civilians in a hostile environment. If you don't come back, if help doesn't come, I want to know what we should do."

Mazer smiled. He liked this kid. "Stay here. Help will come." He brought the helmet down over his head and gave Bingwen a thumbs-up.

The HERC flew away, turning to the south. Mazer looked back and saw that Bingwen was still there on the hilltop, standing on the access road, watching them go.

He wants answers I can't give, Mazer thought. He wants something definitive to fall back on. He doesn't know I don't have answers, that there is no contingency plan, that I'm making this up as I go along.

Maybe Shenzu was right, Mazer told himself. What were he and his team accomplishing out here? Saving a few people who very well might have saved themselves? A fully loaded HERC with a combat crew could protect whole villages or cities. Yet here Mazer was, using it as a bus, shuffling people around.

He wasn't thinking big picture. He wasn't thinking about maximizing the resource and saving the greatest number of people. Logic told him to think statistically, to be objective, to abandon this current course and get the HERC back to the Chinese as quickly as possible where they could put it to better use. Yet even as he considered it, he knew he couldn't do it. There was Bingwen. That was one life that hadn't ended because Mazer had been here. Statistics couldn't argue with that.

The lander was in sight now, the top of it still open. A few more Chinese aircraft were circling it. The skimmers and troop carriers had pushed on to places unknown. Mazer looked below them, searching for survivors.

Reinhardt swore.

Mazer looked up. A second column of alien aircraft was shooting up out of the lander, moving as one, twisting and climbing like a swarm. Troop carriers, skimmers. Hundreds of them. A second wave.

"Get us to the ground!"

But even as Mazer gave the order, he knew they wouldn't make it. They were too high, and already the skimmers at the front of the column had reached the column's zenith and were shooting off in every direction, a cluster of them heading straight for the HERC.

The HERC dropped. Alarms sounded as Reinhardt put them into a fast descent.

The skimmers didn't hesitate this time. They opened fire. The HERC should have been obliterated, but somehow, Reinhardt altered their descent at just the right moment to avoid the blasts, which zipped by and exploded somewhere below. Fatani was at the guns, screaming, opening up. One skimmer took a direct hit, spun off, and slammed into another. The two bounced off each other, damaged, broken out of control. Patu was firing as well. Mazer fumbled with the front guns and fired, missing wide as the HERC spun and dropped. The skimmers were on them now. There was a flash, they were hit. The front windshield exploded, heat and shrapnel rushed into the cockpit. Reinhardt slumped forward. The gravlens was out. They were in a dead drop. Wind, fire, alarms. Mazer reached for the stick, his body was weightless, his helmet visor cracked. He was dazed, disoriented—a ringing in his ear. There was a scream of metal and the fire of an engine. A *chop chop chop*. The emergency rotor blades were up and going. They continued to fall, spinning, twisting, the blades wouldn't stop them.

Mazer saw a flash of treetops, heard limbs snapping, felt the heat of fire. Then impact, a violent jolt shook the world apart and left only blackness.


Mazer coughed, a deep painful cough that squeezed his lungs so tight it felt as if they had shriveled like raisins. He was engulfed in black smoke. He couldn't see. He had passed out. He was pressed in tight from all sides, squeezed in a world of balloons. Then the pain hit him, a searing, white hot explosion of pain in his lower abdomen. He cried out, coughed again. He was blind in the smoke.

"Reinhardt!"

No answer.

"Patu! Fatani!"

He heard the crackle and spark of flames, felt the heat of it near him, all around him. He fumbled with his hands, found his harness, unlatched it, coughing, hacking, desperate for clean air. He pushed at the balloons. They gave a little, deflating slightly. Airbags, he realized. He pushed at them again, scrabbling for the door. He couldn't find it. The smoke was suffocating. His lungs were on fire.

The door came free. He tumbled out, falling to the ground. The pain shot through him like a knife, cutting him in half. He put his hand to his abdomen. It came away red, soaked in blood. He was bleeding in other places, too. No time to see where. He had to get the others out. He pressed a hand to the abdominal wound, and the pain was like a thunderclap. He held it there, his world spinning. He steadied, got one foot underneath him, pushing the pain to some other place, some place deep inside. It felt like a charcoal fire had been built inside his stomach. He fought it, focused his mind.

He got the other foot under him. He could barely stand. He saw Patu. She was slumped in her chair, head to the side. He knew at once that she was dead. There was blood and injuries. Her face was lifeless. He staggered to her, wincing, gritting his teeth, putting one foot in front of the other. The flames were growing. The heat was intense. Mazer ignored them. He grabbed the med kit from under Patu's seat and tossed it out. Then he reached up and unfastened the latch on Patu's harness. She fell forward into him. He wasn't ready for it, didn't have the strength for it. They both fell to the ground.

Mazer came to. He had blacked out again, only for an instant, but he had no time to spare and willed himself to wake. It was the pain. It teetered on the point where it was so unbearable that the body shuts down, like a switch has been flipped. Mazer pushed himself up into a sitting position. He grabbed the fabric of Patu's shirt and dragged her toward him, scooting backward on his buttocks, pulling her away from the flames. She was dead weight, her limbs limp, her head lolled to the side, a trail of blood behind her.

The earth exploded to Mazer's right.

A shower of dirt and rocks and heat rained down on him.

Mazer looked up. A skimmer flew by overhead, having just missed him with a burst of its laser fire. The skimmer flew on for a hundred meters then abruptly turned back, changing its course with unnatural speed. It opened up its gun at a distance, unleashing a barrage of laser fire that tore into the downed HERC and slung shrapnel and burning wreckage in every direction. Hard, hot projectiles struck Mazer in the arm, the shoulder; a heavy, burning piece of metal fell across his leg. He cried out. The pain was immediate and unbearable, the heat intense. Panicked, Mazer pulled at his leg, desperate to free himself. But the fabric of his pant leg was snagged on the metal and held him fast. Screaming, burning, his body coursing with pain and adrenaline, he found the strength to sit up, push the metal off him, and pull his leg free.

The skimmer flew by overhead again, but Mazer didn't track it with his eyes this time. He knew it would be coming back. Patu's assault rifle still hung from her shoulder. He had dragged it out here with her. He crawled to it, pulling himself forward in the dirt. A part of him wanted to lie still and let the inevitable happen, to get it over quickly. Better to die in an instant than to suffer a long lingering death from a gut wound out here in the open. He knew help wasn't coming. He knew he wouldn't survive. His wounds were too serious. He was losing too much blood.

But there was the other part of him as well. The soldier. The warrior. The part that had been shaped by drills and exercises and mottos and principles. The bigger part of him, the stubborn, angry, Maori part of him.

He reached the rifle and pulled it free. It was hot to the touch, scorched in places. The screen said it still held three hundred rounds.

Mazer turned over onto his back. Sure enough the skimmer was coming for a third pass. The earth to his left exploded. Rock, dirt, heat. Mazer ignored it. The ground in front of him exploded, partially blocking his view. He waited a millisecond for the debris cloud to disperse, then he pulled the trigger. The gun screamed, shaking in his hands. He didn't have the strength to hold it. He held it anyway. The vibrations felt as if they were ripping him in half inside, which they probably were. He fired anyway. A continuous burst of armor-piercing slugs.

The skimmers weren't as durable as the troop carriers. The bullets ripped through the hull and pinged around inside in a violent ricochet. The rifle clicked empty. The skimmer flew by. Mazer turned his head to watch it pass. It descended rapidly, crashed, rolled, and took out a half-dozen trees before finally coming to rest in the dirt. Mazer watched it a moment. The wreckage smoked and hissed but didn't move and nothing emerged from inside.

Mazer dropped the rifle. He could feel himself going into shock and losing consciousness again. He blinked his eyes, trying to stay awake, to focus, to use what time he could. He turned his head, searching for the med kit. It was there to his right. He reached for it. It was just beyond his fingertips. He didn't have the strength to move any closer to it.

He reached again, straining.

His fingers brushed the handle. He reached again and this time the tips of his fingers curled around the handle and brought it close. It seemed to require an enormous effort. His eyes were heavy. He could feel his strength draining from him like a dying battery. He was going to bleed out. If he didn't stanch the bleeding immediately he was going to bleed out.

His mind went to Kim. She would know exactly what to do here. She would know how to handle this. She would get into that medic mode, that laser-focused place her mind went to whenever there was serious trauma that needed fast, mistake-free action. He had seen her do it several times and marveled at how she could turn off the world that way and move like a preprogrammed machine. No doubting, no indecision, just go go go. Syringe, meds, pressure, equipment. Boom boom boom. Like a soldier. She had saved countless lives that way.

She couldn't save his now.

He fumbled with the latch to the kit until the lid sprang open. He turned it over, and the contents spilled out, giving him a better view of everything. He found the packet he needed. He lifted it and brought the corner of it to his teeth, ripping the packet open and spitting out the torn edge. He pulled up his shirt and poured the powder in and around the wound. It burned, and he nearly lost his grip on the thing. But he held on and emptied the packet. Next came the wound gel. Mazer unscrewed the large cap and scooped the gel out with his fingers. Gingerly he spread the thick gel over the wound. The anesthetic worked almost immediately. Like a valve of pain had suddenly been turned to a lower setting. He couldn't see the wound in his arm and shoulder, but his arm felt dead now. He scooped more of the gel and lathered it around the general area, not even sure if he was doing any good.

The gauze was self-sealing. He had the packet out. He tried to bring it to his lips to rip it open, but his hands weren't working right anymore. They were heavy and clumsy and too weak to hold anything. The world was fuzzy at the edges. The sounds of the fire and the wind were fading.

He didn't want to sleep. If he slept, he wouldn't wake up.

But the sleep pulled at him, lulled him, and in his mind he saw Kim kneeling over him and sadly shaking her head. Sorry, my love, she seemed to be saying. This one is beyond even me.

# CHAPTER 16

# Last Chance

The latest transmission from Luna came in, and Victor read it aloud. Imala floated nearby, listening. Landers had set down in China. They had carried skimmers and troop carriers and flyers. The aliens were spraying defoliants all along the countryside, killing vegetation and crops and civilians, leaving everything to rot in the sun. Flyers from the landers were dumping bacteria in the South China Sea, killing marine life. The Chinese Air Force was creaming the flyers, but the land war was a different story. Air strikes against the landers were completely ineffective. The landers were shielded somehow. Direct hits inflicted no damage whatsoever. Chinese ground troops were engaging the aliens in the open, but always at heavy losses. Early estimates put casualty numbers in the thousands.

Victor stopped reading, turned to the monitor, and started digging through the ship's archives for a map. "Where is China exactly?" he said.

"You don't know where China is?" Imala said.

He turned to her, his cheeks flushing, embarrassed and angry. "No, Imala. I don't know where China is. I've never been to Earth, remember?"

She blinked. "Of course. Sorry. Here, I'll show you."

She came forward, but he put up a hand, stopping her. "You know what? Never mind. I'll find it myself." He turned back to the monitor. As soon as he did so, he regretted it. He was being overly sensitive, rude even. Imala was trying to help, and he was snapping at her because he was ashamed of his own ignorance. He rubbed his eyes, waited for the hot flush of embarrassment to subside from his face, then turned around to apologize. Imala was on the other side of the shuttle with her back to him now, rereading the news feeds on the other monitor. Victor opened his mouth to speak, but then said nothing. She was probably angry with him. She had every right to be.

He turned back to his monitor and dug around until he found a map of Earth. It took him a few minutes to decipher it. The map had been designed for commercial ships moving between Luna and Earth, so it was loaded with superfluous information like trade routes and atmospheric entry and exit vectors. Victor made all that invisible and then found China quickly. It was a big country.

The map included several wiki entries, and Victor read through them, feeling more ignorant by the moment. He had known China was a country— there had been a few Chinese corporate miners in the Kuiper Belt. But China's nationhood had been the extent of his knowledge on the subject. He had not known that China was in a continent called Asia, or that it was the most populated country in the world, or that the Chinese language spoken by the corporates was actually one of many variations of Chinese, or that the language was written in ridiculously difficult to decipher characters instead of letters. In other words, he hadn't known what every schoolchild on Earth probably knew.

Again, he felt stupid and frustrated. How was he supposed to get into a university when he couldn't even name the continents? An admissions committee would laugh him to scorn. All their perceptions of free miners as dumb, bumbling grease heads was true. It wasn't a stereotype, it was him.

Oh sure, he could fix things. He could take a busted water pump and rebuild it with nothing but scrap metal and discarded circuits, but he couldn't tell you the capital of Japan. And now that he thought about it, he wasn't even certain Japan was a country. Was it a state somewhere? Or a province? He looked it up.

Country.

Yeah, you're a real brain, Victor. A genius.

He was sure Mother had taught him all of this at some point. He remembered lessons on geography when he was little. But he had been, what, seven years old at the time.

Then again, maybe he had missed that lesson. He had started apprenticing with Father at a young age, much younger than was the norm. So he had been absent for a lot of the classes. Mother and Father had argued about it. Mother had wanted Victor to stay with the other children and sit through the lessons, but Father had wanted Victor's help and had said that the survival of the family took precedence. Mother had been insistent however; Father would just have to find someone else.

Father had tried that, using a fifteen-year-old boy for a while named Gregor. But it hadn't worked out. Gregor had initially been assigned to the kitchen, and it soon became clear to Father why. "The boy doesn't think," Father had said. "He's slow. He can't work his way through a repair. The parts are all pieces to him. He can't see how they go together, how they intertwine and function as one."

"So teach him," Mother had said.

"I'm trying," Father had said. "That's the problem. I spend half my day trying to drill a simple principle into the kid's head, and the other half of the day I'm redoing what he did wrong. I'm losing time. And all the while, this ship is continuing to break down. I've got a backlog of work orders now, some of them critical. This kid isn't helping. He's dragging me down. I do more without him. I need Victor."

And so on special repairs—ones that needed a second person to hold a pipe while Father tightened it, or ones that needed a tiny child's hand to reach into a small space and remove something—Victor had tagged along. At first these had been exceptions, but slowly, over time, Father had become more and more dependent on Victor until Victor was going with Father more than he was going to class. And then eventually, without anyone acknowledging it aloud, Victor was going with Father every day.

So perhaps Mother had taught all the children about China, and Victor had simply been elsewhere on the ship at the time, crawling through an HVAC duct or squeezed into an engine room or packed tight beside a water heater, making some repair to keep the ship moving and the family alive.

"I didn't mean to offend you, Vico," said Imala. "I was just surprised you had never heard of China before."

She was behind him, hovering there, which of course only made him blush again. He should have apologized earlier. It should be him instigating this conversation. He turned around, not caring now if she saw how embarrassed he was. "I've heard of China, Imala. I just didn't know anything about it. I shouldn't have snapped at you. I was out of line. I'm sorry." He sighed. "I just can't help but feel like an idiot. I should know all of these things about Earth, but I don't."

"You're space born, Vico. Earth has never been your world. You grew up on a ship in the Kuiper Belt. You think I know anything about the Kuiper Belt? I couldn't tell you two facts about the Deep." She smiled. "Let's help each other. Isn't that how a free-miner family works? Everybody has their expertise, and you work together, sharing skills and information. Stronger together than alone, and all that?"

He smiled. It should be him making this argument. He should be the peacemaker. "That's the gist of it, yes. Although if we were a real miner family, we'd also be yelling at each other and threatening to kill each other. You'd be calling me a pig-faced rockhead, and I'd be crying and saying how I wished I'd never been born in this family."

She held her smile. "Something tells me your family isn't like that."

He shrugged. "Not usually, but we have our moments. It wasn't a very big ship. When you have that many people in that tight of a space, everyone's faults are glaringly obvious. Believe me, we had our disagreements."

In truth, El Cavador had never felt tight or close-quartered to Victor. It was simply the life he knew. People crammed in together to sleep. That's what you did. You stacked four or five or even six hammocks on top of each other—so close together that turning over in your sleep would likely brush your hammock up against someone else's. It wasn't always comfortable—there were smells and other annoyances occasionally—but that's how you lived.

Now that Victor had spent time on Luna, now that he understood Imala's world and all the space it afforded, he realized how confining this shuttle must seem to her. It made her sacrifice to accompany him all the more selfless and significant. She was doing this for him, suffering for him, and he was acting ungrateful.

"Let's dock at the depot," he said. "A few umbilicals have opened up. Let's go inside and stretch our legs. We'll take a holopad and read the feeds in there for a while."

"They're charging ridiculous docking prices," said Imala. "They bill you by the hour. We don't have that kind of money."

"I do," said Victor.

"Yeah, money for your education."

"Which I'm not likely to get. Please, Imala, let me buy you lunch. We could both use a breather."

They docked and floated down the umbilical to the café. There were few people inside. Victor launched toward a table near the back, away from everyone else, and strapped himself in. Imala followed, and soon a waitress floated over.

Victor looked at the menu, but then returned it to the waitress. "Would you do a specialty order?"

"Depends," said the waitress.

"White rice, black beans, shredded beef, fried *platanos,* and an *arepa* with butter."

The waitress looked up from her wrist pad. "I don't know what *platanos* and *arepas* are, so we probably don't have those."

Victor wasn't sure what the English word was, so he looked it up on the holo. "*Platanos* are plantains. You know, like giant bananas, only starchier?"

The waitress looked annoyed. "I know what a plantain is."

"Do you have any?"

"I'll have to check. What's an *arepa*?"

He had been looking it up. It wasn't in the dictionary, which meant it was unique to Venezuela and had no English equivalent. "It's a round corn patty, maybe four to five inches across. Really thick, not thin like a tortilla. They're not hard to make."

"They are if you've never made one before. I'll have to check." She turned to Imala. "Let's hope you're easier."

"I'll have the same as him," said Imala.

The waitress sighed. "Of course you will."

She floated back toward the kitchen.

"A family dish?" asked Imala.

"The unofficial plate of Venezuela, where my family's from. We ate it all the time on the ship, although truth be told, we usually ate it without the shredded beef and plantains. Both were practically nonexistent in the Kuiper Belt. Our diet was more about quantity than quality. We ate whatever was cheapest and would last the longest. Sometimes we'd eat nothing but rice and beans for weeks on end. Even your sweat starts smelling like beans after a while."

Imala scrunched up her nose.

"Sorry," said Victor. "Not good table conversation."

She smiled. "You miss your family."

Victor was folding his napkin into odd little shapes just to keep his hands busy. "Yes. I do. Very much."

"We'll find them, Vico. We'll get you back to them."

Victor sighed and looked up at her. "I'm not sure that we should now."

"That's why we came out here, isn't it?"

"I'm saying everything is different now, Imala. Everything we hoped and prayed wouldn't happen is happening. I never thought it would come this far. I thought I'd give the world the evidence, and they would respond, they would do something to prevent it from getting this bad."

"That's not your fault, Victor. You gave the evidence. The world didn't listen. You can't blame yourself for that."

"Well I do, Imala. If I had done more, if I had—"

"What else could you have done? You were hurt, barely alive. Your body had wasted away to nothing. You were under arrest. You couldn't go anywhere. All things considered, I'd say you did a bang-up job."

"If it had been someone else, the world would've listened. If my father had come—"

"Your father wouldn't have survived the trip. No one would have found the data cube. Or if they did, they would've thrown it away. The world would've been caught totally unawares."

"Their current situation isn't any better."

"Yes, it is," said Imala. "We don't know all the ways people have been preparing, Vico. We can't see everything. I can assure you. There are armies out there that have been training for this because of you."

"Yes, and I want to join them."

She looked surprised. "You want to join the military?"

He felt stung by her obvious disbelief again. "I'm eighteen, Imala. I'm old enough to enlist."

"Yes, but with what army? You're not a citizen of any country, Vico. You're space born. No one will take you."

"This is a fight against the human race, Imala. Last time I checked I was human."

She shook her head. "It's not that black and white, Vico. Earth doesn't work that way."

"Well why not? Why does everything have to be so constricted by regulations? It drives me insane. If there's a problem, you fix it. You don't set up fences around it and make rules about how it should be fixed. You fix it. Maybe that requires a little bit of ingenuity and doing it a way that's never been done before, but so what. If the problem's solved, why does it matter how it's done?"

"This isn't the Kuiper Belt, Vico. You can't do whatever you want and expect people to agree to your terms. There has to be an order to things."

"And look what that order has done for Earth, Imala. Look at the situation now. Stagnation. Infighting. Disagreements. Inaction. And thousands of people dead on the sidelines."

"So what, you think you can waltz in, join the military, and fix the problem?"

"I'm not useless, you know. I have skills I can offer."

"Of course you do. But that doesn't change the fact that the system is what it is. I doubt NATO would even take you."

"What's NATO?"

"An intergovernmental military alliance. A bunch of countries who agree on defense measures and military action as a combined force."

"Why aren't they doing anything already?"

"I'm guessing they will, eventually, though not in China. Not unless the Chinese change their mind and allow outside troops, which isn't likely to happen any time soon. NATO will be focused on space, taking out the mothership."

"That's perfect for me. I'm built for space. That's where I can help."

"If they'll take you," said Imala, "which I doubt they will. And even if they did take you, you're not likely to see action any time soon. They'll want to train you, specialize you, shape you into what they need you to be."

"Fine. As long as I'm helping."

She watched him for a moment. "Are you sure about this?"

"I wasn't five minutes ago, but I am now, yes."

"And what if we go back and NATO won't take you?"

"Then I'll do my own thing."

She laughed. "Your own thing? Meaning what? Take on the mothership by yourself?"

"If I have to."

Imala laughed again, and then her smile faded. "You can't be serious."

"Why not? Why should we sit back and accept someone else's inaction or failure? I have just as much right to protect the human race as they do."

"And how do you propose to take on the mothership by yourself, if you don't mind me asking?"

"I have no idea. I haven't thought that far ahead yet."

"And what about your family?"

"I'm doing this *for* my family, Imala. If we lose Earth, we lose everything. How long do you think miners would last without supplies? If Earth loses, my family loses."

"The landers are only in China, Vico. Earth is a big planet. It doesn't hang in the balance just yet. We don't even know what the aliens want."

"The report said the aliens were dropping bacteria into the sea, right?"

"Yeah. So?"

"Why would they do that?"

"Kill marine life? I don't know."

"Terraforming, Imala. They're seeding bacteria in the oceans for the same reason they're using defoliants to kill all plants and animals. They want the planet. They want Earth. But they can't have it in its current state. It has to be a planet that conforms to their biology, not ours. All existing life in the sea, all biology on land, evolved here without them. That makes it hazardous to them. They don't have natural defenses against our biota. Our strains of bacteria are different from theirs. So they're going to change Earth to be more like the world they do know. They're going to burn it down and start all over. If we were going to seize a planet, we would do the same thing. We'd drop stuff in the atmosphere, wipe out all existing biological life, seed Earth-born plants and animals, make the new planet as much like Earth as we could. It's the ecosystem we were engineered for. Why else would they have come, Imala? Why else would they be acting the way they are? They don't want to communicate with us. They don't want to negotiate. They're not going to ask us for Earth. They're already taking it. And I've seen these creatures, Imala. I've seen how they attack and how they think, how relentless they are. If they can land on Earth, if missiles and weapons can't hurt them, they won't quit until Earth is theirs."

The waitress floated back over. She wasn't carrying any food. She looked embarrassed. "I'm sorry, but I'm going to have to ask both of you to leave."

"Why?" said Imala.

"Someone is renting out the entire depot. They want everyone else off."

"We paid a docking fee," said Victor. "We just got here."

"I know. I'm sorry. We'll refund the fee."

"Why does someone need the entire depot?" asked Imala. "Do they have that many people in their party?"

"No," said the waitress. "There are just the two of them. They docked a few minutes ago. They said they needed their privacy. I guess when you have that kind of money, you can do whatever you please."

"Who is it?" asked Imala.

"Lem Jukes," said the waitress.

# CHAPTER 17

# Transmissions

The supply depot was exactly what Lem had expected it to be: a dump. A sad excuse for an outpost that didn't appear to have been renovated since the first days of space commerce. The whole structure looked like it might break apart at any moment. There were metal plates crudely welded at random spots all along the inner walls, supposedly sealing off leaks or breaches that had occurred over the years. There were lines of grime where all the walls met, as if the mops they used to clean the place didn't reach the corners. There were several old neon signs for brands of alcohol or travel food that Lem had never heard of and that probably didn't exist anymore. None of the signs were turned on. Lem doubted any of them could.

All this gave the lobby a scarred, postapocalyptic vibe and made Lem more than a little uneasy. He was suddenly wishing he had come in a spacesuit just in case the whole thing split apart and dumped him and Chubs out into the black.

"Mr. Jukes. A pleasure to have you. Welcome. Welcome."

A thin, balding man was floating toward them from across the room. The proprietor. Lem disliked him immediately. He was the kind of person you could read in a blink. False expression, false demeanor, false cadence in his voice. Everything about him said dishonest.

The man's clothes weren't helping either. They had been fashionable at one point, years ago, but never together. The pants and shirt screamed at each other, fighting for attention, one fluffy and exploding outward with fabric, the other tight and form fitting. It was like he had won both in two different poker games and had convinced himself they were a matching set.

The man caught a handhold nearby and righted himself so that he had the same orientation as Lem and Chubs.

"Felix Montroose, Mr. Jukes. At your service. Welcome to Last Chance."

"The price we settled on over laserline will have to be renegotiated," said Lem.

Felix's face fell a little, though to his credit, he tried hard not to show it. "Oh? How do you mean, sir?"

"I mean I'm not paying you what I told you before. I was expecting a nicer establishment." He gestured to the room. "No offense, but I don't exactly feel safe here."

Felix smiled. "Oh, I assure you, Mr. Jukes. Last Chance is one of the most structurally sound outposts this side of the Belt. She was built in the early days, you know, back when ships were made by hand."

"Yes, and she should be dismantled by hand. I'll give you half of our original price."

Felix gave a sharp intake of breath and put a hand to his chest, aghast.

Lem suppressed a smile. He wasn't even sure why he was being a stickler about the money. It was hardly a large amount. Lem's investments had likely made that much in the time it had taken him and Chubs to dock the shuttle from their ship.

Yet Lem also hated it when people thought they could take advantage of him. It was silly, he knew, but he had always carried the belief that people assumed he was a less intelligent, weaker shadow of his father. And as such, he would be easy prey in a transaction. It made Lem more than a little shrewd. At the negotiation table he was downright deplorable, showing far less mercy even than Father at times. But it also made him a brilliant businessman and was largely the reason he had amassed such a large fortune independent of Father.

"That strikes me as most dishonest, sir," said Felix. "We had an arranged amount. We agreed upon the terms. I've ordered all other patrons off the depot to give you the privacy you requested. I will not settle for anything less than the predetermined sum."

"And I will not settle for anything less than a decent establishment. I suppose that puts us at an impasse. Good day to you, Mr. Montroose."

Lem turned on his heels and made as if to launch for the docking airlock.

"Wait," said Montroose. "Surely we can reach an agreeable amount. I remind you that we are the only laserline link with Luna. You can't get a message through any other way."

"My message isn't critical. I'm on my way to Luna now. I can wait to deliver it in person. Besides, from the reports I've heard in the Belt, your bucket-brigade system isn't as foolproof as you implied. I should expect heavy data deterioration."

Felix waffled then, seeing his sale slip away. He and Lem argued for a moment on the price, and when they finally agreed, Felix dabbed at his forehead with a handkerchief, as if he had just surfaced from a feverish bout with an enemy, which, Lem supposed, he had.

"And I have your absolute assertion that the ships in your bucket brigade will relay my conversation with Luna as promised?" said Lem. "I don't want my messages held hostage, Mr. Montroose. I assure you that a legal battle with Juke Limited attorneys would result in you losing everything, including your personal freedom as a result of the criminal charges they would place against you."

Montroose swallowed and checked his watch, as if this whole affair couldn't end soon enough.

Lem tapped the amount into his wrist pad and held out his hand. Felix extended his own, and the two bumped pads. There was a transaction sound, and then Lem smiled. "Now, Mr. Montroose, I would appreciate you escorting me to your laserline transmitter."

Montroose began leading them to the far side of the room toward another corridor.

"Murderer!"

There was shouting behind them. Lem turned. A man and two women were approaching from the opposite entryway. One of the women looked at a loss, as if she had tried to stop the other two, but failed. The man was hardly a man at all, now that Lem got a look at him. Seventeen, maybe, if that. And by the look of his clothes, Lem pegged him as a free miner. Great. More grievances. Another angry rock sucker wronged by Juke employees. Lem was tired of this business. Every pebble picker who heard he was Lem Jukes always came rushing to complain as if it had been his personal fault. Must he bear the burden of every act committed by his father's men?

The boy was coming fast, but Lem didn't flinch. He didn't have to. The gun was in Chubs's hand before the boy had crossed half the room. The boy saw it and caught himself on a handhold near the ceiling. His body swung forward with the momentum and then he righted himself, his eyes boring straight into Lem. The two women stopped beside him.

Lem smiled at the boy, amused. "My goodness, but you are angry."

"I'm sorry, Mr. Montroose," said one of the women. "I tried to get these two back to their shuttle, but they wouldn't listen."

"What is the meaning of this?" demanded Felix, facing the boy. "Get out of here! You've been asked to leave."

The boy never took his eyes off Lem. "I paid to be here."

"And your money will be returned." He waved his arms, as if shooing off a wild animal. "Now get out. Both of you. Leave Mr. Jukes alone."

The boy spoke directly to Lem. His voice was calm, but there was steel behind it. "I wouldn't expect you to remember me, Lem. I doubt you got a good look at my face before you hit me."

Lem suddenly felt uneasy. There was something about this situation that didn't sit well. "Mr. Montroose, will you and your employee please excuse us?"

Felix looked at Lem with surprise. "Are you sure, Mr. Jukes? I can have this boy thrown out."

"Thank you, but that won't be necessary. Some privacy is all we need."

Felix looked unsure, then motioned for the woman to follow him. They went out the way the boy had come in and sealed the door behind them.

Lem regarded the boy and the woman with him. They were an odd pair. The woman was a few years older, though still quite young, midtwenties maybe, and ethnic, perhaps Native American. The boy was a Belter, no question.

"You clearly know who I am," said Lem. "But I don't have the pleasure of knowing you."

The boy just stared, seething.

"I'm Imala," said the woman. "Imala Bootstamp. This is Victor Delgado."

The names meant nothing to Lem. "Victor, I think you may have me confused with someone else. I don't hit people. Not in my nature. I don't even know how to throw a punch."

"Not with your hand. With your ship. Asteroid 2002GJ166. Kuiper Belt. Ten months or so ago. You killed a man. This ringing a bell?"

Lem felt the blood drain from his face.

"You killed Marco. He was my uncle. He had a wife and children."

Lem's mind was racing. He wanted to believe that this was blackmail somehow, that someone had heard about the bump with El Cavador, and that they were now trying to take Lem for money by acting like a member of the crew. Lem wished that were the case. Blackmailers he could handle. Chubs might even have a special treatment for them.

But he knew it wasn't true. The kid wasn't lying. Lem could spot a dishonest person in a blink.

But how was that possible? Lem had seen El Cavador destroyed. Every man on El Cavador had died in the assault on the Formic ship. Lem had watched it happen. The women and children had been placed on the WU-HU ship, but this kid wouldn't have gone with them. He was too old. He would have stayed with the men. He *was* a man. He would have joined in the assault.

And then Lem remembered. "You're the one they sent. The one who was supposed to warn Earth." Lem had dropped the suave exterior. Now he was panicked. "What the hell are you doing here? You should be on Luna or Earth. You should be telling them what we know, sharing the evidence. Why didn't you push on?"

The boy stared at him, confused now, his anger evaporated. "How do you know my family sent me?"

"Because they told me. They told me they sent you in a quickship. I didn't expect you to survive, quite frankly. I figured you were a lost cause. But you obviously made it. You shouldn't be here, though. You should be home. You should've gone to my father."

"We did," said Imala. "We saw your father. Victor's evidence is why Ukko made the announcement."

Lem felt as if a hundred things were bouncing around in his head at once. "What announcement? What are you talking about?"

"That the alien ship was coming," said Imala. "It was your father who told the world and alerted STASA."

Of course, thought Lem. Father would pounce on something like this. It was the perfect opportunity to paint himself the hero and tout the company's strength. Lem could almost picture Father all over the news feeds, humbly offering up all of Juke's resources to "protect Earth from harm."

"When did my family tell you about me?" Victor said.

It was then that Lem realized that Victor knew nothing about what had happened, which should have been immediately obvious to Lem. Of course Victor didn't know. How could he? He had left before El Cavador contacted Lem, before the attack on the Formic ship, before . . .

He looked at Victor. Logic said not to tell him. Victor was a loose end. He was a witness to Lem's attack on El Cavador. And not only that, but he had also been directly assaulted. He was the person Lem had rammed with the ship right before they had stopped. That set off a whirlwind of legal alarms inside Lem's head. Victor was every corporate lawyer's nightmare. And what was worse, Victor sounded as if he were already an international figure. He had brought the warning to Earth. There was notoriety there, which would skyrocket any legal issues to the forefront of the news. The fallout would be enormous. In corporate terms, cataclysmic. It was all of Lem's buried fears risen from the grave.

He knew how Father would handle it. Lem had never heard of his father ending someone's life, but that was probably because Father was too smart to ever reveal his intentions to do such a thing. That didn't mean Father wouldn't do it. In fact, it was far more likely that Father had. You don't get to a position like his without cracking a few eggs. And Lem had to admit he saw the logic of it. There wasn't a more absolute and final resolution to a problem. Stop the heart of the problem, the physical beating organ, and you've stopped the problem, too.

Only here it would be messy. There were two of them. And this was a public place.

Lem pushed the thought away. I am not my father, he told himself. Not now, not ever.

He squared his shoulders and faced Victor. "Your family contacted me after you left. They were heading to Weigh Station Four when it was destroyed by the Formics."

"Formics?" said Imala.

"The name we've given the aliens," said Lem.

"Are they all right?" said Victor, his voice almost frantic. "My family, I mean. Were they hurt?"

"They asked us to join them in an assault on the Formic ship. Us and a third ship, a WU-HU vessel."

Victor's face was grave, as if he knew what was coming.

"The women and children from El Cavador were placed on the WU-HU ship, which stayed out of the fight. The men and Concepción manned El Cavador. We tried to plant explosives on the Formics' hull, but one went off prematurely. It ripped through the hull, and the Formics came pouring out. I lost twenty-five men. El Cavador was destroyed. We barely got out with our lives. I don't know what happened to the WU-HU vessel. I'm pretty sure they were at a safe distance, but there was too much interference. We lost contact with them. I'm sorry."

Victor stared. All the life seemed to have drained out of him. His hands were trembling. If he weren't already floating in zero-G, Lem doubted Victor would've stayed on his feet. Imala put an arm around him, and Victor buried his face in his hands.

Lem moved for the door. He needed to get out. He was invading privacy now. Chubs followed. Outside they found Felix alone in the corridor, waiting.

"To your transmitter, Mr. Montroose," said Lem. "And this time, let's get there without interruption."

There were a few technicians in the comms room, which was impressive considering it was the size of a closet. They all hovered at different orientations around the transmission equipment so as to maximize space. "These men are at your service, Mr. Jukes," said Montroose.

"Tell them to leave," said Lem.

Felix blushed. "Of course." He shooed the men out then turned back to Lem. "I take it you're familiar with this type of equipment then."

Lem looked at everything with distaste. Some of the panels were as old as he was. He had wanted to do the transmission from Makarhu, his own ship, but Felix had insisted that that wouldn't be possible. All of the ships in the bucket brigade were using "closed-circuit transmitters" and the messages would have to be sent from here.

It was probably a lie, of course. Felix had merely wanted Lem here as an assurance of getting paid.

"We'll manage," said Lem. "Assuming your equipment doesn't catch fire."

Felix laughed until he realized it hadn't been intended as a joke. He cleared his throat and said, "The bucket brigade is standing by, Mr. Jukes. They will relay whatever message you send. I've given them strict instructions not to read the text or try to correct any deterioration."

"They can't read it," said Lem. "It will be encrypted."

"Oh," said Felix. "Of course. Shall I leave you then?"

"Please."

Felix bowed and backed out the door. Chubs was already setting up the encryption equipment, attaching it to the necessary panels. Then he got out a sniffer wand and passed it around the room.

"It's clean," he said.

So no one was eavesdropping. Lem nodded, and Chubs went out into the hall to keep Montroose from snooping.

Lem entered the coordinates and commands that would send the message from Luna's receiver into an encrypted relay system that went directly to Father's handheld. It would be a tedious process. There would be a lot of lag time. Lem would send three copies of each message, so that if data was lost by one, it would be filled in by the second or third transmission, hopefully making the messages appear seamless. Then Father would dictate a reply, and the process would go in reverse. If this actually worked, Lem was going to be here a while. He spoke into the dictation device, starting small.

"Father, it's Lem."

An hour later he received a reply. It came faster than he expected. THANK GOD!! I'VE BEEN WORRIED SICK. WHERE ARE YOU?

Lem read the words several times, and his heart lifted. Father had worried about him. Lem had known that of course. He knew Father would be concerned, but to hear, or rather read, those words made it more real somehow. He found it so surprising in fact, that he began to wonder if it was really Father on the other end. Maybe one of the ships along the chain had figured out the encryption and was impersonating Father in the hope of garnering valuable information. Lem decided to play it safe. He sent one word.

"Apple."

"For crying out loud, Lem. It's me. Your father. You're using my encrypted line. You're sending an encrypted message. You don't have to use the stupid corporate code words for verification. Now you've wasted two damn hours, and you still haven't answered my question. WHERE ARE YOU?!!"

It was Father all right.

For the next message Lem started talking and didn't stop for forty minutes. The dictation software turned it all into a lengthy e-mail. He told Father how they had bumped El Cavador off the asteroid; how the bump had resulted in the death of a free miner; how they had successfully decimated the asteroid with the glaser; how they had encountered El Cavador again and conducted an assault on the Formic ship; how they had failed and lost men and rushed back toward Luna; how they had found evidence of the Battle of the Belt; how they were only a week away; how they had decelerated to the depot to make sure there was still a Luna to come home to. He didn't tell Father everything, such as his struggles on the ship to keep authority.

Any lingering doubt about it being Father on the other end vanished when the reply came.

"I've always known you to be an intelligent person, Lem, so I can't for the life of me begin to understand what would compel you to do something so monumentally stupid, so enormously idiotic as bumping a free-miner ship off an asteroid. I don't care that the next closest asteroid was four months away. I would much rather have you sit on your butt during an eight-month round-trip than have you risk damaging a piece of equipment worth several billion credits. What were you thinking? Did you not consider what such a violent jolt might have done to the glaser? Did it not cross your mind for a second that the glaser is more precious to this company than your time? It's a prototype, Lem. One of a kind. For your sake, I hope it's in perfect working condition. If it isn't, you will have a hard time proving to our attorneys that your jolt isn't responsible."

Lem shook his head. So like Father. No mention of the dead free miner. No congratulations for having conducted a successful test. No praise for having gone the extra mile and figuring out a way to extract the minerals from the debris cloud. No inquiry as to the safety of the crew. All Father worried about was his precious glaser.

And then to have the gall to threaten Lem with legal action? All the bitterness and frustration he felt for Father began to well up inside him again.

But then Lem reread the last sentence of the message and saw another meaning. Father might be insinuating that he didn't have control over the legal team, that his grip on command of the company might be slipping. That gave Lem a small measure of delight. Lem still fully intended to seize the company, and any potential weakness in Father's standing was welcome news.

Another message from Father appeared.

"I like the name 'Formic,' by the way. No one has given the species a name that sticks. Everyone keeps saying 'aliens,' which I've always thought is a ridiculous word. Formic I can get behind. A nice hard *K* sound at the end. And I like the connection with ants. Tell Benyawe we're going with that. I'll have it on the networks in the morning. As for the skirmish with the Formic ship, you did good. I'm glad you're alive. Once again, it was astronomically stupid, but it demonstrated great courage. I'm sad it didn't work. Had you stopped the ship, you could have prevented a lot of heartache and disaster. Thousands are dying in China. It's surreal."

Father was answering Lem's message in pieces, probably responding to it as he read it. Again, it was classic Father. Give an inkling of praise and then squash it with stated disappointment. It took courage, then "had you stopped it, all these people wouldn't have died." As if it were Lem's fault that the Formics were killing civilians, as if all those deaths were on Lem's hands because he had failed in the battle.

Nobody else would probably read it that way, Lem knew, but nobody knew Father as well as he did. Pat you on the back with one hand, stab you in the back with the other.

A third message. A short one.

"Send me the names of the crewmen you lost. I want to notify their families immediately."

It surprised Lem. A bit of humanity from Father. Lem hadn't intended to share that information, but of course he should have. He had been the insensitive one this time. Why hadn't he thought of that? It should have been the first thing he shared.

Lem typed in the names he remembered. Only two-thirds of them came to mind, and some of those were probably wrong. Was it O'Brien or O'Ryan? Canterglast? Or Caunterglast? He needed to get the spelling right for Father to find them in the company's database and look up the next of kin. Lem searched through his holopad. The names weren't there. Embarrassed, he stepped out into the hall and found Chubs, hovering by the door. Lem explained the situation.

"I'll type them in for you," said Chubs. He pulled himself into the room and tapped away at the keyboard, making corrections to the names Lem had put in and adding in the ones Lem had forgotten. No hesitating, no stopping to jog his memory; the names just came out of him. He knew these people. They had meant something to him.

He finished. "There you go."

Lem didn't meet his eye, embarrassed. "Thank you."

"You ready for some food? You've been in here a few hours."

"Please," said Lem.

Chubs nodded and left. Lem watched him go, feeling a pang of guilt for having taken away the man's authority. Chubs deserved to be the captain. He knew the crew. They respected him, followed him.

Lem pushed the thought away. Chubs would have his reward. When the company was Lem's, he would need good men, and if Chubs were willing, Lem would have him at his side.

Lem closed the door and pushed send. Ten minutes later Chubs returned with a container of pasta. "Don't expect much from this. The café is no better than the lobby."

Lem offered his thanks and said, "What happened to the free miner? Victor and Imala?"

"They left. Their shuttle took off toward Luna or Earth. I had the ship track them for as long as we could. I figured if you had wanted me to stop them you would have said so in the lobby."

Lem nodded, wondering what Chubs meant exactly by "stop them." Had Chubs killed for Father before? Would he have killed for Lem if Lem had asked?

Lem ate in silence. When he finished, a final message from Father came through.

"I've been talking with the Board. Get to Luna in eight days. That's a Tuesday. Come to the Juke north port at three p.m. Luna time. I'll be waiting for you. I need your help with this Formic situation, son. We've got work to do."

Lem reread the message. Father was actually asking for his help. The great Jukes was actually admitting that Lem had something to contribute, that the two of them would work as a team. He had even called Lem "son."

For half a second Lem believed it was genuine. Then all rational thought returned. Father was intending to use him somehow. That was obvious. How, Lem wasn't sure, but experience had taught Lem to expect the worst and be on guard. He shook his head. You laid it on too thick, Father. Calling me "son"? You're getting sloppy in your old age.

Lem typed. "Understood. Leaving now."

He waited for the message to send, then he logged off. His messages had passed through each of the ships in the bucket brigade as encrypted messages, so he wasn't worried about those. But he had entered them as original text here. The system immediately had encrypted them, but somewhere on the memory drive was the original text. Lem couldn't allow that. He took the surge device from the packet at his hip, plugged it into the system, and pressed the button, melting all the circuits. There were a few harmless sparks, a bit of smoke, and everything shut down.

Lem and Chubs found Felix back in the lobby near the docking airlock.

Felix was all smiles. "Mr. Jukes, I take it you were able to contact Luna?"

"It worked fine, thank you," Lem said, extending his wrist pad. "Here, Mr. Montroose, allow me to pay you more for your troubles."

Felix blinked, surprised. "How kind."

Lem bumped the two wrist pads together, making the transfer, then Montroose read the sum.

"Mr. Jukes! My goodness. Thank you. This is most generous!"

"That's probably two to three times what a new transmitter will cost you," said Lem. "The rest of it you can use to pay some good technicians to install it for you."

Felix was hardly listening now. He was staring at the numbers on his wrist pad.

Lem and Chubs floated into the airlock.

"He doesn't understand," said Chubs. "He doesn't know we just fried his current system."

"He'll find out soon enough," said Lem.

# CHAPTER 18

# Rescue

Bingwen stared at the place where Mazer's aircraft had fallen below the horizon, willing it to come back up again. He knew it wouldn't happen. He had seen everything. He had watched Mazer's aircraft take the hit. He had seen the antigrav give out. He had witnessed it drop like a bag of rice out of the sky. A cluster of alien crafts had dived after it, firing at it, pounding it downward. Those ships had dipped below the horizon as well. But a moment later, they had come up and flown on. Mazer's hadn't. Instead, a line of black smoke rose, twisting upward like a charmed snake.

Bingwen sprinted back into the farmhouse. "They went down! We've got to help them."

Everyone turned toward him. Grandfather shuffled over, hunched slightly. "Who, Bingwen?"

"The soldiers. The ones who brought us here. A new column of ships rose up out of the big disc. Hundreds of little ships. They're everywhere. They shot down the soldiers. Their plane went down over there, to the south." He pointed. "We need to get over there. They need our help."

No one moved. The old woman who had given the soldiers clothes bowed her head and offered a prayer. The others looked worried and defeated again. The small light of hope the soldiers had given them was extinguished in an instant. Grandfather put a hand on Bingwen's shoulder and kneeled in front of him. "There's nothing we can do, Bingwen."

Bingwen recoiled a step, shrugging off Grandfather's hand. "They saved my life." He turned toward the others. "They saved all of our lives. Aren't we going to do something?"

No one spoke.

Grandfather's voice was calm. He reached out again. "Bingwen, listen—"

"No," Bingwen said, jumping back. He took a few steps away, facing everyone. "We can't leave them out there to die."

"If they were shot down, they're already dead," said another of the women. "There's nothing we can do."

"We don't know that," said Bingwen. "They might be hurt. I saw where it went down. I can take us straight there."

The old man with the bag of clothes said, "They said they would be coming back. They said they would send help our way. Doctors and supplies. Now help won't be coming."

"He's right," said his wife. "No one is coming with supplies now."

"Is anyone even listening to me?" said Bingwen.

"We listened, boy," said the old woman. "You told us what we needed to know, now let the grown-ups talk for a minute."

The teenage girl was at the open windows, looking down at the valley below. "Look," she said, pointing downward. Everyone came over. Bingwen muscled his way to the front and looked down. Several of the alien aircraft had landed in the valley and opened their doors. Aliens were stepping out into the rice fields, shooting out mists from their backpacks. The rice shoots withered and turned black as the mist wafted over them. The aliens were over three hundred meters away, well out of earshot, but the old woman spoke in a hushed tone anyway. "That's the mist the soldier spoke of."

They watched a moment longer then backed away from the window, fearful of being seen . . . and fearful perhaps that the wind might carry up whatever was killing the rice below.

Bingwen ran to the old woman's bag of clothes and pulled out an old shirt frayed at the edges. He moved it in his hands until he found a small tear. Then he gripped the fabric on both sides of the tear and pulled. The old, brittle cotton fibers put up little resistance, and the shirt ripped in half. The pulling motion sent a shot of pain down Bingwen's bad arm, however, and he almost dropped the fabric.

"What are you doing?" the old woman demanded, rushing over and raising a hand to strike him.

Bingwen offered her half of the shirt. "Wrap it around your mouth and nose, like a bandana. To breathe through."

The woman paused, then understood. "Yes, yes. Of course." She called her husband over. "Find more pieces," she said, gesturing to his bag. "Tear up your shirts. Make masks for all these people."

"Why don't we tear up your clothes?" said the old man.

"Just do it," said his wife.

Bingwen wrapped the other half of the shirt around his face. He waited a moment while everyone gathered around the old man, their attention focused on the prospect of fabric, then Bingwen rushed outside to the barn. If Mazer or any of the soldiers were hurt, he would have to move them, which of course he couldn't do without help.

Bingwen sized up the two water buffalo in the barn. The one on the right was fatter and wider and therefore stronger. But that didn't necessarily make it better. Bingwen clapped loudly and whistled and waved his arms for the water buffalo to come to him. The smaller of the two stepped toward him until the rope around its neck pulled taut and stopped it. The bigger one merely stared at Bingwen, slowly chewing something.

Obedience trumps strength, thought Bingwen.

He untied the smaller of the two and threw a burlap tool pouch over its back, the kind with two wide pockets on the sides for carrying supplies. Bingwen looked around him. He didn't know what he needed. He wasn't even sure he needed anything. There was a coil of rope in one corner, covered in dust and spiderwebs. He packed it in the pouch. There was a hatchet on the wall, old and rusted and probably not very sharp. He put that in the pouch as well. There were huge cotton harvesting bags with a single shoulder strap piled in one corner. If he needed to dress wounds, those might come in handy. He stuffed as many as he could into the pouch.

"Bingwen."

The voice was mild and kind. Bingwen turned around and faced Grandfather.

"You cannot go, little one. You cannot help the soldiers."

"Why not?" asked Bingwen. "Because I am small?"

Grandfather gave a rueful smile. "Size is no measure of ability, child. See how you chose the smaller of these two water buffalo."

"Because he obeyed me."

"Just as you must obey me. It is not safe in the valleys."

"Which is why I need to hurry. The mist will get them if I don't reach them first." He untied the animal and pulled on the lead rope. The water buffalo responded, falling into step behind him.

Grandfather sidled to his left, blocking Bingwen's path, his face hard now. "You disrespect your elder, child."

Bingwen stopped and bowed his head, staring at the dirt.

"I disagree with my elder, Grandfather. There is a difference. I have nothing but love and respect for you. You are wise beyond wise. Loyal and of great courage. You find strength despite your injuries. I can only hope to become half the man you are. But virtue does not make a man right every time. Please, Grandfather. Without these soldiers, who will protect us? Who will lead us?"

"If they are injured, Bingwen, they can do neither."

"We don't know the severity of their injuries, Grandfather. And even if they are gravely wounded, do we not owe them our lives? If injury discounts a person's worth, then you and I are worth nothing. We're the most wounded of our group."

Grandfather chuckled. "Such a tongue. Look at me, Bingwen."

Bingwen lifted his head. Grandfather knelt down in front of him, putting a hand behind his head. "I think only of you, little one. I cannot let you go. I could not live with myself if something happened to you."

"Survival is why I must go, Grandfather. We need these men. Mother and Father are still out there. And right now these soldiers are the only ones trying to bring us all together."

That gave Grandfather pause. He pursed his lips, considered, then painfully got to his feet. "I will go then." He held out his hand for the lead rope.

Bingwen sighed. This was wasting time. Every moment counted. "Grandfather, you might be able to walk down this mountain, but you can't walk back up it. Not yet anyway. Not until you've mended. We both know that."

He didn't wait for Grandfather to respond; he tugged on the lead rope and led the water buffalo onto the access road.

"And how will you bring back a wounded soldier?" Grandfather asked.

"Very carefully," said Bingwen.

He hurried down the road, eager to get away before Grandfather made some additional argument and forced Bingwen, out of respect, to stop and address it with a rational rebuttal—neither of which Bingwen had time for. The water buffalo didn't like the speed and kept yanking back on the lead rope and forcing Bingwen to slow down. Twice the animal stopped altogether to stick its nose in the air and smell the smoke that kept wafting across their path. Bingwen gave it a hard slap on the rump and got it moving again.

At the top of the mountain Bingwen had been fearless. But the farther he went down the road, the more his courage failed him. The trees that covered the road were suddenly hiding places for the aliens. The thick scrub on the shoulder was suddenly the perfect place for an ambush. The thin braches that stuck out from the forest were suddenly wands waiting to spray a mist into his face. There were aircraft sounds as well, loud and fast, some close, others far away, and every time Bingwen heard one, he was convinced the aircraft was falling toward him, like a burning meteor, targeted directly to his position. The water buffalo seemed to feel the same way. The closer they got to the valley floor, the more resistant and agitated it became.

Soon the trees began to thin, and the whole of the valley plain came into view. It was the back side of the mountain, a valley Bingwen hadn't been able to see from the farmhouse, and the sight of it stopped him cold.

There were bodies on the ground. People. Not clumped together in a big group, but spread out all over the valley in ones and twos and threes, as if a big crowd of villagers had all decided to find a spot away from the others to lie down and go to sleep.

Only, they weren't sleeping. There was no rise and fall to their chests, no casual repositioning of their bodies as sleeping people do. No movement of any kind except for wisps of hair and corners of clothing blown back and forth in the wind.

The closest body was thirty meters away under the shade of a tree. A woman, Mother's age, lying on her side, facing Bingwen, her shirt hanging loosely off her shoulder in a way that no modest woman would ever consciously allow. One of her shoes lay on the ground beside her. Her eyes were open, her mouth slightly ajar, as if she had been waiting for Bingwen to arrive and was just calling out his name when time had stood still and frozen her in that position.

Around her, the rice shoots were curled and black and dead.

The mist had caused this, Bingwen realized. The chemical the creatures sprayed from their wands had killed everything it had touched: the crop, the fleeing villagers, even a few animals here and there: dogs and birds and two water buffalo. There were large patches of healthy crop as well—

green rice shoots that had been spared the mist, some of them as tall as Bingwen's shoulders—but these were in the minority. Most of the valley floor was mud and death and withered shoots of rice.

On the far side of the valley, a downed Chinese aircraft billowed black smoke and ash into the air. Bingwen could hear the crackle and sizzle of the flames and the popping and breaking of components inside. He could smell it, too, an acrid stench of melting plastic and rubber and other synthetics.

It wasn't Mazer's aircraft, he knew. That crash had occurred elsewhere, at least another kilometer away and probably farther. Yet the sight of this one didn't fill Bingwen with much confidence. The aircraft was barely recognizable as such. Perhaps it had been a helicopter once, but now it was nothing more than a heap of twisted, burning metal, with the entire front half of it crushed by the impact. It lay on its side like a wounded animal, burning and hissing and spewing black smoke.

Bingwen wondered how many people had been aboard. Ten? Twenty? It was certainly big enough to carry that many. Perhaps it had been loaded with supplies: fresh water and food and medical equipment, everything he and Grandfather and the others would need to survive at the farmhouse. Whatever it had held, there was no salvaging it now. Nor would there be any survivors.

Maybe Grandfather was right, he told himself. Maybe this was a fool's errand. Why should Mazer's crash be any different? All he would likely find there was more fire and death.

Beside him the water buffalo raised its head and sniffed at the air. It must have caught the scent of death or smoke because the next instant it pulled so hard on the lead rope that it yanked Bingwen off his feet. Bingwen landed hard on his good arm, but the jolt sent another shot of pain through his bad one. He cried out in agony despite himself. The shout spooked the animal further, and it took off back the way it had come, yanking the lead rope free of Bingwen's grip and giving him a serious rope burn.

It took Bingwen fifteen minutes to corner the animal and catch the lead rope again. By then he had taken strips of fabric from the makeshift bandana around his face and wrapped the strips around his hand to form a sort of bandage and glove for holding the rope. The animal began to resist again, but Bingwen gave it a violent tug and reminded it who was leading whom. Then he took one of the harvesting bags from the pouch and made a sort of face mask for the animal, like a giant feed bag that covered most of its head.

The water buffalo calmed after that, smelling only the scent of the barn in the bag's fabric.

Bingwen guided it back down into the valley. He wasn't turning around, he had decided. He had come this far; he would see it through. He wouldn't give up as quickly as the water buffalo had.

They moved toward the nearest patch of healthy crop. If they crossed the valley by sticking to the green shoots, maybe they could pass through without contaminating themselves.

Bingwen took the first few tentative steps into the tall shoots and waited to see if he felt sick or light-headed.

Nothing happened.

He pushed on, pulling the water buffalo behind him.

The healthy green shoots crumpled and broke under their feet. Damaging the crop like that went against everything both of them had ever been taught, but they walked on nonetheless.

They passed dozens of bodies. The first few faces were strangers: men and women from other villages. Then Bingwen began to see people he knew: neighbors and friends of Grandfather. Yi Yi Guangon, one of the elders from the village council. Shashoo, the only woman in the village who owned a washing machine. Bexi, the nurse who made herbal remedies for Bingwen whenever he got sick. All of them were lifeless and lying in unnatural positions, their skin red and blistered, as if they had worked for days in the sun without a hat.

A suffocating fear gripped at Bingwen's chest whenever he saw someone new: What if the next person's face was Mother's or Father's? What would he do then?

Once he was sure he *had* found Mother. The dead woman lay in the mud with her back to him and her face turned away. She had hair like Mother's and a shape like Mother's and the same plain, faded clothes like Mother's.

But when Bingwen walked around her and saw her face, he realized it wasn't Mother. The relief was so sudden and overwhelming that Bingwen broke down and sobbed. His chest heaved, and his body shook, and it took several minutes to compose himself again. By then the water buffalo was growing restless and pulling on the lead rope again. Bingwen wiped at his eyes and nose with the sleeve of his good arm. He had been crying for everything: his arm, Hopper, Meilin, the dead woman who looked like Mother, Mazer's ship. Everything. When he finished, he felt better, braver even. I've had my cry, he thought. My final one.

He kept walking.

There were dead children as well, though Bingwen couldn't force himself to look at them. He made his eyes defocus whenever one came into view, always looking above the body, never directly at it . . . until a bright shirt caught his attention. A shirt he recognized. A shirt he had seen up close when the person wearing it had put him in a headlock once.

Zihao.

Alive, Zihao had always worn a bullish, condescending sneer. But here, lying on his back in the mud, he looked afraid: wide eyes, rigid body, a dirty face streaked with tears. He seemed younger, too. Like a child. Bingwen looked away.

A faint hiss from behind caused Bingwen to turn around suddenly. Back at the end of the access road, a few hundred meters behind him, four aliens were spraying the healthy grass and moving in his direction. They seemed unaware of Bingwen, but he knew that wouldn't last.

Bingwen yanked on the lead rope and got the water buffalo moving. He didn't stop to look at faces. He didn't step carefully. He ran.

The water buffalo sensed his urgency and ran as well, big lumbering strides that weren't fast enough for Bingwen, who kept yanking and pulling on the rope. The animal stumbled once, but quickly regained its footing. They ran for fifteen minutes, never slowing until the valley turned south and the aliens were long out of view. They stopped, both of them wheezing and breathing heavily, the water buffalo moaning and mooing. Bingwen's broken arm felt as if it were on fire; all the jostling and running had aggravated the break. A stitch in his side burned so hot Bingwen was convinced he had torn something inside.

The water buffalo wavered, and for a moment Bingwen thought it might keel over. Then it shook its head and gathered itself.

Bingwen looked to his left and saw that they had arrived. There was wreckage a hundred meters away. Mazer's aircraft. Bingwen was sure of it. A fire had consumed it and burned it black, but the flames had long since died out, and the familiar shape of the aircraft was still intact. The only new feature was the four rotor blades on the top of the aircraft, which must have snapped open as the aircraft fell.

Bingwen's heart sank at the sight. There couldn't possibly be any survivors. The aircraft had exploded, sending shrapnel and debris in every direction. Even if someone had survived the impact, they couldn't have gotten clear of the explosion in time. Nor could they have ejected before impact, not with the rotor blades, not in a dead drop.

Bingwen felt ashamed. He should have listened to Grandfather. He was foolish to have come out here.

Something near the wreckage caught his eye. A rifle perhaps? That would be useful. And where there was one, there might be others; and if not other weapons, then perhaps other tools. He pulled on the rope. The water buffalo didn't want to move; it still wheezed and whined from their run. Bingwen pulled anyway with his good arm, and eventually the animal walked.

The wreck smelled like ashes and burning things and what might be the scent of charred human remains. Smoke still hung thick in the air and stung Bingwen's eyes. He didn't want to look inside the cabin or cockpit. He knew what he would find there.

The ground was littered with shrapnel and debris, some pieces as big as Bingwen, all folded up and bent in odd shapes with torn edges that looked dangerously sharp.

Bingwen's eyes were locked on the rifle ahead of him, but as he approached it, moving through the smoke, something else near the weapon caught his eye. A body.

Bingwen ran forward, frantic, the lead rope dropping from his hand.

It was Mazer. There was blood and mud all over him. His arms, his head, his side. His side was the worst. A bloody bandage lay draped across his abdomen, soaked through and deep red. The contents of a med kit lay scattered around him. Someone had administered first aid. Someone was alive and helping. Bingwen looked around.

"Hello?"

No one answered.

To his left was another body. The female soldier. Bingwen instantly knew she was dead, even without seeing her face, which was turned away from him. She had too many wounds. Her skin was white and lifeless. Her clothes were burned. Her arm was twisted behind her.

In the fields, the corpses had looked asleep, peaceful even in some instances. Not so here. This had been a hard death. Quick most likely, instantaneous even, but it terrified Bingwen more than anything he had seen thus far.

There were lines in the dirt from the aircraft to the woman's body where her boots had dragged across the soil. Mazer had pulled her from the fire, Bingwen realized. Wounded as he was, Mazer had pulled her from the flames. Bingwen could think of no other explanation. And then somehow Mazer had tried to treat his own wounds. Bingwen knelt beside him. Yes, one of the packets from the kit was still in Mazer's hand. Bingwen should have noticed that instantly.

"Mazer."

No answer.

Should he try shaking him awake? No, that might tear something inside him. Instead, Bingwen reached out a tentative finger and poked Mazer in the arm. The skin was warm. The tip of Bingwen's finger came back bloody. Mazer didn't respond.

Then Mazer's chest rose, just slightly, almost imperceptibly. A shallow intake of breath. Then an exhale. He was alive. Barely maybe, but he was breathing.

Bingwen had to get him back to the farmhouse, back to Grandfather. But how? He had hoped to find the soldiers awake and able to walk. And if they couldn't walk, Bingwen would build a travois for the water buffalo to pull and then ask the wounded soldier to climb up onto it. But Mazer couldn't even do that; he couldn't move at all. Bingwen would have to lift him somehow onto the stretcher.

Bingwen ran back to the water buffalo, tied it to a tree, and came back with all the supplies from the tool pouches. He found a grove of bamboo nearby and chopped down three large stalks with the hatchet. It took him forever because he had to do it one-handed, using only his good arm. He then chopped one of the three stalks into shorter lengths and built the travois, lashing the bamboo together with the rope. The shorter pieces went between the longer two, making a ladderlike surface for Mazer to lie on. Bingwen then cut out the bottoms of a few of the harvesting bags and pulled those up over the two shafts, creating a flat surface like the bed of a cot.

The travois was heavy when Bingwen finished, almost too heavy for him to drag with one hand, but he heaved and strained and pulled it across the dirt until he had it on the ground beside Mazer. He had hoped to pull Mazer's body up onto it, but after a few tentative tugs it became obvious that wouldn't work. There was too much dead weight, and he couldn't pull with his broken arm. He'd have to lift the body, suspend it in the air, slide the travois underneath, and then lower Mazer carefully onto it.

By now Bingwen was sweating and thirsty and tired. He hadn't brought any water; he hadn't wanted to take any from the little supply the group at the farmhouse had. Now he wished he had. There wasn't any drinkable water nearby, and even if there had been, he wouldn't have drunk it, not with the mist in the air and the threat of contamination.

He ignored the thirst and got back to work. He had built pulley systems out of bamboo before—he and Father had made a small towerlike structure to lift the bags of harvested rice up onto the load trucks last season. But this would be different. Mazer was twice as long as a bag of rice and far more floppy and collapsible. Nor did Bingwen have Father helping him or two good working arms.

It took him hours to prepare everything, chopping down the bamboo, cutting the proper lengths, separating the threads of the rope into twine because he needed more rope than he had. He used scrap from the wreckage as well. There was a winch in the cockpit with cable and D-rings and fasteners. He was aware of charred human remains in the seats, but Bingwen held his breath, averted his eyes, and retrieved the equipment quickly.

Then he started building. He made a series of A-frame structures with a long shaft between them, then slid several thinner bamboo shafts underneath Mazer at his shoulders, lower back, buttocks, and bend of the knee. He made a special pouch for Mazer's head so that it wouldn't loll back sharply when Bingwen lifted him. He lashed both ends of the bamboo shafts underneath Mazer to a lifting pole that hovered above Mazer, running the length of his body. Then Bingwen threaded the rope through the three pulleys he had made from narrow cuts of bamboo.

The sun was far in the western part of the sky, dipping toward the horizon, when he finished. He was hungry. His arm ached. His whole body was slick with sweat and covered in dirt and soot.

The structure was elaborate; it looked like a giant bamboo spider standing over Mazer, ready to seize him and wrap him in its webbing.

Bingwen pulled on the ropes, and Mazer's body lifted gently off the ground, his head holding steady. All that work for so little movement, he thought.

Bingwen tied off the line, slid the travois underneath Mazer, and lowered Mazer onto the stretcher. Then he moved the pulleys up the crossbeam toward Mazer's head and lifted the front end of the travois high enough to tie it to a harness he had made for the water buffalo. The hardest part proved to be getting the water buffalo to stay still long enough for Bingwen to do the lashings. Finally, though, everything was set.

Bingwen gathered all the supplies from the med kit, including the small, flat digital device that Mazer had used to scan Bingwen's broken arm. Bingwen examined it, brushing off the mud and grime from the screen. There was a crack across the glass, but the device turned on at Bingwen's touch. The home screen was bright and colorful and gave him a variety of options: SURFACE TISSUE SCAN, ULTRASOUND, BLOOD EXAM, SURGERY TUTORIALS, PHARMACY. Bingwen put it in his saddle pouch then did a final scan of the wreckage for more supplies. He didn't see anything else worth taking until he spotted the combat vest the female soldier was wearing. It held several cartridges of ammunition like the one currently snapped into the rifle.

Ammunition they could use. Without it the rifle would be useless. But retrieving the cartridges wouldn't be easy; Bingwen would have to turn the woman more onto her side in order to undo the straps that held the cartridges. And that meant touching a dead person. The idea made Bingwen sick to his stomach; he couldn't bear to look at the woman, much less touch her.

He was being ridiculous, he told himself. Selfish even. They were dead without a weapon, dead without ammunition.

He ran to the woman, his eyes half shut, his lips pressed together tight, and pushed the woman's shoulder to rotate her body. She was stiff and bloody and didn't roll easily with her arm bent back behind her. But Bingwen dug in his heels, and finally the woman's torso moved enough for him to reach in and pull the cartridges free. They clattered to the ground in front of him, and Bingwen scrambled back a heartbeat later, scurrying away on all fours and hating himself for being such a coward.

His eyes were wet with tears, he realized, and he wiped at them quickly. He got to his feet, collected the cartridges, and dropped them into the tool pouch. Next he tied a rope around Mazer's chest, securing him to the stretcher; then, after one final look back at the wreckage, he took the lead rope and pulled hard. The water buffalo moaned in opposition and resisted, but after another hard jerk from Bingwen, the animal followed.

Bingwen had heard aircraft all day, most of it far away, but now the skies were quiet. It was dusk, and he figured he wouldn't reach the farmhouse until well after dark.

They arrived at the valley of corpses and found that the aliens had killed all the remaining crops. Without any healthy grass to walk on, Bingwen cut north, looking for another place to cut back toward the mountain. He found one a kilometer later, another wide field of crop without much standing water.

There were more bodies here: people and animals. A family of pigs. Three water buffalo. A group of children.

And Mother and Father.

Bingwen saw them from fifty meters away and stopped dead. They were lying facedown in the mud, Father's arm draped across Mother's shoulder, as if comforting her.

Bingwen didn't move. He couldn't see their faces, but that was Mother's shirt and Mother's back and Mother's shape. And that was Father's clothes. And Father's boots and Father's hair. And the glint of sunlight was off Father's watch on his left wrist where he wore it.

Bingwen felt as if his body were made of air. His eyes couldn't focus. His knees felt flimsy and unstable. He stood there, staring at them, him upright and alive and breathing and them not. Their hearts weren't beating, their lungs weren't taking in air, their mouths weren't moving, telling him how much they loved him and that they would protect him and that he would be safe with them. Their arms weren't wrapping around him and pulling him close to their chests. Their bodies weren't doing anything except lying there in the mud and misted grass.

Bingwen stood there for a long time, how long he did not know. An hour perhaps, maybe double that. The water buffalo mooed and pawed at the ground, impatient. Bingwen ignored it. He ignored everything. If aliens were coming, he wouldn't run from them.

He breathed in and out. No tears came. No wails. No cries of anguish. Everything was broken inside. Everything was empty. He wouldn't make tears anymore, *couldn't* make them. He wasn't going to allow that. Tears belonged to the old, dead version of himself, the previous Bingwen, the boy who sneaked into the library and who worried about tests and going to school and who had a friend with a twisted foot and parents who loved him and sat him by the fire when he was wet and cold. That Bingwen was gone. That Bingwen was lying there in the mud with Mother and Father, his arm draped across Mother's shoulder just like Father's was.

He would make Mazer well. Yes, he would make Mazer well, and then Mazer would stop everything. Mazer would end the mists and the fires and the bodies in the fields. And Bingwen would help him. He'd give Mazer the cartridges, and he'd carry Mazer's water, and he'd do anything to put an end to it, to make it all go away. Then he would allow himself to cry.

It was full dark when he reached the farmhouse. Grandfather ran out to greet him, embracing him, kissing him on the cheek, cursing himself for letting Bingwen go. Only then did Grandfather see that the water buffalo was dragging someone behind it.

The others came outside as well. They saw Mazer and the travois and they stared at it all, as if they couldn't understand what they were looking at, as if the rational part of their brain were telling them it wasn't possible. The old woman turned to Bingwen and regarded him with an expression Bingwen couldn't read. Confusion? Awe?

No one moved. No one jumped to help.

They didn't know how to respond, Bingwen realized. They didn't know what to do. "He's alive," Bingwen said. "We need to help him."

Grandfather took charge. "Untie the stretcher. Pull him inside. Quickly now. But gently, do it gently."

Bingwen stood there and watched as they untied the travois and pulled Mazer into the farmhouse still on it. They laid the whole structure on the floor and surrounded the body.

"I need light," said the old woman.

"She's a nurse of sorts," Grandfather said to Bingwen. "A midwife. Do you know what that means?"

"She helps women deliver babies," said Bingwen.

"Yes," said Grandfather. "She knows things about medicine."

"Not enough," said Bingwen. He took the digital device from the pouch and approached Mazer. Everyone was crowding around the travois. The old woman's husband was holding a lantern.

"Back up," the old woman said. "I need space." She bent down, pulled the lantern close, and poked around, lifting the corner of the bandage and looking at the many wounds. "This is bad. Very bad. More than I can do. I can't help him."

"You have to," said Bingwen.

"Boy, you did a brave thing to bring this man back, but he is beyond help. He won't live to see morning. He's lost too much blood. His wounds are too many."

"Then we'll give him a blood transfusion. We'll find a match among one of us and give him blood."

The old woman laughed. "And how do you propose we do that?"

"With this," said Bingwen, holding up the device. He turned on the screen and selected BLOOD EXAM. It asked him if he wanted instructions. Bingwen selected YES. The machine started to talk in English. It startled everyone.

"What is that?" said the old woman.

"A medical device to tell you how to treat someone."

"That sounds like English," said the teenage girl.

"It is," said Bingwen. "I know English. I can walk us through the steps." He didn't wait for them to object. He listened to the recorded voice. It was female, calm and soothing, the kind of voice you would want to hear in a traumatic situation. The device told Bingwen to pull certain items from the med kit. Bingwen obeyed. He used the tiny tube he found to extract a drop of blood from Mazer. He put the drop on the corner of the device's screen where it indicated.

"Type O positive," the device said. "This blood is only compatible with types O positive and O negative."

"What is it saying?" asked Grandfather.

"I need to prick my finger," said Bingwen. He dug through the supplies until he found another thin straw and finger pricker.

"Test mine," said Grandfather, offering his hand. "You're too small to give blood."

"You're too weak," said Bingwen.

"I know my strength better than you do, boy. Prick my finger."

Bingwen wiped Grandfather's finger with the gauze, pricked it, and tested the blood. When the results came back he said, "It's a match."

Grandfather nodded, pleased with himself, as if he had accomplished something. "Then let's get a move on."

"We need to stitch him up first and remove the shrapnel," said the old woman. "But I think it's a waste of time. This man isn't going to live. You'll lose blood for nothing, blood you have no business losing at your age."

Grandfather frowned. "My grandson risked his life to bring this man to us. And this man risked his life to save us. We are going to save his life and you are going to help."

The old woman's husband stepped forward. "Watch your tongue, old man. You don't command my wife."

"I'm doing it because you're not," said Grandfather. "She's duty-bound. She owes this man. We all do. And if Bingwen says we can save him, then we can." He turned to the old woman. "You've stitched up women before. This is no different."

"This is plenty different," said the old woman. "The shrapnel wounds are simple enough. It's the man's stomach that I can't fix. I don't know what's injured inside. His organs could be all cut up. It looks deep. I'm not a doctor."

"The device will tell us," said Bingwen, not knowing if it were true. "Let's at least try."

The old woman hesitated, looked into the face of her husband, then sighed. "Fine. What do we do first?"

Bingwen wasn't sure. There was a button for help. He pushed it.

"State the problem," said the device.

"His stomach is cut and was bleeding a lot. Maybe his organs are cut, too. We're not sure."

"Have you stopped the bleeding?" asked the device.

"Yes."

"Have you washed and sanitized the wound and your hands?"

"No."

"Let's do that first. Do you know how?"

Bingwen knew how to wash his hands certainly, but there might be special instructions so he said, "No."

There *were* special instructions. There were chemicals to use and gloves to wear and sterile gauze to unwrap. Bingwen and the woman did what they were told. They cleaned the wound and stanched the blood. They wiped down and sterilized the device as well.

"Now I need to scan the wound," said the device.

Bingwen held the device over the wound for several seconds.

"I detect serious trauma," said the device. "A portion of the small intestines has been severed. This requires immediate surgery. Is there a qualified doctor available who can perform a small bowel resection?"

"No," said Bingwen.

"What's it saying?" said the old woman.

"Let the boy listen," said Grandfather.

"Can you transport the patient to a hospital where a qualified doctor can be found?" the device asked.

"No," said Bingwen.

"Can you notify a doctor and have one come to you?"

"There are no doctors anywhere. We can't move him."

"Is there someone present who is willing to attempt the surgery?"

Bingwen looked into their faces. "What will happen if we don't?"

"The small intestine is part of the body's digestive tract. When severed it will release harmful waste into the body. If not repaired immediately, and if the wound isn't properly cleaned, the patient will not survive."

"Nobody here has ever done something like this before."

"I will walk you through the steps. You will need the following items from the med kit."

A long list of supplies appeared on the screen.

"What will we have to do exactly?" asked Bingwen.

"The damaged section of the intestines will have to be cut off and removed. The bowel will then need to be stitched back together to reestablish the continuity of the digestive tract. The wound must be properly cleansed and treated for infection. The abdominal wound must then be stapled and treated for infection as well. The patient will need to be under general anesthetic the entire time. I can help watch the patient's vitals and coach you through the process."

"How long will it take, knowing that we're completely untrained and have no idea what we're doing?"

"Anywhere from four to twelve hours."

Bingwen was quiet.

"Well?" said the old woman. "What did it say? Is this something we can do?"

Bingwen looked at them. They were ready to give up. He could see it in their faces.

"Yes," he said. "We can absolutely do this. It won't be hard at all."

Kim hated status meetings. They felt like a complete waste of time. She had gone to school to be a doctor, to help people, to save lives, not to sit around a conference room and look at spreadsheets and due dates and discuss the minutiae of every project. That was an administrator's job. That's what managers did. Doctors got their hands dirty. Doctors rushed to bedsides, giving comfort, cheating death. Meetings like this *were* death, slow and painful and mind-numbingly boring.

"Kim? Are you with us?"

She looked up. Everyone around the table was staring at her. She had been doodling on her holopad, making swirls all over the spreadsheet. She blinked and sat upright. "Yes. Sorry. Go on."

The group went back to it, chattering away about some production issue: the manufacturers in China who were assembling the most recent round of Med-Assists weren't going to meet their deadline; the workers weren't coming into the plant.

"Can you blame them?" said Kim. "There *is* a war on. Alien civilization. People dying. I wouldn't want to go into work either."

"Business must go on, Kim," said one of the project managers. "There's no telling how big this could get. The military might deploy troops. If New Zealand gets in this fight, we need to be ready with the Med-Assist."

He was right, Kim knew. She had seen all the statistical reports; the Med-Assist reduced combat casualties by as much as sixty percent in some studies. Yet even so, it struck Kim as absurd that they would sit here and discuss something as frivolous as labor disputes while thousands of civilians died in rural China. There were aliens out there, for crying out loud. Malicious, highly advanced aliens. The world had changed overnight. They were fretting over a burning tree while the forest blazed all around them.

But she said none of this aloud. Instead she smiled politely and pretended to listen as the meeting continued and the discussion moved on to other production issues.

This had never been in the job description, she told herself. They had said nothing about her helping to manage logistical concerns or labor disputes. And yet here she was, enduring another mindless meeting on those very subjects.

She had tried to get out of them, she had pled to upper management that they excuse her from all management duties, yet her request had been denied. She knew every function of the Med-Assist. An issue in another department might affect what she was doing. She needed to stay in the loop, she needed to be aware.

For the hundredth time she questioned if coming to New Zealand had been the right decision. They had promised her that she would be helping more people through the device, and technically that was true. But now those words felt like a misleading promise. She was helping more people, yes, but she never got to *see* any of them; she never got to give their hands a reassuring squeeze before surgery, or watch their faces light up when she told them all would be well. They were numbers, not names. All the humanity and thrill and reward of being a doctor were missing. It was the work of saving lives, but the work felt lifeless.

Mazer had made it tolerable. When they were together she had ignored the doubts about the job. All the mindless meetings and administrative crap was bearable if it meant having him at her side.

But now even that was gone.

Mazer. She couldn't think of him without four different emotions assaulting her at once. She was angry still, of course. Furious even. How could he think that what they had could be snipped in two and so easily ended? Had it meant so little to him? Then there was the sorrow and the empty loneliness of it all, the vacant feeling she couldn't seem to shake.

But most of all was the worry. The fear that he was dead somewhere in China. He was right at the center of it. Of all the places in the world to go, the Formics had landed there. And not just one lander, but all three.

She had seen him pull the boy from the mud. The press was still playing it over and over again. When she heard that the Formics had landed in China, it was as if her heart had dropped out of her chest. She had glued herself to the feeds, hoping to see something that would reassure her that he was all right.

And then there he was. Right on the screen. Right in front of her. Right there in the mud and thick of it, right at the epicenter. And she had burst into tears.

That had been twelve hours ago, and since then no word. She wasn't sure what she expected. A call from him? A message of some sort, reassuring her that he was all right?

Her wrist pad vibrated. She was getting a call, and for an instant she thought it might be him. Then she looked at the photo and saw that it was the front desk. She considered letting it go to her message box, but then she realized it was her ticket out of the meeting. She got to her feet, smiled apologetically, and left the room.

Outside in the hall she put in her earbud and tapped it. "Dr. Arnsbrach," she said.

The voice on the line said, "Sorry to bother you, Doctor. It's Marnie at the front desk. I've got another one of those misdirects on the line. It sounds urgent. What should I do?"

Kim sighed. Misdirects were calls intended for doctors but which were misdirected to company headquarters instead. Early versions of the Med-Assist device were to blame. They had included a feature that the company couldn't sustain: If the Med-Assist saw that it needed outside help for a procedure, it would make a sat call to a switchboard. That switchboard would then connect the Med-Assist to a real doctor within the Med-Assist network. The doctor would then stay on the line with the soldier who had the device and help him complete whatever dicey medical procedure he was trying to perform.

The problem was, the contracts to build the network of doctors had fallen through at the last minute. So there were no doctors taking live calls. There was nobody.

The company had removed the sat-call feature from subsequent releases of the device, and an update of the software had erased that feature on those devices that had originally had it. Yet every so often an old Med-Assist device surfaced that hadn't been updated. And when it tried to contact the nonexistent network, it failed and called headquarters instead.

"Where's the device?" asked Kim.

"The boy says he's in China."

Great, thought Kim. China. That meant it was probably a device that had made its way to the black market. The company didn't have a contract with the Chinese military. What else could it be?

"Should I tell him we don't offer that service? He's a kid. He's clearly not military."

"No," said Kim. "I'll take the call. Patch him through."

Technically she had no responsibility for whoever was on the line, and there were all kinds of shaky legal issues here. But it was a living, breathing person who needed help. And wasn't that what she was missing?

"Hello?" said a small voice.

"Hello. I'm Dr. Kim Arnsbrach. Who I am speaking with?"

"My name is Bingwen."

"You have a Med-Assist, Bingwen?"

"Yes. I found it. You have to help me. My friend is hurt. We've been following the instructions, but we had a problem and it called you."

"How old is your friend, Bingwen?" If the patient was a child, Kim
would alert one of the pediatricians on staff and get them involved.

"I don't know," said the boy. "Does it matter?"

"Is there an adult there I can speak with?"

"I'm the only one who speaks English."

"Where are you?"

"In a farmhouse. South of Dawanzhen."

That meant nothing to her. "Okay, Bingwen. Maybe I can help you." She
was moving back to her office. "I'm going to talk to the device now for a
minute, all right? I'm going to download some information from it and see
what the problem is. Stay with the device. I'll be with you in a minute. Can
you do that?"

"Yes. But hurry. He's hurt bad. No one thinks he's going to live."

Kim's fast walk became a jog. This was more serious than she thought.
She reached her office and put her wrist pad on the holodesk. All of the
information from the Med-Assist appeared in front of her. Images, video,
steps completed.

It was a small bowel resection. Kim swore. She had expected a skinned
knee or a broken bone perhaps. A child's injury. This was full-on invasive
surgery. How old was this kid? He didn't sound older than seven or eight. It
was lunacy. She waved her hand through the holofield and made a call. A
man's head appeared. "Itzak," said Kim, "I need you up in my office immediately."

He didn't ask questions. "On my way."

He was the best gastroenterologist they had on staff and a brilliant sur-
geon. He was in her office less than a minute later. He quickly scanned the
information in the air in front of him. "They're halfway through the surgery," he said. "Who are these people?"

"Not soldiers," said Kim. "The kid's the only one who speaks English.
None of them has any medical training." She had read the boy's responses
to all the questions the device had asked. "Can we do a shadow surgery?"

He looked unsure. "Maybe. I don't know their skill level."

"They have no skill level. But they're already halfway through it. We have to try." Kim took the line off mute. "Bingwen, can you hear me?"

"Yes. I'm here. I thought I had lost you." He sounded afraid.

"No, Bingwen. I'm here. I have another doctor with me. We're going to try something. It's called a shadow surgery. Dr. Mendelsohn and I are going to show you exactly what to do. We'll have a holo of your friend here in front of us. We'll perform the rest of the surgery step by step and the person on your end just has to mimic everything we do. You're very close. You've been doing wonderfully."

"The woman here who's doing it wants to give up. She doesn't think she can finish. She's been going for hours."

"She *can* do it, Bingwen," said Kim. "You have to convince her to keep going."

"I'm trying. She's not listening."

Itzak spoke quietly. "I need a visual."

"Bingwen," said Kim. "I need you to point the pad over the wound for me and hold it there."

"Okay."

Itzak moved his hands through the holofield, and a holo of a man's midsection appeared on the table. Kim had never gotten used to this part: performing surgery this way, without scrubbing up first, without a wall of equipment and monitoring devices around you.

"Good, Bingwen. We can see your friend now," said Kim. "What's the name of the woman who's helping you?"

"Mingzhu."

"Is Mingzhu ready to begin?"

She heard him speak in Chinese. A woman answered. Kim could here the stress in the woman's voice.

"She says she can't go on." The boy sounded panicked.

"We need to get moving on this," Itzak whispered. "There's some light hemorrhaging here."

"Bingwen," said Kim. "Listen to me. We need to do this right now. Do you understand? Tell Mingzhu that if she doesn't act now your friend is going to die."

She heard Bingwen speak in Chinese again. But this time, he said a word that Kim *did* recognize, not a Chinese word, a name. It froze her heart.

"Bingwen," she said, her voice suddenly shaky. "What did you tell her? Give me the exact words you just said."

"I told her that if she didn't help Mazer would die."

It was like the floor had dropped out beneath her. This couldn't be. It was impossible, and yet completely possible.

"Bingwen," she said slowly. "What is your friend's name? His full name."

"Mazer," said the boy. "Mazer Rackham."

# CHAPTER 19

# MOPs

Wit stood in front of the Chinese lieutenant's desk at Khunjerab Pass, watching the lieutenant study Wit's passport. The lieutenant was young, fresh out of officer's training school probably, which was bad for Wit because it meant the kid would likely try extra hard to prove to his superiors that he was a capable commander of the border crossing. And what better way to prove his abilities than to arrest forty special-ops soldiers posing as civilians and trying to sneak their way into China?

"You are American," the lieutenant said. It wasn't a question, so Wit didn't respond.

The kid's English was good. A slight accent, but that was to be expected. Well educated obviously, and the perfect cut of his hair and the immaculate state of his uniform suggested a life of discipline. Wit figured he was probably the son of some well-to-do high-ranking officer or perhaps the nephew of some party official. A kid with connections. Someone had put in a good word and gotten him a decent command position right out of school. Not that Khunjerab Pass was any Shangri-La. It wasn't. It was barren and cold and isolated and completely uninteresting. There were no forms of entertainment whatsoever, nothing to keep a soldier occupied after hours. There was the gate, there were the trucks that passed through the gate, and there were the mountains. The only break in the monotony was the occasional mountain goat sighting.

But it was a command position. It might be a crappy one, but big careers had to start somewhere.

"Why are you traveling into China?" the lieutenant asked.

"We want to study the Formics," said Wit. Which was true.

The whole world was using that term now. Formics. It was all over the news.

"Your name does not show up on our databases," said the lieutenant. "There's no file for you at all in America. No credit reports. No address. You're an anomaly."

Wit had no address because he was never *in* the U.S. If he had leave time, which was almost never, he passed it elsewhere. Or, in the rare occasion in which he did visit the States, he went to his parents' house in upstate New York. He didn't own property. Why would he?

The rest of his personal data had been erased when he had joined MOPs.

Wit sighed inside. He had wanted to do this the polite way, but the lieutenant wasn't going to let them in. Wit could see that now. It was all over the kid's face; he was picturing himself arresting forty highly skilled soldiers. He was seeing a commendation in his future. Maybe even a promotion.

Wit said, "I'm sure the United States would be thrilled to know you're invading the privacy of its citizens."

The lieutenant looked up from the passport, his lips pressed tight together. "The information is public record, Mr. O'Toole. Anyone with access to the nets can acquire it. You are requesting permission to enter my country. I have every right to know whatever I want to know about you. Your privacy laws don't apply here." He closed the passport, placed it on his desk, and steepled his fingers. "Why do you want to study the Formics?"

"Because we want to stop them," said Wit. "Which will probably involve killing them or driving them back into space. But between you and me, I'd rather kill them. It's easier that way. You don't have to worry about them coming back with their friends."

The lieutenant blinked, surprised by Wit's candor.

"My companions and I are soldiers," said Wit. "As you likely have already deduced. We're MOPs. Mobile Operations Police. We're here, dressed as civilians and passing through your gate as a courtesy to you. We don't have to come through this way. There are hundreds of ways to get into China. I would prefer to do it legally, as I'm attempting to do now. But should you deny us entrance, we'll get in the other way. Easy."

The lieutenant smiled, as if he found Wit's confidence amusing. "You think you can sneak by me and my men, Mr. O'Toole?"

"In my sleep," said Wit. "And if you deny us entrance here and force us to enter the country illegally, it will reflect very poorly on you, Lieutenant. You can be sure of that. Because once we're in the country we'll tell the Chinese military how we crossed right here, right under your noses. We'll tell them how lax your security is. We'll tell them how a whole fleet of foreign vehicles honking their horns and shooting off fireworks could pass through the gaping holes in the border here without any detection whatsoever. We'll tell them it was easy. We'll tell them all sorts of things. We'll be very thorough and very convincing. It will paint you, I'm afraid, in a rather negative light."

The lieutenant looked angry, but Wit was far from finished.

"And you and I both know that the blame won't stop there," said Wit. "Whoever helped you get this position will be culpable, too. He'll be tainted for putting an incompetent in charge here. He'll take the fall. It will annihilate any chance either of you have of ever getting promoted again. If you can't maintain a border crossing in the middle of nowhere, they'll say, then you can't do much of anything.

"However, if you *do* let us cross, you now have a story to tell. They passed as civilians, you'll say. They weren't carrying weapons. Their passports checked out. I had no reason to deny them access. In fact, I was doing my duty correctly by letting them in. And if the Chinese military asks me and my men why we would pretend to be civilians and cross over this way, we'll tell them that we had no other choice. We'll tell them the borders are so tight up there under that lieutenant that we had no choice but to abandon our weapons and go right through the gate. We'll tell them how the level of security here made us uneasy, how a mountain crossing was out of the question because the men at the border are too well trained and too savvy and too watchful of the passes. They'd catch us for sure. We'll tell them all sorts of things, Lieutenant. And it will reflect very well on you. They might even give you a shiny medal."

The lieutenant was quiet a moment. "I could arrest you right now," he said finally. "That would get me a medal, too."

"See? Now you're being stupid," said Wit. "You have no right to arrest us. We've committed no crime. We're not even on Chinese soil yet. This office is neutral territory."

"I could arrest you as soon as I let you in. Right over the border."

Wit shook his head, as if feeling sorry for the kid.

"Your stupid meter keeps going up. Think. If you arrest us right after we're through, then it's obvious you let us in only for that purpose. Again, we'll have committed no crime. My men and I represent thirty different countries. Do you really want the embassies of thirty different countries calling your superior officers and asking why China arrested citizens who legally crossed its borders?"

"You're soldiers. Your very presence in China is illegal."

"You're missing the point," said Wit. "Everything you're suggesting puts a target on your head. When this becomes an international incident, who do you think the Chinese are going to blame to pacify all parties involved? Us? The people who valiantly crossed into China to help its citizens and save lives? No. It will be you. You will take the hit. You'll be stripped of rank, honor, and any affiliation with the military. You'll have to get a blue-collar job. Maybe loading boxes somewhere. Or chopping the heads off fishes in some rancid-smelling market. You *won't* meet and marry that daughter of a party official. You *won't* rise to a position of station. You'll waste away in a one-room apartment with a bad back and no pension. Those are the facts, Lieutenant. You can let us in or you can send us away. The choice is yours."

Five minutes later Wit and his men were walking east into China. They stayed on the shoulder of the road in a long line as cargo trucks streamed past, heading toward the airfield. Wit stuck out his thumb, and it didn't take long before a truck picked them up and gave them a lift.

They slept on the plane, squeezed between crates and boxes. The pilot had accepted their offer without a second thought and promised to take them only as far as Hotan. From there they caught a flight to Jiuquan, and then to Zhengzhou. They ate when they were hungry and slept when they were tired.

Through it all Wit tracked the progress of the war. The Chinese were touting great successes and victories but supplying no evidence for either, which suggested it was all bogus, or at least highly exaggerated. The Russian army had offered to enter China and assist in the war, but China had refused. Probably because the Chinese worried that the Russians might not leave when the war was over. Kick out one invading army only to have another one to deal with.

The nets were flooded with vids. The Formics were relentless. Their skimmers were fast and lethal. Their troops were calm and methodical. They burned the countryside wherever they went, spraying their defoliants like farmers. The Chinese tried to take down the vids and paint a different picture, but you couldn't stop the floodgates of information.

Wit searched for more vids from Mazer Rackham but found none, which concerned him. It had been days now. There was no official word from New Zealand or the Chinese that Wit could find, which either meant that Mazer had been discreetly pulled back from the frontlines, or that he was MIA.

On their third day in the country they landed in Changsha. It was the last flight they were going to get. Commercial flights were grounded now, and no pilot would fly any farther south no matter how much money Wit offered.

Wit made a few calls from the airport. He needed all-terrain vehicles, and the black market in Changsha seemed like as good a place as any to find them. His contacts in Hunan province put him in touch with some shady people, who put him in contact with some even worse people, who suggested Wit go to a used truck lot in the southern, industrial part of the city called Winjia Alley. Wit took Calinga and Lobo with him and left the rest of the men at the airport.

The old man who greeted them at the lot was in his eighties maybe, with a slightly hunched back and a broad sun cap and a pair of exoskeleton braces on his legs to assist him with walking. He introduced himself as Shoshang.

"I'm Captain O'Toole of the Mobile Operations Police. These are two of my companions Calinga and Lobo."

Shoshang smiled. "Soldiers, eh? Come to fight the Formics."

"We've come to help as much as we can," said Wit.

"You think China needs help? You think China isn't strong enough?"

"From what I've seen, no country is strong enough. Not the U.S., not any nation in Europe, not Russia, no one. We all must help."

"Help is what I do best," said Shoshang. "What are you looking for?"

"Armored transports. Off-roaders. All-terrain. Enough to carry forty men and supplies. And they need to be airtight."

"War machines?" Shoshang frowned and shrugged. "Sorry to disappoint you, Captain, but I'm not licensed to sell that kind of vehicle. What you see on my lot is all I have." He gestured to the vehicles behind him. "Big utility trucks and dozers for commercial contractors. Perhaps you would like to test-drive one of those?"

Wit wasn't buying the innocent-civilian act or the weak-old-man act either. He had busted enough drug lords and gunrunners to know that it was normally the ones who didn't look the part who were the nastiest.

"Perhaps this will remind you of some inventory that may have slipped your mind," said Wit, tapping his wrist pad to the old man's.

Shoshang read the amount on his wrist, then smiled. "Ah yes. Now that I think about it, I might have what you're looking for."

He escorted them to a tall, rusted metal wall that encircled a junkyard at the back of the lot. The wall was topped with concertina wire and looked like it could withstand a small army. Shoshang waved his hand through the holobox beside the gate, and from somewhere on the other side a crank turned, and a chain pulled, and the heavy metal door swung open.

"A lot of security for a pile of junk," said Wit.

Shoshang smiled.

They walked through the junkyard—weaving through a labyrinth of scrap iron, crushed cars, and long-dead industrial equipment. When they reached a warehouse at the center of the maze, Shoshang stopped and faced them. Wit saw several armed men perched atop the warehouse roof and a few others among the piles of junk around them. Wit wasn't impressed. The men weren't professionally trained. They were all carrying themselves the wrong way, standing in the wrong places, brandishing their weapons like amateurs. Wit was beginning to think this had been a waste of time.

Then Shoshang ordered one of the thugs to open the warehouse, and Wit saw that the trip wasn't a total loss after all. There were five armored Rhinos inside—which were big, six-wheeled ATVs built for the Chinese military. They were much faster than light tanks and ideal for quick strikes and maneuvering. Shoshang had painted them a deep green to cover the army's insignia, and welders had attached additional armored plates and modifications to make them look like original vehicles instead of stolen government property, which is what they obviously were.

"If I drive those through a military checkpoint," said Wit, "I'm liable to get arrested. The army doesn't take kindly to thieves."

Shoshang looked offended. "These aren't stolen, Captain O'Toole. They were surplus, purchased legally on the open market. I have all the papers in order."

"Falsified papers," said Wit. "There *was* no surplus of Rhinos. The manufacturer was bought out by Juke Limited before production of the initial fleet was complete. Then Juke renegotiated with the Chinese and changed the design."

Shoshang smiled. "I see you are a student of military commerce, Captain O'Toole."

"I'm a student of a lot of things."

Shoshang scratched at his cheek then sighed. "Very well. I'm willing to drop the price because of the *legality* issue." He said the word like it annoyed him.

"What about fuel?"

"I am feeling generous today," said Shoshang. "I will give you all five vehicles and enough batteries and fuel cells for a year of constant use."

"For how much?"

Shoshang told him. It was ten times what the vehicles were worth, even on the black market.

"We'll take them," said Wit.

Shoshang looked surprised. He had expected a brutal negotiation, an argument even. But Wit had neither the time nor the inclination. Strategos auditors would likely sniff out Shoshang and seize the money back anyway. It wasn't Wit's concern.

"We also need supplies," said Wit. "I'm told you're a man who can acquire anything."

"I'm a man of many talents, yes. What else do you need?"

"Containment suits, for starters. With HUDs, targeting capabilities, and plenty of oxygen."

"I take it you've seen the mist the Formics spray."

"We'd rather not breathe it," said Wit. "We also need weapons. Small arms. Antiaircraft. Smart grenade launchers."

"What type of grenade munitions?"

"Whatever we can get. HEABs, flechette-laden, thermobaric. Low-velocity, twenty-by-forty millimeters."

HEABs, or high-explosive air-bursting grenades, would be ideal. It was easier to program the munitions, and air detonations usually had the greatest kill count. But Wit wasn't getting his hopes up.

"I'll need to make a few calls," said Shoshang. "It will take a few hours. It's not every day I'm asked to outfit a miniarmy. But don't worry, Captain, I will get you what you need." Shoshang removed his hat, dabbed at his forehead with a cloth, and smiled. "I can't help but wonder, however, why your own agency isn't supplying you. Not that it's any of my business."

"You're right," said Wit. "It's not your business."

Four hours later a convoy of five Rhinos and forty MOPs were heading south out of Changsha on secondary highways. Wit and Calinga were up in the cab of the lead vehicle. The northbound lanes were packed, but the southbound lanes were wide open.

Calinga gestured to the containment suit he was wearing and the rifle in the seat beside them. "Dare I ask where you got the money to buy all this?"

"MOPs has emergency accounts all over Europe," said Wit. "I emptied a few of them. If we help win the war, the expense may be forgiven. If we die in the process or if the Formics seize Earth, it won't much matter anyway."

"Such confidence," said Calinga.

"This won't be an easy fight. No reason to avoid that fact."

"So what's the plan? You said we'll strike key targets and sabotage. What are our targets exactly? The landers? They're shielded. Missiles can't touch them. The air force is hitting them with everything they've got and not putting a scratch on them."

"Then we'll have to find a way inside one."

"How?"

"No idea. If we can reach one, we can do some recon and investigate." He brought up a map of southeast China on his holopad. "We'll hit the second lander first. The one in the middle. The northernmost lander near Guilin is where the highest casualties are, but it's also where the military is concentrating. I'd rather avoid direct contact with the army right now. Let's accomplish something first. Let's prove our worth to the Chinese. Then they'll ask us to stay."

"Why not go for the southernmost lander, where the flyers are seeding bacteria into the sea? That's serious ecological damage. The faster we stop that the better."

"That lander is more isolated," said Wit. "It's at a higher elevation and harder to reach. That's better left to the air force. Plus the casualties there are in the hundreds, whereas they're reaching the thousands and tens of thousands at the other two. The second lander is the best strategic position as well. We can easily get to either of the other two if we suddenly have to."

They drove for a hundred kilometers without any problems. Traffic on the northbound lanes became increasingly more congested. Soon the cars and trucks were moving over into the southbound lanes and driving in the wrong direction in an effort to scoot the traffic. Calinga kept laying on the horn and flashing his lights to prevent a head-on collision. Most of the cars swerved, but soon the traffic took on a fast and frantic pace.

"Pull over," said Wit.

Calinga took them off the road, and by the time the other Rhinos in the convoy had followed, the oncoming traffic was in a frenzy. Two trucks collided, blocking the road. The car behind them rammed them, trying to push its way through, getting stuck in the process. A pileup resulted. Four cars. Five. Seven. Horns blared. People screamed at each other. The congestion spilled over into the roadsides, where more cars got stuck in the mud and blocked any further passage. Drivers then abandoned their vehicles and ran north on foot.

Wit then saw why. A line of six Formics with mist sprayers was walking up the grass median of the highway, spraying the vegetation and anything that moved. The mist was coming out strong in thick, steady streams, rolling across the ground at waist height like a dense fog just above the surface.

Wit spoke into his radio, addressing the convoy. "Helmets on. We're in a hot zone. Stay put until I verify that these suits work."

He slid the helmet over his head, and it sealed itself to his containment suit. The oxygen valve initiated, and cool air filled the helmet. Wit dropped down from the cab onto the blacktop and closed the door behind him. Crowds of people ran past him, heading straight up the highway in a panic. A few of them were staggering, coughing, wheezing, dying from the mist. A woman collapsed into his arms, eyes rolling back in her head. Wit felt helpless. He had nothing to offer her. He laid her gently on the ground away from the rushing crowd so she wouldn't get trampled. Then he turned and pushed his way through the crowd toward the Formics. The pieces of his rifle were strapped to his hip. He snapped them together as he pushed his way forward, then he extended the barrel and popped in the magazine.

"Calinga, get on the radio. See if you can find any EMTs in the area. We need medics here immediately."

"On it," said Calinga.

Wit forced his way through the crowd, which was in chaos now, the people pushing and screaming and knocking others aside in a mad panic. Some of the fallen got back to their feet. Others were stepped on, kicked, and trampled. Wit helped one woman up, but he nearly got knocked down in the process.

He pushed on. The targeting system on his HUD told him the Formics were eighty-two yards away and closing the distance, coming toward him shoulder to shoulder, casually spraying the mist, as if treating the ground for weeds. It was the first time Wit had seen one in person, and the sight of them was like cold water down his spine.

He raised his rifle, but the civilians kept running into his line of fire. No good. He ran to his left and climbed up onto the hood of one of the wrecked trucks. Now, with some elevation, he had a clear shot. He put the stock to his shoulder, and all kinds of thoughts ran through his head. He didn't like using a weapon he had never fired before. Maybe Shoshang had acquired these guns because they were DOA, duds, Chinese rejects. Maybe the sight was a foot off target. Maybe the barrel was bent. Maybe the thing would blow up in his hands.

He zoomed in with his sight, aimed at the head of the Formic on the far right, and squeezed the trigger.

The rifle fired and recoiled. The back of the Formic's head exploded in a gray mist. Its legs buckled, and it dropped from Wit's sight.

Field test was over. Rifle passed. Time to get to work. Wit squeezed off five more quick headshots, one after another, straight down the line, right to left, *bam-bam-bam-bam-bam*.

The five remaining Formics dropped one after the other, their wands falling from their hands, their bodies crumpling. Wit watched the wand tips. A moment later, the mist stopped spraying.

The misty fog was thick around him now. Wit blinked a command to test his suit for leaks. The sensors beeped and indicated the all-clear; the suit was airtight apparently. Shoshang hadn't skimped them. His goods were legit. Miracle of miracles.

Wit hopped down from the truck and ran ahead through the mist to where the Formics lay. He stood over them, weapon up, ready to plug them with more rounds if they so much as twitched. None of them did.

Calinga's voice sounded in Wit's helmet. "Emergency personnel aren't coming. We're too far from an urban area. They say they don't have a treatment for the mist anyway, and they're short on people. They've got more calls like ours than they know what to do with."

"Move the people several hundred meters upwind," said Wit. "Get them away from mist until the air clears."

Wit squatted down and examined the Formics as Calinga relayed the order and mobilized the men. The Formics weren't wearing any clothing. Nor were they carrying any equipment other than the mist sprayers. No radio transmitters, no receivers, no comms equipment of any kind. Wit turned one over with his boot to be sure he wasn't missing anything. He hated touching the things, even with his boot—he disliked feeling the weight and thickness of them—but he couldn't afford to have any such reservations.

He noticed slight differences in their insectlike faces. Subtle things. A wider mouth here, larger eyes there. Darker fur on one than the other. At first glance they had all looked exactly alike, but now Wit could see that they were as different from each other as any group of humans.

He couldn't tell if these were male or female. They had no visible sexual organs. Maybe they were asexual, like parasites.

Wit snapped several photos with his HUD, first of the whole group, then of an individual headshot wound. Then he blinked a command to take down his dictation. He spoke for five minutes into his helmet microphone, describing the weapon he had used and where he had hit each of the Formics. They had all been headshots, yes, but he was specific about where each bullet had entered. He used medical terminology for the human head as a context, like a doctor describing an ER gunshot victim. Then he stated his conclusions. The Formics could be killed. Their landers were shielded, but their infantry was not. Headshots did the job nicely. He would try other ways in the future.

Wit then uploaded all the text, photos, and geotags to the nets. He created his own site using a minimalist theme design and the URL StopThe-

Formics.net and signed it "The Mobile Operations Police." He then ordered the site to translate this entry and all future entries into Chinese, and to place the Chinese text first in the post, followed by the original English. Then he used push software to send the same information to hundreds of social platforms and media venues across the world, including all the forums and sites used by servicemen in the Chinese military.

The military no doubt already knew that a headshot was fatal, but Wit wasn't going to assume anything. If he had information, he would share it, regardless of how obvious it might seem.

Wit returned to the Rhinos. Calinga and the rest of the men had moved the crowd upwind. The panic had subsided. Now the people were mourning. Fifty-four people were dead, most of them had been killed by the mist, though a few had died in the rush of the crowd.

"Now what do we do?" said Calinga. "These people are asking for a ride north to the nearest city. Some of their cars can't be driven anymore. We obviously can't give everyone a lift. The moment we start carrying people north, every other car we passed on the way down here is going to stop us and ask that we do the same for them. And we can't fit all these people anyway, not unless we're going to pile them on top of the Rhinos and take five trips."

"Tell the crowd everything you've told me," said Wit. "Explain that we're moving south, not north. We're going toward the Formics, not away from them. Tell them they'll move much faster if they help each other. We'll use the Rhinos to clear the wrecked vehicles and open up the highway. Those who have a functioning vehicle should make room for those who don't."

"What about the bodies?" asked Calinga.

"We'll dig a massive grave. The survivors can help, but we should lead that effort. We'll record everything, edit it down, and upload it to the site."

"We have a site now?"

"I'll explain while we dig."

They went to work. Soon the air cleared enough for the MOPs to remove their helmets, which made digging and breathing easier. Many of the civilians joined in. Some of them had tools and shovels in their trucks. Wit had sent MOPs out in a wide circle to form a perimeter. Just when the grave was done, the warnings came in over Wit's radio.

"Incomings!"

Wit was out of the hole with his helmet on when the skimmers came flying in over the trees. There were three of them: small, single-manned aircraft, moving fast. The lead one fired a burst of laser fire. An explosion to Wit's left knocked him off his feet. Dirt clods and rock rained around him. His ears were ringing.

All three skimmers were firing now. An explosion hit the crowd of civilians, sending bodies into the air. The others scattered, screaming.

Wit was on his feet with the grenade loaded two seconds later. The lead skimmer came around for a second pass, and Wit aimed and fired the HEAB at a point in the air ahead of the aircraft.

It wasn't a direct hit, but it was close enough. The HEAB detonated and blew out a burst of shrapnel that ripped into two of the skimmers flying in close formation. The skimmers jerked violently to one side, lost control, and crashed. No survivors. Not a chance.

Wit turned and scanned the sky for the third skimmer and saw that a troop transport had landed behind him, near where the six dead Formics lay. The transport doors opened, and Formics poured out. Several of them carried wands and began spraying immediately, unleashing steady streams of mist into the air. A squadron of MOPs hurried toward them, firing their weapons. Other Formics exited the transport and began recovering the Formics Wit had killed, carrying their corpses and equipment back inside the transport.

Wit turned back to the sky and saw the third skimmer retreating toward the horizon, well out of range. He then ran toward the transport. The new Formics with mist sprayers were going down, taking fire. It was easy pickings; they were right in the open and took no measures to conceal themselves. For a moment it looked like the skirmish would end quickly. Then the transport lifted, rotated, and opened its guns on Wit's men, who were using the cars and trucks as cover.

Sustained lasers from the transport sliced through the cars and cut through the asphalt, leaving deep, gouged lines in the earth. Globules of a laserized substance then shot forth from side-mounted cannons. The globules seared straight through whatever they hit, leaving gaping holes through engine blocks, people, the highway guard railing. Windshields shattered, parts and shrapnel blew in every direction.

MOPs went down.

The doors of the transport were still open. Wit fired in a grenade just as two other MOPs did the same. One grenade went in one side door and out the other, but the other two ricocheted right and stayed inside. The explosions blew fire and smoke out the doors in a deafening boom. The transport rocked to one side, wavered a moment, then dropped from the sky. It hit the ground and stayed upright, spilling out dead Formics.

MOPs were on it in an instant, unleashing gunfire inside the cockpit to make sure the job was done. Wit ran to where he had seen some of his men go down. The mist rolled through like smoke, obscuring his vision. The remnants of four men lay on the decimated blacktop, all of them in pieces. Wit had to resort to body scans to identify them. Toejack, Mangul, Chi-Won, and Averbach. Wit had handpicked each one of them. He had studied their backgrounds, tested them, trained them, shaped them into the soldiers they were. Two of them he had known for years.

Wit closed off the part of him that allowed him to mourn. There was no time. He spoke fast into his headset.

"Calinga, we need to get these people out of here. The Formics collect their dead. More might be here at any moment. I want this highway cleared, the bodies buried, and the people on the road immediately."

Everyone moved quickly. The civilians were in a state. Confused, terrified, panicked. Seven more civilians had died in the attack. Others had run off into the forests and not come back. Calinga found the ones who were coherent and could take orders and put them to work, gathering and calming the others. MOPs fired up the Rhinos and moved the vehicles blocking the road. Other MOPs pulled the bodies into the grave and pushed in the dirt. The most recent deaths were lowered in, some of them piece by piece. It was crude and fast and no way to handle fallen soldiers, but it was better than leaving them out on the road.

Calinga and his team gathered the surviving civilians and put those who didn't have vehicles with those who did. Once everyone was loaded up, the MOPs directed the traffic and got everyone moving north.

Wit and his team didn't pause to mourn those they had lost. There was no time. They drove the Rhinos farther off the road, concealing them in the nearest trees. Then they hiked back to the downed troop transport and waited.

Their containment suits were a bright yellow, probably made for field research, certainly not for combat. But they were tight fitting without being uncomfortable and offered plenty of mobility—perfect for the job at hand, really, except in terms of camouflage, and that could be easily remedied. Yet even with non-chameleonic suits, the MOPs were still able to hide themselves. In moments all of them were invisible, even to Wit. Trees, brush, abandoned vehicles. They melded with the landscape.

Ten minutes passed. Then twenty. The transports were silent, so Wit watched the sky. Finally he saw them. Two transports, flying low on approach, moving fast. At first Wit thought they wouldn't stop—they showed no sign of slowing. Then they descended quickly to the right and left of the downed transport.

Doors opened. Formics emerged. Alien hands picked up the fallen Formics.

Then Wit gave the order and all hell broke loose. He had been clear in his instructions. Do not let the transports in the air. That's where the firepower was. Take out the pilot first. Cripple the ship. Then mop up the others.

The men moved fast and efficiently. The transports remained grounded. Formics fell. It was over in less than ten seconds.

When the smoked cleared, Wit stepped up into the transport. There were dead Formics at his feet, their blood on the floor of the ship thick like syrup. Wit took video of everything. The flight controls, the switches and levers. He had no idea what anything did, and he did not experiment. He did the same outside. Every inch of the machine.

His preference was to get the aircraft into human hands for examination, but that wasn't going to happen. Instead, once they documented as much as they could, they fired two incendiary grenades and burned the vehicles.

Then they headed south, sticking to secondary roads and avoiding people as much as possible. As they went, Wit updated their site. He explained the new "kill, bait, and ambush" strategy: Take out a few infantry Formics, then lie in wait for the transport to collect them, and hit the corpse-recovery team. He stressed the importance of hitting the pilot first and avoiding the transport fire. He uploaded video, photos, and directions of attack—it was best to rush the transport from behind and slightly to the left or right, giving you a clear shot of the cockpit where the pilot was positioned as soon as possible. Attacking from the front was suicide.

Wit then checked the site's forum. He already had five different media requests for interviews. They all wanted the same thing: the face behind

MOPs, the human-interest story, the juicy details that would set the ratings on fire.

Wit's typed response was the same for all. "Who we are is irrelevant. Help the effort by broadcasting what we've learned. Show the vids. Share the tactics. Invite others in the fight to share their tactics, too. Focus on saving lives instead of offering useless entertainment."

Some would honor his request. Most wouldn't. What did they gain by playing the same vids as everyone else? They wanted *exclusive* content. They wanted exposés on MOPs, bios of its members, photos of loved ones back home.

Wit programmed the forum to filter any future media request and reply with his rote response.

Soon there were other posts as well. Anonymous messages from Chinese soldiers. Some expressed gratitude. Others shared information they had gleaned.

THE FORMICS DON'T SEEM TO USE RADIO. WE CAN'T DETECT ANYTHING. THEY DON'T SEEM TO RECOGNIZE OUR RADIO EITHER. OR IF THEY DO, THEY DON'T SEEM TO CARE.

THE FORMICS HEARING IS ODD. IT'S NOT ACUTE LIKE OURS. IT SEEMS TO BE BASED MORE ON PERTURBATIONS IN THE AIR, WHICH THEY CAN DETECT. LIKE BATS.

THE MIST IS LETHAL WITH ANY CONTACT. YOU DON'T HAVE TO BREATHE IT IN. WE'VE LOST MEN IN GAS MASKS. BUT THEIR WRISTS WERE EXPOSED, OR THEIR NECKS. THAT'S ALL IT TOOK.

Wit posted every tip onto the main site to give it more visibility.

Then he read the last forum entry. It was a spam post, offering life insurance. There were misspelled words and bad punctuation. It was not unlike the millions of other spam posts out there clogging the nets. Except . . . it *was* different. Subtly so. It took Wit a few minutes to decipher the code. He then entered the code into his browser and waited. The screen went white. Then a command appeared: READ THE POEM ALOUD. A Shakespearean sonnet materialized on screen.

Voice recognition, Wit figured.

He began to read the text aloud. He hadn't finished the first stanza, when the poem disappeared and a vid began. Colonel Turley of the U.S. Delta Force—and current member of Strategos—faced the camera. It was a prerecorded message.

"Since you've cut off all communications with us, Captain, we have no choice but to reach you by other, less-secure means. You should know that a majority of Strategos is calling for your court-martial. Some are calling for your head. You've illegally used MOPs funds. And you've forced our hand. If we admit to the Chinese that we sanctioned your insertion, we'll take a serious beating in the Security Council for ordering an unauthorized, unlawful military act. If we *deny* that we sanctioned your insertion, then we look dangerously inept and incapable of controlling rogue operatives. We order you to turn yourself in and allow the Chinese to extradite you. Your heart is in the right place, Captain. But your behavior is not conducive to the policies and procedures of the Mobile Operations Police. Please act accordingly."

The vid winked out. Turley had been reading the statement, Wit noticed. Wit had seen how the man's eyes scrolled right to left. His heart wasn't in it either. A majority of Strategos might be calling for Wit's court-martial, but Turley almost certainly wasn't one of them. He was a hawk if there ever was one.

What surprised Wit most was that Strategos hadn't figured out the solution. He opened the site's e-mail and sent an encrypted message directly to Turley.

COLONEL, WITH ALL DUE RESPECT, I CANNOT IN GOOD CONSCIENCE ABANDON THIS EFFORT. TODAY WE WERE ABLE TO HELP HUNDREDS OF CIVILIANS AND DEVELOP A TACTICAL MANEUVER THAT INFLICTS HEAVY ENEMY CASUALTIES. YOU CAN SEE EVIDENCE OF EFFORTS AT OUR SITE. TO LEAVE NOW WOULD BE TO ABANDON THE THOUSANDS AND TENS OF THOUSANDS OF CIVILIANS WE INTEND TO HELP AND PROTECT IN THE FUTURE. FOR THEIR SAKE, I MUST REFUSE YOUR DIRECT ORDER AND SUFFER THE PERSONAL CONSEQUENCES.

IN THE MEANTIME, MAY I MAKE A SUGGESTION THAT MIGHT SOLVE YOUR DILEMMA? LIE TO THE WORLD. LIE TO THE SECURITY COUNCIL. TELL THEM CHINA REQUESTED OUR INSERTION. TELL THEM

THEY ASKED FOR OUR HELP. PRAISE THE CHINESE FOR TAKING
SUCH SWIFT ACTION IN THE DEFENSE OF THEIR CITIZENRY. HONOR
THEM. SHOWER THEM WITH COMPLIMENTS. USE OUR VIDS AS EVI-
DENCE. GIVE THE CHINESE BRASS ALL THE CREDIT. THE CHINESE
WILL HAVE NO CHOICE BUT TO VALIDATE THE CLAIM. TO DENY IT
IS TO TURN THEIR BACK ON THEIR PEOPLE AND CONDEMN WHAT
HAPPENED TODAY.

He didn't sign it. He didn't want to use his name in any communications.

They found an abandoned hotel that night north of Chenzhou. Looters had ransacked the lobby. Wit took keys from behind the front desk and divvied them up among the men.

It was a nice hotel. There was hot water and soft beds. The air checked out. Calinga and a few others went out and returned with several cans of spray paint. Greens and browns and black and grays. Wit didn't ask where they had gotten them. They all met in the courtyard and camouflaged their containment suits. Then they returned to their rooms, hung their suits, and allowed them to dry.

Wit checked the news. Strategos had made a public statement praising the Chinese for requesting assistance from MOP troops. The press was directed to the footage of the transport ambush and rescue of Chinese civilians. It wasn't Wit's e-mail exactly, but it was close. The Chinese had wasted no time in responding. They praised MOPs' actions and promised that the government would continue to pursue all avenues to protect its people. It wasn't exactly a corroborative response but, more important, it wasn't a denial either.

Wit shut down his holopad and lay on his bed, staring at the ceiling. He had lost four men today, a tenth of his army on his first day of war. He couldn't sustain those losses. His whole unit would be wiped out in a little over a week at that rate. No, likely sooner. The fighting would get worse and more intense the closer they came to the lander. Plus the Formics would wise up to whatever tactics Wit and his men implemented. The enemy would adapt, reevaluate, change their MO. They would come at Wit in ways he hadn't considered.

Wit pushed all thought of the Formics aside.

He exhaled deep.

He let his muscles relax.

Then he allowed himself to think of those he had lost. He opened that part of him. He pulled from his memories. He brought to mind all the ridiculous moments they had shared. The pratfalls and dumb mistakes. The pranks and slips of the tongue. The dares given and the dares performed. All the moments that only he and they would find remotely amusing.

He had thought perhaps that such memories would make him laugh all over again, that he could stir up a cheerful mourning.

But no laughter came.

And when sleep finally took him and the Formics came in his dreams, the only laughter he heard was theirs.

# CHAPTER 20

# Post-Op

Mazer's eyelids slowly opened and he squinted at the light. Colors appeared in his vision, dark at first, blurred and melted together like soup—browns and blacks with speckles of white. Then the colors slowly took shape, solidified, and came into focus. They were timbers, Mazer realized, structural braces, trusses seen from below. He was lying on his back, looking up at a ceiling. Holes in the roof let in thin shafts of piercing sunlight. He heard voices. Hushed and to his right. He turned his head. The grandfather and Bingwen were ten meters away, sitting on the floor, eating rice with their fingers, using wide jungle leaves as bowls. Their bodies were turned slightly away from him. They didn't see him. Mazer knew this building, he realized. He had been in here before. Twice. It was the farmhouse.

Mazer opened his mouth to speak, but it took a moment to find his voice. When it came, it was raspy and quiet and weak. "How did I get here?"

The old man and the boy turned, startled. Then they smiled.

The old man spoke in Chinese, "Well, look who's returned to the land of the living."

They came over and knelt beside him. The old man lifted a cup to Mazer's mouth. "Drink this. Slow sips."

Mazer drank. The water was room temperature and had a tinny taste to it.

"You've been asleep for four days," said the old man, putting the cup aside. "Five, if you count the day you spent out by the crash. You're lucky to be alive."

Crash, Mazer thought. Yes, there had been a crash.

"My unit," he said in Chinese.

The old man's face became grave. "Your friends did not survive the accident. I am sorry. You would have died as well if not for Bingwen." He put a hand on the boy's shoulder. "He brought you back here. Then he and a few others brought you back from the grave."

There was a blanket draped across Mazer. The old man pulled it aside and revealed heavy bandages wrapped around Mazer's midsection. The bottom layer was gauze, but the additional layers were strips of fabric of various colors. He wasn't wearing a shirt.

"They operated on you," said the old man. "A midwife and Bingwen here."

"It was mostly the midwife," Bingwen said. "I just held things open and translated. She did all the cutting and stitching."

Mazer's hand carefully went to the bandage. There was a dull ache in his abdomen he hadn't noticed until now. A tightness.

"Your insides were damaged," said the grandfather. "The machine said we had to fix it or you'd die."

"What machine?" Mazer asked.

Bingwen reached to his side and held up the Med-Assist. "The batteries died three days ago."

"It dictated the surgery to you?"

"In English," said the old man. "Lucky for you Bingwen speaks good English."

"Lucky for me," said Mazer. "How did the surgery go?"

The old man shrugged. "It took a long time. Mingzhu, the midwife, did not want to do it. She cried and refused and said it was a waste of time. Bingwen and I and your friend made her finish."

"My friend?"

"The doctor," said Bingwen. "The American. Kim. She helped us."

Mazer was confused. "You mean her voice. Her *voice* helped you." But how did they know Kim's name?

"It was her voice on the device, yes. But she was on line, too," said Bingwen. "The device called her. She was very concerned for you."

"You spoke to her? The actual person?"

"She took us through the surgery. She saved you. And she helped us monitor you afterwards until the batteries died. She tried to get us evacuated, to bring a ship to our position. But she was unsuccessful. There are hundreds of such requests, she was told, and no medevacs are getting through. She was ready to come herself, but no private pilot would bring her here."

Mazer could hardly believe it. Kim. Was that possible? They had spoken with Kim. She had guided them, saved him. He looked down at the bandages around his stomach. He wanted to call her, thank her, hear her voice, not the impersonal voice of the device, but the voice that spoke to *him,* the voice that had feelings and promises woven into it.

"How was I afterwards?" he asked.

The old man squirmed. "In a lot of pain. Delirious. You cried out many times. You ran a fever. Kim had us give you antibiotics and keep you asleep. I thought you had died on two different occasions, your breathing was so shallow. There were other medicines we needed but didn't have. I've been feeding you water and nutrients. The machine said you had a thirty percent chance of survival. I thought your chances were far worse."

"I'm glad I proved you wrong."

"You're a fighter. Even when you sleep," said the grandfather.

"Fight has nothing to do with it," said Mazer. "It was the medicine, your efforts, and a good dose of luck." He reached out and put his hand on the grandfather's arm. "What is your name, friend?"

"Danwen," said the grandfather.

"Thank you, Danwen." He reached out with the other hand and took Bingwen's, squeezing it with what little strength he had. "Both of you."

He removed his hands. The motion took an enormous amount of energy, as if his hands were four times as heavy as normal. He looked to his left and right. "Where is Mingzhu? I'd like to thank her too."

Danwen and Bingwen exchanged looks. The boy scowled.

"They left three days ago," said Danwen. "In the night. Bingwen had brought back a rifle and ammunition from the crash. We had food as well, cans and things that Bingwen and I had buried and stockpiled and went back to the village for. Mingzhu and the others took it all. Even the water buffalos. They left us with nothing."

Mazer looked at the cup. "You have water."

"Rainwater," said Danwen. "We catch it off the roof and boil it. We dare not drink from the streams. Not with the mist."

"Smart," said Mazer. "For boiling what you caught and for avoiding everything else."

"It doesn't taste very good," said Bingwen.

"Beats dying of thirst," said Mazer. He turned to the old man. "Where did the others go?"

Danwen shrugged. "North. With everyone else. All the survivors are moving that way."

"You two didn't go with them."

"We weren't going to leave you," said Bingwen.

Mazer squeezed the boy's hand again. "Again, thank you." Then his brow wrinkled and turned to Danwen. "How did you move me here? The crash site had to have been several kilometers away."

Danwen answered eagerly, as if he had been waiting to share this story. He told Mazer everything, throwing in tiny details that he knew would build the drama. Bingwen looked down at the floor at first, then excused himself, busying himself elsewhere in the farmhouse. When the old man finished, Mazer called the boy over and extended his hand. "I owe you my life three times over, Bingwen. I can't thank you enough. What you did was very brave."

Bingwen took the offered hand and shook it. "Repaying the favor," he said, wiggling his cast in the air.

"How's your arm?"

"Fine. It doesn't hurt anymore. Not if I don't use it, that is."

Mazer felt exhausted then, his eyes heavy, his muscles weak, as if the world was slowing down again.

"Leave him be," Danwen said to Bingwen. "He needs his rest."

Mazer wanted to argue. He had been resting for four days. He needed to move, he needed to get his body up again. He was useless lying here. He was endangering Bingwen and Danwen. They should move on. There was nothing else they could do for him.

He felt his breathing slow into the rhythm of sleep. He fought it, but the darkness pulled at him and wrapped him in its silent blackness.

The crack of thunder woke him, loud and booming and rolling through the valley. He was still on his back on the farmhouse floor. It was dark out. Rain was pounding the roof, leaking through half a dozen holes in the ceiling and forming puddles on the floor. Mazer turned his head. Bingwen was asleep beside him, his back to him, practically touching him. At one point Bingwen may have enjoyed a corner of Mazer's blanket, but it had since fallen off, and now Bingwen lay huddled in a fetal position, cold and shivering.

Mazer lifted his arm and pulled the blanket off himself and onto the boy. The night air felt brisk and biting against Mazer's exposed skin, and he wished the old midwife had left him with his shirt.

Mazer turned and saw Danwen standing at a window, looking out into the storm. The old man held a long thin object in one hand, over a meter in length, with the end of it resting against his shoulder. Mazer couldn't tell what it was until lightning struck, and a flash of light lit up the man's front. The sword was old and thin with an ornate hilt of a dull, unpolished metal. A family heirloom perhaps, or a costume piece for cultural events. Not a very good weapon. Certainly not much against a squadron of aliens, should they arrive.

I should be the one standing guard, Mazer thought.

Only, he didn't have the strength to stand. He barely had the strength to move his head and look about. And when his eyes began to droop again—despite the cold and damp and roar of the storm—he couldn't muster the strength to fight back the pull of sleep.

When he woke, it was daylight. The storm had moved on, and sunlight stabbed through the holes in the roof, reflecting off the puddles on the floor and casting sprinkles of light onto the walls. Bingwen and Danwen were nowhere to be seen, but someone had draped the blanket back across Mazer's chest. He forced himself to get up, rolling to one side and then pushing up with his arms. The movement sent a jolt of pain through his abdomen, but he knew, considering what he'd been through, the pain could have been much worse. He got on all fours, feeling shaky and a little unsure of himself. Whatever they had given him to keep him asleep was taking its sweet time getting out of his system. He felt something hanging from his hip, and he realized then that he had a catheter in him. He had been wearing it all this time and hadn't even noticed. He reached down, winced, and pulled it out.

He got one foot under him, then another, and stood. His legs were shaky and weak; he felt light-headed. He shuffled to the doorway and braced himself against the jamb. Danwen and Bingwen were right outside, squatting by a small cook fire, boiling more water and rice.

"You shouldn't be up," said Danwen. "The machine said you should stay off your feet for five to six days."

"Close enough," said Mazer. "Who put a catheter in me?"

Danwen looked confused. He didn't know the word.

"The bag that catches my urine," said Mazer.

Danwen reared back his head and laughed. "That was the old midwife. Of all the instructions the machine gave us, that was the one step she didn't fuss about."

"That's not true, Grandfather," said Bingwen. "She fussed plenty about that, too."

"Well, her heart wasn't in it," said Danwen. "It took little arguing to convince her."

"Tell me what's happened since the accident," said Mazer. "With the war."

Danwen put down the pot he was holding. "Better if I showed you." He walked past Mazer through the door, dipping under Mazer's arm as he went, and crossed the room to the open windows. He waved Mazer over. "Come, if you can walk now. See for yourself."

Mazer shuffled over to him, and Danwen gestured out the window. The valley below was stripped of vegetation. Where there had once been rice fields and thick tropical vegetation on the edges of the valley was now scarred earth—mud and exposed roots and puddles of dirty rainwater, as if someone had peeled back the skin of the world.

"The aliens did this?" asked Mazer.

"They call them Formics now. That's the name the army has given them."

"How do you know that?"

"I've gone down to the valley a few times now to search for supplies. I usually take from the dead. I am not proud of it, but that is how we have survived. I've found clothes for you. There is a shirt over there in that box, if you're ready to wear it." He pointed to a crate over in the corner. "The people ran from their villages with what little they could carry. I've brought up bags of food, pots for cooking, necessary things. I'm not the only one who picks from the dead either. I've seen other people as well, survivors like us, digging through the people's belongings. They tell me things. The Formics are peeling away the land, they say. All of the biomass. Plants, animals, people. All biological matter. They're scooping it up and collecting it all into a giant pile. A mountain of biomass, rotting in the sun beside the lander. I believe them. When the wind blows north from the lander, you can smell it. A rotting stench. A smell so powerful, it turns the stomach. Two days ago the machines came through this valley. Bingwen and I watched them. They stripped the land without even touching it. The machines drove forward and the scorched land peeled away."

"Shields," said Mazer. "That must be how they're stripping the land. It's the same technology they're using to protect the lander."

"I do not know technology," said Danwen. "I only know that they are evil. Destruction and death is their only business. First they spray the mist. Whatever it touches wilts and dies quickly. Then the wind carries it elsewhere. Over time the plants touched by the wind wilt as well, sometimes an hour later, sometimes as much as a day. Soon everything shrivels and dies. Then the Formics return and scoop it all away." He looked behind him, saw that Bingwen was still squatting by the fire twenty meters away, and spoke almost in a whisper. "The boy's parents are dead. I found them a few days ago in the valley behind us. They had been killed with the mist. I went back the next day with a shovel to bury them, but the land had been stripped. They were gone. Their bodies are there in the rotting mountain. I have not told Bingwen. No boy should have to know such things."

Mazer was quiet a moment then said, "Is that where you found the sword? Down in the valley?"

Danwen nodded. "Off a dead man from our village. It is not much. Hardly any edge to it. But we needed something when we lost the rifle. I will protect Bingwen with my life."

"He's lucky to have you," said Mazer.

Danwen smiled. "Yes. And you're lucky to have *him*."

A sound of an aircraft in the distance made them both turn in that direction.

"What about the war?" asked Mazer.

"For the first few days there were many planes and battles in the air. Our fighters were better than theirs. I saw two Formic flyers destroyed in a dogfight. I watched the whole thing from right here." He pointed west. "They crashed five kilometers or so in that direction. I felt like dancing. But these are little victories. The rumors are that wave after wave of Chinese soldiers are dying. Great battles northwest and southeast of here. The Formics mow them down. It is a one-sided war, and we are losing."

"What about the lander?"

"What of it?"

"Has anyone attacked it?"

"The air force made a great show of it. Dozens of aircraft, flying in formations and firing every kind of missile and laser. We heard the explosions for days. Boom boom boom. Nothing gets through to the lander, though. It is protected. After a while the air force gave up. They haven't come back."

"What about Chinese infantry? Have you seen any tanks or military presence near here?"

"I have seen nothing," said Danwen. "Not a single Chinese soldier."

"You should have left me here and moved north with the others," said Mazer.

"Bingwen wouldn't hear of it. I suggested having the water buffalo pull you again, but you were too weak. Too sick. You probably wouldn't have made it. Bingwen refused. He can be very stubborn."

"And very smart."

"Yes. That too."

"I'm sorry I kept you. You can move on now. There's no reason for you to stay."

Danwen laughed quietly. "Bingwen says we are safer with you than we would be out in the open. He says you'll protect us. That's why he brought you back. For protection. Again, a very smart boy."

"I'm not going north," said Mazer. "When I'm well enough I'm going south, toward the lander."

"Why?"

"To destroy it."

"You are one man. Wounded and without any weapons. How can you destroy such a thing?"

"Find a hole in their shield and exploit it."

"And what if there is no hole?"

"Then I'll make a hole."

Danwen shook his head and laughed sadly. "You are as stubborn as the boy, Mazer Rackham. As stubborn as the boy."

# CHAPTER 21

# Homecoming

Lem's ship, the Makarhu, landed at the Jukes North Dock on Luna just as Father had instructed, arriving precisely at the appointed hour. Lem could have arrived twelve hours earlier, and he had been tempted to do just that to throw Father off his game. But in the end he had decided against it. To ignore Father's specific instructions would be to fire the first shot of whatever war would play out between them, and for now Lem thought it best to play the part of the conciliatory son. Better to see first what Father was playing at and then react accordingly.

Lem stood at Makarhu's airlock in his best uniform. He had not yet turned on his greaves, and he could feel the light gravity of the moon pulling at his feet. It was a welcomed feeling. The first sign of home.

Outside, the anchors clicked and locked. The umbilical extended and pressurized. The airlock beeped and opened. Then Lem took a deep breath, switched on his greaves, felt the stronger pull of gravity at his feet, and walked down the umbilical toward the terminal gate and whatever Father had up his sleeve.

It was not what Lem had expected. As he stepped through the final door and into the terminal, the cheers and applause of several hundred people and the flashing cameras of several dozen reporters assaulted him from all sides. It was a media frenzy. To his left, a group of perhaps a hundred females, some as young as ten years old and others old enough to be their mothers, screamed like rabid fans at a red-carpet event, waving signs and banners expressing their undying love for him or asking for his hand in marriage. To his right, applauding with much more restraint and yet still showing a great deal of enthusiasm, was a crowd of Juke employees, some of whom Lem had known on a casual basis before setting out, but most of whom were complete strangers to him. The press was bunched together behind a roped-off section of the terminal, their faces hidden behind their rapidly clicking cameras. And there, in the center of the whole circus, fifteen meters away, directly in front of Lem, smiling ear to ear with his arms extended in that universal invitation of an embrace, was Father.

Lem knew instantly the role he was supposed to play here. He made eye contact with Father, smiled, walked briskly toward him, and threw himself into Father's embrace. The cameras went crazy. The crowd gave a collective *Ahh,* as if nothing plucked at the heartstrings more than the reunion of a father and son.

Father's embrace was tight, pressing them hard into each other, as if Father feared something might suck Lem back out into space. They stayed that way for at least thirty seconds—not too long so as to be awkward for those watching, but long enough to erase any doubt of their absolute love and devotion for each other.

Then Father broke the embrace and stepped back, holding Lem at arm's length, smiling and regarding his son. Lem was surprised to see tears in Father's eyes, and for a moment Lem even thought them genuine. Then he reminded himself that Father had orchestrated all of this, including this moment, and that Father never left anything to chance. If tears were visible, then tears were meant to be seen.

Lem briefly considered conjuring up watery eyes of his own—he could do so easily and rather convincingly—but he figured Father would want him to play the role of the strong, masculine one, the son who leaves for war as a boy but who gallantly returns as a man. That was probably the plan anyway.

The cameras went into high gear again. Tears in Ukko Jukes's eyes? Unprecedented! *Click-click-click-click-click.*

"It's good to see you, Father."

"Welcome home, son."

Ukko put an arm around Lem, and they moved for the exit, pushing their way through the crowd. Six or seven men from Father's security detail kept the reporters and screaming fans at bay, making a path.

"Lem, what was it like to fight the Formics?" one reporter yelled, his arm extending from the crowd, holding a recording device.

"Lem, will you assist your father in his personal fight against the invaders?" yelled another.

"Did you and your crew really take on the whole Formic ship?"

"What will you say to the families who've lost loved ones?"

Lem and Father were moving toward a skimmer Father had parked inside the building. There were more security guards around it. The windows were tinted.

Just before they reached it, Ukko stopped, turned back, and faced the crowd, his face still plastered with a smile, his voice loud enough to be heard over the din. "Ladies and gentlemen, please. My son just returned home from nearly two years in space. He and his crew have been through a series of traumatic events. He will be happy to answer all of your individual questions on another occasion. For now, please respect a family's privacy. He and I have a lot of catching up to do."

A security guard opened the skimmer door. Father ushered Lem inside and squeezed in behind him, taking the seat opposite. The door closed, and the skimmer took off. It was quiet and luxurious inside. The seats were wide, deeply cushioned, and covered in leather. Even the lap belts and shoulder straps were the height of comfort, yet another reminder that Lem was truly home. He buckled himself in so as not to be thrown about in the low gravity, then addressed his father. "You just promised those reporters personal interviews with me."

"You'll need to give a lot of those, Lem," said Ukko. "People want to hear your story."

"And what story is that?"

"Don't tell me you've forgotten it already."

"What story are they expecting, Father?" said Lem. "What did you tell them? You obviously fed them something. They were asking about my involvement with the Formics."

"Again, good name choice there. The media loves the word 'Formic.' The whole world's using it. It's the hard *K* sound. You can't argue with a hard *K*. Like 'tank' or 'kill' or 'Juke.' "

" 'Formic' was Benyawe's idea," said Lem.

Father smiled. "Noloa Benyawe. How is she?"

"Fine. She was playing second fiddle to my chief engineer, Dr. Dublin, the ditherer, until I put her in charge of testing the gravity laser. At first I thought it was one of your life tests for me."

Father frowned. "Life tests?"

"Come now, Father. All the games you've played with me ever since I was a child, all the obstacles heaped in my path in some ridiculous effort to impart some of your wisdom to me."

"You flatter yourself, Lem. I have far more important things to do than constructing elaborate scenarios that might teach you a moral or two. You're not a child anymore."

"No, I'm not. Which is why I was somewhat disappointed when I learned that you had told Dublin not to do anything that might endanger me. And don't deny it. He told me so himself."

"Why would I deny it?" said Ukko. "You were testing an unproven, potentially volatile device, Lem. I asked Dublin to use caution, if not because of the sheer value of the prototype then at least for the welfare of my only son. Pardon me for such an offense. Next time I'll give little regard for your life and have my engineers be reckless and irresponsible, if that's more to your liking."

"You made Dublin doubt his every move. He was paralyzed with fear. That's why our first round of tests took so long. Dublin wouldn't take any risks. He had the fear of harming me and therefore displeasing you hovering over his head."

Ukko laughed. "So I'm responsible for another man's fear now? What else am I guilty of, a child's nightmares? Really, Lem, you're blaming me for your inability to conduct the initial tests? Dublin is a grown man. He makes his own decisions and accepts full responsibility for them. So should you."

"You gave Chubs, my second in command, the same instructions: Do nothing that will endanger Lem. You essentially told him to supersede my authority. You made me look weak in front of my crew."

"You seem to forget, Lem, that when you're piloting one of my ships, you're acting as an employee of this company. You don't get special privileges because you're my son. You have responsibilities as a captain, and your first priority shouldn't be how elevated you remain in the minds of your crew. Your first priority *is* your crew, twenty-five of whom died under your watch and as a direct result of your reckless orders. Do you have any idea how damaging that is to the company? Now there will be lawsuits. And regardless of how we respond, regardless of how fairly we treat the grieving families, regardless of how generous we are in the settlement, the press will skewer us. They will label us insensitive and careless. You can't win those battles, Lem. Sooner or later, the press will stop caring why we did it. It won't matter that we were trying to stop the Formics. We'll look negligent. We'll look like the bad guy. And when that happens, our stock will dip. Do you have any idea how much money is lost when we go down one one-hundredth of a percentage point?"

Lem didn't answer.

"Well do you?" Father insisted.

"Of course I do, Father. I own shares in this company, and I'm the primary shareholder in quite a few others. I know how the market works."

"Well good. I'm glad to see that your expensive education is affording you some awareness of the world. When you told me you had bumped those free miners off the asteroid, I thought you might have lost control of all your mental faculties."

"Your precious prototype wasn't damaged, Father."

"You're right about that, Lem. It is precious. Several billion credits worth. The Makarhu is rather valuable as well. It's one of our fastest, most luxurious ships. Which is why I can't for the life of me understand why you would be irresponsible enough to risk damaging all that. This is piloting 101, Lem. These are fundamental principles that every captain knows. Rule number one: Don't destroy the ship. Rule number two: Don't kill the crew. Surely someone reviewed this with you before you set out."

Lem turned away from Father and gazed out the window. They had left the terminal now and were flying over the lunar landscape back toward the city. To their right were the massive Juke production facilities where most of the ships in Father's mining fleet were built and tested prior to their departure for the Belt. A massive Juke logo was prominently displayed on the largest and tallest of the buildings.

"Yes, I gave Chubs special instructions," said Father. "I told him not to follow any order of yours that might put you in danger. I did so to protect my property and to protect you."

"Protect me from what, Father? My own poor judgment? My own stupidity? Don't you realize that by giving that order, you not only stripped me of true command, you also demonstrated your complete lack of confidence in me?"

"Is that what you want, Lem? Do you want me to tell you how *confident* I am in you, how sure I am that you can do it? Do you honestly need that kind of coddling?"

Lem wanted to scream. He wanted to beat the back of his head into the headrest. But he kept still and said nothing.

"And why are you complaining anyway?" said Father. "Chubs obviously ignored my order. You attacked the Formic ship, for crying out loud, an alien vessel a hundred times your size. I'd say that constitutes dangerous orders. Chubs clearly didn't supersede you then. He followed *you*, not me."

"He refused my orders on other occasions."

"So you were giving out *multiple* dangerous orders? Well, in that case, it sounds like you were more reckless than I expected and that I was right to give him the instructions I did. You should be thanking me. I might have saved your life."

Lem turned back to the window. Nothing had changed. Father was as critical and impossible as ever—fixated on Lem's mistakes and blind to all of Lem's accomplishments. Lem had intended to tell Father how Lem and the crew had mined the asteroid, how they had developed a method for extracting the ferromagnetic minerals from the rock after it had been pulverized, which was a potential industry breakthrough. Yet now Lem had no desire to tell Father anything. Why should he? Father would only see the errors. He would only shoot the whole premise with holes.

Lem suddenly felt angry with himself, realizing now that he had wanted to tell Father the good news not because he knew the extraction technique would help the company, but because he so desperately wanted to win Father's favor.

How pathetic, thought Lem. After everything, I'm still poking about for Father's approval. Well, not anymore. Enjoy your comfortable seat, Father. If I have my way, this won't be your skimmer or company much longer.

They flew over the northern outskirts of Imbrium and then continued south over the Old City. Then the skimmer banked to the left and headed east. Soon the city was behind them, and they were once again over untouched lunar surface. Finally, they came to one of the entrances into the tunnels of Juke Limited.

The entrance was a wide, circular landing pad with a giant letter-number combination on its center, signifying where in the intricate tunnel system they would be entering. The skimmer touched down gently, and the landing pad descended like an elevator. After thirty meters, the landing pad stopped at a brightly lit docking bay, where robot arms lifted the skimmer and carried it off the pad and into the bay airlock.

Lem could see a shuttle and a few technicians waiting in the bay just outside the airlock. He and Father sat in silence a moment while the airlock pressurized.

When Father finally spoke, all the bite was gone from his voice. "I *am* glad you're home, Lem. Despite what you may think, I am glad you're safe. I know I'm not the easiest person to get along with, but everything I've done, I've done because I thought it was best for you. I didn't have an easy upbringing, Lem. You know that. What I've built, I've built from nothing. And one of my fears has always been that your life would be too soft, that *you* would be too soft. Not because of who you are, but because of what we have, because of the luxuries our fortune affords us. I didn't want you to be a child of privilege, Lem. I didn't want a silver spoon in your mouth. I wanted a bitter spoon for you. Like I had. You may think that makes me a terrible parent, and maybe you're right, but you're a better man because of it. There's no arguing that."

The airlock buzzed the all-clear, and without another word, Father opened the door and stepped out of the skimmer. He walked through the airlock door and climbed into the waiting shuttle. It whisked him away immediately and disappeared down a corridor.

Lem sat there a moment, too stunned to move. Not because Father had just abandoned him—Father was always zipping off somewhere—but because Father had never spoken to Lem that way. He had never discussed their relationship or broached the subject of their fortune. Not that Father had made any attempt to conceal their fortune from Lem. How could he? Everything around them bore witness to it. And yet to hear Father mention it and, more significantly, for Father to acknowledge that Lem was any measure of a man felt completely foreign to Lem.

And yet Father had seemed sincere. There was no hint of irony or sarcasm in his voice.

What was this? Lem wondered. Another test? Another exercise in humiliation? Or was Father actually speaking from the heart?

"What's the matter, Lem?" a voice said. "You got space legs?"

Lem looked up. Father's assistant, Simona, was outside in the airlock, bent forward and looking inside the skimmer, holding her holopad.

"You're not stuck in there are you? Do I need to call someone?"

"My legs are fine," said Lem. He climbed out of the skimmer then brushed a nonexistent speck of dust off his sleeve.

"Little atrophy is nothing to be ashamed of," Simona said. "Two years in zero-G is a long time."

She was talking to him like he was a boy, just as she always had, even though she was only five years his senior. He hated that. "I'm fine," he said.

He hadn't noticed her standing there among the technicians earlier, but that didn't surprise him. Simona had a way of suddenly appearing at Father's side exactly when he needed her, usually without making a sound. Lem had jokingly called her a jungle cat once, which she had mistakenly taken as some flirtation. She had then proceeded to tell Lem that she wouldn't be one of his conquests and flatly denied him. Lem had laughed at that, which Simona had taken as yet another insult. It was all a silly misunderstanding, but it had soured the air between them, and Lem could sense that two years apart hadn't mended that.

Simona looked exactly as she did when he had left: conservative skirt, conservative blouse, flat functional shoes. She was not one for fashion. She usually found the latest trends insulting and ridiculous. Lem agreed with her, but that didn't raise her in his esteem. She was not particularly pretty either. Not plain, but not the kind of woman that would earn a second look. Her hair was arranged to keep it out of her face, and that was the extent of attention she gave it. Her nose was small, her cheeks freckled, her chest flat. She was like an awkward twelve-year-old girl who had made a wish to stay that way her whole life.

"Father left in a hurry," said Lem.

"He won't be coming," said Simona. "He has meetings."

"Coming where?"

"Didn't he tell you?" She looked down at the schedule on her holopad and started walking away from him down the corridor. "No, of course he didn't. He has too much on his mind." She snapped her fingers. "Come."

He hurried and fell into step beside her. "I'm not a dog, you know."

She didn't look up from her pad. "I snap. I give quick commands. That's how we move things along."

"Yes, well, it's not very polite."

"Your father doesn't mind it."

"I'm not my father. I'm nothing like my father."

She shot him a glance and a wry smile. "No, you're not."

He stopped. "What's that supposed to mean?"

She faced him. "It means what I said. I was agreeing with you."

"Yes, but when you say it, it sounds like an insult."

She folded her arms. "Agreeing with statements you make is insulting. Noted. I'll argue and disagree more." She motioned down the hall. "Now, shall we move on?"

They got walking again. Lem grit his teeth. Same old Simona. Ten seconds, and you wanted to strangle her.

"Why the rush?" he asked. He practically had to jog to keep up with her.

"We keep a tight schedule, Lem. Your father is managing the largest corporation in the world and trying to stop a war. It's a full plate. I'm glad you're home, by the way."

"Thanks."

"Your father is glad as well. He's been concerned about you."

"So he said."

She cast him a look. "You don't believe him?"

He didn't want to answer. Whatever he said to Simona would doubtless be echoed to Father. "Where are we going?" he asked, changing the subject.

"We're not going anywhere anymore," she said. "We're here." She stopped and opened a door to her left. Lem followed her in. They stood inside a small anteroom where there was a director's chair, a mirror, and a woman with several boxes of cosmetics. Beyond the anteroom was a much bigger space, where production lights and cameras were set up. A crew of five people was moving about, fussing with various equipment.

Simona pointed to the director's chair. "Sit."

Lem sat, gesturing to the cameras in the other room. "What is this?"

The woman with the cosmetics draped a paper bib around Lem's neck and began dusting his face with powder.

"This," said Simona, "is your first interview. Gun Chen. He's Chinese. He has an early-morning program. Very popular. Here are your talking points." She ticked them off on her fingers. "One, you were in the Kuiper Belt testing a Juke Limited proprietary device. You learned of the Formics, and you made plans to stop them—"

"It wasn't my idea to stop them," Lem interrupted. "It was someone else's."

"Whose? Another crewmember?"

"Another ship. Free miners. They came to me and asked us to help."

"In that case, you will say that you were in contact with another ship, and that 'we decided to attack the Formics.' They couldn't have done it without you, so you should give yourself more credit."

"There was a third ship as well," said Lem. "A WU-HU vessel."

Simona's face soured. "Were they in the fight?"

"Not technically. They stayed back with the women and children."

She nodded, considering this. "All WU-HU ships have been grounded to the Belt, so it doesn't matter anyway. Don't mention WU-HU. Say 'another mining vessel' if you have to. Or don't mention them at all."

"In other words, don't mention a competitor."

"The PR and legal teams have to vet the interview before it goes out, Lem. So if you said WU-HU, we'd cut it anyway. Let's save the audio engineers some overtime and keep it simple. When Chen asks you why you rushed back from the Kuiper Belt, your response is that you returned to deliver this proprietary device back to Juke. You believe this device can help in the war effort. Maybe even end the war."

Lem pushed the powder brush out of his face, and the makeup lady backed off. Lem got out of the chair. "Is that what this is about? Is that why father had all the fanfare at my homecoming? The media and the screaming Lem fans and the big phony embrace? To put me in the spotlight so I could be the pitchman for his damn glaser?"

He yanked the bib off his neck, tossed it aside, and was out the door, moving fast down the corridor in the direction Father's shuttle had been heading.

Simona was practically running to keep up. "Wait. Where are you going?"

"To have a word with dear sweet Dad."

"He's in a meeting."

"Where?"

"Will you stop for a moment and let me talk to you?"

"Where's the meeting?"

"I'm not going to tell you that."

"Then I'll find someone who will." He kept walking, looking up and down each corridor he passed, desperate for a passerby.

"No, you won't," said Simona. "None of the people in this wing know where your father is. And even if they did, all I would have to do is send a universal text to them, which takes all of two seconds, and no one would talk to you. They'd clam up."

"Yes. More of Father's obedient little sheep. Just like you."

"Will you stop for a second? I can't run in this skirt."

He stopped and spun around. She ran into him and dropped her holopad, which hit the floor but didn't break. Lem bent down and picked it up immediately to look at the schedule, but the screen went dark as soon as he touched it. He tapped it, but nothing happened.

"It won't respond to your touch," Simona said, yanking it out of his hand. "Biometric security." She tucked it under her arm, brushed a stray hair back, and said, "What is your problem?"

"My problem is that my father thinks he can use me in his little war-profiteering effort. And I've got news for him: I am not playing along."

"What are you talking about?"

"The glaser! He wants to use the glaser in the war."

"And that's a crime because . . ."

"I am not going to sell the glaser to the Chinese. Or to the Russians. Or to whomever it is Father wants me to pitch it to. I know what he's doing. This is classic Father. He fed the reporters my story of how I took on the Formics in the Kuiper Belt to make me out as a hero. He's trying to boost public opinion of me so he can use me to sell the glaser. He's doesn't want a son. He wants a celebrity endorsement. And you know what? You know what the saddest part of that whole scenario is? I actually fell for it. For a fleeting moment I actually entertained the idea that those misty eyes of his at the terminal were real. Which is ridiculous. He arranged the whole thing. It was a performance. A fabrication. He set the stage. He brought in the audience. He called action."

"Let me get this straight," said Simona. "You're the celebrity of a celebrity endorsement?"

He folded his arms across his chest. "You're mocking me."

"I'm trying to follow your train of thought," she said. "I'm not questioning your celebrity status. Son of the wealthiest man in the world. Hounded by the paparazzi in his earlier years. Voted most eligible bachelor by some teenage-centric pop zines on the nets. Good hair. White teeth. I can see why you might reach these conclusions."

He turned around and started walking again.

She hustled to keep up. "Okay, you're right. I was mocking you. But I shouldn't. Because you're partially right."

He stopped and faced her.

"But only partially," she said. "Your theory's wrong in a lot of ways."

"Enlighten me."

She sighed. "Your father *does* want you to tout the glaser. He does want to give it a lot of attention. But not to sell it. He's trying to convince the U.S. not to kill themselves."

"What are you talking about?"

"It's faster if I show you." She gestured him to follow and turned down a side corridor. They walked twenty meters and went through the first door they came to. It was a conference room with a holotable in the middle. A team of six engineers was studying a holo of some intricate mechanical part in the air between them. One of them was poking it with his stylus and leading the discussion.

"I need this room," said Simona.

The engineers looked at her and then at Lem. Then they turned to the chief engineer with the stylus, clearly the most senior among them.

"Now?" the chief engineer asked.

"No, yesterday at brunch," said Simona. "Yes. Now."

"But we reserved this room."

"And I'm unreserving it," said Simona. "Now please leave." She snapped her fingers again, and the engineers hopped to it, gathering their things and hustling out the door. They knew who she was and to whom she reported.

When they left, Lem said, "You have such a pleasant way about you."

"It worked, didn't it?" She moved to the holotable, wiped the holo away, and entered a series of codes and gestures. A ship appeared in the holo-space, smooth and small, with a long tube-shaped device mounted on its underside.

"This is the Vanguard drone," said Simona. "The biggest product launch we've had in years. It's a prospecting drone, designed to seek out viable asteroids. If it finds something worth digging, it alerts us, and we send a manned craft out there to dig up the lugs. It's been in development for over a decade."

"Why have I never heard of it?" asked Lem.

"It was on a need-to-know basis. You weren't on the list. Try not to be offended."

"Okay."

"Your father introduced the Vanguard to the world literally minutes before he found out about the Formics. Ukko was not pleased. The Vanguard was set to reignite the company. The interference had been killing business for months. We had two dismal quarters. Stockholders were antsy. We needed a victory. The announcement of the Formics couldn't have come at a worse time. It threw the Board into panic mode. Everyone knew the news would eclipse any momentum we might have gained with the Vanguard."

"Sounds like the Board," said Lem. "More concerned about the bottom line than about an imminent alien invasion and the possible annihilation of the human race. Classy. What's this tube underneath the drone?"

"That's the glaser," said Simona.

"Glaser? You have more than one prototype?"

"There's only one prototype, and it's on your ship. This is the real thing. Your father moved the glaser into production as soon as we heard that you had a successful field test in the Kuiper Belt about nine months ago."

"You moved it into production?" said Lem. "But we weren't finished with the testing. The results we sent you were from the initial test only. We had dozens of field trials to go."

"Which you never got around to doing," said Simona. "We lost contact with you because of the interference, and your father grew impatient. We did some more tests here, made some tweaks, shrunk the design, wrapped the whole thing in armored plates, and that was the end of it."

"So you didn't wait for us?"

"It was nine months ago, Lem. We weren't even sure if you were still alive. It was very valuable tech. We weren't going to sit around and hope you showed up. We took what we knew and we moved on."

"If you could've done all the testing here, why did my father send me to the Kuiper Belt in the first place?"

"Because the K Belt is still the ideal place to conduct field trials secretly," said Simona. "Your father wasn't trying to get rid of you, if that's what you're thinking. The Deep is still our preferential testing ground. We only tested here because we had to. We didn't have the time or the communications capabilities to launch another crew."

Lem leaned on the table and stared at the holo. Two years in space, and Father could have just as easily done the tests here. Not as thoroughly perhaps, not as reliably, but that hadn't stopped Father from doing them. It made Lem feel as if all that time on the Makarhu had been an utter waste. "If it's a prospecting ship, then why is it outfitted with a glaser?"

"Because it's not a prospecting ship anymore," said Simona. "Now it's a warship."

Lem regarded her, an eyebrow raised. "You're joking."

"Ukko plans to attack the mothership," said Simona, "and he's going to use a fleet of drones to do it."

"A fleet? How many of these drones does he plan to make?"

"Fifty. And he's already made them. The glasers are produced as well. The only thing left to do is mount the glasers onto the drones. Our assembly lines are working around the clock on that as we speak. It's proving trickier than we thought, though. We're having to modify the drone's flight controls to accommodate the glaser."

"How extensive was your testing of the glaser?" Lem asked.

"Mostly lab work and computer models," said Simona. "We couldn't exactly go outside and blow up a few asteroids. There aren't any around here. That's why fields tests are best."

"You need to speak with Dr. Benyawe and Dr. Dublin, my chief engineer. All of our computer models for the glaser were wrong. When we hit a big asteroid in the Kuiper Belt, the resulting gravity field was far bigger than any of us expected. It almost consumed our ship. The Formic ship is much bigger than that rock, and its composition is unknown. Benyawe convinced me that it was too dangerous to hit it with the glaser. There's no telling what kind of gravity field would result. Hitting it with fifty glasers at once could be suicide."

Simona made a few notes on her holopad. "Anything else?"

"Yes. You still haven't explained why I need to pitch the glaser in interviews and what this has to do with the U.S."

Simona wiped her hand through the field, and the drone disappeared. After a few more gestures, the Formic ship appeared in its place. "Our sources inside the U.S. Joint Chiefs tell us that the Americans are planning a strike against the Formic mothership," said Simona.

"We have sources that high inside the U.S. military?"

"We have sources everywhere, dear. And these are particularly reliable ones. Although the strike isn't much of a secret, truth be told. Everyone expects it. The U.S. has been preparing for it out in space ever since word of the Formic ship was confirmed. And as you know, it's very hard to do anything in space without the whole world noticing. What *isn't* common knowledge is when and how the strike will happen, which is what our sources have told us."

"What's the U.S. planning?"

"They've weaponized about fifteen shuttles, and they've added these to their existing space fleet. Right now they have twenty-two ships. We caught wind this morning that the Russians, British, and Chinese are adding ships as well, bringing the total to fifty-three."

"I saw the Formics take on sixty ships at once in the Belt," said Lem. "It wasn't pretty."

"The U.S. is doing it anyway," said Simona. "Their military dismisses the Battle of the Belt as blue-collar scrubs acting like soldiers."

"Then the U.S. military are idiots," said Lem. "Asteroid miners are far better space pilots and far better prepared for space combat than soldiers and pilots brought up from the planet."

Simona shrugged. "I'm not a strategist. I just keep your father informed."

"Why doesn't the U.S. military just pound the mothership with nukes?"

"They have. Or rather they tried. Three days ago. It didn't work. The Formic guns picked off the missiles on their approach, long before they reached the Formic ship. The missiles detonated and emitted massive electromagnetic pulses that took out about three dozen satellites and created artificial radiation belts that will annoy everyone for years to come."

"If the nuke strike failed, then why is the U.S. going through with a manned strike? If the Formics can hit missiles, taking out shuttles and ships will be child's play."

"The U.S. doesn't think so. The Formic weapons systems are hidden inside the ship and only emerge when the ship is threatened. STASA footage of the Battle of the Belt and the footage of the Formics taking out the U.N. secretary showed us where those weapons are concealed."

"How? The surface is round. Every square inch of the ship looks identical."

"I don't know. They must have some way. Maybe the ship's close enough now to detect small discrepancies on the surface. All I know is they intend to target those places where the weapons are stored and cripple the guns before they can emerge. A second team of ships will be striking the Formics here, at the tip, where the shield-generation equipment is located. The

U.S. is confident that with those two objectives achieved, they can easily push on with a full-scale assault."

"They're wrong," said Lem. "The Formic guns are only the first line of their defense. The ship itself is a much more lethal weapon. There are apertures all over the surface. Any of them can open and fire laserized gamma plasma in any direction. I've seen it happen. The shuttles don't stand a chance. When do they plan to do this?"

"In about forty-eight hours," said Simona.

"You have to stop them."

"That's your job. That's what the interviews are for. Tell the world what you know. You don't have to exaggerate. You don't have to lie. Be honest. You and your crew have seen the Formics up close. No one else has. Convince the U.S. to withdraw and let Ukko conduct a drone strike."

"I've already told you. Drones with glasers could be a bad idea. I'm not endorsing that approach. If you want me to say that in an interview, forget it. You'll have to find someone else to do that."

"Fine. We will. Say what you think is best. But if you say anything against the drones, we'll only cut it out later, so don't bother. Just help us stop the U.S. assault. You'd be saving lives."

"Spare me the saving-lives argument. You and I both know that Father wants to be the hero here. He doesn't want the U.S. and its allies taking out the mothership because he wants that glory for himself. I know how my father thinks, Simona. If it doesn't benefit him, he doesn't care."

"You really don't think much of him, do you?"

She would echo everything he said to Father, but at the moment he didn't care. Right now his mind was racing. A spark of an idea had ignited. What if this was the opportunity he had been waiting for? The drone strike was destined to fail. And yet Father was putting all his eggs in that basket. Fifty drones and fifty glasers. A massive fortune. Not enough to bankrupt the company, but certainly enough to pass a vote of no confidence in Father and boot him off his throne once the glasers and drones were destroyed. The Board couldn't ignore a mistake like that.

It would take some time and effort to rebuild the company, of course, but Lem had rebuilt companies before. Never on this scale, but the game was the same regardless of the company's size.

Booting Father wouldn't be enough, though, he knew. Lem also had to position himself as the rightful successor, and having Father elevate him as a national hero certainly wouldn't hurt in that effort. The Board would have their eye on Lem. They would be desperate to rebuild the company's image, and what better way to do that than with a media darling with proven business success who just happens to be the founder's tenacious son?

Granted, the Formics would still be an issue. That would need addressing as well. But they were an enemy for another day. Right now Father was the one with the exposed flank, and Lem wasn't about to ignore it.

Lem straightened his jacket and gestured to the door. "Let's get this over with."

She looked relieved. "You're doing the right thing, Lem. People need to hear this story. And don't edit yourself. Give it some drama. People want drama."

"Relax, Simona. I'll have them biting their nails."

# CHAPTER 22

# Crows

The airlock was small, but all fifteen women managed to squeeze inside it.

Rena pulled the interior hatch closed—sealing them off from the cargo bay—then she spun the wheel and secured the lock. The exterior hatch, on the opposite wall, was now all that separated them from the vacuum of space.

"Check the suit of the person beside you," said Rena. "Look for punctures, scratches, any sign of structural deterioration, especially at creases: elbows, armpits, back of the knees. Make sure everyone's suit is airtight." Their pressure suits were newer and nicer than anything they had ever had on board El Cavador, but Rena wasn't taking any chances.

The women obeyed without hesitation. They had come to trust Rena's leadership when it came to the equipment. "Check your oxygen levels," said Rena. "Fiddle with the air valves, make sure you have manual control of your air intake if you need it. Know what you're breathing. Monitor your mixture. Ask your helmet to run a full scan of life support. If any of your biometrics are off, if you sense the tiniest of glitches, speak up now. This is not a drill this time. This is the real. No mistakes."

Their faces were visible through their visors, and Rena could see that many of them were nervous. Rena didn't blame them. She was afraid as well. Most of them hadn't done a spacewalk in years; it was the men on El Cavador who had done all the mining. Worse still, crows didn't use lifelines—or the long hoses that connected to the back of a spacesuit and kept a person anchored to the ship. On El Cavador, going outside without a lifeline was suicide, the most dangerous, reckless, stupid decision a miner could make. The lifeline was exactly what its name implied. Power and air came down the lifeline, and if you were ever in trouble, if you needed a quick rescue, the lifeline was the means by which you were pulled back into the ship.

But lifelines were impossible with scavenger work. The wreckage constantly moved; lifelines would knot and twist and kink once everyone got on board. Plus the insides of ships were mazes, with corridors extending in any direction; lines would too easily twist and tangle and tie into knots. Then there was the risk of severing a lifeline on the sharp edges from torn metal and wreckage.

No, portable oxygen and batteries were better for scavenger work. Yet lifelines were the only type of spacewalking any of the women had ever done. The idea of going out into the black without a tether was terrifying.

"We're going to be fine," Rena assured them. "We've been practicing for this."

She moved to the exterior hatch and looked out the small porthole at the wreckage outside. It was difficult to tell what type of ship it had been. The alien weapons had blown most of it to bits during the battle, leaving only this rear section intact.

She turned back to the group and lifted her arms high over her head. "Stretch out. Muscles need to be loose for takeoff and landing."

The women complied, bending their legs and getting loose. Rena took a moment to reposition some of the gear she had strapped to her shoulders and belt. Arjuna had loaded each of them with salvaging tools. Rena carried a rotating saw, industrial shears, and a dozen other smaller tools stuffed into her suit's many pockets.

Arjuna's voice sounded in their helmets. "Move quickly. Don't waste time on parts of little value." He was up in the helm, monitoring them, tracking the wreckage. "When you enter a room, look at everything. Put a price on every piece you see. And remember that the most valuable pieces may not be out in the open. Look for pipes, wiring, conduit. Follow them to their source. Find whatever they're powering or pumping from. Rip back panels. Expose everything. Then go to what's worth the most and start cutting." He was repeating himself. He had drilled this into them for weeks now. "And how much extra do you cut away?"

He meant extra wiring or pipes, all the replaceable pieces that fed into the part and anchored it to the ship. Cutting a power cord was fine. Cutting the part wasn't.

The women all answered in unison, some with a tired rhythm in their voice. They had been over this so many times already. "At least half a meter," they said

"At the *least*," Arjuna repeated. "At the least. More is better. Err on the side of caution. If you cut the part too short or if you damage it when you cut it free, it's junk. We'll get nothing for it."

Rena looked to her right and saw Abbi beside her. Abbi had come to El Cavador as a young bride from a Peruvian free-miner family that had never allowed their women to do spacewalks. She looked terrified.

"Stay close to me," said Rena. "We'll go everywhere together."

Abbi nodded, grateful.

Rena's heart ached for the woman. Abbi had lost her only son, Mono, when El Cavador was destroyed, and the loss had been devastating. Ever since then Abbi had been detached and distant. Rena had tried comforting her on a few occasions, but Abbi had always brushed off the gestures and preferred to be left alone. Now, however, she was terrified and desperate for companionship.

"We'll help each other," Rena told her. "No one's alone on this."

Abbi nodded again, putting on her best face. She was trying at least, thought Rena.

Arjuna's voice returned. "We'll have the nets open. Once you pull a part, bring it outside and push it to the nets."

The nets had been a source of contention among the women. Arjuna had ordered his original crew to man the nets and catch the salvaged parts while he had ordered the women of El Cavador to go inside the wreckage and retrieve the valuables.

"You see what he's doing, don't you?" Julexi had said. "He's giving us the dangerous work and giving the light, safe labor to his own family."

"We're better cutters than they are," Rena had said. "We know the parts better than they do. He's doing this for practical reasons. We'll move faster and salvage more this way."

It was true, but no one liked it.

"You see how she always takes his side instead of ours?" Julexi had said. "Arjuna can do no wrong as far as Rena is concerned."

It was a ridiculous accusation. Rena had argued privately with Arjuna on a half-dozen issues, usually winning those arguments and getting what the family needed. But she never bragged about these small victories to the women. No one else even knew they had occurred. That would only fuel those who still griped about being here. They would use those arguments as proof that coming along had been a mistake. It didn't matter that *all* ships had arguments like the ones Rena had with Arjuna. It didn't matter that all families operated that way. It had happened every day aboard El Cavador. People argued. Disagreements were voiced on how things should be done. Opposing viewpoints were considered. Compromises were made.

But people like Julexi seemed to forget that fact when they were so desperate to build a case against their current situation.

Arjuna said, "Hatch is opening in five . . . four . . . three . . . two . . . one."

The hatch cracked, and the rush of oxygen in the airlock was sucked out into the vacuum of space. With the bolts pulled back and the seal broken, Rena pushed on the hatch, and it swung outward, revealing the wide, infinite expanse of space beyond. She had told herself that she would be the first one out, leading by example, showing the women that they could do this without lifelines, that all would be well.

But fear paralyzed her. The blackness was a well she would fall into and continue on forever. It had taken Segundo. It would take her, too.

"What are you waiting for?" said Julexi. It was an accusation as much as a question. It was as if she were saying: You see how she hesitates? You see how she's afraid?

It was exactly the motivation Rena needed to shatter the fear. She reached up, pulled herself through the hole, got her feet outside on the hull of the ship, and pushed off hard toward the wreckage, moving a little faster than was necessary to prove she wasn't afraid.

She flew, heading straight for the flat side of the wrecked ship's hull, which they had determined was the safest place to land.

She knew the others were behind her. She could hear their grunts and exhalations as they launched from the Gagak's hull and made for the wreck.

Right at the last moment, Rena tapped the retros on her shoulder pack, which shot out small bursts of compressed air and slowed the forward movement of her upper body. As she had hoped, the lower half of her body continued forward and she rotated so that her feet were now in front of her. She landed expertly feetfirst with her boot magnets turned on, anchoring herself to the wreck. Then she quickly turned around, saw the others coming, and shuffled back out of the way.

Abbi came next, but she didn't land nearly as gracefully. She failed to get her feet under her in time and hit the hull with her shoulder and bounced away, nearly spinning off into space. Rena caught her by the arm and pulled her back, helping her to a standing position. Abbi was breathing hard, eyes were wide with terror, but she nodded her thanks and worked to compose herself.

Julexi twisted her ankle on her landing, and when Rena approached her to help her up, Julexi waved her brusquely away. "Don't pretend to care. I'm fine."

They found a hatch and went inside, entering into the airlock of a cargo bay. It was completely dark, and when Rena shined her spotlight around the room, the beam fell upon two corpses twenty meters away. They had expected this, but Rena still gave a quick intake of breath. The bodies were both men. One of them was turned away from them, but the other seemed to be looking at them, his expression pained. They wore heavy, nonmatching jumpsuits, which meant they were probably part of a clan; corporates would have had uniforms.

The women crowded around Rena, staring at the bodies. Rena lowered her beam and faced them. "We knew we'd find corpses in here. Ignore them. Let's focus on the equipment."

A quick scan of the cargo bay revealed all sorts of useful tools and heavy equipment: suits, helmets, mining tools, even a few digger mechs that looked to be in perfect working condition and worth a small fortune each. Most of it was anchored down tight and thus had not been thrown around and damaged during the battle. Rena radioed back up to Arjuna and rattled off what they had found.

"Not a bad find for your first wreck, Lady of El Cavador. We are opening the nets now. I'll send down some men with cables and wenches to pull in the mechs. What about elsewhere?"

"We haven't explored beyond the bay yet."

"Leave most of your team there to recover what you've found and send a few out to check the rest of the ship. This is a sizable wreck. There might be more worth taking."

"Roger that."

Abbi was shining her light at the two dead men. "Doesn't seem right, Rena. Taking from the dead like this. These were free miners like us."

"We've salvaged from dead ships before, Abbi. A lot of our equipment on El Cavador came from things we found."

"Yes, but I never had to be the one to take it. And anyway, we were doing that to stay alive. Crows take to make a profit."

"It's no different, Abbi. It's all survival. Now come on, I need your help." She pulled her away from the corpses. Several of the women had their drills out, removing the anchor bolts to the equipment they were hoping to bring in. "Julexi," said Rena. "Abbi and I are going to scout the rest of the ship. You're in charge of the recovery here."

Julexi seemed surprised then narrowed her eyes, suspicious. "Why me?"

"Because if anyone can handle a big job like this, you can." Rena figured it would help Julexi to feel some ownership for their success today. Arjuna had agreed to give them 30 percent of whatever they recovered, so today's haul would be a decent sum. It was nowhere near what they would need to buy their own ship, but it was a start. If Julexi felt responsible for that, it might mend things between them.

"So *we* work while you two play explorer?" said Julexi.

"We won't be poking about," said Abbi. "We're looking for other parts. That's why we came."

Abbi's response surprised Rena. Usually Abbi was all too eager to echo Julexi's complaints, but here she appeared to be siding with Rena. Maybe the infighting was beginning to subside.

"We'll hurry back if we don't find anything," said Rena. She launched toward the hatch on the far side of the cargo bay, and Abbi followed. Out in the corridor they found two more bodies, one of them a woman about Abbi's age, the other an old man. Rena pushed them aside without looking at their faces, and the corpses floated to the opposite wall.

"You paint," said Rena. "I'll lead."

Without lifelines or a lot of light to see by, it would be easy to get lost in the labyrinth of a ship, so Arjuna had supplied them all with spray paint. They were to mark the walls wherever they went and use the painted markings to lead them back to the ship.

Abbi painted a circle on the hatch they had come through while Rena moved down the corridor, scanning right and left with her light, searching for anything useful. She followed pipes for a while, but they turned upward into the ceiling, heading up to another deck. They passed several less-valuable items—compressors and filters and purifiers—but Arjuna had given them strict instructions not to waste their time on those. Big-ticket items were their goal. They moved through a series of hatches, turning right or left. Abbi sprayed arrows whenever they changed direction. The size of the ship surprised Rena; it had seemed much smaller at a distance.

They passed more bodies: men, women, some young, some old. Rena made a point not to look at their faces. She paused, however, when they came upon the corpse of a young women clutching a bundle wrapped in a blanket. The expression on the woman's face was earnest and desperate, as if she had passed her final moment pleading to God in prayer. Rena didn't dare pull back the blanket flap; she couldn't bring herself to see a dead infant.

The signs on the walls were all in French, and the people had a European look about them. Rena passed door after door of living quarters. The rooms were decorated with colorful paints and bright fabrics and framed portraits, as if everyone had worked hard to make their little corner of the ship their own. There were hammocks and containers of food, children's toys and holopads. Rena even saw a few paper books floating in the hall.

They had been a wealthy family by the look of things. Rena couldn't tell if they had belonged to a big clan or were a single-ship operation, but either way they had been a successful outfit. More importantly though, they had been happy. She could see it in their faces in the portraits. Husbands holding wives, children clinging to parents like monkeys held to trees. It was as if each portrait held all the love in the world.

Her thoughts went to Segundo. Her rock, her other self. She had never been afraid with him at her side. When he held her, all anxiety melted away. There was nothing they couldn't face together, no pain they couldn't endure when they shared the burden and held each other tight. And yet when he had needed her most, she hadn't been there. He had been alone. His last moments, his last breaths, he had passed and taken alone.

Rena opened the door to a mechanical room and found something worth salvaging. The electrical generator was tucked neatly in the corner, and appeared to be undamaged. Generators didn't usually bring in a lot of money, but this one looked fairly new, only a few years old at the most, with decades of life left in it.

Rena moved closer and examined it, noting the many bolts and anchors that held it fast to the wall. Cutting it free wouldn't be easy, and carrying it back to the bay would be a cumbersome task—the generator was tall and bulky, and maneuvering it through the corridors without damaging it would be tricky.

For a moment Rena considered not calling it in and ignoring it completely, but the thought left her just as quickly. To come back empty-handed would be to invite the wrath of Julexi. No, she needed to prove that she was pulling her weight while the others salvaged what was in the cargo bay.

Rena clicked on her transmitter and radioed it in, sending photos and vids directly to Arjuna. The crow captain sounded pleased by the find and asked her to bring it in as quickly as possible. Rena anchored her spotlight to the wall and used her juice meter to ensure that the generator didn't currently have power. Then she unstrapped the saw from her leg and got busy. The room was tiny, so Abbi waited out in the hall while Rena cut.

The blade screamed as it sliced though the steel braces, shooting sparks back toward the hand guard. Rena cut the first two braces away easily, but the third and fourth ones were behind the generator and the saw wouldn't reach them. Those she would have to do by hand. She set the saw aside and got out the hacksaw. The space was barely wider than her arm. When she reached back with the hacksaw, she didn't even have room enough to turn her bulky helmet to the side to see what she doing. She felt around blindly with the hacksaw until she found the brace and started cutting. It quickly became apparent that this would take forever. By the time she stopped to catch her breath, she was hot and sweating and frustrated.

She called Abbi on the radio to give her a hand.

Abbi didn't answer.

Rena tried calling her again, but still got no response.

She retracted her arm from the tight space and went out into the corridor. Abbi wasn't there.

"Abbi?"

"I'm here." The voice was quiet. It sounded like she had been crying.

"Where?"

"The corridor to your left."

Rena's light was still with the generator. She left it there and moved to her left. Light from Abbi's suit spilled from one of the rooms up ahead. Rena moved toward it. When she reached the doorway she saw that it was a room for young boys. The walls had been painted with mining ships and planets. Five child-sized hammocks were positioned along one wall. There were toy figurines and plastic helmets, sports balls, and stuffed animals. To Rena's relief there were no children here; perhaps they had been moved elsewhere on the ship before the battle.

Abbi floated in the middle of the room holding a toy hand drill. She didn't look up. "Mono had one of these," she said softly. "It was broken when we gave it to him. He was only about two years old then. He played with it for hours, flying around the room, making the drill noises, pretending to unscrew everything." She turned it over in her hands. "I think that's why he wanted to be a mechanic. He had this stupid little plastic drill and then he saw Segundo and Victor using the real thing, and his eyes lit up."

Rena said nothing.

"He was going to be a mechanic," said Abbi. "That's what he told me all the time. He was going to be like Victor. It was always Victor this and Victor that. He asked me more questions about Victor than he asked about his own father."

She let go of the drill. It floated there in the air in front of her. She stared down at it. "If I had given him something else, a different toy, everything would have been different. He wouldn't have wanted to be a mechanic. He wouldn't have snuck off that day. He would've stayed with me. He wouldn't have been on El Cavador."

She lifted her head and looked at Rena. There were tears in her eyes. "We should have died with them, Rena. All of us should have died."

"They didn't want that, Abbi. They wanted us to survive. Segundo said so."

"Who cares what Segundo said!" She was yelling now. "Mono was a child! He died alone! Everyone else was outside the ship. He would've been afraid. He would've wanted me with him. He would've screamed my name."

Rena didn't know what to say.

"You keep telling us *somos familia, somos uno.* We are family, we are one, we need to stick together. Well why didn't we stick together when it mattered most? Huh? Why did we ever leave the ship? Why weren't we *familia* then?"

Rena moved to embrace her. "Abbi—"

"No! Don't touch me!" She shoved Rena away. The action pushed them both away from each other. Rena caught herself against the far wall.

She kept her voice gentle. "Abbi—"

"GET OUT!"

Rena didn't move.

"I SAID GET OUT!"

Rena left. She moved back down the hall to the room with the generator. She didn't pick up her hacksaw. She stared at it. She had been kidding herself, she realized. They were not *familia*. That had died with Segundo and Mono and Pitoso and all the others. What they had before was forever broken. Even if they were to get another ship one day, what would that change? That wouldn't mend anything. They'd still be who they were; they'd still be missing that other part of themselves.

Arjuna's voice on the radio startled her. It was fast and frantic. "Everyone get back to the ship now! Drop what you're doing and move! Now!"

"What is it?" asked Rena.

"Don't ask questions! Move!"

"Abbi and I are still several minutes away. We're deep in the ship. Tell me what's going on." She grabbed her light and rushed back to the room Abbi was in.

"Khalid," said Arjuna.

"What's a Khalid?"

"It's not a thing. It's a person. A Somali. A vulture. The worst of them all. He's coming. He must have heard our transmissions. He will kill us if he finds us here. How far away are you?"

Abbi was still in the boys' room. She had picked up the toy drill again. Other than that she hadn't moved.

"We're ten minutes from the cargo bay," said Rena. There were hatches to open and corridors to traverse.

"You don't *have* ten minutes," said Arjuna. "I need you in the ship now. Find a faster way out."

"And if we can't?"

"I can't wait for you. I'm sorry. Hurry. I'll give you five minutes." He clicked off.

This wasn't happening. Five minutes. "Abbi. Let's go. We have to move."

Abbi didn't look up. Rena flew to her, grabbed her by the shoulders, shook her. "Move! We need to go now!"

"So go then," Abbi said casually, shrugging off Rena's grip.

She was giving up, Rena realized. She was choosing to die here. Rena grabbed her by the shoulders again. "Listen to me. I am getting off this wreck and you are coming with me."

Abbi brushed Rena's arms away. "Leave me alone." She tried to turn away, but Rena wasn't having any of it. She grabbed Abbi and threw her toward the door. It was easy to do in zero-G; Rena's feet were grounded, and Abbi's weren't.

Abbi spun awkwardly but caught herself in the doorway. "You can't force me. So don't even try."

Abbi was right, of course. Rena couldn't force her. She couldn't drag her back to the ship with Abbi kicking and resisting the whole way. But what could Rena do?

"I'm not leaving you here," said Rena.

"Then we both die."

The resignation in Abbi's voice was as frightening as what was coming. It was as if she were dead already. There was no convincing her, Rena realized. Abbi's mind was set.

Rena moved to her. "I'm sorry, Abbi."

"For leaving me? Don't be."

"Not for leaving you," said Rena. "For doing this." She reached behind Abbi's helmet and yanked out the oxygen line. Abbi's eyes widened with panic as the air in her helmet was sucked out the valve. She opened her mouth, gasping desperately for breath, then she lost consciousness, and her head lolled to the side. Rena thrust the oxygen tube back onto the valve and checked Abbi's vitals as Abbi's helmet refilled with air. Abbi's heart was beating. Pulse was weak, but there. Rena grabbed her and pushed her limp body out into the hall. If Abbi wouldn't come voluntarily, Rena would pull her back to the ship. The question was how. Rena couldn't have Abbi's appendages sticking out and snagging on things or hitting walls and hatches. They'd move faster if Abbi were tight in a fetal position.

Rena grabbed the coiled harness strap on her hip and pulled out several meters of slack. She bent Abbi and bound her legs up tight to her chest. Next came the arms. Rena folded Abbi's arms inward and strapped them down as well, as if Abbi were hugging her knees. It wasn't ideal, but it would have to do. Rena checked her watch. One minute already spent.

*I'll give you five minutes.*

Rena looked to her left, the way they had come. The spray-painted arrow on the wall at the end of the hall pointed her back toward the cargo bay. Ten minutes that way.

She looked to her right. The corridor extended another twenty meters and then stopped, allowing her to turn either right or left. She had no idea what was in that direction. There could be a hatch to the outside. There could be a dead end.

*I'll give you five minutes.*

She launched to the right, heading into the unknown. The harness strap attached to her hip pulled taught, and Abbi followed. They weren't going fast enough. Rena hit the propulsion button on her thumb. It was lunacy to do that inside. She shot down the hall. Abbi banged into the side of the wall but kept coming, pulled by the straps. Rena had Abbi's vitals on her HUD. The pulse was there. Don't die on me, she thought.

She reached the end of the corridor. Abbi slammed into her back, knocking her against the wall. Rena recovered herself, unhurt. She looked right and left, hoping to see a hatch to the outside. There wasn't one. It was another corridor, extending twenty meters to the right, maybe forty meters to the left. She looked behind her. Way down at the end of the hall was the spray-painted arrow, calling to her, pointing the way.

*I'll give you five minutes.*

She launched to her left, moving farther into the blackness, farther into the maze of the ship, farther away from the only escape she knew. They should have stayed on WU-HU, she told herself. Julexi had been right. What business did they have among crows? She was going to die in this scrap of a ship—her and Abbi both—and it was all her own fault. This Khalid and his crew would find them here and they would do their business, and the family would be broken even more.

Or worse, Khalid would catch Arjuna's ship and everyone would die. Edimar, Lola, Julexi, the children, the babies. Everyone.

She should have followed the arrows. That had been the right choice.

Her light flickered and then shut off, leaving her in total blackness save for the small light in her helmet. She swore, shaking the light, jostling the batteries, trying to get it working again. She flew forward, essentially blind. Ten meters, twenty meters. She smacked the light hard against her palm, and the light came on again. She reached where the corridor bent to the left and caught herself on the wall, bracing her back for the impact with Abbi. Half a heartbeat later Abbi collided and bounced off, though the foam of their suits took the brunt of the impact.

Rena turned to the left and found . . .

A bathroom.

It was a dead end. There was no hatch here. No way out. No exit. They had come the wrong way. She had taken a risk and lost the bet.

*I'll give you five minutes.*

She couldn't tell him to wait for her. That was as much as killing everyone else. She would tell him to go. Now. Don't wait for us. Run. Get out. Protect the children, damn you.

She wanted to cry. Segundo had told her to stay alive. He had asked her to keep them together. And she had ruined everything. She had failed. She couldn't even do that much. She was nothing without him.

Abbi was floating there in the corridor in a ball beside her, wrapped up in the straps. Part of Rena wanted to kick her. The other part of her wanted to roll up into a ball and join her.

She clicked on her radio, her voice calm. "Arjuna."

He answered immediately. "Rena! Where are you? The others are loaded up. We need to launch now!"

The others were back on the ship. They would get out at least. That gave Rena some comfort.

"Go," she said.

"What?"

"You heard me. Go. We can't get out in time. Promise me you will take them to a depot. Promise me you'll keep them safe."

He was quiet a moment. "On my life, Lady."

There. It was done. He would keep his word. She knew it. The *familia*, however broken, would survive. She pushed lightly off the wall and headed back the way she had come. The strap pulled taut and Abbi, still unconscious, followed. She and Abbi would find a room, she decided, somewhere where they could be together and wait for this Khalid. Maybe Rena could talk to him and offer to serve on his ship. Perhaps he would let them both work for their lives.

But no. She was kidding herself. He was a vulture, a killer. There would be no mercy, no joining his ship. He would do what vultures always did.

Nor could she fight them, not armed vultures. Rena had no weapons and no skill for combat. I have to cut Abbi's air, she told herself. And for good this time. That would be the greatest mercy: let Abbi slip peacefully from sleep before this Khalid comes and has his way with her. Yes, thought Rena. I will cut her air and then my own.

She passed a room on her left. She turned her head casually and saw that there were cabinets on the opposite wall filled with supplies. She continued on. She passed a second room. She turned her head again and saw that there was nothing on the opposite wall.

There *was* no wall.

There were only stars. Millions of stars. Where the wall had once been was a gaping hole. She must have passed it when her light went out.

"WAIT!" she shouted into her radio. "WAIT!"

She turned her body and hit the propulsion. She shot out through the hole. The harness strap was tight. Abbi was behind her. They were out of the ship, space all around them. Free.

"Don't leave us! We're out!"

"I see you," said Arjuna. "I'm coming to you."

The Gagak was a big ship but a nimble one. It swooped toward them. Retros fired, slowing it as it neared. The airlock hatch was open, thirty meters away from her. Lola was there at the hatch, waving her to come. "Now, Rena!"

Rena punched the thumb button. She shot forward like a bullet. She came in fast. She fired retros at the last second, but it wasn't fast enough. She hit the hull hard. Abbi was right behind her, careening into her. It knocked the breath out of Rena this time, and she thought she might ricochet off into space. But Lola was faster. She grabbed Rena's hand and pulled them inside. Abbi was in. Lola slammed the hatch shut. "I got them!"

The ship vibrated. The engines roared. Rena braced herself, ready for the force of acceleration. But no force came. "We're not moving," she told Lola.

Lola was unwrapping the harness straps and freeing Abbi. "It's a trick. Help me unwrap her."

Rena was confused but she didn't argue. They pulled the straps free. The airlock was pressurizing, filling with oxygen. Then the lights went out. Rena was panicked a moment. And then they were moving. Rena was nearly thrown backward in the blackness, her hand scrabbling for a handhold. She found one and steadied herself. Then her body adjusted to the acceleration and all was still. The airlock beeped the all-clear, and the interior hatch opened.

Rena was flooded with personal spotlights. The other women were waiting in the cargo bay, shining their lights in the hatch. They helped Rena and Lola and Abbi into the cargo bay and got their helmets off. By then Abbi was coming to, rousing, her eyes slowing blinking open. Alive.

Arjuna arrived a moment later with his own light, rushing in from the helm. "We are safe for now."

"What just happened?" said Rena.

"We fired a heat bomb and went black."

"I don't know what that means."

"When we leave a site, we go black. We give off no heat signature, no light, nothing that could cause the buzzards to locate us. Buzzards always look—not at the original wreckage—but at the ships *leaving* the wreckage. So we give a strong signature on a particular straight course, but just as we go black, we jink in a different direction, a sharp move to one side that makes it hard to guess what course we're actually on."

"So they think we went somewhere else."

"We give off a false heat signature in another direction. It will show up on Khalid's instruments as if *that* were the real direction of the rocket blast, so they'll search for us in the wrong part of space."

"Won't they detect our jink rocket?"

"It's as focused as possible, so it can't be picked up unless you're in a very narrow range, while the heat bomb is large. It looks like a rocket firing once and quickly. But actually it makes no change in our trajectory because it's detached from the ship before it blows."

"Clever," said Rena. "I'm assuming this has worked before."

"I'm alive, aren't I?" He regarded Abbi, who was fully conscious now, the other women crowded around her, consoling her.

"Now what?" asked Rena.

"Now the real work begins. Now we sort through everything and get rid of what we don't want."

"We can't simply jettison things of little value," said Rena. "That's dangerous. Other ships will fly into it. Debris like that is the equivalent of a landmine."

"I am not like other crows, Lady of El Cavador. Other crews may do this, but not us. We carefully put unwanted items on the surface of asteroids so as not to leave a trail of ship-wrecking debris."

She nodded, impressed with him yet again.

"I did not mean to frighten you back there," he said. "Khalid came out of nowhere. He must have been following us. He will not follow us now. I am glad you made it back."

"Makes two of us," she said.

"Are you all right? How do you feel, Lady?"

Rena's heart was still pounding in her chest. "Alive," she said. "I feel alive."

# CHAPTER 23

# Camouflage

As soon as their shuttle was close enough to Luna to send and receive transmissions, Victor sent a laserline and contacted Yanyu. It was sleep-shift on Imbrium, and when Yanyu appeared in the holofield above the dash she looked unkempt and half asleep. Then she realized it was Victor and Imala on the other end, and she was awake in an instant. "They told us you were heading to the Belt."

"We were," said Victor. "The situation changed. We turned back at Last Chance. We haven't had any contact with anyone in seven days. We were hoping you could bring us up to speed. We didn't know who else to call."

"Do you have a place to stay?"

"Actually no," said Imala.

"Then you will stay with me. Where are you docking? I will meet you there."

"We don't want to impose," said Imala.

"You must stay here. Where else will you go? Which dock?"

"Lunar Guidance hasn't grabbed us yet," said Imala. "We can go to whichever is nearest you, though we'd rather not go to a Juke dock. We were supposed to take this shuttle to Midway."

"There is a public dock south of Old City in Covington Square. Do you know the place?"

"I know it," said Imala.

"Meet me there in one hour," said Yanyu.

Imala flew them toward Old City, and Lunar Guidance brought them in the rest of the way. They docked, deboarded, and found Yanyu waiting for them in an all-night café, dressed and presentable. They took a booth in the back away from everyone else.

"You left without saying good-bye," said Yanyu.

"Ukko was eager to get us on our way," said Victor.

"That is what we assumed," said Yanyu. "He would not want you talking about Lem. Lawyers came to Dr. Prescott and me when you left. They made us sign nondisclosure agreements saying that we would never speak of Lem or of any attack his ship may have made."

"Is that legally binding?" asked Imala.

Yanyu shrugged. "We could argue that we signed it while under duress, but it would not matter anyway. It would never get to court."

"I'm sorry you got involved," said Victor. "I didn't mean to drag you into it."

Yanyu shrugged again. "I do not think about it. There are more pressing matters elsewhere."

"Tell us about the past seven days," said Imala.

Yanyu frowned, grim. "First there was the nuclear strike."

Victor and Imala stiffened. "Against the mothership?" asked Imala.

"Do not get excited," said Yanyu. "It was a failure. The Formics destroyed the missiles long before they reached the ship. Their guns hit them, and the bombs exploded. The blast of electromagnetic radiation destroyed dozens of satellites and damaged much of the existing communications grid. It is a miracle Luna can still contact Earth. It could have wiped out the whole system."

"The Formics weren't hurt at all?" asked Imala.

"Not that we could detect," said Yanyu. "And it gets worse. Yesterday the U.S. and a few other nations launched an assault against the mothership using a fleet of over fifty manned ships. That attempt failed as well. Now debris from the destroyed ships and shuttles is floating around the mothership. Thousands died. It was awful."

"Why is the debris collected around the Formic ship?" asked Victor. "The wreckage should have shot off in every direction when the ships broke apart."

"The Formic ship has some kind of field around it," said Yanyu. "Magnetic somehow. It's not strong enough to catch everything, but it catches the smaller pieces. It's a mess up there. The debris field is several hundred klicks thick."

"Did the Formics sustain any damage?" asked Imala.

"Not exactly," said Yanyu. "There are a few scorch marks from laser fire, but no structural damage that we could see. For us, however, it was a massacre. People are calling it the end of any large-scale space-based offensive."

"What about China?" asked Imala. "What's the status on the ground?"

Here Yanyu became solemn and quiet. "It is terrible. The casualty estimates are now above the two-million mark, and the military has not landed any major victories. The three landers still stand. The air forces have hit them with everything, and every attempt fails. Now the Formics have built mountains of biomass from stripped vegetation, dead animals, human corpses, all thrown together like giant piles of garbage. No one knows why, but there are plenty of gruesome photos on the nets, which I suggest you avoid."

"Have you heard from your family?" Imala asked.

Yanyu nodded. "My mother and father fled Guangzhou on a shipping boat to Vietnam. From there they flew to London. They only got out because they're wealthy. All of my friends and extended family are still in China. My father is trying to get out as many as he can, but the boats are few and the price for passage grows every day. There are thousands that gather at the shipyards every morning, but only a few ships get out. The crowds have turned violent. Some people literally kill to get passage."

"Survival instincts," said Victor. "Parents will do anything to save their children."

"It's too horrible to think about," said Yanyu. "That is not the China I remember."

"What else have you heard?" asked Imala.

"Nothing good. I have many friends in China on the nets. They send me images and vids they've taken of the destruction. I used to open their attachments. I don't anymore. I don't have the stomach for it. I have some net friends who haven't answered my e-mails or logged on in weeks. I don't know if they're dead or alive." Her eyes misted, but she kept her voice steady. "I feel so helpless here. My country burns, and I can do nothing. I cannot even enlist." She held up her gimp arm. "I tried, but they would not accept me."

"Take me to the recruiting office," said Victor. "That's why we came back. So I can join in the fight."

Yanyu looked surprised. "But what can you do? You are not Chinese. My country is not letting in other soldiers, and the fight out here is over."

"My family's ship was destroyed," said Victor. "My father and half my family were killed. The Formics did that. I'm not going to watch them do that to someone else. I'm going to stop them."

Yanyu reached across the table and took his hand. "I am sorry for your loss, Victor."

It was her touch and the gentleness of her voice that nearly pushed him to tears. For days he had buried all thoughts of Father. It was too much to think about, too painful to dwell on. Father was dead. The most constant person in Victor's life was gone. Day after day they had spent every waking hour together bouncing around the ship and making repairs, learning together, laughing together, arguing at times yes, but always apologizing and feeling stupid together afterward. Always together. Not even Mother spent that much time with Father.

And now Father was gone.

Victor wondered how Mother was taking it. A part of him felt guilty for not rushing back and looking for her and the others on the WU-HU ship. Wasn't that his duty as the last surviving male? Not going back was like abandoning Mother, wasn't it? She needed him. She would be broken inside without Father.

And yet Victor also knew that Mother's spine had more iron than his. If anyone could survive and keep all the women and children together, Mother could. She didn't need Victor's help for that. In fact, he would only add to her burden because she would be consoling him, not the other way around.

That was Mother's gift. Father fixed broken machines, Mother fixed broken people.

"Come," said Yanyu. "I will take you."

They took a track car to the center of Old City where the recruiting offices were located. They got out at the NATO building and stood in the artificial sunlight.

"You want me to come in with you?" asked Imala.

"No," said Victor. "I can do this."

"We'll wait here," said Yanyu. "I'll take you both back to my place when you're done. They won't ship you out for a few days at least."

"*If* they ship me out, you mean."

"Think positive," said Imala. "The world is desperate. They'd be insane not to take someone with your talents."

Victor entered the building and told the woman at the counter why he'd come. She directed him to a room where a handful of other men around Victor's age were waiting. An hour passed as more men trickled in. They were from all nationalities. Some were nicely dressed. Others wore mismatched hand-me-down garments as was the norm among most free-miner families.

Eventually a uniformed soldier entered and addressed them. "NATO does not take walk-ins," he said. "We take trained soldiers only. Our forces come from the existing armies of our member countries. So we can't enlist any of you into our service. However, through that far door we have recruiters from every member country. You can enlist in their army, and once you've received training, you can request a transfer to a NATO force. If you are not a citizen of any country, if you don't have a birth certificate, I'm afraid no country is going to take you. Please exit back this way." He pointed to the door they had come through. "Give your contact information to the woman at the desk. If our policy changes, we will make an effort to contact you."

"How?" said Victor. "How will you contact us? My ship was destroyed, and how would you contact a ship anyway? Most communications are down."

"Sorry. That's what I've been asked to say."

"You mean that's what they told you to tell us space borns to make us go away."

The room was quiet. The soldier said nothing.

"What difference does citizenship make anyway?" said Victor. "People on Earth are dying. Do you think they care if their rescuers have a birth certificate?"

"Look, I don't make the policy," said the soldier.

"No, you just follow it. You'll let the world be destroyed because of a *policy*."

"With all due respect, friend, one person can't stop the world from being destroyed."

Victor was on his feet. "With all due respect, friend, you're wrong."

He went through the door and passed the front desk without stopping.

Outside, Imala and Yanyu instantly saw that it hadn't gone well. "You okay?" asked Imala.

All the rage and disappointment in Victor fizzled out, replaced with embarrassment. "I'm not even a second-class citizen, Imala. I'm nobody."

"Not true," said Yanyu. "You are a first-class citizen. First-class friend. Come. I will cook you my turnip cakes. They will make you happy."

Cakes made from turnips? The idea didn't sound promising. But Victor put on his best smile for her sake and followed them toward an available track car.

Yanyu's apartment was cramped but well organized, adorned with trinkets and art prints from China. There was plenty of food to go along with the turnip cakes—pan-fried noodles with bean sprouts, congee with dried minced pork, and sweet tea, all of it in sealed containers that magnetized to the table. Victor never would have thought of it as breakfast food, but it was all good nonetheless.

The turnip cakes, as Yanyu had promised, did in fact make him happy. They were thick, pan-fried, square-shaped rice cakes filled with sausage and Jinhua ham. Victor had eaten four of them before Yanyu explained that they weren't actually made with turnips.

"Then why call them turnip cakes?" Victor asked with a mouthful.

Yanyu shrugged. "Why do Americans call them hamburgers if they're made from beef and not pork?"

"She has a point," said Imala.

When they had eaten and cleared the dishes, Yanyu asked, "What will you do now?"

"If an army won't take us, we'll form our own," said Victor. "The three of us."

"What can three people do against the Formics?" asked Yanyu.

"Tell us more about yesterday's attack on the mothership," said Victor. "What did the Formics do exactly?"

"They won," said Yanyu. "They fired at anything that moved. Some of the shuttles came in slowly and got close, but the Formics vaporized them before they reached the ship. It made humans look foolish."

"Do you have any footage from the battle?" asked Victor.

"We recorded it with the Juke scopes." She pushed off from the table and moon bounced into the family room, where she pulled up several vid files on the holoscreen. "Help yourself, though you will only find it depressing."

Victor took the controls and began studying the footage. The attack was well coordinated. The first wave targeted the shield generators and other defensive targets on the ship's surface, but the rockets fired by the human ships detonated before they reached the mothership, hitting whatever shielding surrounded the Formics. Laser fire broke through the shielding, however, and this seemed to spur the human shuttles forward. Any hope of victory was dashed a moment later as plasma erupted from the surface of the Formic ship on all sides and decimated the entire human fleet in under a minute.

"It's like they're not even trying," said Imala. "We give them everything we've got, and they shrug us off."

Victor replayed the footage. On the second viewing he asked the computer to monitor the human ships' speeds, their angles of approach, and the number of times each ship fired. On the third viewing he saw the pattern. On the fourth viewing he was sure he was right.

"Look at this," he said, starting the vid again and playing it at a slower speed. "The apertures on the surface of the Formic ship open, but look, they target the fastest ships first."

"So," said Yanyu. "That's what I would do. The fastest ships are the ones that will reach them first and are therefore the most immediate threat."

"That's just it," said Victor. "Some of these fast ships aren't even heading toward the Formics. A few of them are moving in an arc, getting into position, preparing to come at the Formics from another direction. So their trajectory is taking them to a spot in space on the other side. A few of them aren't even firing yet."

"What's your point?" said Imala.

"My point is, it doesn't make tactical sense. Humans would defend themselves differently. We would target those ships that pose the biggest, most immediate threat, right? The ships that were firing. But the Formics don't. They target the ships that are moving the fastest."

"They wiped out every ship," said Imala. "Does it matter what order they did it in?"

"It absolutely matters," said Victor. "Look." He sped up the vid to the end of the battle. "Watch. The ships that were destroyed last were the ships that were moving the slowest. And yet some of these ships are scorching the surface of the Formic ship with laser fire. So in some instances, the Formics took out ships that *weren't* firing before they took out ships that *were*."

"Meaning what?" asked Imala.

"Meaning their defense is somehow built on motion detection," said Victor. "They identified all the ships and destroyed them in the order of how fast they were moving. Which means if a ship was moving slow enough and inconspicuously enough, it might be able to reach the Formic ship."

"That doesn't make sense," said Imala. "If it's moving toward the ship, it's in motion. That would set off the Formic sensors."

"Not if it's moving very, very slowly," said Victor. "Here, look at the debris around the Formic ship. Most of the debris from the destroyed ships is gone, blasted off and moving away at a constant speed. But you still have hundreds of pieces of debris surrounding the mothership. Now, none of these pieces is completely inert. They're all spinning or drifting slightly, so they have some motion. And yet the Formics don't blast them. Why?"

"Because they're not ships," said Imala. "They're debris. They're not a threat anymore."

"Exactly," said Victor. "They have some motion but they're being ignored because they're debris."

"If you're making another point, Vico," said Imala, "we're not seeing it."

"This is the answer," said Victor. "This is how I can reach the Formic ship."

"How?" said Imala.

"By camouflaging a tiny shuttle to look like debris and then piloting it very slowly, as if it were drifting, right up to the surface of the ship. It would blend in with all of the other drifting debris. The Formics would completely ignore it. And if the motion was slow enough, their sensors wouldn't detect it."

"Theoretically," said Imala. "You don't know how sensitive their sensors are."

"Actually," said Victor, "we have a pretty good idea. My father and all the men from El Cavador, along with Lem's men, reached the surface of the ship. How? By having their ships match the Formics' speed, which meant their ships looked stationary to the Formics. And more importantly, for whatever reason, the men passed through the shield. I can get on that ship, Imala."

"And do what exactly?" asked Imala. "Blow it up? Your family already tried that, Vico. It didn't work."

"My family tried damaging it from the outside. They didn't go inside."

"So you'll go *in* the ship? How?"

"I don't know yet. I just came up with the idea. I'll figure something out."

"I know you're upset about not being able to enlist, Vico," said Imala, "but let's think rationally here. What you're suggesting is suicide. We don't have any of the supplies you'd need. We don't have a shuttle. We don't have camouflage for a shuttle. And we certainly don't have weapons for doing any damage inside the Formic ship even if you were, by some miracle, able to get inside."

"What is it with you planet people?" said Victor. "All anyone ever does around here is say something can't be done. We don't have this. We can't do that. That's against the rules. Well guess what? This is how we live, Imala. This is how free miners think. When there's a problem, we don't sit around and take note of everything that *can't* be done, we do something. We find a way, and we fix it."

Imala folded her arms. "You and I are on the same team, Vico. I've made sacrifices for you, and getting snippy with me doesn't help. Everything I've said is true. You may not like it, but those are the facts. We *don't* have those supplies. Just because I question your idea doesn't mean I'm wrong. Are you telling me that every free-miner idea is a good one?"

"No. Of course not."

"Then let's think this through instead of arguing."

Victor exhaled. "You're right. I'm sorry."

Imala turned to Yanyu. "Does the observatory have a shuttle we could use?"

"I thought you were dismissing the idea," said Victor.

"I'm figuring out if it's feasible," said Imala. "I'm trying to help." She turned back to Yanyu.

"No," said Yanyu. "We sometimes have the scopes serviced, but there's a repair crew that does that. They have their own shuttles. I've never even seen them before. I wouldn't know how to acquire one."

"What about the Juke shuttle?" said Victor. "The one we just docked?"

Imala shook her head. "It's in the system now. We don't have authorization to reboard it or take it anywhere. Juke Limited wouldn't let us near the thing. How would you camouflage a shuttle anyway? Maybe we start there."

"Space junk," said Victor. "There are thousands of pieces orbiting Earth. Old satellites, retired space stations, discarded shuttle parts. We simply scoop up some of that and then weld it all over the surface of the shuttle to make it look like a big chunk of a destroyed ship."

"Weld it?" said Imala. "Who's going to loan us a shuttle and then allow us to essentially destroy it by welding junk all over it?"

Victor shrugged. "I don't know. I have some money. Maybe we buy a used one."

"You don't have enough," said Imala. "Not even a fraction of what we would need. Operating shuttles are expensive. Even old ones. Especially now. With the war on and people in a panic, you can bet the price of shuttles has skyrocketed. I'd give you everything in my account as well, but we'd still be shy. Plus there's the cost of fuel to go out and recover the space junk. That's probably nearly as expensive as the shuttle itself. It's a good idea, Vico, but we don't have the money for that."

"I'd give you everything in my account too," said Yanyu. "Maybe the others at the observatory would chip in also."

Victor and Imala exchanged glances.

"It's worth a shot," said Imala. "But I still don't think it will be enough."

"Let me conference with everyone," said Yanyu.

She hopped to the holofield and began a chat with her coworkers. Several of them pledged money, but most of them were skeptical and politely refused. They had the same issue that Imala did. Once you reach the Formic ship, then what? What good is it to invest in a shuttle if you can't do anything once you get there? Imala spent the time looking on the nets at shuttles for sale, becoming increasingly more convinced that they couldn't afford to buy one.

After the conference, Yanyu and Imala shared notes. They were still far short. They didn't even have enough to buy the shell of a shuttle someone was selling. No engine. No flight controls. Just the body of the ship.

"We need a benefactor," said Imala. "Someone with resources. Someone who could give us a shuttle and a weapon."

"If you're going to say Ukko Jukes," said Victor, "I'll politely remind you that he wants us off the grid. He practically threw us out to the Belt."

"Not Ukko," said Imala. "Lem."

"Absolutely not," said Victor. "He's a murderer, Imala. He crippled my family's ship. He tried to kill me."

"He helped your family later, Vico."

"He abandoned them. He left them to die."

"He has what we need, Vico. And he wants to get rid of the Formics as much as we do."

"We don't even know if he's on Luna. He was still at Last Chance when we left."

"I already checked while Yanyu was on the holo," said Imala. "He arrived several days ago. It was all over the news."

"He can't be trusted, Imala."

"He came clean about your family, Vico. He didn't have to. He told the truth."

"His *version* of the truth. And that doesn't make him an ally."

"Anyone who wants to destroy the Formics is an ally, Vico. I don't like it any more than you do. I find the man as repulsive as his father, but he can get us what we need if we can convince him to cooperate."

"He'll only take the idea and do it himself."

"All the better," said Imala. "Let him take the risks if he wants to. It doesn't matter how the Formics go down. It only matters that they do."

Victor was quiet a moment. "If he refuses I want permission to punch him in the face."

"If he refuses," said Imala, "you'll have to get in line."


Lem agreed to meet them at a botanical garden in the Old City an hour after the facility closed. Imala suggested that Yanyu stay behind and continue the search for a reasonable shuttle.

Victor and Imala arrived at the appointed hour, and the man at the gate escorted them through the azalea garden to a bench beneath a crabapple tree and then left them there. Lem had not yet arrived, so they settled onto the bench and waited.

Imala pointed out all the flowers she knew. Azaleas and rhododendrons lined the path all around them. White, pink, coral, magenta. Huge lilac plants swayed gently in the artificial breeze, their purple blossoms giving off a sweet scent. It mixed with the smells of damp earth and grass and other flowers, and was so powerful and so foreign to Victor that it made him a little sick to his stomach.

Lem showed up ten minutes later with a retinue of security guards who hung back at a distance. He took the bench opposite them and settled back languidly.

"Why meet us here?" said Imala. "Why not somewhere more public?"

"Because he doesn't want to be seen with a filthy rock sucker," said Victor.

Imala put a hand on Victor's leg to calm him.

"Wherever I go I get assaulted by paparazzi," said Lem. "It's annoying. I figured you didn't want cameras shoved in your faces."

"Yes, you're a big hero now," said Victor. "We watched some of your interviews this afternoon. You were so brave to abandon those free miners. Wherever did you find the courage?"

Lem rolled his eyes. "Is this why you asked to see me? To insult me? Because I really don't have the time." He started to get up.

"No," said Imala. "That's not why." She shot Victor a look, and Victor put his hands up in a show of surrender.

Lem settled back on the bench. "Look," he said, "whatever your agenda is, let me begin by saying that this company has the finest legal team in the world. If your intent is to blackmail me, you're making a mistake. It won't work. My father would never allow that to happen. If you go to the press, they'll ignore you. If you go the nets, it will be removed, and you'll be slapped with a lawsuit that would pretty much guarantee a very dismal financial future for yourselves. Trust me. I know how my father works. I know you're not wearing listening devices because I had the gardener sweep you when you came in, but if this is your intent, let me save you a lot of heartache and end the conversation right now before you say something you'll regret. Because whatever it is, my father will hear of it, and it would not bode well for you."

"You see, Imala?" said Victor. "All he has for us is threats."

"I'm not threatening you," said Lem. "I'm warning you. I'm doing you a favor. You don't want to make a spectacle of what happened in the Kuiper Belt. You'd lose. There are other ways to do this. I'm willing to settle with the family of the man who died. We would do it privately. In a way that is untraceable back to me. But I will gladly do that. No lawyers. No documents. If the wife and children are still alive, I'll happily set up an account and see that they're taken care of."

Victor was so angry it took everything not to shout the words out. "You think you can buy my family? You think my uncle Marco can be *paid* for?" He turned to Imala. "This was a mistake. He's not going to help us."

"Help you do what?" said Lem.

"We didn't come here to blackmail you," said Imala. "We came here because we think we've found a way to get inside the Formic ship."

"And why would you want to do that?" asked Lem.

"There's a war on," said Victor. "Maybe you didn't notice."

Lem narrowed his eyes. "Your family was far more charming than you are, Victor. I find it hard to believe you're even related."

Victor stood up. "That's it. We're out of here, Imala."

"Sit down, Victor." Imala's voice was sharp as a whip. "Both of you are acting like children. There are people dying. Millions of people. I would like to do something about that. I thought the both of you did as well. If I'm wrong, tell me now, and I'll look elsewhere."

Reluctantly, Victor sat down again.

Imala looked at Lem, who sat back and put his hands up, acquiescing. "I'm listening. What's your plan?"

She told him.

When she finished Lem was quiet a moment. "How do you get inside the Formic ship once you reach it? I've seen it up close. There are no doors. No windows. No entry points anywhere."

"I'll go in where the guns emerge," said Victor. "On our way to the ship, I'll stop at one of the bigger chunks of debris, I'll attach a propellant to it. A small engine of sorts. It wouldn't take much. Then when I reach the Formic ship, I'll initiate the propellant and fly the hunk of debris directly at the Formic ship as fast as it can go. The guns will emerge to blast it to smithereens, and I'll slip in through the hole."

Imala regarded him. "That's actually a good idea. Why didn't you mention it before?"

"Because I just thought of it," said Victor.

"How would you get back out again?" said Lem. "Once the gun retracts, you're stuck inside."

"I'll take braces with me, made of the strongest reinforced steel available. I'll prop open the crevice enough to squeeze back out."

"What if there's no entry point inside the hole?" asked Lem. "The gun could sit in a recessed space without any access to the interior of the ship."

"Then I'll use the opportunity to disable the gun," said Victor. "I'll cripple the ship as much as I can. I'll make the most of my time. I'll do reconnaissance. I'll learn as much as I can."

"And what will you do if you *do* get inside the ship?"

"Find the helm and plant an explosive," said Victor. "Whoever is leading the army will likely be there. Kill him, and you put the army in chaos."

"How would you know where the helm is located?" asked Lem.

"It'll be in the center of the ship," said Victor

"How can you be sure?"

"Because that's where *I* would put it. Look at the shape of the thing.
Where would you want to be if you were the captain and you were moving
at a fraction of the speed of light through space with collision threats all
around you?"

"As far away from the side of the ship as possible," said Lem.

"Right," said Victor. "The center of the ship. The most protected spot."

"Assuming you're right about its location," said Lem, "how do you plan
to reach it? The ship is likely crawling with Formics."

"I won't know until I'm inside," said Victor. "And I'll be recording
everything. So even if I die, the footage would be useful. Whatever team
follows me wouldn't be going in blind."

Lem sat silently for a moment. Then he came to a decision and leaned
forward. "There's a corner of the Juke production facility dedicated to a
project I'm working on. Wing H16. It has its own dock and entrance and
exit. My father's people don't go there. Only my engineers are allowed access. Once you've collected the space junk, bring the shuttle and junk
there. I'll give you space in the facility to camouflage the shuttle and prep
it for launch. I'll have all the tools you need and engineers on hand should
you require them. I'd offer scraps of Juke ships for the camouflage, but I
don't want my father to have any part of this. This is not a Juke mission,
this is *our* mission. Understand? If we use anything from Juke other than
my facilities and private finances, my father would strip this from us and
make it his own. We'd lose control.

"So we can't use a Juke shuttle either. It has to be one you buy from an
outside source. Small so it would blend in with the debris, but outfitted
properly. Something reliable. Not a junker. We're not going to fail because
of faulty equipment. Buy a new one. You'll also need a cargo shuttle or a
dumper to haul in space junk from orbit. You can't load everything into a
tiny shuttle. So get both. A dumper and a small shuttle. We can resale the
dumper if we have to. You'll need fuel as well of course, plus other supplies I'm probably not thinking of. How much do you need?"

It took Imala a moment to find her voice. "Um, I hadn't factored in the price of a dumper—"

"You'll need one," said Lem.

"All right." Imala thought for a moment then gave him a number.

"I'm tripling that," said Lem, tapping digits onto his wrist pad. "You need a cushion. These things are always more expensive than you think. If you need more, let me know." He motioned for her to extend her hand, then he tapped his wrist pad to hers.

Imala looked at the amount. It took a moment to find her voice. "Thank you."

"Don't thank me. I'm not doing this for you. I'm doing it for the human race."

He stood up to leave. "One more thing. I read your file, Imala. You uncovered a lot of dirt on my father. It cost you your job. I know you may think otherwise, but my father wasn't involved in those business practices. He has some dishonest employees, and he's dealing with them. In the meantime, I want to settle the issue. Whatever back taxes and tariffs my father may owe, I want to know about it. I will see to it that it's paid. My father won't be running this company forever. And when it's mine, I don't want any dirty laundry. There's a link in that amount I gave you. Send me everything you found, and I'll take care of it."

Imala nodded, surprised. "I will."

"Good. Now get the supplies and bring them to the dock."

"Wing H16," said Imala.

"Right," said Lem. He adjusted his coat and checked his cufflinks, as if he thought a photographer might be waiting right outside the door. Then he turned and walked out, his security retinue falling into step behind him.

When he was gone, Victor said, "Is it just me or did the smell of flowers go away when he and his stink walked in?"

"I don't trust him either," said Imala, looking down at her wrist pad. "But I'm not going to argue with this." She tapped him on the chest with the back of her hand and moved for the exit. "Come on, space born. You and I just declared war on the Formics."

# CHAPTER 24

# Blood and Ashes

At dinner, Mazer sat cross-legged on the farmhouse floor across from Danwen and Bingwen. It was the third night in a row eating rice and boiled bamboo shoots. Mazer finished his portion and set down his leaf bowl. "I'm well enough to move now. I should set out in the morning."

Bingwen looked panicked. "You can't. We have to stay together. Tell him, Grandfather."

"You do not command your elders, Bingwen," said Danwen. "Mazer must do what he thinks is best."

"But . . . you can't leave us," said Bingwen. "I saved you. You have to protect us. You owe us."

"Bingwen!" Danwen clapped his hands together so loudly it was like thunder inside the farmhouse. "You dishonor me. Outside. Clean the pots."

"Yes, Grandfather." The boy bowed low and scurried off.

"You will forgive my grandson, Mazer. He is young and loose lipped and knows little respect."

"He's right," said Mazer. "I do owe you."

"You owe us nothing. We are alive because of you. There is no debt between us."

"You should go north," said Mazer. "You can't stay here. There aren't any more supplies in the valley. You need food, fresh water. You've only stayed this long because of me, and for that I'm grateful, but I can't allow you to endanger yourselves anymore on my behalf. Let me take you north until we find another group or family you can travel with. Then I'll leave you and come south."

"To the lander? I cannot talk you out of such folly?"

"Destroying the landers is the only way to end this war."

Danwen exhaled. "I am an old man, Mazer. Too old for war, with you or the Formics. If you say you must go south, I will not try to stop you. Although I will allow you to escort us to a family or group. The boy doesn't feel safe with me, and I don't blame him. I can do little to defend us. He deserves better. We will leave at first light."

"Thank you," said Mazer. "Also, and I hope you take no offense at this, Ye Ye Danwen, but after the war, I want to help Bingwen get into a school. He has told me how hard it is to get an education here. With your blessing I would like to enroll him somewhere. In a private school in Beijing perhaps. Or in Guangzhou. I will pay for it. For as long as I can. I owe him that."

Danwen reached out and patted Mazer's hand. "You are a good man, Mazer Rackham. You have my blessing. Bingwen is a rare boy. You will say I am biased, but I believe he is one in a thousand. Maybe one in a million. Do you think a child could be wiser than most adults, Mazer?"

"I do now."

Danwen laughed. "Yes. A very wise boy. You should ask him how to destroy the lander. I would not be surprised if he had the answer."

That night Danwen insisted on taking first watch. He sat in the doorway of the farmhouse with the sword lying across his lap. Mazer lay down near the window on the far side of the room with a view of the night sky. He stared up at the millions of stars, wondering if the mothership had been destroyed. Maybe the Formics here in China were all that was left of them.

"Mazer." A whisper.

Mazer turned. Bingwen was beside him, sitting on the floor hugging his knees tightly to his chest.

"I am sorry for asking you to stay. That was selfish."

"You don't have to apologize, Bingwen. I'd stay if I could. I'm sorry I can't."

The boy nodded but didn't leave.

Mazer waited. Bingwen stared at the floor.

"Is there something else you wanted to say, Bingwen?"

The boy nodded, but he didn't look at Mazer. "You must tell Grandfather something. Before you leave. I cannot tell him. I have tried many times, but the words won't come."

Mazer waited. The boy said nothing.

"What must I tell him, Bingwen?"

In the moonlight Mazer could see tears running down Bingwen's cheeks. The boy didn't make a sound. He wiped at his face with his sleeve then spoke in a whisper. "My parents. They will not be waiting for us in the north. The day I came for you, I saw them." He shook his head, ashamed. "I did not bury them. And now they are in the mountain of death, piled with all the dead things. I have dishonored them."

Mazer sat up and took the boy in his arms. "You have not dishonored them, Bingwen. Don't think such a thing. You have honored them by helping *me*." He didn't know what else to say. The boy shook silently in his arms. Mazer could see Danwen's silhouette in the doorway, looking in his direction. Mazer held up a hand to indicate that all was well.

Sometime later Bingwen fell asleep. Only then did Mazer release him, gently laying him on his mat on the floor. Mazer lay down on the wood planks beside him, eyes weary and body weak. The rice and bamboo were filling his stomach but doing little more than that. His energy was down. He needed nutrients. Judging by how gaunt his body looked and felt, he guessed he had lost about seven kilos, or fifteen pounds. It was weight he couldn't afford to lose—he had had almost no body fat to begin with.

Outside, the night was still and quiet. It had taken Mazer a week to get used to the silence. No birds fluttered; no mice or small creatures rustled in the grass; no insects chirped in the darkness. The Formics had burned the land and everything with it, and left nothing behind but the wind.

Mazer woke suddenly. He had slipped into sleep, but now a sound had awoken him. A soft noise that didn't belong. He sat up and saw it, standing at the door, just outside, its wand leveled at Danwen's face. The old man was asleep, completely oblivious. Mazer was up and running. The wand released a single puff of mist into Danwen's face. The old man moaned quietly. The Formic looked up, sensing movement in the darkness. Then Mazer threw himself at the creature before it could raise the wand again.

They collided and tumbled out into the yard, the creature flailing. Mazer ripped its hand from the wand. Its other hands clawed at him. A leg kicked him. It was strong, Mazer realized. Stronger than he had expected, like an ape. It was scrabbling for him, reaching for him, twisting, fighting, trying to bite at him with its maw. They rolled in the dirt. It struck Mazer on the back, a colossal blow that sent pain ripping though his upper body. The creature was desperate, kicking, bucking. Mazer felt his grip weakening; his strength was not what it was. He twisted and maneuvered himself behind the Formic then wrapped his legs around its torso, pinning its arms to its side. The creature thrashed, desperate, angry. Mazer thought the back-pack of defoliant might break and cover him in the liquid.

"Grandfather?"

Bingwen was at the door, looking down at the old man, whose body had slumped to the side.

"Get back!" Mazer shouted. "Cover your mouth!"

Bingwen retreated back into the darkness. The creature kicked and thrashed. Mazer wrapped his arms around the Formic's head and jerked it violently to one side. Something cracked. Mazer felt muscle and bone or cartilage tear. The Formic went limp.

Mazer held it a moment longer, then released it, kicking it away. His heart was pounding. There was moisture on his arms and legs. He wasn't sure if it was his sweat or the Formic's. He gagged. But then he extended his neck and controlled the reflex.

He heard the soft patter of feet. Footsteps. But not human ones. They were coming from behind the barn. Danwen's sword lay in the dirt near the doorway. Mazer looked for any remnant of the mist, but could see nothing in the dark. It might be there, or it might not. He wasn't sure. The footsteps were getting closer. Mazer reached for the sword, grabbed it, and rolled away, coming up on the balls of his feet, ready to move. He ran for the barn, keeping his steps silent. He put his back to the wall of the barn just as another Formic with a mist sprayer came around the corner to his left, moving right past him. The Formic saw its dead companion in the yard and stopped.

Mazer brought the sword down from behind hard and fast. It sunk into the Formic's head with little resistance and drove down clear to its neck where it stuck. The creature dropped, nearly pulling the sword from Ma-zer's grip. Mazer jerked it free and stepped back against the barn, listening.

More footsteps. This time to his right. He sidled in that direction, his bare feet moving silently in the dirt. The Formic came around the corner before Mazer had reached it. It saw him, hesitated, then fumbled with the wand.

Mazer lunged, skewering the creature in its center mass. The blade struck the backpack and stopped. The creature looked down at the blade protrud-ing from its chest. Mazer retracted the blade and thrust again, piercing the creature through once more. The Formic didn't make a sound. Mazer yanked the blade free again, and the Formic crumpled at his feet.

Mazer crouched again, listening. He stayed that way for a full minute. Then two. He counted the seconds in his head. He heard nothing.

Then he was up, sprinting for the farmhouse. Danwen's body was folded there in the doorway, half inside, half outside. Mazer grabbed the old man by the wrists and dragged him out into the yard, away from where the mist had been sprayed. Danwen was limp. Mazer already knew he was dead. Bingwen appeared near the doorway.

"Don't go through the door," said Mazer. "That's where it was sprayed. Grab my boots and climb out the side window."

Bingwen disappeared again inside.

Mazer knelt by Danwen. The creature had sprayed the old man in the face, and there was moisture on his forehead and cheeks. Mazer wanted to check Danwen's pulse, but he dare not touch the man's neck. He picked up his wrist instead.

No pulse.

He tried the other wrist as well.

Nothing.

He put a hand to Danwen's chest. No heartbeat. Mazer looked up. Bingwen was standing there holding Mazer's boots in his hands, staring down at his grandfather. He had thought to put on his own shoes. Mazer went to him and turned Bingwen's face to his own. "Bingwen, look at me."

The boy blinked. He was in shock.

"Your grandfather is gone. We can't stay here. We need to move now. Do you understand?"

Bingwen nodded. Mazer sat down in the dirt and threw on his boots, tightening the straps as fast as he could.

Bingwen stood over his grandfather's body. "We can't leave him here like this. They will come and take him and put him with the dead things. They will dishonor him."

Mazer took Bingwen's hand. "There's no time to bury him, Bingwen. We have to move now."

Bingwen jerked his hand free. "No. We can't let them take him."

Mazer reached for Bingwen, but the boy was quick and dodged his grasp. Bingwen ran to the fire pit they used for cooking. He grabbed one of the pots and scooped around in the coals. A few of the coals at the bottom were still red hot and smoldering. Bingwen used a stick to scoop them into the pot.

"What are you doing?" Mazer asked.

Bingwen didn't respond. He ran to the barn and dumped the coals in a corner where an old bundle of hay lay rotting. The hay caught fire immediately, igniting like a match. The flames spread quickly, licking at the old, dry wooden wall of the barn. Bingwen dropped the pot and ran back across the yard to where Danwen lay in the dirt. He grabbed the old man by the ankles and pulled with all his strength. Danwen didn't budge, light as he was.

Mazer came over, bent down, and scooped the old man up into his arms, being careful not to touch Danwen's face. Smoke was pouring out of the barn now. Flames crawled up the interior wall like it was kindling. There was a square wooden box on the ground near the back wall where more tools were kept. Mazer laid Danwen atop it and kicked some of the untouched hay around it. The fire was close now. Mazer kicked at a burning plank to knock it free of the wall. It splintered and broke away, burning at the edges. Mazer grabbed a corner that wasn't on fire and placed it at the base of the box Danwen lay on. The smoke was thick and burned Mazer's eyes. The heat was intense. Mazer retreated out of the barn coughing and brushing burning ashes from his clothes.

Bingwen stood outside in the yard, staring at the flames, the sword loose in his hand, blood glistening on the blade in the firelight.

Mazer knelt beside him. "We can't stay, Bingwen. Can you run?"

They needed to move. The troop transports were silent and light as leaves. They could be here at any moment. Bingwen turned to Mazer, his movements slow, as if in a trance. He didn't respond. He wouldn't be able to run, Mazer realized. Not quickly. Mazer took the sword and gently picked up Bingwen in his arms. Then he ran, heading down the mountain, the flames and the farmhouse at their backs—moving north, into the darkness.

They ran for fifteen minutes, cutting through fields that had been stripped of all life. Mazer's boots were soon heavy with mud and ashes. They crossed rice fields, sticking to the thin bridges of earth between the paddies and steering clear of the standing water. The rice shoots had long since wilted and died, and now a thin chemical residue floated atop the water at the paddies' edges, glistening in the moonlight like oil. A kilometer beyond the base of the mountain they found a stretch of jungle untouched by the mist and pushed their way through it, preferring to be in the cover of the thick foliage than out in the open where they could be easily spotted. It was harder to see in the jungle, however. Branches snagged at their clothes and slapped at their faces. Twice Mazer stumbled, nearly dropping Bingwen both times.

By now, Bingwen was coming to himself again. "You don't have to carry me anymore," he said quietly. "I can run."

Mazer didn't argue. He was exhausted. His body was slick with sweat. His arms and legs were cramped, particularly his right arm, which had carried the bulk of Bingwen's weight. The wound in his belly had begun to burn, too, and he worried that he might have torn something. He set Bingwen down, and they collapsed at the base of a tree. Mazer leaned back against the trunk, his breathing heavy.

They sat in silence for a while. Mazer wanted to comfort Bingwen; he wanted to say something reassuring, something to soften the boy's grief. Yet everything that came to mind sounded insufficient or like an empty promise he couldn't keep. They were in danger now, more danger than they had been in before, and any assurance of a happy ending seemed false and disingenuous.

It was Bingwen who finally broke the silence. "I'm sorry you had to carry me," he said. "I . . . wasn't thinking straight."

"It's all right," said Mazer. "I didn't mind. I needed the exercise."

"No. You didn't. You shouldn't be straining yourself. You should be resting. Look at you. You're thinner than you were. You need food, Mazer. Real food. Meat and fruits and vegetables, not rice and bamboo. And a real doctor should have a look at you." He pulled his knees up tight to his chest as he had done in the farmhouse. "You can't go back to the lander, Mazer. You can't. You're not healthy enough to fight."

Mazer took a few more breaths before responding. His heart was pounding. "It's complicated, Bingwen."

"No. It isn't. You're weak. The army has been pounding the lander and gotten nowhere. What can you do that they can't? You'd be throwing your life away. Let the fighters and bombs do their job."

"You just said the bombs weren't working."

"Walking to the lander is stupid. Suicide. If you want to get in the fight, find some troops. Do good elsewhere. You can help and still survive."

"If I go north and find Chinese troops, Bingwen, they'll likely arrest me and ship me back to New Zealand. And that's the best-case scenario."

"Why would they arrest you?"

"Like I said, it's complicated."

"And I wouldn't understand because I'm a child? I thought we were past that."

Mazer exhaled deep and wiped the sweat from his face with the sleeve of his shirt. "All right. They'd arrest me because I'm not supposed to be here. I disobeyed a direct order by rushing to the lander. Three of my friends died as a result of my decision. My military isn't likely to forgive that. I'm not sure *I* can forgive it." He took another deep breath and leaned forward. "That's why I have to go back, Bingwen. I'm not going home until I help end this war. Not because it might absolve me of ignoring the order, but because I owe it to my friends to make their deaths mean something. Because I owe it to you and to your parents and your grandfather and everyone in China who has suffered. Does that make sense?"

"No. It doesn't. It's boneheaded. You're not responsible for what has happened here, Mazer. You're not responsible even for your friends. They wanted to help. It was their decision to disobey that order as much as yours. It's not your fault they died."

"It is actually. I was their commanding officer. I was responsible for their safety."

"So throwing yourself to the Formics is going to change that? What are you hoping to accomplish by getting yourself killed?"

"I don't plan on dying, Bingwen."

"Well the Formics are likely to spoil those plans. It's you against hundreds or thousands of them. You, unarmed and weak, dressed in rags. And them, shielded and loaded with weapons and completely merciless. You don't have to be an adult to see how foolish you're being."

Mazer smiled. "Rest, Bingwen. This is the last break we'll take for a while."

They sat in silence for several minutes. Mazer's breathing normalized, and the burning in his side had dissipated, which suggested it was a stitch in his side and not the surgery wound . . . or so Mazer hoped. They got up and started moving again, this time at a much slower pace. They used the sword to cut their way through the densest parts of the jungle, but every slice was loud in the stillness, so they did it sparingly.

After another hour of walking Bingwen asked, "Do you have a son?"

The question surprised Mazer. "A son? No. I'm not married, Bingwen."

"Why not? The doctor, Kim, she cares for you. Why not marry her?"

Mazer regarded the boy. It was hard to see him clearly in the darkness and shadows of the jungle. "I wish it were that easy, Bingwen."

"She loves you. I could tell. I may be eight, but I'm not blind."

"People don't marry simply because they're in love, Bingwen."

"Of course they do. Why else would they do it?"

"Marriage and family is a commitment to someone. If you can't be absolute in your commitment, you shouldn't make it. I'm a soldier. I'm always away. That would be hard on a marriage."

"So you'll never marry?"

"One day, I hope. After I'm a soldier."

"Would you ever consider having a son before you were married?"

Mazer saw where this was going. When he spoke his voice was kind and quiet. "You can't be my son, Bingwen."

"But I'd work hard," said Bingwen. "And I'd obey. You wouldn't have to scold me or punish me because I would always listen. I wouldn't even complain when you had to go off somewhere on assignment. I could take care of myself. I could cook my own meals. I can cook other things besides rice and bamboo, you know. I can cook meats and vegetables. I could cook for you, too."

Mazer stopped and knelt in front of the boy, placing a hand on his shoulder. "If I have a son one day, Bingwen, I hope he's as brave and smart and strong as you. But China is your home, and New Zealand is mine."

"China *was* my home. But it's a new China now, one that's as strange to me as it is to you. I don't belong here any more than you do."

He's like me, thought Mazer. Displaced, alone, coping with a new culture, having lost the one he knew. It was exactly how Mazer felt as a boy when his mother died. She had angered her Maori family by marrying an Englishman. They were pure Maoris, and they saw Father as an intruder, stealing their daughter from her heritage. So they expelled her from the tribe.

Later, when Mazer was born, Mother repented by immersing Mazer in the Maori culture. She still loved Father—she would never leave him—but she wanted Mazer raised as she had been. So she plunged him into the culture and taught him the language, dances, and songs. She fed him

Maori food, instilled in him the warrior spirit. She made him super Maori.

Then she died when he was ten. And now there was no one to champion Mazer's inclusion in the group. Father, after having been excluded for all those years, certainly wasn't going to do it. Instead, he took Mazer back to England and tried to erase all the Maori in him. Father was the scion of a noble family, and he would make Mazer a proper Englishman with studies in computers and science. Suddenly Mazer went from a fishing/taro-planting/pig-butchering life full of song and story to a life of high-tech computers in British boarding schools.

He learned to adapt. He was never accepted by the pure Brits—they called him a wog and excluded him. But he became more British than they were. He learned every courtesy of British society. He mastered the accent. He became extremely articulate. He consumed every subject he studied. He made himself an expert in two cultures . . . even though he was never really a citizen of either.

Bingwen faced the same issue. He was a primitive farm child who had crossed over and immersed himself in a different culture, learning English, learning computers, soaking up as much as he could. He had passed back and forth between worlds as Mazer did.

"The world will always change, Bingwen," said Mazer. "You become whoever you need to be to fit it."

"So I'm never really a person at all then. I'm just whatever is convenient to the world around me? That's not who I want to be. That's not *me*."

"That's not who you *are,* Bingwen. But that's how you survive. You've been doing it all your life already. It doesn't change who you are. You still get to decide who that is. You get to choose the best of everything. The best of China, the best of what you've learned, the best of your parents. That is still your choice, regardless of what the world is doing, whether this is the China you know or not. You still decide who you are."

"Except I can't decide to be your son."

"No, but you don't have to be my son to mean something to me. You can—"

He stopped. He had heard something. Voices perhaps. Not too distant. He put a finger to his lips, and Bingwen nodded that he understood.

They crept forward, silent as shadows, until they reached the edge of the jungle, just a few meters away. A wide clearing opened before them in the darkness, and far out in the center of it, two hundred meters away, a red dot of firelight flickered. There were shapes moving around the fire, though at this distance it was impossible to see how many people there were or if they were friendly or not. Mazer and Bingwen crouched at the edge of the jungle and listened. Whoever they were they weren't very smart to have built a fire in such an open space. They were practically calling the Formics to their position.

Mazer had hoped to find a group or family that Bingwen could go with, but it wouldn't be this lot. They were reckless and loud and likely to get Bingwen killed. The smart thing to do would be to move on and stay clear of them. Let the Formics find them. Not our problem.

But Mazer was desperate for information. He knew nothing about the Formics' position or movements. He might be walking Bingwen straight toward a Formic stronghold. It was a risk to talk to whoever was out there, but it was a risk Mazer knew he had to take.

For a moment he considered ordering Bingwen to stay behind while he advanced and approached the fire, but he didn't feel comfortable leaving Bingwen alone, and he doubted Bingwen would like the idea either. "Stay close," said Mazer. "And step as quietly as you can until we're certain they're friendly."

They moved toward the light, Mazer leading, sword in hand. When they were halfway across the field Mazer stopped and sniffed at the air.

"What is it?" Bingwen whispered.

"That smell," said Mazer. "It smells like . . . lobster."

Bingwen sniffed. "I smell it too."

Mazer tightened his grip on the sword hilt, and they drew closer to camp. Soon the vague shapes in the firelight took form. There were five men and one woman, all of them crouched on the ground, huddled around something, the fire behind them. There was a spit above the flames with some creature roasting on it. As Mazer drew closer he saw that the cooked creature was the bottom half of a Formic. The people were eating the top half, which they had pulled off the spit and placed on the ground, surrounding it like a pack of scavengers.

Mazer felt sick. He wanted to retreat, but they were close to the fire now, and the woman saw them. She cried out, and the men were instantly on their feet, weapons in hand. They had staves and knives and machetes. They were peasants. Their clothes were torn and stained, their faces wild. They were thin and sallow and desperate.

Mazer didn't move. Bingwen hid behind him. No one spoke.

One of the men with a machete finally said, "This is our food. There's not enough for you."

"We don't want your food," said Mazer.

"He's lying," said the man with a knife. "He wants it all right. Look at his eyes."

"You shouldn't eat that," said Mazer. "It's the wrong arrangement of proteins. It wasn't made for humans to eat."

"See?" said the man with the knife. "He's trying to trick us and take it from us."

"They collect their dead," said Mazer. "They might come for this one."

The men glanced up in the sky around them as if they thought a transport might descend right on top of them.

The woman was behind the men near the fire. She turned away suddenly and began to retch. The men watched her. The woman fell to her hands and knees and emptied her stomach onto the dirt. The men recoiled and looked down at the dismembered Formic at their feet, its skin charred and black from the fire, its chest cut open and steaming in the glow of the fire.

One of the men began to retch, and Mazer grabbed Bingwen's hand and ran.


At dawn they found a highway. There were deserted cars—some intact, other smashed and shattered and wrecked. There were craters in the Earth two meters wide from explosions and laser fire. There were scorch marks everywhere, accompanied by deep cuts in the earth and asphalt. There were no bodies, but there were dark stains of blood everywhere. Mazer tried starting several of the vehicles, but the batteries and fuel cells had been stripped.

They continued on foot, following the highway north for a few hours. They saw more destruction and deserted vehicles. When they heard aircraft, they hid and waited for it to pass.

At midday they found a family with two young children resting in the shade of an overpass. The wife said little, but she offered Bingwen and Mazer soup, which they both gratefully accepted.

"We stayed hidden in an underground storage shed," said the father. "We had enough food for over a week. We thought we could hold out until help came, but no soldiers ever came for us. We're moving north now."

Bingwen was off to the side, playing with the four-year-old boy, tossing wads of rags back and forth to each other like a ball. It was the first time Mazer had ever seen Bingwen laugh.

"Can you take the boy?" Mazer asked.

"Food is scarce," said the father.

"He's smart, resourceful. I can't pay you now, but when the war is over, I will."

"You may not be alive when the war is over. Or we may not win the war."

"We'll win. Take the boy."

The father considered, then nodded. They made the arrangements, and in no time Mazer was kneeling in front of Bingwen, handing him the sword.

"Here," said Mazer, "your grandfather would want you to have this."

Bingwen took it. "I am safer with you at the lander than I am with this family in the north."

"They're good people, Bingwen. They'll feed you. That's more than I can do." He put a hand on the boy's shoulder. "When this is over, I want you to contact me. I'll get you enrolled in a school. A good school, where they'll feed you and take care of you."

"Like an orphanage."

"Better than that. A place where smart kids go. Special kids."

"How do I contact you?"

"Memorize my e-mail and holo address. Can you do that?"

Bingwen nodded. Mazer told him the addresses. "Now recite them back to me."

Bingwen did. Mazer stood and extended a hand. Bingwen shook it. "How long do I need to keep this cast on my arm?" asked Bingwen.

"Another two weeks. Try not to let any more trees fall on it."

"Try not to get killed."

Mazer smiled. "I'll try." He paused a beat, not wanting to leave. "No more heroics, all right? Just get north and stay safe."

Bingwen nodded.

There was nothing more to say. The family was waiting, ready to move on. Mazer smiled one last time then turned on his heels and headed south, not looking back.

He stayed off the highway, moving parallel to it, and made good time. He had been walking slower because of Bingwen, but now he set his own pace. The soup had given him new energy. He found a patch of jungle and slept for a few hours, burying himself among the fallen leaves and staying out of site. When he woke, he got moving again. By now he was dying of thirst. He passed several puddles of rainwater, but he knew better than to drink from them. Late in the afternoon he thought he heard the faint sounds of a battle far west of his position, but he couldn't see anything.

As dusk approached he heard aircraft. He crouched near some wilting shrubs and watched as a Chinese fighter engaged in a dogfight with a Formic flyer directly overhead. The fighter had more firepower, but the Formic craft was more nimble. It swooped and dove and clipped the wing of the Chinese fighter with a laser burst. The fighter was suddenly consumed in flames, spinning out of control, dropping out of the sky. The pilot ejected a few hundred meters from the ground, coming down fast. His parachute opened. His body was limp. The plane crashed some distance to the south. Mazer heard the explosion. The Formic flyer flew on. Mazer watched the pilot's parachute descend out of sight, less than a kilometer away. He jumped up and ran in that direction.

It didn't take him long to find the pilot. The man had landed in the middle of a scorched field, the white, downed parachute billowing in the wind, standing out against the black landscape like a beacon.

Mazer approached the pilot, who wasn't moving. The man lay on his back, head lolled to the side, his helmet tinted so Mazer couldn't see his face. The parachute flapped in the wind. It caught a gust, filled with air, and dragged the pilot on his back a few meters through the dirt.

There was a knife strapped to the pilot's leg. Mazer ran for it, quickly unsheathed it, and cut through the suspension lines. The more he cut, the less pull he felt from the skirt of the chute, until at last it was loose and unable to catch wind anymore. Mazer dropped the knife and knelt beside the pilot. He tapped a sequence on the side of the helmet, and the tint of the visor vanished, revealing the pilot's face behind the reinforced plastic. The pilot's eyes were closed, and he didn't appear to be breathing. Mazer pulled back the chest patch on the man's flight suit to expose the biometric readout. The pliable screen was cracked but still functioning. The pilot had flatlined. Cause of death was a broken neck and severed spinal column. According to the data, it had happened microseconds after the pilot had ejected.

Mazer sat back on his heels. More death.

He looked upward, scanning the sky. He was out in the middle of a field, exposed. If the Formic should return or others pass by, he'd be an easy target.

He grabbed the pilot by the straps of his chute harness and dragged him backward through the dirt toward some wilting scrub. It wasn't much cover, but it was better than nothing.

There was a large auxiliary pack strapped to the pilot's legs, and Mazer loosened it and pulled it free. Inside he found a treasure trove: a sidearm with four clips of ammunition, binoculars, flares, several days worth of MREs, a full canteen plus extra bottles of water, a gas mask, a first-aid kit, a Med-Assist computer, toothbrush, and fresh socks. Mazer quickly opened the canteen and guzzled some of the water. It was cold and clean and so good he wanted to cry. He tore open one of the MREs—a pasta that heated instantly when the air hit it. It had ham and cheese and flecks of sun-dried tomatoes. He didn't find a utensil, so he poured it straight into his mouth. Then he brushed his teeth, which might have been the sweetest relief of all.

He packed everything back into the pack, including the knife and sheath. Then he stood and considered the pilot. The man was tall for a pilot, though not quite as tall as Mazer would have liked. The flight suit was probably two sizes too small for Mazer. Yet even so, a small flight suit was better than the rags Mazer was wearing. If he made a few strategic cuts in the fabric perhaps he could wear it without any problems. He stripped the pilot of the suit then made careful slits in the armpits and crotch. Then he removed his own boots and clothes, down to his undergarments, and dressed in the flight suit, not bothering with any of the biosensors. The sleeves and pant legs were too short, but he could live with that. He was more concerned about mobility. He did a few tentative squats and knee bends and was relieved to see his movement unhindered. He sat back down and put on a new pair of socks and his old boots. Then he loaded the sidearm, stuffed it into the flight suit's holster, and placed the gas mask over his head.

It seemed wrong to leave the pilot here unburied, but he had neither the time nor the tools for it. He gathered up the white parachute and rolled the pilot into it, wrapping him tight like a mummy. It wasn't a proper burial, but it was the best Mazer could do given the circumstances.

He hefted the pack onto his shoulders and headed south again. He hadn't gone far when he heard someone shouting his name. The cries were faint at first, like distant whispers on the wind—so quiet in fact that he initially dismissed them as his imagination. Then a distinct shout of "Mazer!" cut through the quiet, and there was no mistaking it. Mazer turned and ran east toward the source of the sound. He knew that voice. And he sensed the terror and desperation behind it.

His training had taught him stealth and caution and quiet, but Mazer couldn't help himself. He tore off the gas mask and shouted back. "Bingwen!"

They continued shouting each other's names until they found one another moments later. Mazer rounded a ridge and there was Bingwen, running toward him, desperate and dirty, his face streaked with tears. He collapsed into Mazer's arms, exhausted and terrified and too upset to speak.

Mazer carried him to some shade where they'd be hidden from sight and opened the canteen for him. At first Bingwen's breathing was so heavy he couldn't drink, but then he forced himself to calm enough to swallow gulps of water.

"Not too fast," said Mazer. "You'll make yourself sick."

Bingwen lowered the canteen and began to cry anew. When he spoke, his voice was hoarse from shouting for hours on end. "They're dead. The family. All of them. A transport dropped right in front of us. It didn't make a sound. One instant it wasn't there, the next instant it was. Kwong, the father, he shouted for me to run. He and Genji each tried to carry a child, but . . ." He closed his eyes and shook his head, unable to go on.

Mazer took him into his arms, and Bingwen began to sob, his little body shaking with grief and terror and perhaps a dozen other pent-up emotions all flooding out of him at once.

Mazer held him, his arms wrapped around Bingwen in a protective embrace. He wasn't going to lie. He wasn't going to tell Bingwen that he was safe now and that Mazer wouldn't let anything happen to him. Bingwen was too smart for that. So Mazer let him have his cry and made no effort to stop the tears.

When Bingwen calmed again, Mazer opened one of the MREs and watched as Bingwen ate it. "We'll rest here until nightfall," said Mazer. "Then, when it's full dark, we'll move north again."

"No," Bingwen said quickly. "We're not going north. We're going south."

"I'm not taking you to the lander, Bingwen."

"Why not? Because I'm a child?"

"Well, yes. It's dangerous."

"It's dangerous everywhere. It was dangerous at the farmhouse. It was dangerous in my village. It's dangerous in the north. Nowhere is safe. We might as well push on. We're here. It can't be much farther."

Mazer shook his head. "We've been over this, Bingwen."

"Yes, we have. You're not my father. I'm not your son. That means you can't command me where to go."

"If you come with me, you put me in more danger. I'd be watching out for you and not giving the threats around me the full attention they deserve. Plus you'd slow me down."

"I'm not as helpless as you think," said Bingwen. "I can help. I'm slower, yes, but two sets of eyes are better than one. I can watch our rear. I can carry supplies. I'm not useless. I'm an asset not a liability."

"I don't doubt your abilities, Bingwen, but we're not going on a day hike here. This is war. I'm a trained soldier. You're not."

"I'm just as capable of killing Formics as you are."

"Oh really?"

"Yes, really." He gestured to Mazer's sidearm. "How much strength does it take it pull that trigger? I think I can manage."

"Firing a weapon is more involved than that."

"So teach me how."

"No. Children don't fight wars."

"Really? Says who? Is there some child rulebook I don't know about, because I'm pretty sure I've been fighting wars my whole life."

"These are killers, Bingwen. Not village bullies."

"What's the difference?"

"A world of difference. Village bullies don't melt your face off." He regretted saying it as soon as the words had come out. Bingwen had witnessed such things.

Mazer sighed and leaned back against one of the few remaining trees, his voice gentle. "You can't come because I don't want anything to happen to you, Bingwen. And because we don't know what's in that valley, and because in all likelihood I won't be able to do much damage anyway."

"You can do recon. You can learn things, observe things, find weaknesses, see something the airplanes haven't. Then you can take that information back to people who matter. Right now you don't want to go back because you feel like you've failed. Information is a victory, Mazer. And I can help you get it."

Mazer said nothing.

"I know this enemy as well as you do. Maybe even better than you do. And I certainly know the land better than you do."

"There isn't much land left."

"No. Nor people either." He stared at the ground a moment, picking at a rock half buried in the earth. "My parents are in that valley, Mazer. Heaped up with everything else. Maybe Grandfather too. And Hopper and Meilin. And Zihao. And everyone I've ever known. My life is in that valley. You're fighting to save your world. I'm fighting because they've already taken my world from me. Yes, I'm young. Yes, I'm a child. No, I'm not a trained soldier. But if I'm old enough to fight to stay alive, I'm old enough to fight the war."

Mazer said nothing. It amazed him that Bingwen could be so young and so frail in some ways and so old and so unbreakable in others. Children are more capable than we give them credit for, he thought. Yet even so, he knew he shouldn't take Bingwen with him. Common sense and his training told him it was a tactical mistake. Yet what could he do? Bingwen was right. They'd find danger in the north as well.

Mazer reached into the pack and pulled out a small bedroll. He pushed the button on the side, and the pad inflated. "You've been running for most of the day," said Mazer. "Get some sleep. I'll take first watch." He handed him the gas mask. "Put this on first."

"That's for an adult."

"I'll adjust the straps as far as they'll go. It should form a seal."

"How am I supposed to sleep with that on? It will swallow my head."

"You'll breath fine. And it will be cleaner air than what's out here."

"What about you?"

"I'll manage." He slipped the mask over Bingwen's head and fiddled with the straps until the seal was good.

"How do I look?" Bingwen asked, his voice muffled by the mask.

"As alien as the Formics."

Bingwen smiled. "Perfect. It'll be my disguise. We'll use it to infiltrate. I'll be the Formic, and you'll be my weak human hostage. Works every time."

"Go to sleep, Bingwen."

Bingwen lay down on the bedroll. "You'll be here when I get up, right? You're not going to sneak off while I'm asleep?"

"I won't sneak off. You'd only find me anyway."

"You bet I would. I'd track you down." Bingwen rolled over onto his side and pulled his legs up, getting into a comfortable sleep position.

"How long had you been shouting my name before I found you?" Mazer asked.

"A few hours."

"The Formics could have heard you, you know. You could have called them down right on top of you."

"I know. Especially since 'Mazer' in their language means 'Here I am. Come kill me.' "

"Not funny," said Mazer.

"I tried looking for you. It wasn't working. If I had kept silent, I never would have found you. It knew it was a risk. I got lucky."

"Lucky is an understatement . . . But I'm glad you found me. Now close your eyes."

Bingwen did so. "I feel like I have a bucket on my head. This thing is pressing into my ear. I can't sleep this way."

"Then don't sleep on your side."

"I have to sleep on my side. That's how I sleep."

Mazer shushed him. "If you're talking, you're not sleeping."

Bingwen fell silent. Soon, his breathing had slowed and he was asleep. Mazer leaned back against the tree, listening to the wind blow in from the south and rustle the wilted leaves overhead. The wind carried with it faint traces of a putrid smell—a smell Mazer hadn't noticed in a while. He sniffed the air and grimaced. It was the scent of bodies rotting in the sun.

He pulled his old shirt from his pack, ripped up the fabric, and tied a makeshift bandana over his mouth and nose. Then he took the sidearm from his hip and silently removed the clip. He took out the rounds and counted them. Then he reloaded the gun and did the math in his head, adding up the number of rounds from the other clips. About eighty rounds total. Not much at all.

So why was he going to the lander? Why was he being so insanely stubborn? Why did he think he could face an army of Formics?

Because of Kim, he told himself. Because he had left her so that she might have a life she deserved, and he wasn't going to let the Formics ruin that. Because of Patu and Reinhardt and Fatani and Bingwen's parents and Ye Ye Danwen. Because this was Bingwen's China, not theirs.

He settled back against the tree and recited the words of the *haka* his mother had taught him so long ago. A song of the Maori warrior. The dance of death.

*Ka mate! Ka mate! Ka ora! Ka ora!*
*Ka mate! Ka mate! Ka ora! Ka ora!*
*Tenei te tangata puhuru huru*
*Nana nei i tiki mai, whakawhiti te ra*
*A upane! ka upane!*
*A upane! ka upane!*
*Whiti te ra! Hi!*


*I die! I die! I live! I live!*
*I die! I die! I live! I live!*
*This is the hairy man*
*Who has caused the sun to shine again*
*The Sun shines!*


Then Mazer turned his face into an ugly grimace and stuck out his tongue. Let them see the face that will strike them down. Let them see anger. Let them feel fear.

# CHAPTER 25

# Space Junk

The rings of junk around Earth were like the rings of Saturn, only instead of ice and silicates, Victor saw thousands of discarded satellites and long-forgotten space stations and old, outmoded weapons from the time when countries were all arming in Earth orbit.

"Look at all of this, Imala," said Victor. "It's just floating out here waiting for someone to scoop it up and use it. Do you have any idea what my family could have done with all this?"

Imala piloted the shuttle toward a spot in the junk heap where several different satellites were relatively close together. "This is as near as you've ever been to Earth, Victor. You've got a breathtaking view of the planet directly in front of you, and all you see are the completely worthless, broken shiny objects."

Victor was floating at the artificial windshield, taking in the scene in front of him, a sea of metal and plastic and polycarbonates, all glinting in the sunlight. "I see the planet, Imala. It's beautiful. But you have to realize, out in the K Belt, when something broke, we couldn't simply go out and get a replacement part. We had to make one. Or pull the necessary pieces from scrap, which were rare and hard to come by. You have everything you could possibly need out here. And a lot of it is new."

"It's not new, Vico. It's crap. It's old junk."

"If you think this is old, Imala, you should see the scrap we normally worked with."

Imala fired up the retros and started the shuttle's deceleration. Victor was already in his spacewalk suit, a long lifeline extending from the back of it. He wore a propulsion pack and carried a laser cutter, which he would use to snip off pieces of the junk to haul back to the shuttle.

"Some of these pieces were weapons once," said Imala. "So don't go cutting willy-nilly. Use the schematics I uploaded to your HUD. You'll be able to see where it's safe to cut and where it isn't." She had used her LTD access back on Luna to dig through the agency's archives and pull files on as many of the objects out here as there was still a record for.

"Thanks," said Victor. "I'll try not to blow us up."

"That's not even remotely funny," said Imala.

"Don't worry. This isn't explosive material. I know what I'm doing."

Imala moved the shuttle alongside the first of the satellites and Victor excused himself to the airlock. Once outside he got right to work. The reconnaissance shuttle needed to look like a hunk of debris, so Victor was most interested in the worthless guts of the satellites. The conduit and structural braces and insulation, all the stuff that would be exposed to space if a ship were ripped in half. All the really valuable pieces—the processors and chips and fuel cells and lenses—were typically small and therefore unimportant. Even so, Victor couldn't pass up the temptation to cut away a few processor chips and sneak them into his chest pouch.

He also had to keep in mind that while these were satellites, he was camouflaging a ship. He would be wise to ignore the pieces that were unique to sats, such as solar arrays or thermal blankets—all the thin membranous material that might reflect a lot of light and draw attention to the recon ship.

At first he was slow and methodical about what he selected. But as the day wore on, and as they moved from object to object, he cut faster and thought less about what he was gathering. Quantity, not quality was what mattered now. He could be meticulous and selective in the warehouse. Out here he was reaping the wheat. Back on Luna he would make the bread.

After twelve hours, the cargo bay was full floor to ceiling. Victor had convinced Imala to get a dumper shuttle four times as large as she thought they needed, and Victor had filled every square meter of it.

"This is enough junk to camouflage an asteroid," said Imala. "You're covering a tiny two-seater, remember?"

"We won't be using all of this," said Victor. "We'll have to sift through it and find the right pieces. The ship has to look somewhat uniform, Imala. All of the pieces have to appear to have come from the same ship. It can't be a multicolored potpourri of parts. It will look fake and slapped together."

"The Formics don't know human ships well enough to tell the difference," said Imala.

"You don't know that," said Victor. "It's a mistake to underestimate them, Imala. They may resemble ants, but they invented near-lightspeed travel. They're far more intelligent than we are. I'm not taking any chances."

Imala shrugged and didn't argue.

The flight back to Luna was long, but Victor stayed busy the whole time. First he disassembled some of the larger junk pieces that were accessible in the cargo bay. Then he took the smaller, disassembled pieces and scanned them in the holofield, making 3-D models of each. He had already built a holographic model of the small recon ship he and Imala had purchased back on Luna. He called it up now in the holofield and began attaching the 3-D models of junk pieces to it, virtually building the camouflage design in the holofield and trying several different approaches. By the time he and Imala reached the Juke warehouse, he had a pretty good idea of how he wanted to attack the project.

Lem had arranged for the engineering staff to be on hand to help unload the shuttle. So when Victor and Imala stepped out of the umbilical and onto the warehouse floor there was a small crowd of people waiting for them. An older woman of African descent with long gray braids and a slight accent greeted Victor and Imala with a smile and handshakes. "Mr. Delgado, Ms. Bootstamp. I'm Noloa Benyawe." She gestured to the man beside her. "This is our chief engineer, Dr. Dublin."

Dublin's face was kindly, and his expression softened even further when he shook Victor's hand. "I am sorry about your family, Victor. Dr. Benyawe and I were there in the battle. Your captain and family were determined to protect Earth. They have my utmost respect."

Victor nodded. "Thank you, Dr. Dublin. That is very kind of you to say so."

"Lem wants to be certain this remains a private endeavor," said Benyawe. "He asked that I emphasize to the staff that this is not a company project. That means we can't help you during normal working hours. Lem's afraid company lawyers could use that as a basis to seize whatever we do. Silly, I know, but he's insistent. But don't worry, I've spoken with everyone here, and we're all happy to help you after hours for as long as you need us."

"Again, that's very kind," said Victor. "I'd appreciate your input."

"Our understanding is that you hope to place a propellant on a few of the debris objects and fly them toward the ship so that the gun doors will open."

"That's correct," said Victor. "That's how I'm hoping to get inside. That may not be the best idea, though. If you have a better approach, I'd be thrilled to hear it. I'm making this up as I go along."

"We think it's a smart tactic," said Benyawe. "And we've taken the liberty of proposing a few mechanisms that might do the job, if you'd allow us to share them with you."

"By all means," said Victor.

They escorted him and Imala to a corner of the warehouse where a holotable projected a narrow cylindrical thruster two meters in length. "These are designed for quick acceleration," said Dr. Dublin. "Each can produce quite a jolt of propulsion, so you'd want to secure them soundly to the surface of the debris. You don't want them snapping off and zipping through space like a deflating balloon. So the anchor structure is as important as the thruster itself." He waved his stylus through the holofield, and an unadorned cube appeared. "Let's assume this is the hunk of debris you want to use." He grabbed the thruster and placed four copies of it on four sides of the cube. "You can place as many of these thrusters as you like on the surface of the debris. You'll obviously want to place them equidistant from each other or as close to equidistant as possible to evenly distribute the thrust. This will likely be a challenge since the shape of the debris chunk won't be uniform. It will be odd shaped and unstable. You'll also want to install the thrusters so that their orientation is the same. That way, when you reach the surface of the ship and ignite the thrusters via remote control, they will all act as one, swiveling in their anchor braces and responding to your flight commands on the remote. If you position yourself near a gun door, you can fly the chunk directly toward you, which would increase the likelihood that the gun nearest you would open."

"This is brilliant," said Victor. "Let's do this, but may I make a suggestion? Let's not attach these thrusters to a debris chunk already floating in space around the Formic ship as I initially proposed. You've shown me that there are too many issues with that. What if I don't secure the anchors well enough? What if the chunk is so unstable that the thrusters rip it apart? Plus there's the challenge of me doing a spacewalk so close to the Formics. That would require a lot of time, and if I slip up, I might inadvertently alert the Formics of my presence before I even reach them, which for the sake of my health, I'd rather not do. So here's what I propose: Let's do exactly as you suggest and use these thrusters, but let's build the chunk of debris here in the warehouse. Let's manufacture it. That will allow us to control the structure. We can place the thrusters equidistant. We can reinforce the anchor braces. We can ensure the whole thing is fortified and won't break apart when I initiate the thrusters. We'd control all the variables, and most important, we can test it here and be sure it flies how we want it to. That way I won't needlessly endanger myself by trying to do all that in space. We can attach this chunk to the shuttle, then I can release it among the other debris, continue on to the Formic ship, and fly it toward me when the time is right."

Benyawe and Dublin exchanged glances.

"That would be ideal, yes," said Benyawe.

"We can use some of the space junk we just recovered," said Victor.

"We certainly brought back enough of it," said Imala.

Victor smiled. "See, Imala. More is always better."

Back at the dump shuttle, Victor used lifters and cranes to unload all the pieces of space junk and place them on the floor of the warehouse in an organized system. Imala kept trying to help, but whenever she put something on the floor, Victor would tell her it didn't go there and move it elsewhere.

"If you tell me how you're organizing it, I won't keep putting stuff in the wrong place," said Imala.

"You're not doing it *wrong* per se," said Victor.

"Well I'm obviously not doing it right either. Explain what's in your head, Vico, and save us both some time."

He could see she was getting annoyed. "It's hard to explain. I'm separating them by how we're going to use them, either for the recon shuttle or the decoy chunk. Then I'm divvying up *those* pieces into categories of how ready they are for use. Some of this stuff will need disassembling, some of it will need damaging."

"Damaging?"

"The ship will need to look like it's been blasted," said Victor. "It should be dent up and scorched and beaten."

"Where's that pile?"

They crossed the warehouse floor to a heap of junk stacked as high as they were tall. "All these big pieces here," said Victor.

"How do you plan on damaging them?" asked Imala.

Victor shrugged. "Taking a hammer to them. Beating them senseless. Burning them with a blowtorch. Bending them out of shape."

"I'll do that," said Imala, crossing to a wall of tools and pulling a hammer down. "I feel like pounding something at the moment."

"Be sure to anchor your feet and the piece you're pounding," said Victor. "This is Moon gravity. You'll likely get a lot of recoil on the hammer. And you'll want to wear a face shield in case small pieces break off on impact."

She looked at him with a hint of scorn. "I know how to whack something with a hammer, Vico. I'm not stupid."

"I didn't mean to imply that you were. I was just reminding you that—"

"Forget it. I got this." She yanked one of the pieces down from the pile and let it slowly clatter to the floor. Victor backed off and left her to it. He felt like he should apologize, but for what? He *did* have a system in place for the junk, and it *was* hard to explain; it was coming to him as they went along. He couldn't spell it out like she wanted; he hadn't finished defining it all in his head yet. As for the hammering, that was how he and Father had always worked: They talked to each other as they did things; they reminded each other of safety precautions; they watched out for each other. You had to. It was easy to forget things and get sloppy when you were tired, and you couldn't afford to get injured in the K Belt.

Only, we're not in the K Belt, he reminded himself. We're in Imala's world.

Imala was down on her knees, locked to the floor. She began pounding on the piece of metal, and the booming clang of it echoed through the warehouse.

Victor backed off and returned to the crane he had been using. He was surprised to find Lem there waiting for him, a large duffel bag slung over Lem's shoulder.

"You have a unique way with women, Victor. Rather than make them swoon, you make them want to beat you senseless with a hammer. A new approach. You'll have to tell me how that works out for you."

Victor tried to keep the disdain from his voice. "Something I can do for you, Lem?"

"Something you can *take* from me." He unshouldered the duffel bag, set it gently on the floor, and opened it. There were two large devices inside that Victor didn't recognize and a third smaller device that looked like a detonator.

"This is what you'll carry inside the Formic ship to the helm," said Lem. "That is, assuming you can reach the helm. There's enough explosive here to do quite a bit of damage. I'd prefer you had a tactical nuke, but those are hard to come by. I had to pull off a few small miracles to get this."

"How does it work?" Victor asked. His family had used explosives all the time for mining asteroids, but Victor had always felt uneasy around them, even when they were disassembled like this and completely harmless. Lem showed him how the two pieces clicked together. Then, without doing so, he explained how to arm the explosive and trigger the detonator.

"What's the range on the detonator?" Victor asked. "How far away can I get before I trigger it?"

Lem winced, looking uncomfortable. "That's the tricky part. These things are designed for asteroids. They're made for open space, easy communication between detonator and explosive. You drop them into a dig site, back up your ship, then boom. They weren't designed to be placed deep within the bowels of a ship that's—in all likelihood—intricately tunneled and made with layers upon layers of strange metallic alloys. And if you're right about the helm, if it's at the center of the ship, that's quite a distance from the hull."

"You're saying you don't know the detonator's range," said Victor.

"I'm saying there's no way to tell without knowing what's inside the Formic ship. You might be able to get halfway back to Luna and still be in range. Or you might be out of range the moment you leave the helm. There's no telling."

"What about a timer?" Victor asked.

"That's option B. Plant the explosive where it won't be discovered then set it to detonate twelve hours later or twenty-four or however long you think it will take you to get out. Personally, I'm not a fan of timers. We used those when we attacked the Formics the first time. It didn't work out well."

He says *we*, thought Victor, and he means him and my family, him and Father. Victor still hadn't gotten used to that image: Lem fighting alongside Concepción and Father and the other men of the family.

"Thanks," said Victor. "I'll figure it out."

Lem walked over to the recon shuttle that Imala and Victor had purchased. It sat on the floor of the warehouse near the piles of collected space junk. It was a small, boxy two-seater, no bigger than a skimmer. The side door was open. Lem bent his knees and looked inside. It was comfortable and outfitted with all the latest flight controls. "Nice little ship. Seems a shame to trash it."

"We'll only be trashing the exterior," said Victor.

"How are you going to do this?" Lem asked. "There's no airlock in here, and the Formics aren't likely to extend an umbilical. Once you open this door to go outside, you're in a vacuum."

"I'll be in a spacesuit the whole way," said Victor. "I'm carrying all the oxygen I'll need from the moment I leave Luna to the moment I return."

"What about anchoring the ship? How will you keep it from drifting off when you leave it to go inside the mothership? The hull of the Formic ship is as smooth as glass. There's nothing to hook on to. And I don't know that I'd trust a ship to magnets."

"I'll be flying it," said Imala. Victor turned to see Imala approaching. She carried the hammer in one hand and wiped sweat from her brow with the other.

"I'll keep it in position," she said. "I'll make sure it doesn't drift."

"You're not coming with me, Imala," said Victor.

"Yes, Victor. I am. I'm a better pilot than you are. We both know that, and maneuvering this thing through that debris field will require a steady hand."

"I'll be drifting at a negligible speed," said Victor. "I think I can manage."

"A thousand things could go wrong, Victor. We drastically increase our chances of success if there are two of us."

"Absolutely not, Imala. I'm not letting you put yourself in danger like that."

She raised an eyebrow. "You're not *letting* me? You're not my supervisor, Vico."

"I know that. Of course not. What I mean is . . . this is my fight, Imala. I couldn't live with myself if something happened to you because of me. You shouldn't have to take this risk."

Imala breathed out, brushed a long errant hair out of her face, and turned to Lem. "Would you excuse us, please?"

Lem smiled. "As much as I'd hate missing the rest of this conversation, I'll leave you two to figure it out." He moved to leave then turned back.

"But whatever you decide, choose the method that will most likely result in success. I'm not paying all this money to see that tiny shuttle blown to smithereens." He walked away, leaving the duffel bag at Victor's feet.

When he was gone Imala said, "I appreciate you being concerned about me, Vico, and I recognize that you have a lot invested in this fight. You've lost half your family, and I can't begin to imagine the kind of hurt that brings. But you're wrong about one thing. This is not *your* fight. This is my fight, too. I haven't lost my family, true, but if the Formics don't stop, I *will* lose them. I'll lose everything. And I'm not going to sit here and do nothing and allow that to happen when there's a way for me to contribute. You've lost your home, Vico, but I'm losing mine as we speak. Right now Earth is burning, and that gives me just as much right as you have." She leaned against the recon ship and folded her arms. "But even if none of that were true, Vico, even if I had no stake in this whatsoever, practically speaking it makes sense for both of us to go. You can broadcast to me what you see and find inside the ship. That way, if you die I can carry what you've learned and recorded back to Luna. I can make sure that intel gets to people who can use it and act upon it and end this war. I don't want anything to happen to you, of course, but that intel would be more valuable than both of our lives."

Victor was quiet a moment. She was right of course. He couldn't argue with any of it. "We'll both have to wear suits the entire trip, which means we'll have to double our oxygen supply, which means we'll be crammed inside the cockpit practically on top of each other the whole trip. It will be very uncomfortable. There will be zero personal space."

She smiled. "At least we'll have helmets on. That way, if either of us has bad breath, only the culprit will suffer for it."

"I'm serious, Imala. It won't be pleasant. We'll be cramped."

Imala put a hand on his shoulder. "Victor, we're going up against an indestructible alien ship that just wiped out most of Earth's space fleet. Uncomfortable seating is the least of our problems."

# CHAPTER 26

# Biomass

Mazer and Bingwen set out for the lander three hours before dawn under the cover of darkness. Bingwen led the way, the gas mask pulled down securely over his head, his boots padding quietly through the mud. They moved quickly, talking little, Mazer scanning the sky around them for any sign of troop transports.

They weren't likely to see any, Mazer knew—not until it was too late anyway. The transports were near silent and used no exterior lights, making them practically invisible at night. If one did come into view, it would likely be right when the lander was on top of them. And what could Mazer and Bingwen do at that point but fight and hope for the best? They couldn't run for cover. There was none. Not anymore. In the north there had been patches of jungle in which to conceal themselves, but here, near the lander, the Formics had left nothing. Every sprout and sapling and blade of grass had been stripped or burned away, leaving a landscape so barren and devoid of any life that it was as if Mazer and Bingwen had stepped off of Earth and walked onto another planet entirely.

"If I tell you to run, you run," said Mazer. "Do you understand? No questions asked, no hesitating. Immediate obedience."

"Immediate obedience," Bingwen repeated.

"It could mean your life, Bingwen. It could mean both of our lives. If I tell you to drop, you drop. If I say jump in the river, you jump in the river."

"The river's probably polluted," said Bingwen. "All of the runoff from the mist is in that water. I might die if I swim in that."

"You see? That's the type of hesitation I'm speaking of. You can't question my orders. Ever. If I tell you to jump in a polluted river, it's only because every other option means death. It means the chances of surviving a polluted river, however slim, are greater than the chances of surviving *not* jumping in it."

"River. Jump. I got it."

Mazer stopped and took a knee, facing him. "I'm serious, Bingwen. If I give you an order, it's only to keep you alive. It may contradict what you think is best or what you want to do, but you must obey it. That has to be instinct. You have to believe with absolute certainty that anything I tell you will be for your good."

Bingwen nodded. "I believe that."

"So if I tell you to crouch down and take cover . . ."

"I crouch and take cover."

"And if I tell you to hide in a hole . . ."

"I make like a snake and hide."

Mazer unholstered his sidearm. "And if I tell you to take this and go north . . ."

"I thought you weren't going to teach me how to shoot."

"I'm not. Not really. This is a last resort. This is when all other options have failed. But if I tell you to take this gun and run north, you take it and protect yourself and run north. Understand?"

"But why would you give it to me?"

Mazer made a move to speak, but Bingwen continued, cutting him off.

"I wouldn't question you in the moment," said Bingwen. "If you told me to do it, I'd do it, no hesitation. I'm asking the question *now,* when you can still answer it. If you're alive enough to give me the gun and give me the order, then aren't you alive enough to keep fighting with it yourself?"

"If I give you the gun and tell you to run, it's because it's the only way to keep you alive and get you away."

"Me . . . but not you."

"I don't want to die, Bingwen. I will do everything to get back home. But more important to me is that at least one of us survives. If I can hold them off long enough for you to get away, I prefer that than something happening to both of us. Do you understand?"

Bingwen waved his hands. "No. That can't be how it works. That's wrong. If you were by yourself, you'd fight for as long as you could. You'd stay at it. And who knows, because of perseverance or luck or skill or desperation, maybe you would survive, even if you didn't expect to. But giving me the gun is guaranteeing failure. That's giving up. You'd be dying because of me. I can't allow that."

"Listen to me, Bingwen."

"No. I'm not letting you do that. If you have it in mind to give up your weapon, you will do it at the wrong time. You would hold off for as long as you think is necessary to ensure *my* survival instead of yours. And you would overcompensate. You would give me more time than I needed and therefore give up sooner than necessary. You can show me how the gun works, but I'm only going to use it if you no longer can."

Mazer was quiet a moment. "In the military we call this insubordination. People are stripped of rank and imprisoned for it."

"Then it's a good thing I'm not in the military."

"You're making this difficult, Bingwen."

"No. I'm making it the opposite. I'm removing a consideration from your mind. I'm letting you fight with a clearer head. That's in my best interest, too. The more focused you are on staying alive, the better my chances are, too."

Mazer considered then nodded. "All right. No giving up the gun."

"Good."

"But if I can no longer use it, you pick it up." He showed him the weapon. "You see this light? Red means it can't fire, the safety is on. Flip this switch here, the light goes green, it's ready to fire." He flipped the safety back on. "Don't run with your finger on the trigger, even if the safety is on. That's the fastest way to shoot yourself. Keep your index finger flat against the receiver like this until you're ready to fire. And use the wrist brace. Here." Mazer tapped a button on the grip, and the wrist brace extended backward, found Mazer's wrist, and wrapped around it. "It will tighten automatically to fit the diameter of your wrist and help steady your aim."

"Where should I aim?"

"Center mass. Middle of the chest. Two rounds. One right after the other. You'll feel a recoil, but it's slight." Mazer stood, noticing the disquiet in Bingwen's expression. "It won't likely come to that though, Bingwen. You'll probably never have to use it."

Bingwen nodded, but Mazer could still sense his unease. I shouldn't have brought Bingwen south, he told himself. We should have pushed west, away from the patrolling transports in the north and away from the lander. What was I thinking to bring a child here?

"You're reconsidering," said Bingwen. "I can see your gears turning."

"I'm reconsidering because what we're doing is lunacy, Bingwen. This isn't a game. This is war. It's one thing for me to go. It's quite another for you to come along. Soldiers don't take eight-year-olds to war."

"I'm eight and a half."

"I'm not joking. This is wrong. My training says so. Common sense says so. The law says so."

"We've been over this. This is my decision."

"You're not old enough to make that decision. You're a minor. There's a reason why we don't take recruits until they're eighteen years old."

"I'm not going as a soldier. I'm going as a guide. I'm taking you to the lander. If I hadn't course-corrected us already, you would have missed it by a few kilometers."

"I would have found it eventually," said Mazer, tapping the side of his nose. "Just follow the stench."

"It may not be as dangerous as you think," said Bingwen. "Have you noticed that the closer we get to the lander, the fewer transports and skimmers and Formics we see? Maybe the ships and infantry are all moving away from here, pushing outward, expanding the Formics' territory. If it's an invasion force, they're going to keep invading. They might not even be guarding the lander. Why would they? It's indestructible. It has shields. Why waste men and ships defending something that doesn't need defending? It's probably the safest place within a hundred kilometers of here."

Mazer smiled. "I'll put you through school when this is over, but not law school. You're too dangerous."

Bingwen gave him a wide toothy grin.

They pushed on, crossing wide, muddy fields, with stagnant pools of water that smelled of rot and death. Bingwen pointed out a hillside where a small village had once stood. All that remained of it was scorched earth and a single sheet of metal roofing, rattling softly in the wind like thunder.

They reached the base of the hill an hour before sunrise. Beyond it was the lander and the biomass. Scaling the hill wouldn't be easy, Mazer could see. The Formics had stripped it of vegetation, and the heavy rains had softened and eroded the exposed earth, leaving steep muddy slopes that threatened to give way beneath their feet and slide downward like an avalanche. Mazer showed Bingwen how to take sideways steps up the steepest parts to more evenly distribute the surface area of their boot soles, but even with that approach they fell often and slipped constantly and had to pains-takingly claw their way up to the summit. By the time they reached it, the sun was up, and they were covered head to foot in muck, their bodies cold and wet and spent.

Mazer took the binoculars from the pack and crawled forward in the mud to a small outcrop of rock overlooking the valley below. The lander was as he remembered it: impossibly large and completely unscathed, sunk into the ground like a giant unearthed landmine. The biomass stood beside it, a mountain of rotting biota as wide and as tall as the lander had been before it had spun itself into the earth. Mazer had expected to be able to identify the various objects in the biomass—a tree here, a water buffalo there—and perhaps at one time that had been possible. But not anymore. Everything ran together like melting wax as cell walls broke down and the biota disintegrated into a thick viscous liquid.

Above the biomass, a cluster of six Formic aircraft of a design Mazer had never seen before were spraying a mist onto the biomass as dense as a rainstorm.

Mazer watched through the binocs as the mist fell and reacted to the bi-ota, dissolving it into thin trails of goop that rolled down the side and gath-ered into dark pools at the mountain's base. A metal wall had been built there, surrounding the mountain of biomass like a circular dam and feeding the goop runoff into pipes that extended outward to processing machines and small structures spread out over the valley floor like a massive industrial complex.

It amazed Mazer to think that all of this had been built in the last ten days or so. And by the looks of it, the Formics weren't finished building. Con-struction crews were everywhere, adding piping, assembling machines, ex-tending structures. Skimmers carried building materials to the crews. Clawlike cranes held pipes in place as Formic workers welded them to the other structures.

Yet as vast and impressive a site as it was, Mazer had never seen any-thing so disorganized and unattractive. There was no order to the construc-tion at all. Everything looked slapped together haphazardly without any regard to uniformity or design. The metals were all red and gray and rough and rusting, as if they had been used a hundred times previously for other purposes and never once cleaned or cared for.

Nor were the Formics concerned about cleanliness. Filth covered everything. The ground was littered with trash and discarded building materials. And everywhere Mazer looked he saw Formic feces. He knew with certainty what the black substance was because he witnessed a few Formics defecating as they labored, showing no regard for those around them, simply dropping it where they stood. It covered the ground and pipes and the Formics' feet. The stench was not only from the biomass apparently.

Mazer pointed the binoculars back at the mist-raining skimmers, zooming in as far as the lenses would go and having the computer take scans and run an analysis. The results didn't tell him much: The mists were a microbe solution of unknown composition.

"It's breaking down the biota," Bingwen said, who had crawled up beside and watched as he worked. "What are they using it for? Fuel?"

"That, or food," said Mazer. "Or maybe both."

Bingwen grew quiet, staring at the biomass. His parents are in there somewhere, Mazer thought.

"Here," Mazer said, offering Bingwen the binocs and hoping to direct his thoughts elsewhere. "Earn your keep. Check out the lander. Tell me if you see anything interesting."

Bingwen took the binocs and pressed the eyepieces against the visor of the gas mask. "This would be a lot easier if I could take this mask off." He glanced thoughtfully at Mazer. "But considering the green, sickly look on your face, I think I'll keep it on."

"Wise choice."

Bingwen adjusted the focus and gazed down at the lander. "For an advanced alien species, they're not too concerned about housekeeping. The metal is all gross and rusted looking."

"And covered in Formic dung, if you haven't noticed."

"Yes, thanks for pointing that out."

"At least you're not smelling it."

Bingwen slowly panned the binocs across the lander then stopped when something caught his eye. "Okay, this is interesting. Near the base of the lander there's a hole in the ground. Maybe a meter in diameter. I just saw a Formic crawl into it. And there's another hole about four meters away from the first one, closer to the lander. A Formic crawled out of the second hole, and at first I thought it was a different Formic. But it wasn't. It was the same one. I could tell because it had a limp in one of his legs. He crawled into the first hole, went underground for about four meters, and then came up through the second hole and moved on toward the lander. That's strange, isn't it? If he was heading for the lander, why not walk straight to it? Why bother going underground?"

"Unless he *can't* walk straight to it," Mazer said.

"Exactly. There must be something there in his way, something invisible, which forces him to crawl under it to get through."

"A shield." Mazer gestured for the binocs, and Bingwen passed them to him. Mazer focused the lenses and looked where Bingwen was pointing.

"You see that big red metal thing that looks like a water tower?" said Bingwen. "There's a pipe at its base. Follow that west for about fifty meters, and there's the hole."

"I see it." Mazer watched the hole. In time, a pair of Formics came carrying a beam of metal between them. They crawled into the hole, dragging the pipe behind them, and disappeared. A moment later, they emerged through the second hole. Once on their feet, they shouldered the beam and moved on toward the lander.

"You know what this means, don't you?" said Bingwen. "It means the shield doesn't go underground. It's only covering what's above the surface."

"Did you see any other holes?"

"No, but it can't be the only one. There are hundreds of workers down there. If they sleep in the lander, that one hole would bottleneck at the beginning and end of every shift. There have to be others."

Mazer scanned for several minutes. "I've counted three other sets of holes, all of them like the set you found. One hole outside the shield, one inside."

"And those are just the ones we can see from here," said Bingwen. "There are probably dozens of these holes all around the lander. This is it. This is the answer. We have to tell the army. They can send in soldiers through the holes to take the lander."

"No," said Mazer. "We're not going in through the holes. The holes aren't the answer."

"But . . ." Bingwen's voice broke off suddenly, and Mazer saw a look of horror on the boy's face. He was staring at something over Mazer's head, behind him. Mazer spun onto his back and saw that a troop transport had landed on the hilltop. Formics poured out of it, running in their direction, riflelike weapons in their top sets of arms.

Mazer was on his feet in an instant, lifting Bingwen and pushing him back the way they had come. "Run!"

Bingwen ran.

Mazer rushed forward, dropped to one knee, his gun in his hand, the wrist brace snapping into place with a *click-click-click*. The Formics were sprinting toward him, thirty meters away. Mazer fired a dozen shots, and five Formics dropped. Seven more kept coming. Mazer turned and was on his feet again, sprinting. He scooped up the pack as he ran past it, throwing it over one shoulder, then another. He dropped the clip from the gun and snapped in the second magazine. He fired a four-round burst behind him as he ran. Another Formic fell.

Bingwen was ahead of him, running along the ridge of the hill as fast as his legs would carry him, which wasn't nearly fast enough. Mazer caught up to him almost immediately. To their left was the lander and hundreds of Formics. To their right was the steep muddy slope they had so painstakingly ascended. There was only one thing to do, Mazer realized. They had no cover up here, nowhere to dig in and fight. They couldn't make a stand. They were completely exposed.

Mazer scooped up Bingwen into his arms. "Hold on tight!"

Bingwen wrapped his arms around Mazer's neck and buried his face into Mazer's shoulder. No hesitation. Immediate obedience.

Then Mazer cut hard to the right where an outcrop of rock extended beyond the edge of the hill.

He ran to the end of it at a full sprint.

And jumped out into space.

The hill was steep, and Mazer and Bingwen dropped ten meters before hitting the slope and shooting down the mud on Mazer's back, using the pack like a luge sled. The ground gave way all around them, sliding off the slope like a sheet pulled from a bed. Mazer could feel the mud gathering around them like a wave, threatening to consume them, swallow them, bury them alive. Mazer kept his legs stiff out in front of him, toes pointed, clinging to Bingwen, trying to maintain as much speed as possible.

They would have to hit the ground running, he knew. They couldn't be caught at the base of the hill on Mazer's back. The mud behind them would cover them in an instant.

They were nearing the bottom. Mud and grit and dirt sprayed up into Mazer's face, making it hard to see. He would have to time this right; come up too soon and his feet would sink into the muck at the bottom of the hill.

Pop up too late, and he would be too prostrate on the ground with the weight of Bingwen on top of him, unable to climb to his feet in time.

He pointed his right foot forward, then dug his heel hard into the earth at what he hoped was the right moment. In the same instant he threw his upper body forward, harder than he thought was necessary since Bingwen was in his arms.

It worked. He popped up from his semirecumbent position into a somewhat standing position, falling the last meter or so to the level earth. He was on flat ground, but his forward momentum was more than he had anticipated. He stumbled. Bingwen fell from his arms, down to one knee. The mud was sliding all around them like beached surf, and Mazer could hear the rumble of more mud behind them. He high-stepped, lifting his feet up hard with each step, not allowing them to become swallowed up in the pool of mud at his feet. His hand reached down and grabbed the front of Bingwen's shirt, lifting him up again. They stumbled, fell, rose up again, running forward, moving, surging a microsecond ahead of the wave.

And then they were free of it, running on level, hard-packed dirt, Mazer's feet steady and sure-footed beneath him.

A valley of scorched earth stretched out in front of them. There was no cover here either. No trees. No ditches. No holes to climb into. They were completely in the open, standing out in the full bright of day like two brown dots on a vast black canvas.

Mazer never stopped running, his heart hammering in his chest, Bingwen clinging to him tightly.

The troop transport dropped out of the sky twenty meters in front of them. Four Formics jumped out before Mazer had even changed directions or slowed down. The sidearm was still strapped to his wrist—he would have lost it otherwise. He raised it and fired, the shot going wide. It was nearly impossible to carry Bingwen and run in one direction and shoot in another and hope to hit anything.

They couldn't keep running. The transport could easily follow them wherever they went. They had to take out the crew. Mazer stopped dead and dropped Bingwen from his arms. "Get behind me!" Mazer spun and lowered himself to one knee again, preparing to take aim, when the net slammed into him, knocking him back onto Bingwen.

A surge of paralyzing electricity shot through Mazer's body, constricting all of his muscles at once. The heavy fibrous net had him pinned down on his back, with Bingwen beneath him, the net crackling and hissing and pulsing with energy. Mazer couldn't move. His body felt as if it were burning up from the inside. His face was contorted in a painful rictus, his jaw clenched shut, his fingers bent and frozen in awkward positions as the energy surged through him. He hoped he was taking the brunt of it; Bingwen's smaller frame couldn't handle this. Better Mazer die than the both of them.

A Formic's face appeared above him, gazing down at Mazer, its head cocked to the side, regarding him, or mocking him, or both.

The gun was still strapped to Mazer's wrist. He had to raise it, aim it, fire it. The Formic was only a meter away, he couldn't miss. It would be easy. They would kill Bingwen if he didn't do something. They would spray the mist in his face as they had done to the boy's parents and to Danwen, and they would toss Bingwen's body onto the pile of biomass and melt it into sludge.

Mazer's mind ordered his arm to move, screamed for it to obey, to animate, to twist a few centimeters, just enough to point the barrel in the right direction, but nothing happened. His hand remained mockingly still.

A loud *crack* sounded, and the side of the Formic's head exploded. Tissue and blood and maybe brain matter blew out in a spray. The Formic crumpled, dropping from Mazer's view.

A cacophony of sounds erupted all around Mazer: the roar of an engine, automatic gunfire, shouting, an explosion. All of it happening in rapid succession.

"Hold on!" someone shouted. "Don't move."

Mazer felt weight placed on the net to his left, pressing the net slightly tighter to his face. Then there was a pop, and the energy surging through him stopped in an instant. He had never felt a sweeter feeling or a greater relief. It was as if his mind had been squeezed in a fist and now the fist had released him. Only . . . he still couldn't move his body. He was limp, his fingers and toes tingling. He told his feet to move, but they didn't listen.

Gloved hands ripped back the netting, pulling it off him. A man in a mottled black-and-gray body suit and mask—not an inch of his skin exposed—was above him. "Bax, help me get him inside. Calinga, grab the boy."

The man in the mask rolled Mazer off of Bingwen and onto his back, then he got his arms under Mazer's armpits. Another man in a matching suit and mask grabbed Mazer's ankles. They lifted him. He was dead weight. Mazer's head lolled to the side, showing him Formics on the ground, bleeding out, dead. Smoke billowed out of their transport. It lay flat on the ground, no longer hovering, burned out. The netting was on the ground too, discarded in a heap. A crude-looking device lay on top of it, something to short-circuit the net, perhaps. The air was thick with smoke and the stench of dead Formics.

The men carried him into a large vehicle and laid him on the floor, the metal surface cold and hard and unforgiving. A third man in a black suit rushed inside behind them, carrying Bingwen. The instant he was in, another man slammed the door shut and yelled to the driver. "Go go go!"

Tires spun. The vehicle shot forward, bouncing, rattling, accelerating. The man holding Bingwen—Calinga they had called him—lay Bingwen down on the floor beside Mazer, bunching up a piece of fabric under Bingwen's head as a pillow. Bingwen appeared limp and frightened, but when he made eye contact with Mazer, a look of relief washed over him. We're safe, it seemed to say. We're alive.

There was a long bench in front of Mazer, where several men sat in mottled gray-and-black containment suits, feverishly working with their holopads. "No movement from the lander," one of them said. "Sky's clear."

Someone behind Mazer responded. "Keep watching. And keep tracking that transport we saw heading north. If it so much as decelerates to head back this way, I want to know."

"Yes, sir."

"Air is clear," said another man. "Ninety-seven percent. We're good."

"Masks off," said the man behind Mazer.

The men removed their masks. Mazer didn't recognize any of them, but he could tell by the way they handled themselves that they were all soldiers, expertly trained. They instantly began caring for their gear, checking their weapons, reloading, readjusting sights, cleaning their masks, getting ready for the next fight as soon as the last one was over. Their movements were quick, disciplined, and automatic. They had done this a hundred times. The dead Formics behind them were already forgotten. They weren't congratulating themselves or celebrating their victory like amateurs; they were calm and procedural, going about business as usual.

They're expert Formic killers, Mazer realized.

It was only after their weapons were ready again that the soldiers saw to their own needs, taking a drink from a canteen, ripping open an energy pack.

None of them were Chinese, Mazer noticed. They were as diverse a mix of ethnicities and nationalities as Mazer had ever seen in a small unit. Europeans, Americans, Latinos, Africans. And yet their clothes revealed nothing as to who they were. No uniforms, no insignia, no rank. And yet Mazer knew at once who they were.

Calinga knelt beside him, preparing a syringe. "The paralysis is temporary. Residual effect of the zappers. This will help." He stuck the syringe into the meat of Mazer's arm. Almost at once, Mazer felt the knot in his muscles relax and the jittered shake of his hands subside. He hadn't even realized he had been trembling until he no longer was.

Calinga did the same for Bingwen.

Mazer could feel his fingers and toes again. His wrist responded when he told it to move. "Thank you," he managed to say.

"Talking already," Calinga said, as he packed up the syringes and supplies. "Good sign. Means they didn't cook your brain. Ten more seconds and you were heading for the gray mountain." He turned to Bingwen, his expression warm and cheery. "And you, little man, are lucky this guy took the brunt of the net. I know he's heavy and smelly and covered in mud, but it's better to be flattened by him than a zapper. Believe me." He patted Bingwen lightly on the arm.

"How long have MOPs been in China?" Mazer asked.

"Since right after the invasion," said the voice behind him.

Mazer knew that voice. He turned and faced Captain Wit O'Toole on the bench behind him.

"Hello, Mazer," said Wit. "I'm glad to see you still alive."

"So am I," said Mazer. "I have you to thank for that."

"You two know each other?" said Bingwen. He pushed himself up and removed the gas mask. His face was the only part of him not covered in mud.

"We tested Mazer for our unit," said Wit. "But instead of incapacitating my men and escaping the test, he endured nearly an hour of torture."

"You tortured him?" Bingwen was suddenly angry.

"Only a little," said Wit. "It couldn't have been worse than the zapper. And you are?"

"Bingwen."

"Captain Wit O'Toole. Mobile Operations Police. I'd say it's a pleasure to meet you, but that would be a lie considering the circumstances." He turned to Mazer. "You brought a civilian into a hot zone, Mazer. Not smart. And a child, no less."

"It's not his fault," said Bingwen. "He tried to get rid of me, but I kept coming back."

"You must have already been at the lander when you saw us," said Mazer.

"We arrived last night," said Wit. "Observing. Undetected. We blew our cover to save you."

"You shouldn't have," said Mazer. "Don't think me ungrateful, but destroying the lander is more important than our lives."

"I'm glad to hear you haven't lost all sense," said Wit. "Because you're right. Strategically, it would have been smarter to let the Formics kill you."

"Well I for one am glad you didn't," said Bingwen.

"The shield only goes to the surface," said Mazer.

"We know," said Wit. "We saw the tunnels. We counted twenty of them around the lander. We'll have a hard time using them, though. Transports patrol the area, and the holes have a lot of traffic. Plus they're too narrow for us. They're Formic sized."

"*I* could fit through," Bingwen offered.

"Those tunnels aren't the answer," said Mazer. "But the principle is. What's the range on this vehicle? Could it get us fifty klicks south of here?"

"Why?" asked Wit. "What's to the south?"

"Drill sledges. We're not going to use Formic tunnels. We're going to dig our own."

# CHAPTER 27

# Launch

There was little heat in the shaft and only the standing lights of the construction crews to see by, but Lem was more worried about secrecy than comfort. Father had ears throughout the Juke complex, but he didn't yet have them here. The shaft had been dug only twelve hours ago. The walls and floor were still barren rock. The dust in the air was still thick and chalky. It seemed the perfect place to meet with Norja Ramdakan, longtime member of the executive board, who now stood opposite Lem, hugging himself in the cold.

"I should have told you to dress warmly," said Lem.

"You should have told me what this is about," said Ramdakan.

He was a plump man who cared far too much for fashion and far too little for his own health. Fine fabrics and colorful little boutonnieres didn't make you any less round in the midsection and thus more attractive to the womenfolk. No doubt Ramdakan's three ex-wives had told him exactly that as they stormed out of his life with a good chunk of his fortune.

Lem had known it would be this cold, and he could have easily passed the information on to Ramdakan, but he rather liked watching the man squirm.

According to the map on Lem's holopad, they were standing in solid moon rock, fifty meters from the nearest Juke tunnel and thirty meters below the surface. The tunnel was to be a connector between two of the wings, but since the excavation and construction were far from complete, the company map had not been updated to include it.

"I'm worried about my father," said Lem. "And I didn't know who else to talk to but you who know him best."

Ramdakan had been with Father since the beginning, handling most of the finances in Father's early mining ventures. He had even spent a few years in the Belt with Father, though Lem could hardly imagine that. Ramdakan recoiled from any discomfort. He must have been a bear to live with aboard a mining vessel.

"Why should you worry about your father?" asked Ramdakan, trying not to look suspicious. He was one of Father's most trusted lieutenants, but he was also the most transparent. The man couldn't act to save his life. He had no sense of his own face, no awareness of how to conceal emotion. It made him seem enormously stupid. For an instant Lem tried imagining the man doing King Lear or Prospero, and the idea was more than a little revolting. Falstaff is more to your liking, chubby, except sapped of all wit and humor.

"I think someone in the company may be trying to usurp my father by discrediting him to investors," said Lem.

Ramdakan laughed. "They'll have a hard time of that. Your father is loved by investors. They all care about one thing, Lem. Coin. And your father gives them plenty of that."

"Yes, but Father could quickly fall out of favor. Everything could turn in an instant. You no doubt know about this business with taxes and tariffs, for example."

"I know we *pay* taxes and tariffs," Ramdakan said cautiously.

Oh you stupid little man, thought Lem. Is that the best you can do? Is that the face you make when you're pretending to be innocent? Has that ever once worked with anyone?

Lem's face of course revealed nothing. Instead, he showed concern. "You haven't heard then? I thought for sure that you, of all people, with such control of the finances, would know." He gave Ramdakan the holopad with Imala's findings already pulled up on the screen. "The LTD recently found billions in unpaid taxes and tariffs," said Lem. "And worse still, there were people both inside the LTD and in Juke Limited who not only knew about the discrepancies, they also took steps to cover it up."

It was absurd to call the illegal accounting of billions of credits mere "discrepancies," but Lem knew that was exactly the term Ramdakan himself had used when the Board was scrambling to keep the news silent. The evidence hadn't implicated Ramdakan directly—he was too smart for that—yet Lem could see the man's dirty fingers all over it. Ramdakan had likely done all the up-front work himself. And if not him then at least his weasely finance teams who had taken his explicit direction.

But regardless of who had gotten the ball rolling, it was obviously a vast undertaking that involved far more people than Imala even knew about, with Ramdakan and Father likely right up at the top.

"Ah yes," said Ramdakan. "I had heard something about this."

Lem wanted to laugh. Ramdakan was acting as if illegal activity with that much money was mere office chitchat or casual gossip. "That's a lot of money, Norja," said Lem. "It takes whole departments of people and no small amount of money to conceal something like this."

Ramdakan shoved the holopad back into Lem's arms suddenly angry. "Is this why you called me into a freezer, Lem? To show me what the idiots at the LTD do with their spare time?"

Not in their spare time, moron, Lem wanted to shout. They're a government agency. This is what they're supposed to do *all* the time. That is, when they're not taking bribes from you and doing whatever dance we tell them to.

But he said none of this. Instead he kept his expression calm. "I called you here, Norja, because I'm worried. Father would never have agreed to this. And yet, the evidence insinuates that Father was complicit in this. Some may even conclude that Father orchestrated the whole thing."

"Not true."

"Of course not. But if the press were to ever hear about this . . ."

"They won't," Ramdakan said. "We have people on this right now, Lem. They're making it go away. And if the press ever did catch wind of it, the PR folks would handle it and make sure it didn't go to the nets. That's their job, and they do it very well. This is old news, Lem. We've got it under control."

"Good. I'm glad to hear it. So how much of it have we paid?"

Ramdakan blinked, confused. "What do you mean?"

"The back taxes, the unpaid tariffs. How much of it have we paid thus far? Surely we've begun the process of meeting the required debt."

"It's complicated, Lem. We're talking about massive amounts of money. It's not like buying a pair of shoes."

Or a bigger belt, Lem thought.

"There are lawyers involved," said Ramdakan. "There are thousands of pages of documentation to sift through. These things take time, Lem. Our people will handle it. That's their job. It's not your concern."

"But it *is* my concern," said Lem. "People in this company are threatening to taint my father's reputation. I won't stand for that. Have we at least made an initial payment, to show our good faith, to keep the LTD from taking this public?"

"I told you. No one's going public with this. Trust me."

Because you've silenced them with threats and bribes and that pig-ugly grimace of yours. "Information has a way of getting out," said Lem. "I'm told these discrepancies were uncovered by a no-name, low-ranking junior auditor at the LTD. If someone that insignificant can dig up this dirt, anyone can. Sooner or later this is going to leak. We need to prepare for it."

"How?"

"We go on record that we as a company are doing all we can to meet this obligation. If we wait until the leaks do that, we'll look like unrepentant snakes trying to cover our own asses."

Ramdakan's teeth were near chattering. "Fine. I'll look into it."

"How much will you give?"

"I said I'll look into it. We haven't allocated funds for this, Lem. It will need some examination. This has been a rough quarter, in case you haven't noticed. We don't have vaults of liquidity that we can dip into whenever we want. This has to be budgeted and approved. I'll have to consult with the Board. *They're* the ones who will decide." The emphasis was an attempt to remind Lem that Lem had no authority in the matter, that he was a minor-league scrub throwing pitches in the big leagues, but Lem pretended to have taken a different meaning.

"You're right," he said. "We don't have time for delays. The last thing we need is boardroom bureaucracy miring this in indecision." Lem thought for a moment, or rather acted as if he were thinking and then pretended to reach a decision. "You may think me a great fool, Norja, but I don't think we can wait for the Board. I want to make a good-faith payment from my own personal fortune on behalf of the company."

Ramdakan chuckled. "You can't be serious."

"I *am* serious. I'll have my people do it immediately. A tenth of what we owe should be enough to keep the LTD content for now."

Ramdakan's eyes widened and he nearly choked on the word. "A tenth? But that's . . . an enormous amount. You can't possibly—"

"—have that much money? I do, Norja. You forget, I've managed a few companies myself. I've done very well. No one seems to remember because Father's shadow is quite long, which is fine by me. But that's how committed I am to this company and to my father."

"Yes, but . . . a *tenth*?"

"Anything less would backfire in the press. It wouldn't be a show of good faith. We'll call it a loan. The company can pay me back over time once the funds have been budgeted."

"Your father won't approve of you doing this, Lem."

"He doesn't have to know. I fear he'd be embarrassed by it. And no one else on the Board must know either. I don't want to do anything to diminish Father's standing among them. It would shame him if the Board and investors knew his own son had to bail him out. Promise me you'll keep this quiet, Norja. My father has spent his entire adult life building this company from nothing. I'm not going to allow a few cheapskates or crooks to tarnish his reputation. He's already poised to take a hit with this drone nonsense."

That gave Ramdakan pause. "Drone nonsense?"

"This business about loading the drones with the glaser. You have to talk to him, Norja. He won't listen to me. The glasers will fail. I've seen the Formic ship in action. Our drones will be decimated. The Vanguard project will tank after the war as a result. The idea of us producing and using drones will be dead. Father's intentions are good, but that will be an ax blow to the company. It could very well cost him his position and all of us our jobs." He stepped closer and put a hand on Ramdakan's shoulder. "You have to help me prevent that from happening. We must protect Father. He has always trusted you. Do I have your word that you are still his man?"

"Of course, Lem."

Lem visibly relaxed. "Good. I'm sorry to make you endure this cold, but Father's precarious position right now can't be heard by those who might try and take advantage of it."

"Yes. Of course."

Lem gestured back toward the corridor. "You go on ahead. We shouldn't both be seen coming out of the shaft at once."

"Smart. Good luck, Lem." He pushed his way through the sheets of plastic hanging from the ceiling to keep the dust and cold out and made his way back to the corridor, his steps bouncy and light without a magnetic floor beneath them to compensate for Luna's low gravity.

Lem watched him go. If Ramdakan was smart, he'd see Lem's game and play along, knowing that his best chance of staying afloat when Lem took Father's place was to prove himself now as Lem's loyal servant. If Ramdakan wasn't smart—which was more likely—he'd believe Lem was sincere and do exactly as Lem had asked. Either way, Lem won.

He tapped into his holopad and sent the message to his assistants that the good-faith payment they had already prepared for the LTD was a go. It was an enormous amount, yes, a very large portion of Lem's fortune, but like everything else Lem spent his money on, it was an investment. You don't make money without spending money, and if this worked, if Lem ascended to Father's position at this ripe young age, he had a lifetime ahead of him to make back a hundred times that or more.

And if it didn't work, well, that's what lawyers were for. He'd get back most of it in the end. Then he could leave the company and go turn that investment into a bigger fortune elsewhere. It wasn't hard, really. Once you had your first few hundred million, the money did most of the work for you.

But it *would* work. He knew it would. He had made gambles like this before, and he'd always been right. He would release Imala's findings to the press in a week or so, going first to the underground press on the nets, away from the journalists Father owned. And he'd leak the news of his good-faith payment to the LTD as well. He would spin it to give the impression that he had made an enormous personal sacrifice to save the thousands of jobs that would have been lost as a result of the company's poor performance. There were all kinds of human-interest stories there. He made a mental note to have a video crew start shooting B-roll of blue-collar types working in the factories. The press ate that crap up.

And of course none of the leaks would be traced back to him. In fact, he'd do all that he could to give the impression of avoiding the press, which meant exiting buildings where he knew they would be gathered and then rushing to his car to avoid their barrage of questions. "My father is a good man," he would say. "Any mistake he's made now can't overshadow a career of enormous success."

There would be a plant in the crowd, naturally. A reporter who would shout over the others, just as Lem was climbing into the skimmer: "Mr. Jukes, what do you say to the rumors that the Board is considering you as a replacement for your father?"

And Lem would look somewhat hurt by the question—stung that anyone would dare to suggest that Father was no longer fit for the position. "I'm honored the Board thinks me capable, but no one can replace my father." And then he would zip away, leaving them with a response that wasn't exactly a confirmation of the rumor and yet wasn't a denial either. And if there's one thing the press loved, it was a mystery. They would pounce on the rumor like sharks and as a result of all the attention they gave it, they would give truth to it. And yet there would be Lem, the dutiful son, passively acknowledging that, yes, he was capable and, yes, the man for the job.

He waited another five minutes then caught a skimmer to the Juke production facility where crews were mounting glasers to the drones. Father was scheduled to check in on their progress, and Lem was more than a little curious himself. He didn't have access to that wing of the facility, despite his requests to Simona to give him one, but if he simply showed up, Father wouldn't run him off.

Probably.

He arrived before Father, as planned, and met the foreman, a stout man named Bullick, in the lobby. Bullick fidgeted nervously as they waited, and Lem tried to put the man's mind at ease. "I'm sure you're doing a fine job. My father doesn't bite too fiercely."

The skimmer arrived on schedule. Simona was out first, followed by Father, who had replaced his suit for a more casual workingman's slacks and blue oxford shirt. He tried to hide his surprise when he spotted Lem. "Did you hack my schedule, Lem, or did you just happen to be in the neighborhood?"

"Both," said Lem, then he frowned at Simona. "Really, Simona, you should guard that holopad of yours more closely. It's a gold mine of information." He winked at her, and she answered him with a nasty glare. In truth, he had acquired the information elsewhere, but it amused Lem to see her face turn that red. It was kind of cute.

"Why are you here, son?"

There he goes with the "son" again, Lem thought. Really, Father. There are no cameras here. Let's drop the façade. Aloud he said, "I wanted to see these drones for myself and allow Mr. Bullick here the chance to convince me this isn't an enormous mistake."

Bullick looked appalled.

Father kept his annoyance concealed—he wasn't the buffoon Ramdakan was. "I appreciate your concern, Lem, but this is my decision, not yours."

"Obviously, Father. And I don't want to get in your way. I only want to ensure that precautions are being taken."

"Why wouldn't I take precautions, Lem? And whom exactly should I be taking precautions for? These are unmanned vessels. If they blow up, no one dies."

"If they blow up, the entire drone enterprise blows up with them."

"I'm glad to see you taking an interest in management, Lem. But the company's bottom line is taking a temporary backseat to saving the human race."

"So this is a closed tour?"

For an instant it looked as if Father would ask him to leave, but then he smiled and made a sweeping gesture with his hand toward the warehouse. "On the contrary. I don't see you enough as it is." He put an arm around Lem's shoulder. "Mr. Bullick, it appears we're a party of four now. I hope that's not a problem."

"It's your building, Mr. Jukes. This way please." He turned and led them down the corridor. As Lem passed Simona, she gave him a look of pure contempt. He couldn't help himself. He winked at her.

The factory floor was immense. The entire fleet of drones filled the space end to end, with hundreds of workers crawling on the surfaces of drones, or standing in bucket lifts, or hanging suspended from harnesses, all of them building and cutting and welding and fastening, working feverishly to finish the order. Sparks flew, tools whirred, cranes panned left and right, carrying supplies.

Bullick moved to the drone nearest them. It sat in a large cradle, suspended in the air, with the glaser attached to its underside in a metal grill that encircled it like an iron cell. "This is the new cage system we've designed to hold the glasers in place," said Bullick. "Extremely tough. The drone will rip apart before this does. We shouldn't have any more detachment problems with this setup."

"Detachment problems?" asked Lem.

Bullick glanced at Father, unsure if he should reveal anything.

"We had a mishap a few days ago in testing," said Father. "They took a drone out in space, gave the glaser too much juice, and the glaser detached."

Lem looked appalled. "Was it firing?"

"Only for a fraction of a second after it detached. Then the fail-safe kicked in and it stopped. Nothing was damaged, son."

"You're lucky," said Lem. "What if it had been pointed at a ship? Or worse, at Luna or at Earth? This thing creates a field through the continuity of mass, Father. It stops gravity from holding things together. Do you have any idea how catastrophic that could have been?"

Father was annoyed. "I know what it does, Lem. I had the damn thing built."

"And you want to put fifty of these in space *near* Earth?" He suddenly realized the horror of that idea. "What if one of them deviates or the glaser breaks off and it fires at Earth? Have you considered that?" He suddenly didn't care about unseating Father or taking the company. The image of Earth separating into dust like the asteroid in the Kuiper Belt had him in a panic. "These things are planet killers, Father."

"We're taking precautions, Lem."

"The only right precaution is not to do it."

"And what would you suggest, Lem? Millions of people are dying. The Formics are moving into cities now. They're gassing everything. People's faces are melting off their bodies and turning into bloody puddles of goo. That's happening. As we speak. Are we taking an enormous risk here? Yes. But what else are we going to do? The military are idiots. Nothing they throw at the Formics is getting through. Not on Earth, and not up here. Shuttles, missiles, nukes. Nothing works. Space is our territory. *Ours.* We own it, not the five-star morons who run armies. We're far better equipped to take action than they are."

"Not with the glaser, Father."

"Yes, with the glaser. You want to throw coconuts at that ship? Be my guest. The rest of us adults will be saving the planet."

Lem walked away. It was old Father now, immovable, pigheaded, loud and blustery. And he was wrong. Lem saw that now, more clearly than ever. Initially he had worried solely about the economic risks of a drone attack.

Now he worried about the *real* danger of it. The image of Earth disappearing into dust resurfaced in his mind, and it left him feeling sick.

He took the skimmer to the facility where Victor and Imala were working. He found them both kneeling by their ship welding a piece onto it, their faces covered in blast masks. Lem was shocked at the sight of the ship. They had completely transformed it. It looked like a piece of wreckage, down to the ship's markings on the hull and scorch marks from laser fire. Wires and conduit and structural beams stuck out everywhere. Had he not known what it was he would have dismissed it as junk.

"How soon can you be ready with this?" he asked.

Victor and Imala faced him and raised their blast masks. "We're moving as quickly as we can here."

"How soon? Two hours? Two days?"

Victor and Imala stood. Victor brushed the dust and fibers off his shirt. "Dublin and Benyawe are finishing up the decoy with the thrusters. We've got a few more hours on our end. Then we can do a test flight."

"Scrap the test flight," said Lem. "There's no time. We launch in a few hours, the instant it's done."

Victor and Imala exchanged glances. "All right," said Victor. "Why the sudden panicked urgency?"

"The Formics have begun gassing cities," said Lem. "We need to move now."

Victor removed his blast mask and studied the ship, gauging how much work remained. "Give us two hours," he said.

Lem nodded and left them to it. He hadn't lied exactly. The Formics were gassing cities, and that was reason enough. But it wasn't the *real* reason, not the *main* reason. Father had to be stopped. He couldn't launch the drones. And the only way to prevent him from doing so was for Lem to do the job first, to remove the need for drones. He would get Victor inside, have Victor destroy the helm, and then the ship would be crippled and theirs for the taking. Father could keep his little drones with their glaser death sticks docked in that warehouse of his.

But what were the chances that Victor would actually reach the helm? And if he did reach the helm, what were the chances that he would successfully detonate the bomb? Or even reach the bloody ship to begin with? It was more likely that the Formics would blast them before they even got there. Well, that was the risk they were taking, wasn't it?

He stepped into an empty office, set up his holopad, put his face into the field, and made the call. A moment later Simona's face appeared, and as he expected she didn't look pleased.

"Have you been wearing that scowl since I saw you last?" asked Lem. "That can't be good for the lines of the face."

"What do you want?"

"You know I'm right about the drones, Simona. Father is playing with a weapon he doesn't understand."

"If you're calling me to make me pick sides, Lem, you're wasting my time."

"You answered the holo, and you knew it was me. That means deep inside you know I'm right."

"It means I'm a civil human being who answers holos, even from obnoxious jackasses."

"This bickering, Simona. It's unhealthy."

"What do you want, Lem?"

"Information."

"And you think I'll give it to you?"

"Father certainly won't."

"Then I won't either."

"When does Father plan on launching his drones?"

"Why should I tell you that?"

"I may have a way to disable the Formic ship," said Lem.

She paused. "I'm listening."

"But I need to know when Father plans to launch his drones. I need my people in and out before Father makes his move. He can't attack while my people are in there."

"How do you plan to get people inside? No ship can get close to it. It blasts anything that approaches."

"You're right. My tactic will probably fail, so it doesn't hurt for you to tell me how much time I have."

Simona said nothing.

"I can get the information elsewhere, Simona. It wouldn't be difficult. But I'm coming to you because you're the most reliable and accurate source of information."

Simona remained quiet, considering.

"You heard my father. Thousands of people are dying every day. I'm ready to move now. We are set to launch. I'm ready to stop those deaths right now. But I can't unless you give me information."

She sighed. "Bullick says the fleet of drones won't be ready for at least five days."

Lem breathed out. "Thank you."

"So are you going to tell me how you're getting people inside?"

"I'll give you the whole rousing narrative some other time." He retracted his face from the field and ended the transmission.

Five days. That was more than enough time for Victor to drift to the ship, do his business, and get out. Or so they had calculated. Victor had estimated three days and thought it might be as much as four, but no more than that. Then again, anything could go wrong.

But no, five days was an eternity away. If they started to approach that, if it looked like they would be delayed, then Lem would radio them to abort.

He went back out to the warehouse and tried busying himself with other things while they finished. Nothing held his attention, and he eventually returned and hovered over them until it was done. Men with lifters came and took the camouflaged ship into an airlock. Benyawe and Dublin had done a good job with the decoy. It attached to the recon ship quite nicely and looked as realistically like junk as the recon ship did.

Victor and Imala were waiting by the airlock entrance already in their spacesuits. "You have the explosive?" Lem asked.

"Wouldn't be much of a trip without it," said Victor.

Lem nodded. No one spoke. There was nothing more to say. Lem extended his hand. "Good luck."

Victor considered the hand, hesitated. Imala poked him in the ribs with her elbow and Victor took the hand and shook it. "Thanks."

"Thank me when you get back," said Lem.

Victor and Imala entered the airlock and climbed into the cockpit. Lem stood at the glass and watched them take off. It seemed strange to watch a hunk of junk fly like a ship, but that was the beauty of the idea, Lem supposed. The ship accelerated, getting smaller and smaller as it moved into the blackness. Lem watched it until it was nothing more than a dot in the distance. In less than a day it would decelerate and approach the Formic ship at a drifting speed, but for now it shot away like a rocket.

Now that they were off, the whole idea seemed utterly ridiculous. A ship disguised as junk. It had seemed like such a good idea at the time. Now, with them out of sight, it felt like a fool's errand.

Benyawe came and stood beside him at the glass, looking out into space, her long gray braids dangling to her shoulders. "They're going to do fine," she said.

He turned to her. "You're a scientist. You act and think and decide based on facts. Do you honestly believe that? Do you honestly believe this has a chance?"

"Probably not."

He exhaled and turned back to the glass. "That's what I thought."

"But the scientist is only part of who I am, Lem. There's also the wife part and the mother part and the sister and the friend and all the other parts. Those parts say we cannot lose. And those parts are the ones I choose to believe."

# CHAPTER 28

# Drill Sledges

The military base was little more than rubble and burned earth and bloated, rotting bodies lying scattered in the sun. Most of them were Chinese soldiers, but Wit saw Formics among the dead as well. Wrecked troop transports, downed skimmers, the husk of a burned-out Chinese helicopter. Wit had expected the sight, but it pained him to see it nonetheless. It was further evidence that the Formics were winning the war. The Chinese didn't even have the manpower to bury their dead.

Mazer directed the vehicles to a hangar at the airfield. There were two aircraft inside that Mazer called HERCs. They both appeared undamaged. "We lucked out," said Mazer. "At least one of these is sure to fly."

They then drove northeast of the airfield to a bunker overlooking a muddy valley. There Wit saw the three drill sledges Mazer had told him about during the drive from the lander.

"They're still there," said Mazer. "Miracles never cease."

"Vehicles are not a plan," said Wit.

"The underside of the lander isn't shielded," said Mazer. "So we attack it from the bottom, underground. We tunnel in with these three drill sledges and punch a hole through the underside of the lander."

"And do what?" asked Wit.

"There are too few of us to take on the whole structure with small arms. I say we plant explosives and cripple the lander."

"Not good enough," said Wit. "We nuke it. We wipe it off the face of the Earth. If we only cripple it, they'll realize the underside is their weak spot and they'll extend the shield down. If that happens we'll never penetrate it."

"So all we need is a tactical nuke?" said Bingwen. "Oh, I thought it might be something *hard* to come by."

"I don't like this kid's sarcasm," said Calinga.

"Bingwen has a point," said Mazer. "There are explosives here on base that I'm aware of, but nothing on the scale of a nuke."

"Leave that to me," said Wit.

"You have a secret stash somewhere?" asked Bingwen.

"He keeps talking like he's one of us," said Calinga.

"He is," said Mazer. "I'm beginning to think some children are made for war."

"The Chinese will give us the nuke," said Wit. "We've been building contacts within the military since the start of our campaign. Many are high-ranking officers who have contacted us anonymously. We share tactics, make suggestions, keep the intel flowing. We've saved their bacon, they've saved ours. I'll tell them what we plan to do and ask for supplies."

"And they'll just hand you a nuke?" said Mazer.

"Either that or they'll see the wisdom of the idea and send their own people with a nuke to do it. Either way it gets done."

"We're foreign soldiers on their soil," said Mazer. "Seems unlikely that they'd entrust us with a tactical nuke within their own borders."

"We've earned their trust," said Wit. "And more importantly, they're desperate. The Chinese army has been decimated. They're hanging by a thread now. They need a victory, and we've got a far higher success rate than they do. Plus you know how to pilot the drill sledges. And seeing as how these drills are just sitting here, I'm willing to bet the Chinese don't have a line of trained pilots waiting in the wings to do something with them."

"How will we transport the drill sledges to a place near the lander?" asked Calinga. "The lander's fifty klicks away."

"That's what the HERC is for," said Mazer. "It has talons. It will take three trips, but I'll carry each of the drill sledges north to a site near the lander. Perhaps a few kilometers away from it. Then we tunnel from there and attack."

"You will pilot one of the drill sledges, Mazer," said Wit. "You know the tech. Calinga and I will pilot the other two. You'll start training us immediately. I'll get on the nets and contact our anonymous officers in the military and divulge our intent to destroy the lander with a nuke. We'll see if anyone bites."

"If we broadcast our intentions, someone will try to stop us," said Calinga.

"I won't broadcast it on our public site," said Wit. "I'll use encryption and contact the anonymous officers individually. If they try to stop us, we'll ask them for a better idea."

For the next two days, Mazer trained Wit and Calinga on piloting the drill sledges. The two MOPs mastered the mechanics of the drill sledges quite easily, and it made Mazer wonder if all MOPs were this proficient. "How many different vehicles do you guys know how to drive?" Mazer asked.

"All of them," said Calinga.

On the morning of the third day, a private skimmer carrying a single passenger landed deftly in the valley. A Chinese woman with a briefcase and casual attire climbed out and went directly to Wit. "Captain Wit O'Toole?" Her English was flawless.

"Yes," said Wit.

She handed him the briefcase. "I trust you'll know what to do with this."

Wit set the briefcase on the ground and opened it enough to see the nuke inside encased in foam. So small yet so destructive. The woman was already moving back toward the skimmer. She was up and away before anyone said a word.

"Your anonymous contacts clearly want to remain anonymous," said Calinga.

"She showed her face," said Wit. "That was brave."

"Maybe she's not the contact," said Calinga. "Maybe she's the wife or the mistress or someone else entirely."

"She's a soldier," said Wit. "She had trimmed fingernails and no pierced ears. Plus she moved like a soldier, taking in everything." Wit picked up the briefcase. "We have our weapon. Let's move."

They didn't waste any time. Wit, Calinga, and Mazer dressed in their helmets and cool-suits.

Mazer knelt in front of Bingwen. "You'll stay here with the MOPs and do what they say. I'll be back soon."

"You better," said Bingwen.

Calinga drove Mazer to the airfield. There, Mazer climbed into one of the HERCs, flew it back to the valley, and picked up one of the drill sledges with the HERC's talons. Then he carried the drill sledge north, staying low to the ground and scanning for enemy aircraft. He found a steep hill five kilometers south of the lander where the drill sledges could easily dig into the earth. Mazer then set down the drill sledge by the hillside and flew back to the valley twice more to retrieve the other two drill sledges. On the last trip he brought back Wit and Calinga with him. Three drill sledges, three pilots.

When they were ready to climb into their respective drills, Wit said, "We'll go deep, get directly under the lander, then surge upward. We'll come in at a slight angle and hit the lander in the center. All three of us will penetrate the hull and tear our way inside. I'll carry the nuke with me in my cockpit. Once we're in, I'll exit my drill sledge and leave the nuke inside. Then I'll climb into Calinga's drill with him. The two remaining drill sledges will then dig like hell to get deep and avoid the blast."

"Why leave the nuke in one of the drill sledges?" said Calinga.

"We can't leave the nuke in the open," said Wit. "We don't know the Formics' capabilities. They might recognize the nuke as a threat and disarm it before it detonates. We can't risk that. The drill sledge will act like a vault. The Formics won't be able to reach the nuke if it stays in the cockpit. Detonation is practically guaranteed."

"Fine," said Calinga, "but I'm carrying the nuke with me. I'm much smaller than you, so there's far more room for it in my cockpit. Once we're in the lander I'll leave it behind and climb into Mazer's drill sledge with him. Same plan, just different people. And don't argue, Wit. You know it makes sense. Mazer is a better pilot than you, and again, size matters. You're almost as big as the both of us together. Mazer and I will fit much easier in a cockpit than either of us will fit with you. I know you don't like me taking the risk when you can, but my way is strategically sound."

"You're right," said Wit. "You carry the package. Mazer, how far below the lander do we need to be to pick up enough speed to penetrate the hull?"

"I'm not sure we *can* penetrate the hull," said Mazer. "I don't know what it's composed of. We might cut through it, we might not."

"Assuming we can," said Wit.

"Three hundred meters at least," said Mazer.

"All right," said Wit. "You take point, Mazer. Calinga and I will be on either side of you, tracking parallel."

They climbed into their respective drill sledges and fired up the drills.

Moments later they were each digging into the side of the hill, spewing back hot lava. Once underground, Mazer began a long gradual descent, heading for a spot three hundred meters below the lander. His cool-suit did its best to maintain a normal body temperature, but it erred on the side of cold. In moments, Mazer's fingers felt stiff and he could see his own breath inside his helmet. His visor frosted at the edges, but fans cycled air through the helmet and kept the visor from fogging completely.

The deeper they went below the surface, the more solid rock they encountered and the faster they moved. They tried not to go hot too often since they couldn't communicate when they moved at those speeds, but at times it couldn't be avoided.

Mazer watched the depth-gauge holo on his dash. When they drew close to the lander, the holo filled with crisscrossing white lines. "The Formics must be tunnelers," he said. "It's like an ant colony down here."

"Maybe we'll get lucky and run into a few Formics," said Calinga. "And I mean that literally. We grind them up and spit them out the back."

They finally got into position, three hundred meters below the surface, almost directly below the lander. Mazer was practically on his back in his seat, wiggling his fingers and toes, trying to keep his blood circulating. It wasn't doing any good. "I'm ready, Wit. Give the word before my whole body turns to ice."

Wit's voice came over the communicator. "Calinga, you set?"

"Set and freezing my ass off," said Calinga. "Let's get a move on."

"Punch it," said Wit.

Mazer hit the throttle, and his drill sledge surged upward, spewing back lava and taking off. The cockpit shook, and Mazer gripped the steering bars tighter, holding on, pushing the drill to build momentum. He could feel the heat rising inside the cockpit. It was a welcome relief after the cold, but it quickly became blazing hot. "Two hundred and fifty meters to target," he said.

The three drill sledges surged upward, chewing through rock and earth. Mazer kept his eyes on the depth gauge, but the growing vibrations made it difficult to focus his eyes on the readout. "Two hundred meters," he said.

More white lines appeared on the screen. First there were only a few, but then dozens materialized as the drill sledges drew near to the lander. The Formics were definitely tunnelers, Mazer thought. No doubt of that now.

The depth gauge scrolled up and revealed a huge spot of white immediately beneath the lander. "Wait!" Mazer said. "Slow down. There's a large air pocket right beneath the lander. We'll never make it."

"I see it," said Wit. "Full stop at the air pocket."

Mazer continued to slow, breaking through the last of the earth and coming up into the air pocket almost at a crawl. The drill began to wind down, and the sledge tipped forward and leveled out on what looked like the floor of a massive cave. Wit's and Calinga's sledges appeared beside him. Mazer opened the cockpit and stood in his seat. He shined his helmet lights directly above him and saw the underside of the lander. A few more meters and he could have reached up and touched the metal surface.

The air pocket was huge. Mazer wasn't sure how wide it was; he shined his floodlight all around him and instead of seeing side walls, he saw only blackness.

"Well that was anticlimactic," said Calinga. He was standing in his open cockpit, staring up at the underside of the lander, a giant alien ceiling above them. "Here I thought we were going to bust through that thing, and now we can't even reach it."

There was a crack of ice and a hiss of air, and Wit's cockpit opened. "Talk to me, Mazer. What are our options? Any way we can reach the hull?"

Mazer shined his helmet lights up again. "I wasn't anticipating an air pocket here. This complicates matters." He considered the distance from the floor to the ceiling. "If we came up like planned, we could fly up through the air pocket with enough ejecta behind us to *reach* the lander. But the drill bits would never get a grip on the hull. We'd bounce off."

"So we can't bust through?" said Calinga. "What do we do? Leave the nuke here?"

"We could," said Wit. "But it would do far more damage inside. Our chances of success grow exponentially if we break through. Mazer, could we burn our way in? What if we turn these gophers around and hit the underside of the lander with our lava spew? Could we melt a hole big enough for Calinga to launch through?"

"No idea," said Mazer. "Maybe. It's worth a shot. Trouble is, we'll have to get out, turn the drill sledges around, extend the stilts, and get the sledges in an upright position, with the back end pointed up at the lander so we can hit the lander with our lava spew."

"Calinga, get back in your sledge and go deep," said Wit. "Get into launch position again. Mazer and I will melt a hole. If it works, we'll tell you to surge up and soar through. We'll come right after you. Then we ditch your sledge and the nuke as planned."

"Roger that," said Calinga.

"I'll need to extend your stilts and get you into a diving position," said Mazer.

Calinga closed himself in his cockpit. Mazer went to Calinga's sledge, pulled back the side paneling, and punched in the sequence to operate the stilts. It was a multistep process that took a few minutes, but soon all the stilts were out and in place.

"You're set," said Mazer. "But wait until I'm back in my gopher and out of the path of your spew."

Calinga waited for the all-clear then fired up the sledge and dove into the earth. An ejecta of lava spew shot back and hit the underside of the lander. Where it did, the hull sizzled and dripped away.

"Hull's melting," said Mazer. "I'd say your plan's a go, Wit."

"Show me how to set up the stilts on mine," said Wit.

Mazer waited until Calinga's sledge had disappeared back into the earth and the ejecting lava spew had stopped. Then he rushed to Wit's sledge and opened the paneling on the side and walked Wit through the process. Soon the sledge was up on its spider legs, its back end ready to shower the lander with lava.

There was a hint of movement in the darkness. Mazer turned and shined his light. A crowd of twenty to thirty Formics was scurrying toward them. They didn't look armed, but their clawed hands and maws looked ready to rip Mazer and Wit to shreds. "We've got company," said Mazer.

His weapon was in his cockpit. He ran for it. The Formics rushed forward. Mazer had the gun in his hand three seconds later and fired the first shots from where he stood on the side of the sledge. Most of the shots found targets. Formics dropped. Others scattered into the darkness.

"Hold them off," said Wit. "I'll get your sledge into position." He rushed to Mazer's sledge, opened the paneling, and got busy.

Their helmets were made for piloting the sledges. They weren't designed for small-arms skirmishes in near-total darkness. Mazer had no HUD, no targeting help, no heat-signature capabilities, no night vision. His visor was a pane of glass, nothing more. He had a handgun and a spotlight.

He kept the light moving, searching for Formics trying to sneak up on their position. Occasionally his beam found one, and he squeezed off a few rounds, aiming for the Formic's center mass.

Moments later the crowd of Formics emerged from the darkness and retreated, scurrying back the way they had come. "They're leaving," said Mazer.

"Good," said Wit. "I need two more minutes."

Mazer kept moving, shining his light in every direction, gun up and ready. For a moment he thought they were in the clear. Then his light fell upon hundreds of pairs of eyes in the darkness, rushing forward.

"Formics!" said Mazer. "Two o'clock. Hundreds of them!"

"Thirty more seconds," said Wit.

The first group had been scouts, Mazer realized, sent forward to see what the enemy had to offer. This was the real army. Mazer didn't think he could hold them for ten seconds, much less thirty. They were coming like a swarm.

He flipped the gun to three-round bursts and opened fire. The gunfire echoed through the air pocket. Every shot hit a target. It wasn't hard. The Formics were practically on top of each other, charging forward, scurrying in a frenzy, closing in on Mazer like a wave of eyes and arms and fury.

They were completely fearless, he realized. He was mowing them down, but they didn't care. It was as if they knew they would overrun him eventually, and the individuals up front were willing to sacrifice themselves to make that happen.

"Thirty meters," said Mazer. "You got three seconds."

"All right," said Wit. "You're set. Go go go."

Mazer sprinted toward his drill sledge, firing erratically behind him. More Formics fell. The swarm continued forward, their fallen companions forgotten.

Mazer scurried up the ladder and into his cockpit. He saw Wit out of the corner of his eye climbing up into the other one. Mazer yanked in the ladder and closed the cockpit just as a wave of Formics slammed into the machine, climbing up the stilts and pounding on the canopy. Their weight rocked the drill sledge, and for a terrifying moment Mazer thought they might tip the sledge over or break the stilts. But the drill sledge held, despite the pounding they received.

"This won't work," said Mazer. "Calinga won't be able to get out of his sledge. They'd overrun him. We have to abort."

"Destroying this lander is more important than Calinga," said Wit. "It's more important than all of us. He knows that. If we leave now, the Formics could shield the underside. It's now or never. Let's burn him a hole."

He was right of course. The mission trumped all other considerations, even their lives.

Mazer cranked up his drill. Then he put the drill sledge's tracks in reverse and slowly lowered the drill to the surface. Lava shot upward and hit the lander. The tracks in reverse countered the forward propulsion of the drill, but the opposing forces caused the drill sledge to buck and bounce. Mazer stayed at it. Wit did the same. Lava spewed. The underside of the lander began to melt.

The pounding on Mazer's cockpit had stopped. The Formics had fallen off. Mazer hoped they were getting a hot lava shower. One minute passed. Then two. The sledge bucked and bounced across the floor of the air pocket. Mazer was careful not to eject lava toward Wit's position, and he hoped Wit was doing the same.

A large chunk of the lander's underside fell away, like the floor in a burning house crashing through. A gaping hole remained.

"Calinga!" said Wit. "You've got a hole. I'm sending you scans now. Get in, drop the nuke, and get out if you can."

"Roger that. You two get clear. I don't want to hit you on the way up. I'm coming in hot."

Mazer stopped the reverse motion of his tracks and collapsed the stilts. The drill sledge immediately dropped and shot downward, churning through earth below the air pocket and diving deep.

Mazer called up Calinga's position on the holo. They passed each other, Mazer going down, Calinga going up. At the last one hundred meters, Calinga put on a burst of speed and shot up through the air pocket. He aimed for the hole perfectly. But since he was coming in at a slight angle, the drill sledge hit the lip of the hole as it entered the lander and flew inside. The contact spun the drill sledge in the air, and it crashed on its side in the lander.

"Calinga," said Wit. "Report."

The voice that answered was pained but upbeat. "You two get deep. I'll detonate the nuke."

"Hold on," said Wit. "I'm coming for you."

"Negative," said Calinga. "If you try to make the jump up here, the same thing will happen to you, and we'll both be dead. I got Formics swarming the sledge already. We couldn't make the transfer anyway. You two dive. I got this. I'll give you twenty seconds."

"It should have been me," said Wit. "I should have taken the nuke."

"Time to let someone else have the glory."

"It's been an honor," said Wit.

"It's been mine," said Calinga.

How could they talk about this so casually? thought Mazer. How could they resign themselves so easily?

Because they're MOPs, Mazer realized. Because they're intelligent soldiers, because they know there's no other way. "Ten seconds," said Calinga. "They're starting to tear into the canopy. I can't delay here."

Mazer punched it, going hot. He counted down the seconds in his head, watching the holo on his dash. At zero, the blip that was Calinga's drill sledge winked out.


Mazer headed for the predetermined location on the map where they had agreed to resurface. None of them knew what the blast radius for an underground nuke would be, but the reach of the radiation would likely be wide. The best they could do was pick a spot ten kilometers away, or the maximum distance the drill sledge could travel.

Mazer broke through the surface at the designated spot and was surprised to see a number of vehicles there on the scanners. He unbuckled, stood, and opened the cockpit.

Half a dozen Chinese tanks and assault vehicles were parked at the site, along with a platoon of armed Chinese soldiers in radiation suits. Wit had already arrived. He was down from his drill sledge stepping into a radiation suit two soldiers held open for him, arguing with an officer.

The officer turned and faced Mazer, smiling. It was Shenzu, Mazer's contact at the Chinese base who had threatened to shoot Mazer down for taking the HERC. "Captain Mazer Rackham. Welcome back. On behalf of the Chinese Army, we thank you for destroying one of the landers and the biomass. Here, step into this suit. There's a communicator inside. We're likely safe at this distance, but we will err on the side of caution."

"The blast was a success?" Mazer asked.

Shenzu smiled. "This is a great day in China. We have scored a huge victory. Also, you are under arrest."

For a moment Mazer thought he had misheard.

"We just destroyed the guys who have been slaughtering your people," said Wit. "You're supposed to see what we did and copy it."

"Oh we'll copy it," said Shenzu. "We have people working on that right now. This is only one lander after all. The war is far from over. But in the meantime, there are the charges against you. Illegally crossing our borders, stealing government property, conducting a nuclear strike on Chinese soil. All serious offenses. I am to escort you to a holding facility."

"This is how you show your thanks?" said Mazer.

"Don't worry, gentlemen. Most heroes in China are arrested first. We're used to it."

# CHAPTER 29

# Mothership

Victor got his hand on the shuttle door, ready to open it. The instruments on the dash indicated that the Formic ship was only six hundred meters away now, practically on top of them. "We're going to make it, Imala," he said. "They're not going to vaporize us." He watched the numbers tick down as they drifted in closer . . . closer.

He had known that being cramped in a cockpit with Imala for a few days would be awkward and uncomfortable, but he hadn't expected the experience to be downright miserable. It was worse than being in the quickship for nine months. At least in the quickship he could do whatever he wanted and not have to worry about being indecorous. If he had to belch, he belched. If he had to urinate, he did. Here, not only was Imala practically right on top of him and thus likely aware of everything he was doing biologically inside his spacesuit, but he was also aware of *her* every move and sound.

Plus their bulky helmets were practically touching, so it was as if they were huddled together and staring at each other. Nonstop. For two days.

"Be careful," said Imala. "When you open the door, do it slowly. Sudden movements might set them off."

"Anything could set them off. Heat signatures might set them off."

"They can detect those?"

"They can travel at near-lightspeed, Imala. Who knows what they can do?"

"It would've been nice to have known that before we set out."

"If you wait until you know everything, you never do anything."

"Who are you quoting? Ben Franklin? Sun Tzu?"

"My father."

The dash gave a beep, signaling it was time for him to leave. Imala flipped off the interior lights. "You can do this, Vico. And if it gets to the point where you don't want to do it anymore, then we turn around. We didn't come here for either of us to die. We'll do more good if we live. Remember that."

"Live. Yes. A good plan." He turned the handle and slowly opened the door, easing it outward. When it was wide enough, he pulled himself out, weightless. The Formic ship was like a red mountain in front of him. He was nothing compared to it. A dot. A gnat. How could he possibly stop something so big?

He slowly pulled out the duffel bag with his tools and the explosive, which suddenly felt hopelessly inadequate considering the size of the thing in front of him.

The shuttle drifted forward. Victor eased the door closed.

They couldn't have the shuttle float into the Formic ship. Having the two touch felt like a risk. It was better if Imala stopped the shuttle shy of the ship and Victor flew the remaining distance alone.

"I'm clear, Imala."

"Roger that. Go easy. Come right back if anything feels wrong."

"Everything feels wrong already. You should see the size of this thing. It's like a moon."

"Firing retros," she said.

Near-imperceptible bursts of air slowed the shuttle. Victor continued on, floating toward the gleaming red metallic wall. No guns sprang out. No Formics emerged.

He landed soft as a kiss, the magnets in his hands and feet anchoring him to the surface. Now that he was close, he could clearly see closed apertures all over the surface of the ship. They appeared to be made of the same material as the hull, which kept them invisible from a distance. Each was the size of a dinner plate, and there were tens of thousands of them, all lined in neat rows that stretched from one end of the ship to the other.

His destination was the place in the hull where the gun emerged, and he took a moment to orient himself and locate it. He would have to crawl across the hull a short distance to reach it, he realized. Stepping lightly, he set out. As he moved he wondered if Father had landed near here. He looked around him, searching for any signs of a struggle or a breached or repaired hull but saw nothing.

He found the place where the gun emerged. He could see the seams in the hull where it opened or parted. It was time. He anchored the duffel bag and removed the remote control. He and Imala had deposited the decoy ten klicks away. He flipped on the control and punched the throttle. At first he saw nothing. But soon he saw a dot in the distance among the debris that was moving toward him. He increased the speed. The decoy slammed into a smaller piece of debris in its path, and the two ricocheted off each other. For a moment Victor lost control of the decoy, but he quickly regained it and righted the craft's course.

There was movement beneath him. Gears turning, pieces shifting, a machine coming to life. He could feel it in his feet.

The hull opened silently. The gun extended and unfolded itself from the hole like a giant mechanical flower opening its petals and stretching outward. It was fifty times bigger than he had thought it would be, bigger than a shuttle. It had looked so small at a distance in the vids.

The remote control was long forgotten. He was at the lip of the hole now, shining his light down into the blackness. The space was immense. There appeared to be corners and nooks and passageways down there. Perhaps one of them led into the ship. He couldn't tell from here.

The ground shook. The giant flower was firing. Victor looked behind him. The decoy ship was now a puff of shattered pieces. Victor turned back, working frantically. His window of opportunity was closing. He needed to keep this hole open. But how? He had envisioned a space much smaller than this. He had brought a bar to force into the hole and wedge it open to allow him to climb inside, but the bar was clearly too short. How could he have been so wrong about that?

The giant flower began to fold in on itself, retracting, preparing to disappear back into its hiding place. Victor thought quickly, reaching out and shoving the bar between two braces that had begun to fold inward. The bar stuck, wedged tight, and the flower's collapsing motion stopped. Victor waited. If the bar snapped free after he climbed into the hole, the flower might collapse inward and crush him.

The flower didn't move. The bar held firm. Victor closed the bag, threw it over his shoulder, and grabbed the lip of hole, ready to launch himself inside. He wished Father were with him all of a sudden. Father could lead out and Victor could follow, just as they had done for years on board El Cavador, moving about the ship and making repairs. Father always knew what needed to be done. Doubt was not in his DNA. His solutions weren't always the most efficient, but they always worked, they always got the job done. Yes, Victor was the better mechanic, but Father worked better under pressure. Father never flinched. Father's hands were always steady.

Victor lifted his right hand and saw that it was trembling.

Be with me, Father. Stay with me, fly with me. *Somos familia. Somos uno.*

Then he lowered his hand back to the lip of the hole and pulled himself forward, shooting down deep, disappearing in the darkness.